The Rake's Retreat

Nancy Butler

D0032729

A SIGNET BOOK

SIGNET
Published by the Penguin Group
Penguin Putnam Inc., 375 Hudson Street,
New York, New York 10014, U.S.A.
Penguin Books Ltd, 27 Wrights Lane,
London W8 5TZ, England
Penguin Books Australia Ltd.
Ringwood, Victoria, Australia
Penguin Books Canada Ltd, 10 Alcorn Avenue,
Toronto, Ontario, Canada M4V 3B2
Penguin Books (N.Z.) Ltd, 182–190 Wairau Road,
Auckland 10, New Zealand

Penguin Books Ltd, Registered Offices:
Harmondsworth, Middlesex, England

First published by Signet, an imprint of Dutton NAL,
a member of Penguin Putnam Inc.

First Printing, April 1999
10 9 8 7 6 5 4 3 2 1

Copyright © Nancy J. Hajeski, 1999
All rights reserved

Ⓢ REGISTERED TRADEMARK—MARCA REGISTRADA

Printed in the United States of America

Without limiting the rights under copyright reserved above, no part of this publication
may be reproduced, stored in or introduced into a retrieval system, or transmitted, in any
form, or by any means (electronic, mechanical, photocopying, recording, or otherwise),
without the prior written permission of both the copyright owner and the above publisher
of this book.

BOOKS ARE AVAILABLE AT QUANTITY DISCOUNTS WHEN USED TO PROMOTE PRODUCTS OR
SERVICES. FOR INFORMATION PLEASE WRITE TO PREMIUM MARKETING DIVISION, PENGUIN
PUTNAM INC., 375 HUDSON STREET, NEW YORK, NY 10014.

If you purchased this book without a cover you should be aware that this book is stolen
property. It was reported as "unsold and destroyed" to the publisher and neither the
author nor the publisher has received any payment for this "stripped book."

A Sorry Sinner

"Jemima," he sighed as his eyes probed hers with a curious entreaty.

At his unspoken bidding, she knelt against the padded arm of the chair. Seduction now seemed the farthest thing from his mind, and yet he wanted so badly to take her in his arms. He yearned to hold her, even for the space of a few heartbeats. And he had an inkling she might even understand and not flee from him in dismay.

He let his hand drift down from her hair, settling it on the nape of her neck. And then he slowly drew her forward. Her eyes were brimming with uncertainty, but still held no hint of fear as she gazed up at him. But then he recalled who he was, a man who did not deserve comforting, especially not at the hands of a creature who put everyone else's needs before her own. She was in far more need of comforting than a sorry sinner like himself. . . .

SIGNET REGENCY ROMANCE
Coming in May 1999

Sandra Heath
Marigold's Marriages

Gayle Buck
The Chester Charade

Nadine Miller
A Touch of Magic

1-800-253-6476
ORDER DIRECTLY
WITH VISA OR MASTERCARD

For my siblings—
Richard, John, and Jo-Ann

Laughter is our truest bond

Virtue is a smug estate, without the lure of vice.

Ode to Persephone
Lord Troy

Chapter One

L ovelace Wellesley was delighted with her name.
    Not her given name, mind, though she also thought
Lovelace a particularly pleasing appellation. And so it should be,
considering that the parents who had bestowed it on her were both
actors. They knew full well how a name could capture the imagination of the paying customers. Irmengarde she could never have
been. Or Agrippina.

But it was her surname that brought a blush of pure pleasure to
her fair cheeks. *Wellesley.* She adored it. Especially since, until two
years ago, it had been just plain Potter.

She had been Lovelace Potter of Professor Potter's Peerless
Players. But then an unfortunate series of circumstances, chief
among them the accidental burning down of a boardinghouse by
the current leading man in her father's troupe, had necessitated
their abrupt departure from the town of Basingstoke. Just to be on
the safe side, her papa had prudently changed the name of his
troupe to Wellesley's Wandering Minstrels. In honor of the Duke
of Wellington, of course.

Lovelace squirmed restlessly on the cot in the stuffy prop
wagon, heedless of the fact that she was supposed to be sleeping
off a sick headache. She peeked out through the small window toward the prosperous-looking gray-gabled inn, where Papa, Mama,
young Charles, and the other two members of the Minstrels were
having their luncheon. The inn's sign appeared freshly painted.
The Iron Duke, it proclaimed in bold red letters above a crisply
painted silhouette of a beak-nosed man in a cocked hat.

Lud, she thought crossly, *these days everyone and his brother is
fashioning himself after Wellington.*

She returned to the handbill she had been admiring as she lay
sprawled on the cot. It was a printed flyer announcing the troupe's
latest offering, *Virtue Rewarded, or the Rake's Redemption.* In let-

ters beneath the title ran a credit line, *Based upon the poem of the same name by Lord Troy.*

Lovelace sighed wistfully. She had a vague hope that England's premier poet might attend the opening of the play in London. If rumors were to be credited, he was the most handsome man in the whole breadth of the land. And just to make sure that he would be compelled to attend the new production, she had insisted that her father include a drawing of Lovelace herself on the handbill. Her brother Charles was a dab hand with a charcoal stick, and she had to admit he had done her credit—even if he had made her nose appear ever-so-slightly skewed. She wished the portrait could have been hand-colored—it was difficult for a mere pencil sketch to convey the sheer luster of her dark gold hair or the shining clarity of her pansy brown eyes. But, all things considered, she judged it a telling likeness.

Feeling heartily bored but unwilling to enter the inn and be subjected to her parents' anxious questions on their daughter's—and featured performer's—health, Lovelace slipped out the back door of the prop wagon. After skirting her family's traveling coach, she headed for the lane that ran along the side of the inn.

As she ambled along, she admired the green pasture to her left and the waist-high tassels of ochre wheat that grew on her right. Lovelace knew that both those colors suited her admirably. A narrow stream trickled beside the lane, parallel to the split rail fence that enclosed the cow pasture. A little distance beyond her, on the far side of the fence, lay a wooded grove, shadowy and inviting.

She hopped nimbly across the stream and, without any thought that she might be trespassing, clamored over the fence, careful that the handbill she still carried did not become creased during her transit. She went along the inside of the fence until she reached the grove. The little brook, she saw, had also followed a similar yen to be among the trees—just after the wood began, the stream verged off from boundary duty and entered the cool, sun-dappled glade.

It was a delightful grove, carpeted with lacy fronds of fern and velvety moss. A fit setting for elfin revels in faerie cotillions. And for faerie princesses, she thought wistfully. She settled herself on a rock, letting the peaceful gurgling of the brook calm her tattered nerves.

And they were quite tattered, she vowed, as she fanned herself with the handbill. Rows with her parents were becoming all too frequent for her taste. And the one they'd had that morning had been a dilly. It wasn't her fault that, in addition to being blessed with looks and talent, she drew young men to her like bees to a honey jar. She had no say in the matter. And she certainly had not encouraged that silly squire's son back in Grantley to pursue her. Well, maybe just a tiny bit. She had no way of predicting he would tell his irritable father that he fully intended to wed his blond divinity.

The result of that ardent and impetuous disclosure had been the eruption of the outraged squire onto the stage during the troupe's final performance of *Letitia, or the Governess Among the Banditti*. The squire had all but wrung down the curtain.

It was really most unfair! Letitia was one of her favorite roles, and the landslide scene in the final act was quite taxing. It was hard enough to keep your mind on your lines, she reflected with a frown, without the distraction of your mother shrieking from the wings or watching your father—in full bandit regalia—bulldog a squirming, sputtering squire off the stage.

At least that unpleasant episode was behind her. It was on to London and the production of the new play. And her much-longed-for introduction to the illustrious Lord Troy.

The brook's trilling sound had taken on an unusual undertone, and Lovelace halted her daydreaming to listen. The noise was low-pitched and staccato; like the voices of men engaged in a heated argument.

She left her rock and went whisper-soft through the trees toward the source of the sound. Sure enough, in a small clearing some forty feet beyond her, two men were locked in verbal combat, their muffled voices rising and falling in the cadence of discord.

She crept closer and then peeked around an oak trunk, noting their hostile posture for future reference—she intended to write a play herself one day, and made a point of gathering interesting scenes for her opus. The man facing away from her was tall and dark, she observed, and wore a boxy blue jacket. His hands were fisted at his sides. The other man was fair, of medium height, and wore a claret-colored riding coat beneath a caped greatcoat. As she watched, his face twisted into a scowl. He spat out a word Lovelace had never heard before, his anger palpable even from such a distance, and then he snarled out, "This is all I found, I tell you!"

The dark man responded in a low voice—Lovelace could not make out his words. The fair-haired man immediately launched himself at his companion and they began to fight in earnest, grappling hand to hand. Seconds later a knife appeared in the dark man's hand and, under Lovelace's disbelieving gaze, he plunged it into his adversary's chest. A scarlet stain spread across the pristine whiteness of the victim's shirt until it blended with the darker crimson of his coat.

Lovelace screamed then. A nice, carrying theatrical scream. If she'd had time for reflection, she would have realized it was not the most politic thing to do in that situation.

The tall man swung around, his gaze darting through the trees. He started at once in Lovelace's direction, heedless of the man who now lay unmoving at his feet.

Lovelace spun and thrust herself back against the tree, tucking her skirts close around her. She waited, heart pounding, for what seemed like an aeon. It was quiet in the wood—either the man had gone away or he knew how to move with great stealth.

"Got you!" A hand reached out to grab her wrist.

She gasped and turned to him for only a second—had a brief glimpse of a tanned face and pale eyes—before she twisted violently, wrenching free from his hold, and pelted off toward the field. Lifting her skirts to free her legs, she ran as though the very hounds of hell pursued her. When she broke free of the wood, she ran close along the fence, gasping raggedly for breath with each stride.

In the distance she could see the slate gables of the inn drawing ever closer. What she didn't see was the grass-covered rabbit hole that lay beside the fence. Her right foot slid into it up to the ankle and she went down, tumbling headlong over the grass.

She lay on her stomach, winded and unable to move, waiting breathlessly for the tall man to come up with her and stick his knife in her back. Her heart began to beat a rapid tattoo in her chest as she sensed something large moving over the grass toward her, its shadow blocking out the sun. She closed her eyes and scrunched up her face in dreadful anticipation.

A large, wet, raspy tongue slithered over the back of her neck.

"Aoow!" she wailed, sitting up and pushing the amorous heifer's head away from her. "Go, bossy!" she cried, slapping at the sleek brown neck. The cow blinked at her several times and then moved slowly away to graze.

Lovelace shrank back as another shadow fell over her. This time it was a tall man, backlit by the sun, sitting on a rangy red horse.

"I saw you take a tumble," he remarked evenly in a refined voice. "Never a good idea to run beside a fence. All sorts of creatures burrow along there."

"Someone was chasing me," she said, holding back a sob. "With a knife."

The man dismounted with a graceful motion and came forward to kneel beside her. His hair was dark and his face was tanned. His coloring was not unlike the murderer's, she realized with a shock. But he was dressed more elegantly than the stranger in the woods, and his eyes were full of concern, though in a detached way.

"Sprained it, have you," he said, as he touched his fingers to her swelling ankle, which was revealed beneath the twisted hem of her gown.

Lovelace looked down horrified. A sprain could take weeks to mend, and she had to be treading the boards in the new play in just over a fortnight. Tears began to course down her cheeks.

"Hey, none of that," the man said. He looked beyond her across the field. "At least your pursuer seems to have cleared off. Not that I saw anyone chasing you, mind."

Lovelace felt an overwhelming relief that the man with the knife had opted for caution rather than pursue her across an open meadow where anyone might see him. But she also recalled, with a sickening lurch of her stomach, that she had dropped her handbill as she ran from behind the oak tree. The man had seen her face, and now he knew her identity.

Oh Lord! she groaned to herself. If only Charles had made the portrait a bit less accurate. Given her a hooked nose, sunken cheeks, or beady little eyes. Anything that would have obscured the fact that Lovelace Wellesley, the pride of Wellesley's Wandering Minstrels, was the same young woman who had seen foul murder done.

She was crying full out now in panic. It wasn't fair! She had her whole life ahead of her.

Without so much as a by-your-leave, the stranger hoisted her into his arms and lifted her up onto the back of his tall horse. "Is there someone nearby who can look after you?" he inquired once he had settled her in the saddle.

"My family is at the Iron Duke," she sobbed through her raised hands.

The man made no response, so she lifted her eyes. He was staring back at her, a look of perplexity on his lean face.

"Over there," she said weakly, pointing in the direction of the inn. "Those gray gables."

"Oh, there," he said, as a wry smile of comprehension twisted his cheek. "It was called the Tattie and Snip until last month." He began to lead his horse along the fence. "I don't know what old Tolliver was thinking, to change the name. It's been the Tattie and Snip since I was a lad."

Looking down at her rescuer, Lovelace judged that to have been some time ago. There were strands of silvery gray scattered in the man's dark brown hair—she could see them clearly from her vantage point in the saddle—though she had to admit the loose curls which tumbled over his brow were not without a certain charm. Percival Lancaster, the leading man in her father's troupe, had to resort to heated tongs to cajole his hair into such fashionable disarray.

The man led the horse through a gate in the fence, and then over the brook into the narrow lane. Even before they reached the inn, Lovelace saw with a sinking heart that the troupe's two vehicles were gone from the front yard. She began to cry even louder, for once not caring that tears positively blighted her creamy complexion.

The man stopped. "What the devil is it now?"

"They're gone!" she wailed. "My family's gone."

He followed the line of her vision, saw the empty yard, and then looked up at her. "What sort of people are your parents, that they would hare off and leave their daughter behind?"

"Ac-tors," she hiccuped raggedly, and then realized she hadn't precisely answered his whole question. "I was supposed to be resting in the prop wagon," she explained. "But I went for a walk instead. They clearly thought I was still napping in there and set off for London."

The man rubbed the back of one hand across his chin. "Stay here," he snapped. "I'll go talk to Tolliver."

Lovelace sat in the shadow of a tall beech tree, every so often casting fearful looks behind her. When at last the man came around the corner of the inn, his expression of distemper hadn't lessened.

"They're gone, sure enough. Your mother wanted to look in on you, but Tolliver heard your father say that you needed your rest. You'll just have to wait here until they discover you are missing and come back for you."

"But what of the man with the knife?" She whimpered. "This is the first place he will look for me."

"There is no man with a knife," the gentleman bit out, his patience clearly on the wane. "You must have banged your head when you fell, which has given you this addled notion that someone was chasing you. It's most unlikely that a man with a knife would be lurking in my cow pasture waiting to do harm to young scamps like you."

In spite of her tears, Lovelace drew herself up. As a reigning goddess of the boards, she had never, ever, been referred to as a scamp. "He was chasing me," she uttered in her most acid tone, "because I witnessed a murder."

The man below her rolled his eyes. "In my cow pasture?"

"In the woods," she pronounced. "He was arguing with another man, and then he pulled out a knife and stuck it in the other fellow's chest."

"You've a lurid imagination, I'll give you that." He looked even less convinced than before.

"Take me there," she ordered. "And I will show you where it happened."

The stranger shrugged. "I suppose I can put off inspecting my cattle for another half hour, but if we don't find anything, you're coming right back to the Tattie and Snip."

"You mean the Iron Duke," she huffed, as he led his horse back up the lane.

Lady Jemima Vale held up her drawing of the lightning-struck tree that lay at the edge of the field and frowned deeply, setting a line of wrinkles across her smooth white brow. No matter how much she smudged the pencil marks or even erased them altogether, the sketch still looked more like a skeletal hand reaching up from the ground than a towering, majestic oak. In frustration she turned her sketchbook completely upside down. Now it was a skeletal hand reaching down from the sky.

She sighed. It was a trial to be so absolutely lacking in artistic ability. Especially coming from the family she had been born into. No, that wasn't fair. Some people were blessed with creative talent, and others possessed more practical gifts. At least that was what she told herself when she was feeling blue-deviled. Which was an all-too-frequent occurrence lately.

She closed her sketchbook, folded her canvas stool, and looked about for a more inviting subject. She had already sketched the inn where she was staying, and the wheat field on her left offered little inspiration. As she cut across the field, brushing back the waist-high, tasseled grass, she caught sight of a rider leading a packhorse beside the small wood that lay in the distance. A picturesque subject to be sure—the bearded peddler with his loose blue coat and wide-brimmed felt hat, his pack of goods slewed over a second horse and bound with rope. But, Jemima reasoned, even the best artists found horses a tricky subject, and anyway, the man would be out of sight by the time she reached the lane.

Perhaps she would find something worth sketching in the wood, she thought, as she came out onto the narrow track. A collection of trees might prove less taxing than a single one. She climbed nimbly over the rail fence—an easy feat for a tall, long-limbed woman—and wandered along a chuckling brook, searching for a good vantage point. She had just settled her stool in a small clearing, which offered a pleasant view of quaking aspens, when someone called out, "Hullo there!"

She swiveled on her stool. A man was standing at the edge of the woods, some distance behind her.

In the general way of things, she was quite stouthearted, but there was something about the man's tall silhouette that made her heart lurch.

"Nitwit!" she chided herself. Is this what happens when you near your thirtieth year? she wondered crossly. Did all the missish behavior you detested in others come rising up in your own character at that time? It certainly seemed to be the case.

"Excuse me," the man called out. "But have you seen anyone in the woods?"

Jemima got up from her stool. "I've only just gotten here," she called back. There was a chestnut horse standing behind the man with a young woman clinging to its saddle. She said something to him and pointed to Jemima's right. He then tethered the horse to a branch and came toward Jemima, brushing back the foliage with his riding crop. The closer he came, the more she had to resist the urge to run off.

Not that he looked particularly ominous. He was tall and dressed like your garden-variety country squire, in the fawn buckskins, narrow top boots, and long-tailed riding coat of the sporting gentleman. His cravat was carelessly knotted about his throat. He was hatless, and his breeze-tossed hair had settled into wayward curls over his brow. She imagined the face of such a man would be hearty, open, and a bit vacant around the eyes.

As he came closer she realized she was wrong on all counts. Lord, this man wasn't your garden-variety anything!

Though he wore his clothing with a loose, easy grace, the coat had not been cut by any hand less sure than Weston's and the gleaming boots had probably set him back a pony at least. And his eyes, rather than appearing empty, looked, as they appraised her, to be sharp as a hawk's. And they were a distinctive shade of pale gray, like snow clouds just before a storm. Those eyes, set deep in a face that was harsh and unfashionably tanned, gave the stranger an unsettling aura of menace. She shivered slightly and again had the urge to flee.

He came to a halt a few feet from her, crossed his arms over his chest, and leaned against a convenient tree trunk.

"See anything you like?" he asked in a lazy voice, clearly amused by her overt scrutiny.

"I'll let you know if I do," she retorted with a flash of her own eyes. Her foolish compulsion to bolt had made her snappish.

His face broke into a surprised smile—as though he approved her show of spirit—and Jemima felt her knees start to buckle. She hadn't accounted him a handsome man; he was too rugged-looking for true masculine beauty. But that smile did wonders for all the harsh planes of his lean face.

"I just thought you'd like to know," he remarked evenly, "that you are trespassing on my land. I'm not sure what the penalty is for such a crime—" His eyes danced over her with studied insolence. "But I wager I can think of something."

Jemima too a tiny step back. Was he being purposely rude or was this just his normal manner with strangers?

She was about to make a scathing reply as to what he could do with his infernal "penalty," when he added in a less baiting tone. "You might not want to hang about, actually. My young companion back there claims she saw murder done in this grove. And within the past half hour."

Jemima looked beyond the tall man to the blond girl on the horse. Even from that distance she could hear the sound of staccato sobbing.

She said softly. "Well, then, no wonder she's weeping."

The man hitched his shoulders. "She cries at the least provocation."

"Oh? And have you been provoking her?" Jemima asked, turning her gaze back to him.

"Not any more than I usually provoke unfledged misses." There was testy anger in his tone now. "I believe it is the crime she witnessed that has turned her into a watering pot."

Jemima sniffed audibly as she went past him through the trees, to where the horse had been tethered. The girl who waited there was fashionably, if a bit garishly, dressed in a pink muslin gown heavily sprigged with pansies and violets, which featured a large posy of silk flowers at the bodice and bands of ruched, violet ribbon along the hem. She gazed down at Jemima with limpid brown eyes.

"Are you feeling any better?" Jemima asked.

"Nooo!" the girl wailed. "I have seen foul murder done and have wrenched my ankle in a rabbit hole."

"There, there," Jemima clucked, not sure how one consoled a witness to foul murder. "I'm sure everything will get sorted out."

"I have to be Virtue," the blond keened. "I cannot be Virtue hobbling about on a stick."

As Jemima turned to the tall man who had come up behind her, her bewilderment at the young woman's cryptic lament was written all over her face.

"She's an actress," he whispered, bending close to her ear. "Lovelace Wellesley. Part of a troupe of players. You know, the sort who travel about the provinces butchering the classics."

The man had carried the folding stool and her sketchbook from the wood. He set the stool down and, before she could stop him, he proceeded to open the sketchbook, riffling quickly through the pages.

"These are dreadful," he pronounced with a squint. He raised the book and tipped it slightly. "Is that a mountain top or a lump of pudding?"

She snatched the book from him with an unladylike snarl. "I see," she uttered, "that you are both theater critic and art critic."

He gave an infuriatingly unconcerned shrug and raised his gaze to her. "I know what I like . . ." He let his voice drift. "And I know when I'm looking at something that pleases me."

Jemima had the disconcerting feeling he was speaking about neither art nor the theater.

"Thank you for fetching my things," she said briskly as she bent to pick up her stool. "I will take care not to trespass again."

She was about to take herself off, when Miss Wellesley cried out, "Oh, please, ma'am, don't go. My family has left me here, and I have no one to turn to."

The girl sounded truly desolated. Jemima bit her lip. It would be hours yet before her brother returned to the inn—sometimes in the aftermath of boxing matches, the revelry could go on all night, especially for those lucky souls who had backed the winner. She had nothing to occupy her time, save defaming more of the local landscape with her pencil. And what was more, she had never been remotely involved in a murder, even as a bystander.

"All right," she said, reaching up to pat the girl's hand. "I'll stay for a bit, if you like."

"Thank you," the girl responded in a wavery voice. "You are very kind."

Bryce was striding about in the woods, looking for the particular clearing the chit had described, and grumbling all the while that he had far better things to do with his time than track down nonexistent murderers for teary-eyed, playacting damsels.

This was what came of things, he mused irritably, when you abandoned the sordid pleasures of London for the more bucolic pleasures of the countryside. His father owed him for this. He could be sitting in White's this very minute, sharing luncheon with his intimates, or better yet, getting intimate with his latest paramour and sharing . . . well, best not meander in that direction. He was a long way from the sultry embraces of Tatiana Stanhope. A very long way.

Not that the peppery brunette he'd just met didn't have possibilities. She was definitely to his taste—tall, long-limbed, and nicely rounded. A bit long in the tooth, perhaps, but he himself was well past his thirtieth year, and he knew that age rarely decreased appetite. At least in men. He wondered, as he scoured the landscape for any signs of a struggle, if the lady in question was ripe for a small intrigue. He'd never seen her before in the neighborhood; she was probably staying at the inn, which greatly increased her allure. Birds of passage always made the best meal—so to speak. And as was his habit, Bryce was not seeking entanglement, only entertainment.

He stood uptight and stretched, relieved that he could go back to his less troublesome duties now. There hadn't been any sign of two combatants, let alone a bloodied body.

He made his way back to the two women. Miss Wellesley had finally controlled her tears; she sat silently on his horse, her fingers knotted in its mane.

"Nothing," he uttered with a shake of his head. "I looked in every clearing. I think I'd better take you back to the inn now, Miss Wellesley—the landlord's wife can see to your ankle."

The girl nodded weakly.

He turned to ask the brown-haired woman where she was staying, and the words stuck in his throat.

She gazed back at him with a puzzled frown. "Sir?"

He reached out and gingerly drew the stool from under her arm, and then with his free hand he lifted a fold of her skirt. She looked down and gasped. Small reddish-brown smears marred the prim muslin surface. He turned the stool over. Sure enough a reddish residue still clung to two of the feet.

"I'll be damned!" he muttered.

"You see! I didn't imagine it," Lovelace crowed. "I am not at all the sort of person who makes things up."

"Are you all right?" Bryce was leaning toward the tall woman, whose face had gone a little green. He dropped the stool and swiftly took hold of her arms.

"Yes," she said, holding the back of her hand against her mouth as she closed her eyes briefly. "Yes, it was just a shock. I'm . . . far too old for such missish behavior." She didn't see the amused glance he leveled at her as she made a visible effort to compose herself.

She took a deep breath. "I . . . I gather I was sitting on the very spot where the murder took place."

Bryce released her arms and stepped back, seeing that she was no longer in any danger of swooning. "It would seem to be the case."

He quickly returned to the clearing where the budding artist had placed her stool and found a dark, damp-looking stain on the matted grass. He rubbed at it with his fingers; they came away streaked with a ruddy smear.

Damn! This was just what he needed to make his day. He had a dozen cows ill with milk fever, half his tenant farmers laid low with the influenza, and his housekeeper had reported only that morning that there were death-watch beetles in the wainscotting. But this infernal problem certainly topped them all.

He'd have to alert Sir Walter, the local magistrate, straight off. And once the news spread, he'd have half the district trooping through his cow pasture to visit the spot. A gruesome murder was sure to invite a great many curiosity seekers, especially in this quiet district. He'd be lucky if his entire herd of Holsteins wasn't off its feed by the end of the week.

He also had no idea of what to do with the blond-haired tear factory. Returning her to the Tattie and Snip was out of the question now. He had a fair idea of what he'd like to do with the tall brunette, but that also was not an option, at least for the moment.

Bryce wiped the traces of blood from his hand with his handkerchief and then tied it on a branch beside the clearing to mark the spot for Sir Walter.

He was still scowling when he returned to the edge of the wood. "There is a deal of blood there," he pronounced. "But no corpse."

"There has to be a corpse," Lovelace insisted softly.

"Maybe not," Bryce said slowly. "Maybe the second man was only wounded and went off on his own."

"Oh, no! I saw the knife go in. It was a mortal wound, I am sure of it."

He looked up at the girl. "Well, I can't take you back to the inn now. It is the first place the murderer would look for you. Your parents picked the devil of a time to run off, Miss Wellesley." He gave an exasperated sigh. "I'd best take you to my house for the time being. My housekeeper can see to your ankle." As he spoke, he unhitched his horse's reins from the tree branch.

"Is yours a bachelor household, sir?" the tall woman inquired in a no-nonsense voice.

"Last time I checked," Bryce said with a chuckle. "But I rarely make a habit of deflowering children."

"I am not a child," Lovelace protested. "I turn seventeen this October. And have been playing young ladies on the stage any time these past three years."

"I think she'd do better at the inn," the woman insisted. "Surely she can't come to any harm in such a public place."

He worried at his lip. This whole thing had blown up into a ripping old farce.

"It's not a good idea," he said. "Miss Wellesley told me she had the misfortune to drop a playbill with her picture *and* her name on it, practically under the ruffian's nose. She's safer with me, whatever you may think, Miss—"

"Vale," she said coolly. "Lady Jemima Vale. And you are—"

In response he drew a card from his waistcoat pocket and handed it to her with a brief nod of his head. Her eyes darkened and her mouth tightened into a knot as she read the words.

"Let me see." Lovelace reached down and twitched the card from Jemima's hand. "Beecham Bryce," she read aloud.

"At your service," he murmured.

"I believe I've heard that name before," the girl mused. She fluttered her eyelids coquettishly as she returned the card to his hand. "Are you someone famous, Mr. Bryce?"

Before he could answer, Lady Jemima said sharply. "Oh, he's famous all right. Or perhaps infamous is a more fitting word—he's possibly the greatest libertine in the country."

Bryce bowed graciously as he tucked the card in his pocket.

"You give me too much credit, ma'am. Perhaps in the south of England."

Jemima put up her chin. "That's settled it—she is coming with me to the inn."

"No," the girl cried out. "I want to go with him. He'll protect me." She leaned down from the saddle and said to Lady Jemima, "Can *you* protect me?"

Jemima crossed her arms, glaring at Bryce as she muttered, "I doubt anyone could protect you from the likes of him."

Bryce thought it was time to end the melodrama. "There is an obvious solution," he said smoothly. "If you, Lady Jemima, would also avail yourself of my hospitality, then Miss Wellesley will be properly chaperoned. And as a lady of advanced years"—he paused to let his words sink in—"you will surely be beyond any adverse gossip."

Lady Jemima appeared to be speechless.

"There, now," he said with a patently false smile. "Hasn't that settled things nicely. I'll get you squared away in my house and then ride back to alert the innkeeper that he is only to reveal this young lady's whereabouts to her parents."

He took up the reins of his horse and headed across the cow pasture with Lovelace in tow. Lady Jemima hung back for several minutes, as if weighing her options, and then came after them at a fast clip. Bryce waited at the edge of the meadow, watching her graceful, long-limbed progress over the grass. It did wonderful things to his imagination.

Perhaps his enforced sojourn in the country wasn't going to be so dull after all.

Chapter Two

They reached the man's home—Bryce Prospect, he had called it—after a half mile walk. Jemima was surprised to discover it was a large, baronial manor house, set deep in a hollow like a mourning dove in her nest. Which was an apt simile, since the house was constructed from an unusual taupe-colored stone, rather close in hue to the plumage of those gentle birds, It was perhaps a century and a half old, square and unadorned except for the ivy that traced over the stonework of the lower floors. Someone in a more recent era had added a white, colonnaded walkway to the east wing of the house, which softened the uncompromising lines of the structure. A rolling green lawn, which gave way to dense woodland, surrounded it on three sides. Behind the colonnade lay a large garden, bright with June blossoms.

As they made their way along the pebbled drive, Jemima could see that each individual stone of the facade was carved with an intricate key design, a marvel of workmanship that drew the eye. It occurred to her that the house was rather like its owner—unremarkable from a distance, but richly compelling up close. Compelling and distinctly irritating, Mr. Beecham Bryce was. And probably quite dangerous to impressionable women. Not that she fell into that category, Jemima assured herself. And he was, furthermore, unlikely to make any attempt to impress a woman he considered to be of such advanced years.

Jemima ground her teeth as she followed her host up the shallow stone steps to the uncovered porch.

Bryce had lifted Lovelace from his horse and was now carrying her so as not to tax her injured ankle. Jemima had to admit that his attention to the girl seemed wholly disinterested. Perhaps he was not attracted to overwrought blonds, or perhaps, as he himself had said, he wasn't interested in deflowering children.

Poor Mr. Bryce, she thought wryly. Miss Wellesley was too young for his tastes and she herself was too old. But then, know-

ing his reputation, he probably had a *cher amie* secreted somewhere in the house. In her experience, rakes rarely traveled far
from their favorite recreation.

They were met at the door by en elderly butler. Bryce dismissed
the man's offer of assistance with a shake of his head. He re-
quested only that the housekeeper be summoned to attend his
guest, and then he made his way to the wide staircase that rose up
from the center of the marble-tiled hall.

Jemima followed them up the stairs, noting the exquisite wainscotting and the graceful chestnut bannister that soared up from the
foyer. The shadowed hall retained a comforting odor of domestic
industry—beeswax, linseed oil, and a tangier scent she couldn't
quite identify.

Bryce had finished settling Miss Wellesley on the bed as
Jemima came through the door. He bowed to them and beat a hasty
retreat. She was drawing a comforter over the girl when the housekeeper, a motherly woman in a prim lace cap, came bustling into
the room with a basket over one arm.

"Leave her to Mrs. Patch, ma'am," the woman said with a reassuring smile. "I'll see she's made comfortable."

"I'll be fine," Lovelace said weakly, gazing up at Jemima. "I just
need to rest awhile."

She stood back and watched as Mrs. Patch gently removed
Lovelace's kid slipper, and then began to wrap her ankle in a gauze
bandage from her basket. Everything looked to be well in hand, so
Jemima slipped from the room.

"Tea, Lady Jemima?"

She looked up, startled. Bryce was leaning back against the wall
opposite Lovelace's bedroom door, one booted leg crossed over
the other. "Or would that be too compromising a situation—taking
tea alone with a gentleman?"

"I see nothing wrong with taking tea with a *gentleman*," she pronounced crisply. "But since that isn't likely to be an option in this
house, I will accept *your* offer."

Her host merely grinned and motioned her toward the stairs.

Jemima was too busy observing the interior furnishings, the fine
paintings and richly carved furniture that embellished the hall, to
note the admiring light in Bryce's eyes as he watched her precede
him down the staircase. It would have surprised her to see it, since
she considered herself to be less than remarkable in the way of
looks. "Middling brown hair, and middling green eyes," was how
she had once described herself to a school friend.

Bryce, on the other hand, thought her waving chestnut hair, with its glints of deep red, a glorious contrast to her pale, magnolia skin. He still hadn't decided if her expressive, almond-shaped eyes were green or blue, since they showed a bit of each color in their depths. He'd once seen an Austrian lake that exact shade—clear azure and shimmering with light.

He ushered her into the sitting room, waiting until she had settled herself in one of the chairs beside the hearth before he seated himself on the brocade sofa opposite her. He lounged back against the plump cushions, stretching his long legs out before him. "So what brings you to this part of Kent, Lady Jemima?" he asked in a pleasantly conversational voice.

She looked up from pleating a fold in her gown; she was unconsciously trying to cover the smudged bloodstains. "I came down from London with my brother. He's off at a prizefight, you see, but he should be back by evening. I'd like to send him a note, so he'll know where I've gone."

Bryce's eyes darkened. Not a heartening bit of news. Not that he hadn't seduced women under the noses of their families before, but brothers were the worst sort of obstacle.

"He's quite welcome to stay here," he stated, knowing he was setting himself a challenge even as he made the offer. "I've plenty of room. And it would certainly ease your mind."

"My mind?" Jemima looked up again from her pleating.

"I'm hardly likely to assail your virtue, with your brother under my roof."

Jemima sniffed. She was doing that far too much lately, she knew. Another missish trait coming to the fore. "I thought my age precluded that possibility."

He smiled slowly and then shrugged. "It's so hard to say. We libertines never know who might strike our fancy. I knew a roué once, who hungered for a washer woman." He leaned forward, his hand upon his knee. "Why? Are you hoping I will try?"

Jemima's eyes narrowed. "As there is no point in answering such an absurd question, I will ignore it."

"Yes, and avoid telling me the truth. Neatly done, Lady Jemima." He sketched a salute in the air. "And nicely parried."

They subsided into silence then, Jemima gazing out the French windows, and Bryce surreptitiously gazing at her. He'd cut his eyeteeth on beautiful women, so looks alone rarely gained his attention. He required something more from his conquests—a spark, a challenge, a sense that the winning of favor would be rewarded with spirited play. Lady Jemima's eyes held such a promise, even if her lovely mouth was currently drawn up in a disagreeable pucker.

When the tea tray was brought in, Bryce insisted on pouring. "It's one of my few domestic skills," he told her, as he handed over a cup and saucer. "And I always enjoy seeing to my guest's . . . ah, needs."

Jemima's hand shook slightly as she carried the tea to her mouth. He was toying with her, and she didn't like it one bit. Certainly men had flirted with her before but never with such blatant insinuation. It had a sort of novelty, though she thought a libertine would have cultivated a more subtle approach.

"I am rather less a guest," she stated dryly, "and more a hostage."

He drew back, a wounded expression on his face. "A hostage, Lady Jemima?"

"You coerced me to come here. You knew once I learned your identity, I wouldn't allow Miss Wellesley to stay here unchaperoned. I only pray her parents come to claim her before nightfall."

"Why?" He raised one brow sardonically. "What is going to happen then?"

Jemima nearly blushed. "I mean, I will need to return to the inn by tonight. All my things are there."

"That's easily remedied. When I ride over to see Tolliver, I'll have him pack up your belongings. And as I said, your brother is welcome to stay here." He raised his glass to her and purred, "We'll be a nice, cozy family group."

The expression on his face was neither cozy nor familiar. Wolfish was more like it, she thought, trying to repress a shiver. Jemima had no intention of spending even one night under the same roof as the notorious Beecham Bryce. But she had an uncanny suspicion that Miss Wellesley's family might not discover her absence until that evening, in which case they were unlikely to come back for her until the following morning. Asking Terry to join her at Bryce Prospect seemed like the wisest course to follow. She could see that Miss Wellesely was properly chaperoned, and her brother's presence would surely keep her host in line with regard to herself.

"Very well," she said as she rose to her feet. "I'll ask my brother to come here. He can bring our luggage over in his carriage and save Mr. Tolliver the trouble. Now, if you would just direct me to some writing paper."

Bryce waved her over to an escritoire in one corner of the room. She quickly dashed off a note, asking her brother to collect their things and giving him the directions to Bryce Prospect.

"I'll ride over now," Bryce said as he tucked her note in his coat pocket. "I may be a while—I'm going to drop in on our local magistrate and fill him in on this murder business."

Jemima had nearly forgotten about the murder. She clasped her hands against her skirt. "I still can't credit that a man was murdered in that peaceful grove. Could it be someone from your estate, do you think?"

Bryce tapped his lip with a long forefinger. "I doubt it. Our prima donna told me that neither of the men were dressed like farm laborers, and that both appeared to be fairly young. My bailiff is a bit of a dandy, but he's pushing sixty. No, I think I can eliminate any of my people, either as victim or villain. That section of the pasture isn't far from the main road, so it's possible the men were travelers who stopped to rest, and then fell into an argument."

Jemima leaned toward him. "And do you really believe the murderer will come after Miss Wellesley?"

Bryce's eyes darkened. "Yes," he said with a slight frown. "He knows she got a good look at him. If he doesn't find her at the inn, I suspect he'll start asking after her father's troupe."

"Then she shouldn't be allowed to go off with them to London," Jemima stated forcefully.

"Yes," he mused, elated at the thought of Miss Wellesley and her starchy but delectable chaperon being forced to extend their stay in his home. "I hadn't considered that till now. Well, we'll deal with that issue when it arises."

Bryce headed for the door and Jemima followed him. He stopped, his hand on the latch, and turned to her. "I think perhaps you should go upstairs and have a rest. After all, Miss Wellesley's not the only one who's had a—" His sentence drifted to a halt.

"What is it?" she asked. He was looking at her with an oddly arrested expression on his face.

"Sorry," he said, shaking himself back to the present. "It's just that you've got the most remarkable blue eyes, Lady Jemima. A man could drown in them."

"They're green," she insisted, setting her jaw.

He leaned very close, so that his face was only inches from her own, and peered intently into her eyes. "So they are," he announced blithely, just before he went through the door.

For a long while after he left, Jemima leaned against the door with her hands fisted, trying to regain her composure. And trying to deny the unaccountable fluttering in her stomach his idle compliment had provoked.

No, she vowed, she was not about to let herself become a diversion for some half-baked libertine. She knew far too much about
Beecham Bryce's reputation to ever let herself be coaxed into indiscretion by a few flattering words. The man had been cutting a
swath through the *ton* since before her come-out, making his name
a byword for all that was licentious and low. His first public in-
famy, she recalled, had been dallying with the wife of a professor
while he was at Cambridge. The upshot of that had been a duel between student and don, whereby Bryce had put the man out of
commission for six months. Needless to say his university educa-
tion had rather stalled after that.

There was another scandal after he enlisted in the army and was
sent to the Peninsula—something to do with a Portuguese noble-
man's wife. The husband in that instance had been killed in his duel
of honor, and young Lieutenant Bryce had been court-martialed. He
only escaped a firing squad when it came out that the dead man had
been selling military information to the French. The army had no
idea what to do with a rascal like Beecham Bryce, and so they had
cut him loose; he returned to London, if not actually in disgrace,
certainly without the laurels another man might have earned for rid-
ding Wellington of a poxy spy.

Three years ago the worst of the scandals had erupted—Jemima
remembered the year because Terry had used Bryce as a model for
one of his less-than-virtuous heroes. The man had fixed his interest on the young wife of a military hero. The chit had run off with
Bryce while her husband was in Spain serving under Wellington,
and then had apparently died under mysterious circumstances. To
Bryce's credit, he had not run when the bereaved husband caught
up with him and faced him over pistols. Bryce had taken a bullet
in his shoulder. He'd maintained a somewhat lower profile after
that sordid affair, involving himself in a long line of less-
sensational amours, involving opera dancers, orange girls, and the
like.

But he had resurfaced late last year, as the founder of a private
men's club called Bacchus. It was very exclusive, highly selective,
and, rumor had it, catered to gentlemen with unusual appetites.
Terry was a member, Jemima knew, though she hadn't heard it
from his lips. But by the time her brother had joined, just this past
May, Bryce was off to greener pastures. Literally it appeared. No
one in London knew where he had gone, and now it was her bad
luck to stumble across him in this remote part of Kent.

She only wondered that she had never before encountered him

in the *ton*. Few doors of proper society were open to him, it was true. Few hostesses welcomed him into their homes. According to the tattlemongers, he spent a great deal of time in the less savory reaches of London—the slums of the East End, and the rat-infested wharves of the south bank. Where he could rub elbows, no doubt, with the worst sort of knaves and blackguards. And where he would, furthermore, find innumerable young women who were easy prey for a man with the outer trappings of a gentleman.

But in spite of Bryce's rare appearances at *ton* functions and his bizarre taste in neighborhoods, it was still hard for Jemima to credit that she had spent most of her adult life in London without ever having him pointed out to her.

And who, she asked herself, would point out the king of profligates to a well-bred maiden lady? Certainly not that lady's brother, not her elderly Aunt Sophie. Certainly not any of the artists and writers Jemima gathered for her monthly salons.

She sighed as she crossed the room and went to stand before the fireplace. *Someone* should have pointed him out to her. So she could have been forewarned, so she could have been prepared for the shock of meeting him face-to-face. It was disconcerting, to say the least, to discover that every nerve ending in her body quivered with physical awareness when she was in his presence. She again recalled how he had sat across from her, completely relaxed, to all appearances the genial host. Except for the strange fire that had gleamed in his frost-colored eyes, a fire that had set her insides to quaking. No man had ever leveled such a look at her in all her twenty-nine years.

She was surprised to discover his potent masculine allure had little to do with his looks. One assumed a libertine would need to be an adonis if he was to have any power over women. Not that Beecham Bryce was exactly ill-favored, but Jemima knew a dozen men, including her brother, who beat him all to flinders in that respect. No, it wasn't his lean, roguish face or his wide, muscular shoulders that made him so dangerous—it was something else entirely. He projected an unstudied grace, an ease with his body, as though he were more comfortable in his own skin than other mortals. And he possessed a devilish humor, at once deprecating and flattering.

No! she railed to herself, as she again went pacing across the carpet. *Stop analyzing why he is so dangerous, and admit only that you see the danger.*

She threw herself onto the sofa and began to fret at one of the pillows.

Except for that last comment about her eyes, he had said nothing to her that was overtly flirtatious. And yet she had a strong sense that he had been flirting with her, baiting her, trying to break through her maidenly reserve. God knew, no one had attempted anything even remotely like that for more years than she wanted to count.

That's all it is, she told herself reasonably. *You are imagining his interest in you, because, like all maiden ladies, you see a threat where there is none. Next thing you'll be sleeping with a pistol beside your bed to ward off phantom intruders with amatory intentions.*

It was a pity though, a puckish voice noted from deep inside her. Because if one had a mind to be debauched, Beecham Bryce was not an uninspiring choice.

Muttering to herself, Jemima stalked from the room, intending to look in on Miss Wellesley. She reckoned the girl's tearful prattling could not be more vexing than her own contradictory thoughts.

Bryce returned home just barely in time for dinner. He apologized for appearing in his riding clothes, but he pointed out that neither Lady Jemima nor Miss Wellesley had a change of wardrobe either.

"We will be very informal," he announced over drinks in the drawing room.

The resourceful housekeeper had furnished Lovelace with a cane, and so she had been able to hobble down to dinner. After Bryce had coaxed her from her sullen unhappiness with a humorous story of his first and only attempt at becoming a steeplechase jockey, she began to sparkle with charm.

Jemima could see, now that Lovelace was no longer tearstained and in shock, that she was an extraordinarily pretty girl—and one who had clearly learned to maximize every bit of allure she possessed. Bryce had placed them on either side of him at dinner, and Lovelace—for that was what she insisted they call her—spent most of the meal flirting outrageously with her host. She simpered and preened, cooed and gurgled. She looked limpidly up through her long, suspiciously dark lashes, and gazed wistfully down over her pert but elegant nose.

I ought to be taking notes, Jemima thought ruefully. The chit had it down to an art.

For his part, Bryce seemed to take her chatter in stride. He laughed at the proper times during her gay stories of life on the boards and frowned soberly when she regaled him with some dire tragedy that had befallen her. But Jemima noticed—she was able to observe him freely, as most of his attention was fixed on Lovelace—that when he grinned at his young guest, the smile never quite reached his eyes, and when he frowned in sympathy, they likewise remained unaffected.

Two-thirds of the way through dinner, as Lovelace was prodding at a platter of cutlets with a fork, Bryce turned to Jemima and whispered, "Lay you odds they never come back for her."

"What?" She nearly choked on her ragout of veal.

"Her family," he said over the back of one elegantly manicured hand. "They're probably popping a cork this very minute in celebration. Well, would *you* want her back? She could talk the scales off a haddock and have breath left over to inflate a dozen hot air balloons."

Jemima hid her grin behind her napkin. "She *is* a trifle self-impressed."

Bryce rolled his eyes. "She could give lessons to Prinny himself." And then he added in a more conversational voice. "Now then, Lady Jemima, why not tell us something about yourself."

"Yes," Lovelace crooned, turning from her cutlets. "I am all agog to hear about you."

Jemima realized she was pleating her skirt again. The housekeeper had managed to remove the bloodstains, but she was still fretting at the fabric. "I lead a quiet life in London," she said. "I look after my brother—he has . . . interests in London that keep him very busy." She wasn't going to say anything more about Terry. They'd find out soon enough if he decided to overnight there.

"And occasionally," she added, "I visit with my two sisters who live in Surrey. They both have young children, you see, and appreciate my help."

"I am prodigiously fond of my own family," Lovelace pronounced. "I have been teaching my brother Charles to sing, and he has shown a deal of progress."

"Ah, so you sing, Miss Wellesley," Jemima exclaimed brightly. "Perhaps you would entertain us after dinner. I would be happy to play for you." She felt Bryce's foot kicking against her ankle in protest. *Not very seductive,* she thought, trying not to grin.

Lovelace's eyes lit. "I would adore it. I blush to say this, but my voice has been acclaimed in places as far away as Leeds."

"They could probably hear her all the way up in Edinburgh," Bryce muttered under his breath.

Jemima shot him a look of reproof.

Lovelace continued to monopolize the conversation through the next three removes, and by the time the port was brought to the table, Jemima had a headache pounding across the back of her head.

"I'll take my port in the drawing room," Bryce announced as he rose from the table. He sidled up beside Jemima as they strolled through the doorway. "You're looking a bit peaky."

"She is like a juggernaut," she hissed back. "Maybe she should run for Parliament."

"You had your chance to forestall her, my pet."

Jemima looked up, startled by the casual endearment.

Bryce wrinkled his nose and said, "Somehow your offering of, 'I lead a quiet life in London,' didn't quite enthrall her enough to throw her off her own track." He raised his brows. "Although I cannot for the life of me see why not."

He moved past her and took Lovelace's arm, guiding his hobbling guest into the drawing room. She at once limped doggedly to the piano and began to sift through the sheet music in the bench. It was clear that Lovelace Wellesley was not about to let a little thing like a sprained ankle keep her from center stage.

"Oh, here is one that I quite adore," she said, holding the sheet up. "Do you know it, Lady J?"

Jemima drew a breath to steady her temper. The girl was unschooled in manners, and not used to society. Much had to be forgiven her. But no one in Jemima's life had ever, *ever* called her Lady J!

"I prefer Jemima," she said gently. "If you don't mind. Lady Jemima."

The girl looked crestfallen for a moment. "Oh, I'm sorry. I didn't mean to be forward. It's just that Jemima is a very . . . oddsounding name, don't you think? I liked it much better when I shortened it."

"Nevertheless," Jemima said, in a voice that could have curdled milk, "odd or not, it is what I prefer."

Lovelace turned to their host. "What do you think, sir? I'm sure this lady will defer to your masculine taste."

"My taste?" Bryce echoed as he settled himself in a wing chair—one which happened to be farthest from the piano. "In truth, I give little thought to women's names." His eyes caught Jemima's and held them. There was that strange fire burning again in their gray depths. "They have other attributes that I find more . . . compelling." He dropped his gaze and let it linger on his glass of port. "But as for your question, Miss Wellesley—I think Jemima is a perfectly useful name. I believe my uncle once had a foxhound named Jemima . . . Or was that Jeremiah?" He looked up and shrugged apologetically.

"See?" Lovelace crowed. "He called it useful. That is hardly a compliment."

Jemima thought the back of her head was going to explode. Which was the least of her problems; when Bryce had cast his heated gaze on her, another part of her anatomy, somewhere below her heart, had started to throb quite unaccountably.

Intent on ignoring her traitorous body, she went to the piano and set up the sheet music Lovelace had chosen. She began to play—with perhaps a bit more heavy-handedness than a popular love ballad required. Lovelace sang with great animation, leaning her weight with both hands upon the cane and swaying in time to the music.

It wasn't a bad voice, Jemima had to admit. But somewhere along the line, someone had instructed the girl to sing every note at the top of her register. The result was a falsetto cacophony that sent one's heart lurching up into one tonsils.

After Lovelace finished her song, Bryce clapped politely. "Delightful, Miss Wellesley. Now if I can interest either of you ladies in a game of commerce . . ."

"I have another song," Lovelace announced breathlessly. She turned to Jemima. "Do you know, 'My Bonny Lad that's Gone Today off to War?' "

Jemima nodded weakly. It wasn't in her to lie, but the dashed song had at least seventeen verses.

Bryce got to his feet. "Perhaps tomorrow night, Miss Wellesley, if you are still here at the Prospect, you can again inspire us with your voice. Now I think you'd best give your ankle a rest and sit here on the sofa." He patted the seat invitingly. "And you can tell me again of your success in Shropshire."

Jemima let her fingers wander over the keys, picking out a Mozart sonata, while her host did his manful best to stay attentive through Lovelace's prattling discourse. She was still feeling the aftereffects of Bryce's heated glance. It bothered her that she could respond to a stranger in such a way. No man, libertine or otherwise, had ever made her insides feel as though someone had lit a torch there. Even in her youth, when she had been courted for who she was, and not yet for who her brother was, no one had ever sparked such a deep-seated, aching reaction.

It would have mortified her, except that it was the only thing she had experienced lately that didn't smack of encroaching middle age. She'd been noticing far too many aspects of her behavior altering for the worse. She had become more fearful, for one thing, afraid of stepping from her familiar path. She had become uncharacteristically vain, searching for gray hairs in her dressing table mirror—though happily none had yet been discovered. But just in case, she had taken to wearing lace caps at home. And worst of all, she had started sniffing at things people said, and humphing and tsking fit to beat the band.

In light of those clear signs that she was slithering into old maidenhood, a heavy, languorous ache in her nether regions seemed almost like something to rejoice over. Beecham Bryce may have made a wry reference to her advanced age, but his eyes just now had told a completely different story. She'd seen desire smoldering there and a challenge she dared not even acknowledge.

She was just finishing the Mozart, when the ancient butler appeared at the drawing room door, holding a silver tray in one trembling hand.

"Mr. Bryce, sir," he said in a reedy voice. "A message from Sir Walter."

"Thank you, Griggs." Bryce looked away from the juvenile Juliet, who was caught in midstory with her mouth open. He rose and quickly scanned the note. And then stood with his head cocked for a moment, before he tucked the paper into his waistcoat pocket.

"Well?" Lovelace said eagerly. "Is it something to do with the murder?"

Bryce shrugged. "Only a request from Sir Walter that I ride by and see him in the morning."

Jemima stood up, pushing back the piano bench. "I think I will retire now, if you don't mind."

Bryce moved to the piano and leaned upon it, his arms crossed. "You're not going to wait up for your brother?"

She shook her head. "He might be hours yet. Perhaps one of your footmen will show him to his room."

"Let me see you upstairs," he said, his voice low.

"No, that won't be necessary," she said as she lowered the cover over the piano keys. "Your housekeeper showed me where I would be staying, if Lovelace's family didn't return tonight."

"They're probably nearly to London by now," Lovelace interjected. "Papa always likes to make good time when we travel."

As Jemima went past him, Bryce caught her arm. "A moment, Lady Jemima." He drew her to the doorway and then turned to his young guest. "If you will excuse us, Miss Wellesley."

To Jemima's dismay Bryce kept his hand on her arm once they were outside in the hallway.

"Come into my library, a moment," he said. "No, don't look so shocked. I don't have seduction in mind—at least not tonight. I need to tell you something."

Jemima let him lead her into the firelit library. As he went forward to light the branch of candles on the library table, she gazed around the high-ceilinged room, and then gasped as the upper reaches of the walls were illuminated. Above the towering mahogany bookshelves were displayed a variety of mounted animal heads. It was a surprising sight—Jemima didn't picture her host as a hunter, at least not the sort that used a rifle to bring down his chosen game.

"I know," he said, reading the expression of distaste on her face. "It is rather macabre. When I was a boy I used to call it the morgue. My father shot a few of them, but I believe my Uncle Horatio contributed all of the more exotic animals."

"Was that the uncle with the foxhound named Jemima?" she asked archly, lowering her eyes from the walls.

"No, that was my Uncle Harcourt," he replied, and then added, "I gather that comment rankled a bit."

"It was intended to," she responded. "So you can congratulate yourself."

"I was only getting my own back." He grinned at her. "I can't believe you encouraged her to sing."

Jemima tossed her head. "At least her song was about someone other than herself."

"True enough. I hadn't thought of it that way. Anyhow, while my Uncle Horatio lived in India, he was obsessed with obliterating the local wildlife. Wooden crates would be delivered to this house at regular intervals, every one containing some ghastly trophy. My brother and I started giving them names. Let me think . . ." He raised his arm and pointed to a heavily antlered stag. "That was Angus—shot in the Highlands by my father." He shifted to a tiger, caught in midroar. "And that was Rajah, and the gazelle over there was Delilah. She was my favorite. The water buffalo was called Brutus . . . and the elephant—"

Dear Lord! Jemima hadn't noticed the large gray head near the French windows. Its trunk was raised almost entreatingly, and if it hadn't been dead for decades, she thought she would have wept.

"That was Tusker. He was my brother's favorite." His voice lowered a notch. "We had to make it into a sort of game, you see, otherwise it would have hurt too much. To know they had died to furnish a rich man's library. Such a waste."

Jemima turned to gaze at him. Those were the first words he had spoken to her that were not laced with irony, sarcasm, or simmering innuendo. But his eyes were hooded now, the frank openness gone as quickly as it had appeared.

"Yes," she said. "I don't approve of killing animals for such a pointless reason. But then I expect you ride to hounds."

"No."

There was a moment of silence while she waited for him to expound on his answer. He stood before her, his arms relaxed at his sides, and said nothing—offered no disclaimer, no explanation. She realized then that he was a man who voiced no excuses to the world for the choices he made, either bad or good.

"So you have a brother," she said, trying to lighten the mood.

"Not any longer," he said as he moved away from her. This time, however, he did explain. "He was in the navy, and was drowned off this coast. Late last year it was, before Christmas."

She remembered hearing the tale of Bryce's lost brother last January at a house party. She also recalled thinking at the time that a man as wicked as Bryce probably didn't deserve to have a brother. "That is very sad for you," she said with great feeling, trying to make up for her harsh thoughts of last winter. "I would certainly be devastated if anything happened to Terry."

"Ah, yes, your missing sibling. I'm sure he'll turn up eventually. Now if you would have a seat, I can tell you my news, and then send you off to bed." He sat down across from her. "By the way, I hope your headache is improving."

"I never said—"

"Just an educated guess. I noticed how you kept rubbing the back of your neck. I do the same thing when my head starts to throb."

"It's a little better."

"Here, let me get you a cordial." He shifted to the tray of decanters on the table beside his chair. "Though I believe earplugs would have been more efficacious as a preventative measure."

Jemima chuckled. "Perhaps by tomorrow we will have grown used to her."

"Or have throttled her. It's anybody's guess."

He filled two glasses and leaned forward to hand her one. "To my hostage," he said as he clinked his drink against hers. "The ever-surprising Lady J." He took a slow sip, his eyes watching her as he drank.

Jemima refused to comment on his teasing use of Lovelace's

nickname. She merely inquired, "Whyever would you consider me surprising?"

He lowered his glass. "Because you are still water, my pet. I wouldn't have guessed it when we met in the woods. And I rarely have to revise my first impression of people—especially women."

"Then I can chalk that up as a small victory—that I have mystified the omniscient Beecham Bryce."

He gave her a crooked smile. "I never said you mystified me, only that you surprised me. But keep on as you are doing, and mystification can't be far behind. Now as for this matter I wanted to discuss . . ."

He had switched so rapidly from banter to business, that Jemima had to take a few seconds to catch up.

". . . so you can imagine how amazed I was when I read Sir Walter's note." He tapped his waistcoat pocket. "Apparently the man's body was found and reported only a short time after I left Sir Walter's house this afternoon. A farmer whose land adjoins this estate discovered the missing corpse in one of his hay ricks, an old one, left over from last year. It appears the murderer set fire to it, trying to cover his crime. It was a lucky thing the farmer happened to be working nearby, otherwise the body would have been burned beyond recognition.

Jemima's eyes widened as he continued. "You understand now why I didn't want to bring this up in front of Miss Wellesley—she may be irritating, but she is a young girl and still overwrought. It's bad enough Sir Walter had to identify the body—poor chap must still be feeling the shock."

"How did Sir Walter know who the man was?" Jemima winced as she added, "What I mean is, was there enough left of him to identify?"

Bryce grinned at her squeamishness. "The corpse was only slightly . . . braised. Sir Walter was able to identify him by his possessions—a watch and a signet ring, apparently. And the fellow's appearance matched his much-heralded descriptions."

Jemima blinked her eyes in confusion. "What descriptions?"

"Medium height, fair, athletic build. Everyone's heard him described that way. The newspapers are always rattling on about his gilded looks, whenever his name appears in print. I wager there will be teary eyes aplenty when the news gets out that he's been murdered—especially amongst the female population."

"Mr. Bryce," Jemima cried crossly, "I have no idea who you are talking about."

He shot her a look of impatience. "Didn't you hear what I said at the beginning of my story? The murdered man was that perishing national treasure—Lord Troy, the poet."

Jemima staggered to her feet and took one step toward Bryce. Her glass slid through her fingers, the cordial draining out onto the hearth rug.

"Lady Jemima?" Bryce crossed to her in one stride.

"Troy?" she echoed raggedly.

"Terence Vale—" he started to explain. And then it hit him. Lady Jemima Vale, awaiting the return of her brother Terry. Terence Vale.

"Bloody hell," he muttered as he caught Jemima, just before she followed the path of her spilled cordial and tumbled to the carpet.

Bryce had rung for Mrs. Patch to sit with Jemima until she recovered from her swoon, and had then gone to the drawing room to send a protesting Lovelace to her bed, saying only that Lady Jemima was feeling unwell.

He was now striding agitatedly around the perimeter of his house, trying to sort out what he needed to do. He had one house guest who had witnessed a murder and another whose brother had been the victim. He felt like he was sitting on a crate of explosives. So much for his quiet stay in the country.

Bryce had turned the corner that led to the dark stableyard, when he spotted a man lying in the straw near the haywagon. He quickly reached into his coat pocket for the small pistol he always carried and approached the fallen man cautiously, fearing that the murderer had already traced Lovelace to his home, and coshed one of his grooms. Not that the fellow in the straw appeared to be dressed like a groom—in the moonlight Bryce saw how the man's topboots gleamed.

As he knelt beside the fallen stranger he got a whiff of him. *Christ!* It wasn't a cudgel that had felled the man, it was gin.

"Up you go," he said as he caught the fellow under the arms. "Let's get you sobered up."

The man opened one eye. "Dwy-know-you?" he muttered thickly as he tried to stand and only succeeded in reeling over backward. Bryce caught him before he hit the straw and then dragged him over the cobbles. It was only a few yards to the stable pump.

Bryce held him under his arm while he worked the handle. Once a steady surge of water was issuing from the spout he levered his charge under the stream. There were several loud, inarticulate, sputtering curses, and then the man thrust away from him.

He was managing to stand on his own now, Bryce was happy to see.

"Who th' devil're you?" he growled as he swiped his wet hair back from his face. "And where in blazes is m'sister?"

Bryce nearly laughed. He'd been asked that particular question numerous times in the past.

"Your sister is undoubtedly home, sleeping in her bed," he replied reasonably. "Now if you will just tell me where that is, I can send you on your way."

The man looked up at the house that loomed before him. "S'this Bryce Hall?"

"Bryce Prospect," he corrected him. "I am Beecham Bryce."

The man turned toward him and stood weaving slightly. "Then she's here. Leff me a note—" He fished around in his pockets and then gave up with a wobbly shrug. "Now f'ew will take me to Shemima—"

Bryce stepped forward and grasped the man by the shoulders. "What lunacy is this? Lady Jemima's brother was killed today."

"Not killed," the man muttered irritably, "only foxed."

And then with a beatific smile he slid to his knees and fell slowly forward onto the cobblestones. "Best damn fight I e'er saw," he mused, his face against the ground. "Best damn fight . . ."

Bryce stood unmoving, waiting for his shock to wear off. And then, when the irony of it hit him, he began to laugh. He was soon doubled over—by the sheer bloody humor of it and by the enormous relief he was feeling.

He raised the drunken man up, hoisted him over one shoulder, and then made his way in through the rear door of the house. He'd already carried one Vale this evening, the female sibling, who had felt particularly pleasant in his arms before he'd settled her on his library couch.

There would be hell to pay in the morning, he had no doubt. Weighing up all his crimes against society, this one might just be the capper—when word got out that the man he had so unceremoniously doused under a pump, as though he were a bosky schoolboy, was none other than Lord Troy, England's premier poet.

Chapter Three

Bryce was in the breakfast parlor by nine, and so was surprised when Miss Wellesley joined him only a few minutes after he'd drawn his chair up to the table. In spite of her limp, she looked bright-eyed and chipper, which he attributed to the fact that she knew none of what had transpired last night with Lady Jemima and her brother. She offered him a pleasant "Good morning," asked after Lady Jemima's health, and then busied herself at the sideboard.

Troy appeared soon after, looking less chipper; his eyes were bloodshot and bore heavy shadows beneath them. Bryce had asked his own valet to look after the new guest, and Quigley had done wonders with the man's appearance, almost disguising the aftereffects of a night of carousing.

After a nod of greeting to Bryce, Troy made up a plate for himself, and then sat down opposite the breakfast parlor window. In the sunlight his thick hair gleamed a rich, pale gold, and his eyes shone a pure sapphire blue, in spite of their somewhat inflamed condition. Since Troy had seated himself beside Miss Wellesley, who was herself not an inconsiderable beauty, Bryce was almost overwhelmed by the shimmering splendor that arose from the table opposite him. It made a man long to take up a paintbrush.

"I am Terence Vale," Troy said, holding out one hand to the girl beside him. "Jemima's brother."

Bryce winced—he'd been too distracted by gilded youth to perform the proper introductions.

"And I am Lovelace Wellesley," the girl replied.

"Wonderful name," Troy remarked, still holding her hand.

"Wellesley?" she said. "Yes, I do adore it."

"No," Troy said with a grin. "Lovelace. I assume you were named after Richard Lovelace."

Her face went blank. "Oh! Is he someone you know?"

Troy laughed. "No, he's been dead for over a hundred years."

She frowned. "That's very disagreeable. Why would I be called after someone who is dead?"

"He was a poet," Bryce interjected gently. "A very renowned poet."

"Lud!" said Lovelace with a toss of her curls. "What do I care for horrid old dead poets. Now playwrights, that's a different matter altogether." She gave Troy a wide smile and said with great portent, "I am an actress. I was on my way to London with my family to perform in a new play. We've been traveling the provinces, you see. And to great adulation, I must confess, though I do not like to sing my own praises. Why, only last month, a critic in Wiltshire said that my Ludmilla—that was in *The Valiant Maiden of Wurtenburg*—sent him home in tears."

"I shouldn't be surprised," Bryce muttered to himself.

"What was that?" She turned to him with a wide-eyed expression of inquiry.

"Nothing, Miss Wellesley." He pushed back his chair and rose. "I think I'll go up and see how Lady Jemima is faring." Bryce stood watching Troy expectantly, as though he was waiting for some response.

The young man looked up and said with an easy smile, "She's still asleep—I checked before I came down. But you're welcome to look in on her. It's not like Jemima to sleep in, she's usually up with the birds. I . . . don't recall much of last night, but I do remember she was dreadfully overset by the notion that I had been murdered."

Bryce nodded. He'd only allowed Lady Jemima enough time with her brother to see for herself that he was not yet a corpse, and then had whisked him away to his room before she could detect how truly pickled he was. She'd had enough shocks for one night, he reckoned.

Lovelace had been following their conversation with an expression of charming confusion on her face. "You aren't the man who was murdered!" she declared hotly to Troy.

He bit his lip. "Oh, and why do you say that?"

"Because I saw it happen," she said, tapping one finger against her lace-frilled bodice.

"You're sure it wasn't me?"

She narrowed one eye. "Do I look like a lackwit to you? The man who was murdered had light brown hair. Yours is quite blond." She folded her arms triumphantly.

Troy looked up at Bryce, who was lounging in the doorway, trying not to laugh. "Then I guess I am not dead," he pronounced. "If Miss Wellesley says it is so."

"Well, that relieves my mind," Bryce drawled. "Hate sharing my breakfast table with corpses. Now if you two will excuse me . . ."

Still chuckling, he made his way up the stairs. It was a pity Jemima had missed Lovelace's latest start. It would have entertained her no end.

Jemima awoke slowly, aware only of a feeling of great relief. *Troy was not dead.* The words sang in her heart. Somehow, by some miracle, he had been returned to her. She recalled how Bryce had roused her gently from her stupor and then urged her brother down beside the library couch. She had wrapped her arms around Terry and wept with joy. He had seemed befuddled by her outpouring of emotion, but than he was particularly unsympathetic to a woman's tears. Dear, peevish Troy.

Jemima got up and held one hand to her head. Bryce had plied her with brandy once Troy had gone off to his bed, and she wasn't used to such strong spirits. Or to having her life turned upside down in the space of one day. First, Lovelace's brush with murder, then Bryce's high-handed manipulation, capped off by the erroneous report of Troy's death. She devoutly hoped today offered her nothing more taxing than a peaceful stroll in the garden.

She moved to the dressing table and began to comb the tangles from her hair. She had long ago gotten used to doing without a lady's maid, since it was Troy's habit to go jaunting off to out-of-the-way places at the drop of a hat, which made servants an encumbrance. Their visit to the Iron Duke was a case in point. Two days earlier Troy had come striding into the drawing room of their London town house, insisting that she accompany him to a mill in Kent. She knew he didn't expect her to actually attend the prize-fight, he merely wanted her company on the journey.

He had a wide circle of male friends who were always delighted to travel with him, so it was flattering that he frequently asked her to go along in their stead. Not that her presence didn't offer him compensations other than her companionship. She knew precisely how to wangle the best rooms from an innkeeper, and how to ensure that her brother would get the finest cuts of meat from the kitchen. She smoothed things for him on every stage of a journey, kept him soothed and untroubled, so that he had nothing to focus on but his poetry and his amusing pursuits.

She had been looking after him for so many years—ever since

their parents died—that it never occurred to her that he was taking advantage of her good nature. He was generally so amiable himself that she didn't mind performing those little offices that made his life run without a hitch.

There was a knock at the door. Jemima spun on the bench. "Yes?"

"Are you stirring yet?"

Oh, Lord, it's Bryce. "Yes," she called quickly, "I'll be down in—"

The door opened.

He at least had the courtesy not to enter the room, preferring instead to lean against one side of the door frame. "I wanted to see how you were faring this morning. You . . . had a rough time of it last night."

"I am not dressed," she said icily, disregarding his solicitous remark. She felt a small stirring of guilt—Bryce had been noticeably selfless last night and she owed him some gratitude for that, but that didn't mean he could come wandering into her bedroom at will.

He eyed her voluminous night rail, and the roomy dressing gown she wore over it. His brows rose. "Rather overdressed, if you ask me. Not what I would have chosen for you."

"They belong to your housekeeper," she muttered between her teeth. "In case you have forgotten, my things are still at the inn."

Her fingers itched to draw the lapels of the robe over her chest, but she would not give him the satisfaction of seeing her cringe under his overt scrutiny. It infuriated her that he thought she could own such unflattering garments. Just because he was a maiden lady didn't mean she dressed like a dowd. She had a mind to appear at dinner wearing her most revealing gown, if only to put him in his place.

"That is why I am here," Bryce said, shifting to the other side of the doorway. "I'm off to see the magistrate this morning—to let him know he still has an unidentified body on his hands. On the way back, I can take you to the Tattie and Snip to fetch your things. And your brother's. He was a bit . . . indisposed last night. It must have slipped his mind."

"He was roaring drunk," she retorted sharply. "Though I suppose I should thank you for trying to keep it from me. He's gotten like that a time or two in the past, so it doesn't shock me. And furthermore, I am only his sister, Mr. Bryce, not his watchdog."

Bryce shrugged. "He apparently gives you the same freedom."

She looked perplexed, and so he added, "Most men who sobered up to find their sister staying in the home of a well-known libertine would have at least taken me aside and warned me off. Troy is at present sitting in my breakfast parlor, blithe as you please, making inroads on the kippers. And he didn't bat an eye when I mentioned looking in on you. A less fraternal performance I have yet to see."

"You sound almost disappointed," she observed. "Would you rather he challenged you to a duel over my honor? I should warn you, Troy is a crack shot."

Bryce's eyes darkened. "Shooting wafers at Manton's isn't quite the same as looking down a pistol barrel and staring perdition in the face." He stepped back from the door. "I'm leaving for the magistrate's in fifteen minutes. Meet me on the front steps if you want to join me." He turned and disappeared.

Jemima swung back to her mirror and was dismayed to see that a noticeable pink flush had risen to her cheeks. Drat the man, for having such an effect on her. Making her feel giddy and outraged at the same time. It occurred to her that going for a carriage ride with him might not be the wisest course she could follow, but then she chided herself for being missish. Even in the propriety-conscious *ton,* unwed ladies were allowed to drive out with their gentlemen callers. Not that Beecham Bryce would ever have had a reason, gentlemanly or otherwise, to call on Lady Jemima Vale.

More's the pity, that tiresome inner voice lamented. "Oh, hush," she said aloud.

She twisted her hair into a knot, coaxing a few strands to curl about her face, and then quickly drew on her chemise and gown. Both were freshly laundered and ironed, and she silently saluted her host for the efficiency of his staff, as she caught up her bonnet by its ribbons and went hurrying from the room.

She made a sidetrip to the breakfast parlor, where Lovelace and her brother were deep in conversation. Or more accurately, Lovelace was deep in conversation—Terry looked to be in deep shock.

". . . and then in Basingstoke, the mayor presented me with an honorary wreath, to commemorate my performance of . . . Oh, hello, Lady J. I've been telling your brother a bit about myself."

Troy craned around to grin up at his sister. "Jemima."

"Morning, Troy," she said, as she bent over and kissed him on one cheek. "How's your head?"

"Still attached to my shoulders, more's the pity," he said with a rueful wince.

She patted him on the shoulder. "I gather you backed the winner yesterday—"

"Troy?" Lovelace interjected. "Lady J, did you just call him Troy?"

Jemima looked down at her brother. "Are we incognito this morning?"

He turned to Lovelace with an apologetic smile. "I am known to some as Lord Troy."

Lovelace scrambled up from the table as if there were a serpent on her plate instead of a coddled egg. "*You* are Lord Troy? The poet Lord Troy?"

As he nodded, she raised both hands to her mouth. "Oh . . . this is infamous. And so unfair! I was going to meet you in London, when I performed in our new play. You wrote it, you see . . . well, the poem. And now you have ruined everything! That you should first see me hobbling about on a stick, wearing this wretched old gown, with my hair in positive knots . . . it is beyond mortifying. Oh, how . . . how could you sit here, eating your breakfast, knowing the whole time that you were Lord Troy?"

"Even poets have to eat," he said gently, clearly trying to untangle the source of her distemper.

"I have never felt so dispirited in my whole life. First murderers, then rabbit holes, now poets who pretend to be ordinary people. M-my life has surely become a wretched thing." She raised one hand to her brow and wilted back against the draperies, staggering a little on her bad ankle.

Jemima leaned down to her brother's ear. "She's an actress."

"So the rumor goes," he muttered as he continued to regard Lovelace's theatrics with a dubious eye.

The girl had begun to sob softly, the tears running down her face in tiny rivulets.

"You'd better deal with this, Jem," Troy said as he threw his napkin down and got to his feet. He drew his sister away from the table. "You know I can't stomach weepy women."

"Oh, no," she said, waving away the suggestion. "Bryce is waiting for me—I am already late. Use some of that famous Vale charm on her," she whispered intently. "Tell her about our trip to Greece. Tell her you saw her in Othello and thought she was the best Moor ever . . . Oh, I don't care what you tell her."

She snatched a honey bun from the side table and went hurrying off toward the front of the house.

Bryce was waiting in the drive, in a black high-perch phaeton drawn by four exquisite chestnut horses.

"This is a surprise," she said, as a groom assisted her onto the elevated seat. "Rather bang-up for the provinces, don't you think?"

His cheeks narrowed. "I can always have the hay wagon brought around, if you'd prefer."

"No, this is very nice. As long as you don't overturn us in a ditch."

He made no comment, merely dropped the reins and sent his team out of the courtyard at a brisk trot.

Jemima held on to her bonnet as they rounded the corner of the drive onto the main road. "You needn't show off on my account," she said. "I am sadly unimpressed by driving."

"I see," he murmured, keeping his eyes on the road. "So you are not one of those sporting ladies who longs to take the ribbons from her gentlemen friends. I, on the other hand, live to take the ribbons from my female acquaintances."

She couldn't keep from laughing. "I wonder you can be so full of sauce this early in the morning."

Bryce shot her a wicked look. "I am particularly full of sauce in the morning."

Jemima was spared a reply when an inattentive goose boy let his charges wander into the path of the oncoming carriage. Bryce sent his horses onto the grassy verge and neatly avoided the potential decimation of the local poultry population. Jemima was impressed by his skill, in spite of herself.

"I do enjoy riding, however," she remarked once they were back on the road. "Troy and I grew up in the country and we rode every day. Now we only ride in Hyde Park, which is rather tame."

"If you stay on at Bryce Prospect, I insist that you let me mount you."

Jemima turned to stare at his rugged profile. His face was re-laxed and without any guile. She couldn't see the devils that danced in his eyes. "Thank you for the offer," she said. "But I doubt we will remain past today. Lovelace's family should turn up by noon at the latest."

"You have engagements back in London, then?"

She shrugged. "Nothing pressing, now that the Season is wind-ing down. But you will surely want us out of your hair. Speaking of London," she added. "I am surprised I have never seen you driving in the park. This carriage would be hard to miss."

"I don't drive in the park," he said as he guided his horses past a slow-moving farm cart.

"What?" she said with a chuckle. "Afraid everyone will give you the cut direct?"

He turned to her and she saw his mouth had tightened. "Yes, Lady Jemima. That is exactly the reason."

She started to apologize, and then stopped herself. Bryce had made his own bed, so why should she be sorry he had to lie in it? Still, the expression on his face troubled her for the rest of their short journey.

They soon came to Withershins, a small village whose shops and houses were clustered around a charming green with a duck pond at its center. Bryce slowed his team as they made their way along the high street, pointing out the local livery, the bake shop, and a tavern called the Bosun's Mate.

"You're quite near the sea here," Jemima said. "I'd forgotten that. The countryside looks so pastoral, not maritime in the least."

"We're only five miles from Romney Marsh. Best place to land smuggled goods on the entire coast."

"Have you ever been involved with smugglers, Mr. Bryce?"

He gave her a wry look. "And would I tell you, if I had?"

She laughed. "No, I suppose not. It's just that in London we think smugglers a very romantic lot."

"Well, then," he pronounced musingly, as he drew up in the stableyard of a small manor house. "I might just have to take it up . . . if that's what it requires to impress ladies from London."

A young groom ran out from the stable to hold his horses. "Thanks, Smitty," he called down. He turned to Jemima. "Want to come in and meet Sir Walter?"

"Perhaps not, if you don't mind. I believe you'll be able to sort things out better without a female hovering near by."

"As you like. This shouldn't take long. You can always go for a walk—there's a pretty meadow beyond the stable." He added with a grin, "It's a pity you left your sketchbook at home."

"I know I am not talented, Mr. Bryce," she said with some starch. "I draw only for my own pleasure."

His eyes widened. "I didn't mean to imply anything uncomplimentary. You could . . . come up with a few sketches, and we could make a parlor game of it later, guessing what they were supposed to be."

He swung down from his seat before she could hit him and went around to her side of the carriage. "You can't blame me, Lady J. I only provoke you because it makes your pretty blue eyes light up."

"They're green," she said between her teeth.

He lifted her from the seat and held her a little bit above him, his hands tight at her waist. Then he slowly lowered her, until their noses were nearly touching. "So they are," he whispered. "I don't know how I keep forgetting." He set her on her feet and went striding off toward the front of the house. He stopped before turning the corner. "And don't go wandering near any groves of trees, if you please."

Grumbling to herself about irritating, high-handed, overly confident men, Jemima stalked off behind the stable, to a wide field where acres of wildflowers were just starting to blossom. She settled down on a thatchy spot and took off her bonnet, tipping her face to the sky. The sun felt very pleasant on her cheeks and on her shoulders, where it warmed the thin muslin of her gown.

All around her bees hummed, busy at their nectar gathering. In her girlhood, when she lived in the country, her family had kept honeybees. There was a groundsman, Tom Paulie, who watched over the hives, and he had given her a skep of her own to care for. She had learned bee lore from him. And the one thing she recalled above everything else was that the hive was for the worker bees and the queen. The drones, the male bees that mated with the queen, eventually died, cast out from their hive.

She thought about Beecham Bryce and the empty, licentious life he lived. And how he avoided the park during the prime social hours to save his pride. If he performed any service in the *ton,* it was after hours, in the dark. By daylight he was not welcomed by his peers.

Jemima wondered if she should tell him about the bees.

No, she sighed, he'd probably end up making some ribald comment about the birds and the bees.

Bryce found her sitting in a field of glorious color—pinks and lavenders and soft, shimmering purples. In her pale yellow gown she looked like an overgrown buttercup. He stood at the edge of the meadow letting his eyes drink in the sight of her. She was leaning back, propped up on her elbows, her head tilted up. It put her body in very pleasing relief—her gown clung to her full breasts and the rise of her hips, the fabric molding to the flatness of waist and stomach. He had a hunger to lay her back on those burgeoning blossoms and run his hands over the slim, beguiling length of her.

He was still trying to figure her out. More so now that he'd learned she was Troy's sister. The boy ran with a fast crowd, he knew that much. Sporting gentlemen and gamesters. High-flyers and opera dancers. Troy was even a member of Bacchus, though Bryce himself had wearied of the club by the time the poet had been invited to join. Their paths had never crossed before last night.

He wondered how Jemima had been able to preserve her virtue, in light of all the rascals she must have met through her brother. But the fact remained that she had—he of all men knew an untouched woman when he stumbled across one. And that only heightened her appeal. She was as ripe for plucking as an August peach.

Bryce moved toward her and when she saw him approaching she shifted up into a kneeling position. It took all his strength of will not to kneel himself and pull her up against him.

"That didn't take long," she said, shading her eyes from the sun with one hand.

He sprawled down beside her. "Sir Walter is not much for conversation. And he's not pleased that we are back where we started—with an unknown corpse on our hands. He sent to Bow Street last night to call in the Runners, thinking he needed reinforcements to look into the murder of so famous a man. By now, unfortunately, the word will be all over London that your brother was killed."

Jemima sat back on her heels. "That's dreadful news. All his friends and admirers will be devastated."

"Sir Walter is sending a messenger to London, posthaste, to recant the story. It will become just one more chapter in your brother's not inconsiderable legend."

His legend. Jemima looked amused at his choice of words. "Sometimes it's hard to credit that the headstrong boy who wouldn't wash behind his ears is now elevated to the pantheon of great men."

Bryce broke off a stalk of burdock and began plucking the purple chaff from its head. "What's it like then, being sister to a legend?"

Jemima shrugged. "He's changed very little from the younger brother I looked after. Perhaps he's a bit more full of himself than before. He has money now, which we didn't have when we were children in Sussex. We weren't dreadfully poor, but we had to practice economy every day. Now he has taken London by storm, and I am glad for him. Sometimes dreamers should see their dreams come to pass."

"And what of your dreams? What would Lady J dream if she stepped out from her brother's shadow?"

She frowned slightly. "That's not where I am, is it? In his shadow?"

"Where then?"

"I'm not sure. I have my own life. Through Troy I've met many clever people, men and women both. I have a salon once a month, for aspiring poets and painters." She tipped her chin up. "Just because I am not talented, doesn't mean I cannot recognize ability in others."

"So you are a patron of the arts." He leaned back and grinned. "Is that your dream—to set some young talent on the road to greatness? It must be very ennobling, to have such lofty, selfless aspirations."

Jemima swung her gaze away from him. "You mistake the matter. I am not selfless in the least."

"Sorry," he said. "I didn't mean to bait you. If it's any consolation, I myself have a rather selfish dream."

"Oh," she said, rolling her eyes dramatically. "I can just imagine a libertine's dream. Let me guess—orgies in the seraglio? Primitive revels on a South Sea island?"

"Tame stuff," he said with a wave of his hand. "But until I am with aim's ace of achieving my dream, it's going to remain a secret."

"I doubt I will achieve mine," she said with only a tiny trace of wistfulness. "Which is often the way with dreams. I . . . I think we should be going back now."

She climbed to her feet but Bryce stayed where he was, stretched out on the carpet of flowers. Jemima wished he didn't look so . . . healthy, reclining there at her feet. The breeze was playing with his unruly forelock and the bright sun had turned his eyes the color of platinum. And his mouth, relaxed now into a lazy curl, was beckoning her. She wondered what it would feel like to be kissed by such a man as Beecham Bryce. To have that lazy mouth curve around her own . . . slightly open, tasting her, coaxing her to respond. Not that she would require much coaxing, she thought.

Jemima felt the throbbing start up again, deep, deep inside her, due south of her belly. She fought off the disturbing sensation with an audible sniff.

Bryce looked up. "Head cold coming on?" he asked.

"I'm fine," she said evenly. "Just a bit of pollen. The bees you know. Well, are you coming along? The Wandering Minstrels might have wandered back to the Iron Duke by now."

"There's no hurry," he said, shifting onto his side to face her. "There's something I haven't told you. Wellesley's troupe passed through here late yesterday afternoon. One of the squire's sons saw them drive past the green. They looked to be heading toward Grantley, which is about ten miles south of here."

Jemima cocked her head. "But Lovelace said they were heading to London. Grantley would be in the opposite direction."

Bryce nodded. "It makes no sense to me. But then if the rest of Lovelace's family are as bubble-headed as she is, it's a wonder they can find their way out of a privy, let alone all the way to London."

"Well, that's washed it," she said softly. "Poor Lovelace, fallen out of her nest, just like a baby bird. And her parents clearly haven't spared a thought for her. If they started out for London, and then did an aboutface to head for Grantley, that means they had to go right past the Iron Duke. What would make them drive past the inn and not stop to pick up their daughter?"

He sucked in his cheek. "Good sense?" She gave him a furious glower. "No, no. I'll stop belaboring the point. The child needs looking after . . . and she's welcome to stay on at Bryce Prospect until they return from their quest, whatever it may be."

"Troy and I can take her back to London with us," she said. "She could stay on at our house until her family returns to the city."

Bryce made no comment, but his eyes had lost all their mirth.

"Well, you certainly don't want us overstaying our welcome," she pointed out reasonably. "Troy will eat you out of house and home for one thing. And Lovelace will talk you to death."

"And what will you do to me, Jemima?" he asked softly. He was gazing up at her with those quicksilver eyes, making her stomach go all wobbly.

"I'll—" She looked frantic for an instant. "I'll hang indecipherable drawings over all your walls."

"Surely an undeserved fate," he said as he climbed to his feet and dusted off the back of his driving coat. "But London is not a good option. Our murderer knows she was heading there and he's seen her face, don't forget. Even in a city of that size—full of beautiful women—Lovelace Wellesley is bound to attract notice. I take leave to doubt her acting talent, but her looks are unassailable. Your only recourse would be to keep her with you, inside your home. Day and night."

He waited a moment for the full impact of his statement to sink in. "Yes, I see the look of horror dawning in your eyes, Jem. Prisoners of war have cracked under less strain."

"I could send Lovelace to my Aunt Sophie in Richmond—she's nearly stone deaf, poor dear. But unfortunately, Sophie is in the Lake Country at present, caring for an ailing cousin."

"It looks like you're stuck here," he said as he turned for the stable. "That is, unless you are willing to admit I have no interest in the chit; then your services as chaperone would be unnecessary."

Jemima mulled this over while they walked across the field. She owed nothing to Lovelace Wellesley and wondered that she should feel compelled to look after her.

"Oh, I don't know what to do," she grumbled as she trudged along behind him.

Bryce waited at the edge of the field. "Stay," he said quietly as she came up even with him.

Her head darted up. He was looking away from her over the slate roof of Sir Walter's tidy manor house. "What was that?"

"Stay," he repeated. "Here with me. For now."

"Why?"

"Because," he said as he took her arm and led her to his waiting carriage. "You might be in nearly as much danger as Miss Wellesley."

"That's preposterous," she said as he lifted her onto the seat.

"Not at all." Bryce walked around the carriage and climbed up beside her. "The dead man had Troy's things on him. A most strange circumstance, don't you think? It's possible the murderer was after the real Troy, which places both you and your brother at risk."

"If you are trying to frighten me," she said heatedly, "it's not working. I have very little sensibility in that direction. Lovelace is the one in danger, not me or Troy."

"Still, I think it's best if you all remain at Bryce Prospect, at least until things get sorted out. The man from Bow Street will be here tomorrow. We'll see what he has to say."

Jemima was frowning as they bowled along the main street. She chewed on his words for a time and then asked, "Tell me again, what was the dead man carrying that made Sir Walter think he was Troy?"

"Ah," Bryce said as he fished in the pocket of his driving coat. "I nearly forgot. Sir Walter gave me these to return to their rightful owner."

Jemima took the gold watch and the signet ring from him, and then shook her head. "My brother is so careless sometimes. He leaves his valuables lying about at every inn we visit. I've warned him it's an invitation to theft."

"A man rarely goes out without his watch or his signet." Bryce glanced down at his own unadorned fingers—he had left off wearing his own signet ring for a variety of complex reasons he still hadn't fully come to terms with. "Do you have any idea why he wasn't wearing them yesterday?"

"Oh, he never takes his valuables with him when he goes off to prizefights—too many pickpockets."

"There's some sense to that, though he'd have done better yesterday to have kept them with him. By the way, that's a rather florid inscription in his watch."

She flicked it open and read aloud, " 'My dearest Troy, time only increases my love for you.' "

Bryce made a face. "Obviously a gift from a besotted admirer."

Jemima chuckled as she closed the watch and tucked it into her reticule. "You could say that. Our grandmother gave it to him. Terry is her only grandson, and she lavishes all sorts of gifts on him."

"Your grandmother calls him Troy?"

"I'm the only one in the family who still calls him Terry. He's been Lord Troy since he was seven." Her voice lowered. "Bryce, do you think the murdered man broke into my brother's room yesterday?"

He sighed. "It would seem the obvious conclusion. Tolliver's servants have been with him for years, so I doubt we can look for the thief in that quarter."

"But it makes no sense. There were several well-to-do gentlemen staying at the inn yesterday. Why would Troy have been a target?"

"He might not have been the only one. Maybe there was a rash of robberies at the Tattie and Snip."

"The Iron Duke," she stated, correcting him with a grin.

Once they were at the inn, Bryce went off to discover if Tolliver had heard of any other thefts, or if he'd seen any suspicious-looking characters loitering about the previous morning. Jemima went to her brother's room to see if anything else had been stolen. She checked the top of the bureau and the nightstand and looked through the tall wardrobe that sat in one corner.

"Is anything else missing?" Bryce was leaning against the doorpost, his arms folded over his chest.

"Not one thing," she replied with a sigh.

"How can you tell?" He motioned around the room. Troy's possessions were scattered throughout the small space—random piles of books, heaps of discarded clothing, and a hazard of writing implements and inkpots. "Your brother is a veritable pack rat." A naval officer's bicorn had been tossed onto the window seat. Bryce crossed the room, took up the hat, and gave her a sweeping, theatrical bow.

Jemima grinned. "That hat is rumored to have belonged to Nelson," she explained. "One of Troy's idols." She began stacking her brother's books into neat piles. "So, did Tolliver shed any light on things?"

Bryce had moved to the bed and now sat, idly swinging one crossed leg. "There have been no other complaints of theft. And he thinks everyone here yesterday morning was on the up and up. But since there was so much traffic from the prizefight, he can't swear that no one was creeping about up here."

Jemima set the books on the bed beside Bryce, trying to disregard her heightened awareness of him. Here in this small chamber his presence was overwhelming. And she had a feeling he had placed himself on the bed just to be provoking.

As she turned to lift Troy's valise down from the tall wardrobe, Bryce sprang up, and elbowed her gently aside. "Here, let me." He looked down at her as he lifted the case from its high perch. "Why don't you take care of things in your room, Jem. I'll see that the gilded poet gets packed up."

Jemima went across the hall and began to remove the numerous gowns from her wardrobe. Even though she and Troy had expected to be away from London for only a few days, experience had taught her to pack more than she needed. Her gregarious brother often met up with friends while traveling, which, of course, necessitated a prolonged visit. This wasn't the first time she and Terry had started out booked at an inn and ended up overnighting in an elegant home. Fortunately she had brought several dinner gowns with her, in addition to her day dresses and her riding habit.

When she was finished, she went out to the hall to call for the porter and nearly bumped up against an elderly man in a tight black coat. He was tall, cadaverously thin, with unkempt white eyebrows that thrust out from his brow. He gave her a narrow-eyed look and then his face brightened in recognition.

"Lady Jemima Vale," he said as he bowed.

"Sir?" Her face remained blank. "I believe you have the advantage of me."

"Sir Richard Hastings, ma'am, late of His Majesty's Navy. We met at Lady Hammersmith's rout in May."

"Oh," she said in her best society voice. "Are you staying here at the Iron Duke?"

He pointed to the room beside her brother's. "Came over from Canterbury for the mill. Pleasant little inn, what? And Tolliver does stock a fine cellar. Though it's likely smuggled goods, being we're so close to the coast. But my excise days are behind me, thank heavens. Now I get to drink the stuff, instead of chasing after it up and down the Channel." He chuckled softly. "Well, good day to you, ma'am. I'm heading home this afternoon."

He glanced over her shoulder through the open door of her room. "Ah, I see you are also packing up for home. Which is just as well . . . there are unpleasant things afoot in this place, Lady Jemima."

"What?" A shiver of apprehension sketched over her spine at his tone. "Do you mean the murder?"

He shook his head. "That's nothing you need trouble yourself over, ma'am. Still, you'd do best to return to London."

Bryce had come out into the hallway at the sound of voices. The older man gave him a curt nod, shot Jemima a meaningful look, and then went off in the direction of the stairwell.

"Who was that?" Bryce asked gruffly.

Jemima was still staring after the old gentleman. "I'm not sure. He says he's called Sir Richard Hastings and that he met me in London at a *ton* party. It's just . . . odd."

"Odd that you don't remember him? You can't expect to remember every man you meet, Jemima."

"It's not that . . . He said there were unpleasant things afoot here. And that I should return to London. Why would he say such a thing to me? Do you think he knows something about the murder?"

Bryce tapped his finger over his lower lip. He was sorry now he had tried to frighten Jemima into staying on at Bryce Prospect. She hadn't shown any fear then, but now there was something very like it in her eyes. He drew her into her brother's room and shut the door.

"Listen to me, pet." He set his hands on her shoulders. "If I'm not mistaken, Sir Richard Hastings is a retired admiral. I've never met him, but he's an acquaintance of my father's. He probably heard about the murder from Tolliver, and was merely cautioning you out of gentlemanly concern,"

"But he gave me such a start, Bryce."

"You're just feeling edgy because of what I said back there in the field . . . but that was nothing more than a lot of gammon. Of course the killer isn't after you or Troy. I was only suggesting it to prevent you from going back to London."

"But why?" Jemima immediately discounted the obvious, but highly unlikely, reason that he might have wanted to keep her near him.

Bryce sighed. "Because I feel responsible for what happened in the woods; it occurred on my family's property, after all. And I can't keep Lovelace safe if you whisk her off to London. But I didn't mean to make you start flying at shadows, Jemima. So stop looking so frightened."

"I'm not frightened," she said. He gave her a shake. "Well maybe just a bit." She laid both hands over her face and lowered her head. "You must think me a total loss. There's Lovelace, who witnessed a bloody murder, completely composed by dinnertime. And here I am, totally undone by a bit of petty thievery and a doddering old gentleman."

"Lovelace has the resilience of youth on her side," he said with a grin.

"Oh, and what have I got? The decrepitude of old age?"

"Give yourself a little credit," he said stoutly. "Middle age, at least."

She drew back from him with a chuckle. "You are a wretch, you know."

He was delighted to see that her eyes were now dancing up at him.

"If I had any pretensions to anything," she said, "you would quickly shoot them down. I only wonder that with such a barbed tongue, you are able to attract any women at all."

He gave her a long, intent, and very speaking look. "Oh, I have my moments."

They both returned to packing up her brother's scattered belongings—Bryce realized it would never have occurred to Troy to stir himself to look after his own things. He lifted a slim leather diary from the desktop and was about to place it in the valise on the bed when Jemima backed into him, carrying a stack of shirts. Since he'd much rather have caught her about the waist than hold on to her perishing brother's book, he let the diary go flying and danced her back against the bedframe.

"Thank you," she said politely, trying to tug out of his arms. "I was in no danger of falling."

"Maybe *I* was," he said and gave her an exaggerated leer.

She looked up at him and shook her head in exasperation. "Do your paramours find this sort of childish behavior at all entertaining?"

"My paramours?" he echoed, his brows raised teasingly. "You shock me, Lady Jemima. And no, I don't know if they do—they're usually too busy with . . . um, other things to sit in judgment on my manners."

"Insufferable man," she muttered as he released her and bent to pick up the book.

He smoothed one of the blank pages, which had become creased, and was about to lay it in the valise, when Jemima caught his wrist. "No, wait!" she cried softly. "Open it again."

He did as she bid and saw that four or five pages had been torn from the stitched binding.

"Troy uses this for the poems he's currently working on," Jemima said, running her fingers over the rough, deckled tears. "It's a new notebook—I purchased it for him only last week—and it looks as though everything he's written since then has been torn out." She looked up at Bryce in disbelief. "Why would a thief steal Terry's poems?"

Bryce shook his head. "I couldn't imagine. No one would dare to publish Troy's work under their own name—your brother has too distinct a style."

Jemima sighed. "This is very troubling. I hope that if Sir Walter found Troy's poems on the murdered man, he hasn't disposed of them."

Bryce grinned. "I doubt if Sir Walter knows a poem from a pork pie. He's one of those hearty, hunting mad types. Probably illiterate, for all that he's a magistrate. Don't fret, sweetheart. I'm sure that if the dead man was carrying Troy's papers, they will be returned to you. And speaking of murder, let's get back to the Prospect and see whether your brother has done bodily harm to the Portia of the Provinces."

Chapter Four

They found Troy scribbling away in the library. He was undismayed at the loss of the notebook pages—he was deep into another poem now, he declared—but was relieved to get his watch and ring back.

"Can't think why anyone would bother to take *my* things," he said as he slipped the ring onto his finger. "Jemima would be a more likely candidate—she travels about with all sorts of valuable fripperies."

Bryce eyed the fine pearl necklet that adorned her throat. He'd purchased enough fripperies himself—for various deserving ladies—to know the value of the piece. Not that the pearls could compete with Jemima's pale skin for beauty or luster.

She was frowning at her brother. "Yes, but I never leave my things lying about, Terry. I hide them in a very clever, secret place."

"Which would be?" Bryce coaxed. He was vastly interested in all Jemima's secret places.

"No longer a secret if I told you, sir," she responded with a sniff.

Then, with boyish, bloodthirsty enthusiasm, Troy asked Bryce for the particulars of the murder. Bryce settled into an armchair, poured them each a glass of claret, and launched into the tale.

Jemima drifted out through the open French window, murmuring that she would take a stroll in the garden. Not that anyone appeared to notice her departure. An air of good-natured male camaraderie had already pervaded the room—which pleased her unaccountably.

For some reason—and she chose not to examine this too closely—it was important that the two men grow to like each other. She knew Bryce thought her brother lacked a proper fraternal attitude and she suspected he hadn't approved of Troy's drunkenness last night. Nice judgment, that, coming from a notorious womanizer. But she wanted Bryce to appreciate the finer aspects of

Terry's makeup: his keen intellect—which he went to great lengths to obscure from some people—his wry sense of humor, and his easy charm. And she likewise wanted Terry to admire Bryce, although she hadn't a clue as to why. Except that it was always good policy to be in charity with one's host, and it appeared they would all be living under Bryce's roof until the murder got sorted out.

She strolled around the house toward the gardens behind the colonnade and had only just stepped onto the brick walkway, when she spied Lovelace, sitting in a white dovecote. Once again there were tearstains on the girl's pearly cheeks.

Jemima tried to sneak away—she'd had her fill of melodrama—but Lovelace caught sight of her among the peonies and called out, "Lady J! Please, sit with me."

Jemima sighed and then made her way to the trellised folly.

"Any news of my family at the inn?" the girl asked softly as Jemima sat beside her.

"There was some news, but not from the inn. The magistrate's son saw your family's coach late yesterday afternoon; it was heading south, toward Grantley."

"Grantley?" Lovelace gasped. "They were supposed to be going to London. Papa had booked us into a theater in the West End." Tears filled her eyes. "Oh, this is not possible."

"Please don't cry, Lovelace." Jemima leaned forward and rubbed her consolingly on the back. "I know this is very difficult for you. Shall I ask Troy to sit with you and read you some of his poems?"

The girl drew back with a smoldering expression on her face. "Your brother is not a very nice person, Lady J. He called me a rattle-pated featherwit and said if I was going to prance about like the Queen of Sheba, then it was no wonder everyone went off and left me."

"Oh, dear." Jemima tried not to grin. "Did he really say that?" She knew Troy was not at his most tolerant after a night of carousing. "I'm sure he was only teasing you. He has three sisters, you see, and teasing comes naturally to him."

Lovelace looked slightly mollified. "I know I talk a great deal more than I should, Lady J." Her eyes widened in dismay. "Oh! I forgot, you don't like that name."

"I'm getting used to it," Jemima responded with a sigh. Bryce seemed to have latched on to it in his perverse fashion, though there were times it sounded almost like an endearment on his lips.

Lovelace continued her snuffling discourse. "It's just that I . . . I become nervous around strangers. Before last night, I'd never sat down to supper with a titled lady and a gentleman as polished as Mr. Bryce. My mama just clouts me on the ear when I start in to talking and 'tooting my own horn,' as she calls it."

"My dear, I promise you neither Mr. Bryce nor I will clout you on the ear. My brother, however, I cannot answer for."

Lovelace responded with a watery chuckle. It was the first sign she had given Jemima that she possessed any sense of humor at all.

"How did your parents come to be actors?" Jemima asked, hoping to distract the girl.

"Papa was tutor to an earl's son near Norwich and Mama was the steward's daughter. They ran off together—it was such a scandal." Lovelace grinned slightly. " At first Papa wrote plays to support them. Then a theater owner in York asked him and Mama to perform in one of them."

"I take it they were successful."

"Oh, yes. They started their own troupe after a while. Papa is a wonderful playwright. And my parents were so looking forward to their first London production." She sniffed. "But now everything has gone awry . . . . I only pray the theater manager hasn't booked another play into the Orpheum."

Jemima took up her hand. "I will ask Troy to write to him, if you like, explaining the delay in their arrival. My brother . . . has a certain influence in the city."

"I don't doubt it," Lovelace said. "I'm sorry I made such a scene at breakfast, but I have had an abiding passion for your brother ever since I read 'The Crucible of Byzantium.' It was too oversetting to realize he had been sitting beside me the whole time, and never once mentioned who he was."

Jemima gave the girl an encouraging smile. "You are in the public eye, Lovelace, so you know how people clamor after those who are . . . set apart. My brother does not like to capitalize on his name and often introduces himself as Terence Vale. He didn't intend to deceive you. Now come inside and have your luncheon. We brought my luggage over from the inn, and if you are still here at dinnertime, you can wear one of my dresses. I have a rose-colored gown that would suit you perfectly."

"I don't want to have dinner with your brother." Lovelace grumbled, for once immune to the temptation of appearing in a flattering shade of pink. "He makes me even more nervous than you or Mr. Bryce. And then I will begin to chatter on and on." She lowered her eyes. "And no one really cares to hear about my sorry little life."

Oh, dear, Jemima thought. Lovelace had gone from monumental *hubris* to sniveling self-pity in less than twenty-four hours. It was the girl's age, she knew, that caused it. The wild flights of fancy giving way to the deep valleys of despair. As much as she dreaded the dogged approach of middle age, Jemima vowed she wouldn't be seventeen again, not on a bet.

"If you come along now," she coaxed, "I'll tell you a secret. When you are nervous around people, the surest thing is to ask them about themselves. That way, they think you charming and astute. And Troy is the perfect subject—he'll natter on about himself forever if given half a chance."

As Bryce concluded his tale of the murder and its subsequent aftermath, Troy rose from the desk and went to pour himself another glass of claret.

"Poor Lovelace," he said as he resumed his seat. "She's had a rotten time of it. I gave her quite a setdown this morning—I'm not very tolerant of other people's weak natures. Still, she is a little beauty. Even if she has the brain of a peahen."

Bryce smiled. "Some men might consider that an asset. And speaking of beauties . . ."

Troy looked up from the glass that he was twirling between his ink-stained fingers. "No, no, don't say it. You needn't tell me to mind my manners around Lovelace, old chap. I'm not in the petticoat line, not when it comes to veritable babes in the wood."

"I wasn't referring too Miss Wellesley. I meant your sister."

"Jemima?"

"Of course, Jemima. Unless you have another sister hidden in the house. I find her to be quite . . . enchanting."

"Jemima?"

A slight frown appeared on Bryce's brow. "Stop saying it like that, Troy. You'd think your sister was an antidote."

Troy shrugged. "She's long past her last prayers, Bryce. Anyone can see that. And a good thing, too. I'd be desolated if some old sparky came along and whisked her off. She's the best of sisters, and looks after everything for me. Here, now, I'll tell you what. You know your way around women—if even half of what they say about you is true." Troy gave him an especially speaking look. "Why don't you spend some time with her, you know, do the pretty, dose her with a bit of charm. Poor old Jem could do with a bit of cheering up; she's been rather glum lately, blue-deviled like I've never seen before—though I couldn't tell you why."

Bryce suspected the reason was sitting across from him in blond splendor, knocking back a glass of claret. But he couldn't tell Troy that he, Jemima's own brother, was likely the one who was sullying her spirits. One didn't preach at one's guests, especially when they were offering you carte blanche with their willowy, chestnut-haired sisters.

It was clear that Troy was blind to any allure Jemima might possess and that he was likewise insensitive to her need for some kind of recognition. How wearing it must be for her to always be in the company of a self-indulgent genius, Bryce reflected. Though he didn't much care for Troy's florid poetry, he had a feeling history would judge the man quite differently. Poor old Jem, indeed. She, who couldn't see her own worth beyond the bright light that fairly glistened off her brother.

By the time Jemima peeked into the library, the masculine bonhomie was as thick in the room as the smoke from the cigars the two men were enjoying. It was well past lunchtime—the ladies had been left to fend for themselves and had opted to dine outdoors, on the stone terrace that ran along the back of the house. Terry and Bryce were deep in the throes of reminiscence by the sound of things, and since they couldn't see her through the cloud of smoke, Jemima decided to listen at the door.

"Eleanor Astoria? I remember her." It was Troy's voice. "Never say you had her after Bothwell?"

"I did indeed," Bryce replied in a voice mellowed with claret. "She was a taking little thing."

"Took Bothwell for all he was worth!"

There was the sound of hearty, deep-pitched laughter.

"And whatever happened to . . . oh, what was her name, the opera dancer from Clapham?"

"You mean Harriet Travers? She married some young lordling whose family shipped them off to Ireland in disgrace afterward."

"And was she one of your conquests, Bryce?"

There was a slight pause. "Ireland is a very beautiful country."

Troy gave a shout of laughter. "You mean you had her after she was married?"

"Before and after. Harriet's lordling was a trifle . . . unexciting."

Jemima stepped back from the door, and stood for some time unmoving on the hall carpet. She shouldn't have been surprised, she knew. Beecham Bryce made no claims to being a saint. Quite the opposite in fact. But it was one thing to hear his exploits being recounted over tea by the insatiable gossips of the *ton* and quite another to hear the man himself bragging about them.

She wanted to pack up her newly arrived luggage and storm out of the house, but there was nowhere to go, except back to the inn. And when Terry came to fetch her, there would be a scene when she refused to return. What could she tell him, what excuse could she give? Bryce had not made any improper overtures to her. Oh, he had flirted with her, in his sardonic way, but that was a usual occurrence between men and women of the *ton*. No, Bryce had done nothing that would excuse her fleeing from his home. Nothing except confirm his reprehensible reputation—a reputation she was well aware of before she agreed to stay beneath his roof. But it was most curious that overhearing something she already knew to be true could still cut like a knife.

Behind the partially closed door, the two men began to move about. Jemima barely had time to slip into the front parlor before they emerged.

Troy was clapping Bryce on the back. "I might just take you up on that offer. I haven't done any fly-fishing since Jem and I were in Scotland last summer."

"Your sister might not wish to remain here," Bryce remarked as they walked past her hiding place. "Not once the murder is solved."

"Jem? She's never any trouble. Follows where I lead, just like a faithful hound."

It was a good thing the gentlemen were out of earshot when Jemima left her hiding place or they would have heard her say a most unladylike word.

Dinner was a subdued affair at best. Jemima had entered the drawing room only just ahead of the butler, who had come to announce dinner. During the meal she focused all her attention on Lovelace. Bryce was surprised by that development—the two ladies appeared quite in charity with each other. Lovelace seemed in a less ebullient mood than last night, and when she wasn't conversing with Jemima, she addressed her male companions in a quiet voice, inquiring artlessly about their respective lives.

Jemima, however, continued to pointedly ignore the two men. By the time the custard tarts were carried in, Bryce decided it was time to draw her out.

"Lady Jemima," he said, turning to her with an encouraging smile. "Your brother mentioned that you visited Scotland last summer."

"Yes," she said without looking up from her dessert.

"And did you enjoy your stay?"

"Yes." Her spoon scraped against the porcelain dish.

"And how did you find the people to be?"

"Scottish, for the most part."

She then turned away from him and asked Lovelace about the new play. Bryce recognized a snub when he was handed one. He shot a questioning look toward Troy, who merely shrugged.

Since the lady would not converse, Bryce had to satisfy himself with watching her, which was not a hardship. She had appeared for dinner wearing a gown of pale gold satin that did wonderful things for her rounded bosom and her elegant white shoulders.

After dinner the men opted to take their port in the drawing room, as Bryce had done the night before. With some skillful navigation, Bryce managed to get Jemima out onto the terrace, leaving Troy to entertain a remarkably subdued Miss Wellesley.

"This is my favorite time of night," he said, carrying his glass to the stone balustrade. He leaned back on his elbows, keeping a watchful eye on his guest, who was hovering just beyond the light that spilled from the drawing room. "I like to watch the sky turn from blue to gray to black—that slow, velvety letting go of light."

"You are waxing very lyrical tonight," Jemima remarked from the shadows. "Maybe *you* should take up poetry." Her voice grew clipped. "But then you already have a full-time occupation that leaves you no time for other pursuits."

"What's this?" He moved away from his comfortable perch and headed in the direction of her voice. She was standing beneath a clematis vine that had coiled its way up one of the lilacs that overhung the terrace. "What has put you so out of twig?"

He reached out to touch her arm, and she backed away until the stone wall stopped her retreat.

"I—I shouldn't have come out here," she said haltingly. "I only wanted to give my brother and Lovelace a chance to mend their fences. They got off to a bad start this morning."

"Yes, and you and I got off to a rather good start. So what has happened?"

"Nothing."

"Hmm," he muttered. "When women say 'nothing' in that tone of voice, it generally spells trouble."

"You would know," she said. "Being such an expert on my sex."

He moved a little way beyond her, again leaning against the balustrade. In slow increments he decreased the distance between them. Lateral moves, he knew from long experience, were often more effective with skittish creatures then direct ones.

"I'd think you were vexed with me, Jemima," he said evenly, "but I couldn't help noticing that you've barely said word to your brother either."

"I'm not vexed with anyone." She put her chin up, and he had a lovely view of her profile, the straight nose and fine, lush mouth, silhouetted against the indigo sky.

It was odd, he thought. All his banter seemed to have deserted him in the face of her obviously troubled spirit. He could talk most women around his little finger, but with Jemima, for tonight at least, he had no interest in even trying. He didn't want to charm her, he wanted only to comfort her.

"I had another avocation once," he said in a musing voice. "Before I dedicated my life to l'amour."

"I heard you tell Lovelace," she uttered, "you wanted to be a steeplechase jockey."

Bryce chuckled. "No, my sweet, that was only to win a bet. I wanted to . . . now you must promise not to laugh . . . I wanted nothing more than to enter the church."

Instead of laughing, she spun to him and cried softly, "Don't blaspheme, sir. It is not amusing."

"See, I knew you wouldn't believe me. The fact is, I was studying divinity at Cambridge."

"Oh?" she drawled waspishly. "Was that before or after you seduced the don's wife?"

He tsked. "You've been listening to gossip, Jemima. And as for the don's wife, it was quite the other way round, if you must know. Not that I didn't enjoy it. But it put me right off divinity, I can tell you."

"I don't want to hear this." She swept away from the wall, but he reached out swiftly and caught her by the arm as she passed him. He felt her resist, knew she was longing to slap at his hand where it was clamped on her forearm.

Then she stopped fighting and turned to face him. "All right, I admit it. I am very cross tonight. There now, are you satisfied?"

He slid his hand down to her wrist and let his thumb wander over the pulse point beneath her white glove. "No," he said. "I want to know why you are cross. It's my duty as your host to look out for your comfort. Has someone been putting too much starch in your bed linens? Were the crabcakes at lunch a trifle off?" He had a sudden inkling. "You're angry because Troy and I abandoned you at lunch. That's it, isn't it? We left you to your own devices with the Wrath of the Wellesleys."

Jemima shook her head. "Don't make sport of Lovelace, Bryce. She is just a frightened young girl, who talks too much when she gets nervous. I know she is not very clever, but I feel sorry for her."

"You feel sorry for yourself, is more like." He overlooked her indrawn gasp. "I don't like you maudlin, Jemima. Not one bit."

She tugged back from his hold. "I don't seek to make you like me sir. That is the very *last* thing I desire."

"It's Troy who's made this change in you," he said in a low voice. "I see it clearly now. Before his rather unsteady advent last night, you were quite in charity with me, in your own prickly way. And this morning, driving to Sir Walter's, you gave as good as you got. I enjoy that in a woman, Jem. You're not some mealymouthed little hypocrite who pretends she doesn't know apples from pears. But now that you are in company with your brother, you've put on your Sunday manners. What, Jemima, afraid that Troy will realize his sister is a flesh-and-blood woman, and not his own personal acolyte?"

She gasped again. "My relationship with Troy is none of your concern. And besides, you like my brother . . . I know you do. I heard you and Terry talking in the library. Sounding like two old cronies, as a matter of fact."

"Of course I like him, he's a decent enough fellow. Except for the way he takes you for granted. I only wish that . . . Wait a minute—What was that you just said? Exactly when did you hear us talking in the library?"

Jemima bit her lip and closed her eyes. She'd properly let the cat out of the bag now. Bryce was peering at her in the faint light, his brow puckered, as though he were trying to recall exactly what it was he and Troy had been discussing.

"Oh, Lord!" he said after a moment's reflection. "*That* was a rather salty conversation for a lady's ears. My sweet Jemima, did no one ever tell you not to eavesdrop on gentlemen?"

"I was only looking in for a second," she said primly. "To see if you'd had your lunch."

"And got your ears scorched for your troubles, I wager. Well, at least you know now that your *brother* is a flesh-and-blood person."

She tossed her head. "Terry has always enjoyed the companion-

ship of ladies. But *he* doesn't pursue them to the exclusion of all
else.

"You are referring to me, of course. I . . . um, believe you rate
the merits of your sex a bit too highly if you think that women
alone are enough to fill up a man's time."

"Ah, yes. I left out gambling and drinking."

He turned a little away from her, so that she could no longer see
his face. "I don't make excuses to anyone for the life I lead."

"Yes," she said quietly in a voice that was tinged with grudging
admiration. "And that is one of the few good points in your character."

Jemima went back into the drawing room then, and Bryce didn't
try to stop her.

In the far corner of the room, Troy was making Lovelace giggle
over a game of piquet.

"Discard now, Sheba. And make it a good one. I'm feeling lucky
tonight."

"Don't call me that," she complained, albeit with a trace of
laughter in her voice.

"What, then?" he asked. "How about, 'Fair Cleopatra, temptress
of the Nile, who laid antiquity to dust, with just a smile.' "

Lovelace cooed, "Did you write that for me?"

Troy chuckled and shook his head. "I wrote that while you were
still in leading strings."

Jemima relaxed somewhat. At least her brother wasn't intent on
seduction. His voice contained nothing more than amused tolerance, the same tone he'd used as a boy whenever he was teasing
their two younger sisters, Penelope and Anne. Which had been
often, as she recalled.

She went to the piano and began to play, trying to empty her
mind, as her fingers drifted over the keys. She didn't want to think
about anything, not the talented, amiable brother who thought of
her as a faithful pet. Not the foolish, abandoned girl, who might be
the target of a cold-blooded murderer. And certainly not the tall,
harsh-faced man who infuriated her and stirred her into wayward
thoughts.

Bryce came in after a time and wandered over to the card table.
Jemima watched him from across the room, admiring, in spite of
herself, the impressive set of his shoulders. She noted how the fabric of his elegant evening coat stretched over the sloping muscles
of his back as he leaned down to whisper a playful comment to
Lovelace. His eternally unruly hair had again tumbled over his

brow; as he stood upright he brushed it back with one hand. And his eyes met hers.

For the first time since she'd met him, years ago it felt like, though it had been only yesterday, she saw doubt in their gray depths. All his blithe self-assurance had faded away, leaving behind a curious expression of discontent.

Nicely done, Jemima, she congratulated herself scornfully. *Your bout of melancholy has now rubbed off on your host. Nicely done, indeed.*

It is said a clean conscience makes for easy slumber, but contrary to the edict, Beecham Bryce rarely passed a poor night. Tonight, however, was an exception. He tossed and turned, pummeling his pillows into submission, and still sleep eluded him. Things were percolating inside his head, and he couldn't get quit of any of them.

He hadn't heard from his father since he'd taken ship for Barbados, and even with a swift crossing, it would be weeks before he got word of his safe arrival in the Caribbean colony. He wondered how the old fellow was getting on. The doctors had assured him that six months in a warm climate would clear up his father's lung ailment, but Bryce had little faith in the medical profession—if such a word could be applied to that lot of quacks. For himself, he'd trust his farrier to prescribe for him before he'd let a London doctor make a diagnosis.

And then there was the unsolved murder to tax his brain. He had an uncanny feeling that he was going to be embroiled in the investigation, and not just because the murder had taken place on his property. He suspected he knew more about the matter than he was able to admit to anyone. Another batch of trouble he could lay at his father's door, but much more serious than sick cows or sneezing farmers. It was just like the old man to go off, leaving him in possession of half-truths and thinly veiled warnings.

And tomorrow there would be a Runner on the scene. Bryce prayed he could maintain an air of indifferent curiosity and not rouse the fellow's suspicions. Perhaps the onerous task of questioning Lovelace Wellesley would send the man hying back to Bow Street on the next mail coach.

At least Troy's presence in his home didn't look to be much of a problem, excepting the pressure that was placed on a man when he entertained literary royalty. The poet was an engaging youngster, not unlike the men that Bryce consorted with in London—

sporting mad, up to all rigs, and overly fond of female company. Except that in Troy's case, the pursuit of pleasure was combined with the drive to create and the rare talent to make those creations take flight.

There was only one thing about the man that Bryce misliked. It was as he'd told Jemima—Troy hardly gave a thought to his sister. No, it was worse than that. He belittled her. Bryce recalled Troy's comments with a frown. *Past her last prayers. Follows me like a faithful hound.* It was to be hoped that Jemima had not been eavesdropping during *that* part of her brother's discourse.

And all the gilded poet could think of to remedy his sister's unhappy state was to throw her into the path of a notorious rake. Believeing, no doubt, that Bryce could be counted on not to remove the invaluable Jemima from Troy's life with an offer of marriage. No, he'd just sully her a bit and send her on her way.

Bryce groaned and burrowed his head into the pillow. He couldn't do the pretty, to use the poet's less-than-inspired words, without wanting to do another, less-sanctioned deed. Jemima had gotten into his blood and he had no intention of stopping at mere flirtation. But if he pursued her to his own ends, Troy was sure to be roused from his indifference. Christ, he might even call him out. Still, Bryce reminded himself, Jemima was no simpering schoolgirl who needed her brother's permission to walk in the park—she was a mature woman, one who could certainly make up her own mind about whether or not she wanted to embark on an *affaire de coeur.*

But damn Troy for putting him in such a spot. Bryce felt as though he was the only one who gave a thought to Jemima's honor. If she was *his* sister, he knew, he wouldn't let her get within a mile of a bounder like Beecham Bryce. He grinned in the darkness. Maybe if he'd had a sister—a feisty, outspoken, warm-hearted woman like Jemima Vale—he wouldn't have turned into the licentious care-for-none that the *ton* disdained and the world-at-large shunned.

The clock was striking one when he crawled from his bed and dragged on his dressing gown. These country hours were killing him. If he'd been in London, his evening would have just been beginning.

He went through the dark, silent house, heading, as he'd done in childhood, for the library. Many were the nights he and Kip would sneak downstairs, light a single candle and place it on the floor, and then proceed to make up vivid stories about the animals who dwelt on those walls. His brother had teased him in more recent years over the fact that Bryce had always favored the gazelle, Delilah, precisely because she was the only one to whom they had given a female name. Kip had seen it as a portent of his brother's future proclivities. God bless Kip. Wherever he was.

As Bryce opened the door, he thought perhaps his brother was closer at hand than he realized. A single candle burned on the floor, tilted slightly in its silver candlestick, and a slim, robed figure was huddled before it, gazing up at the stuffed tiger that had place of honor over the mantlepiece.

"Oh!" Jemima started to get up.

"No," Bryce said, moving forward and laying a hand on her shoulder. "Don't let me disturb you. I . . . I come down here, some nights, when I cannot sleep."

"Mmm, I couldn't sleep either." She wrapped her arms about her knees. "Troy was in my room talking nonstop about his new poem. And after he left, I just couldn't settle down. It's all this country air, I expect. A bit too invigorating."

"Were you looking for a book to read? There's something for everyone in this library. Poets, playwrights, slumber-inducing sermons." He forbore to mention his own private collection of erotica, which was locked away in one of the library cabinets.

She shook her head. "You will think me daft," she said sheepishly. "I was talking to Rajah."

"Not daft. It's a Bryce tradition, talking to the animals. My brother and I told them everything."

"But I am not a Bryce," she pointed out as she started to nervously pleat the skirt of her robe.

The garment was quite an improvement over what she'd been wearing this morning, he noted appreciatively. Both robe and night rail were made of a delicate lawn, in a creamy shade that glowed in the candlelight. But not quite as richly as her smooth, white skin.

"You are a guest of Bryce Prospect," he pointed out. "And can make free with our traditions. So what have you been telling the fearsome Rajah?"

"Oh . . . just that I was sorry I was so disagreeable tonight. Grumbling guests are the very devil, and I know this can't be easy for you—"

You have no idea, he thought with wry amusement.

"Having three people underfoot, who were strangers to you before yesterday. I had no reason to take my ill-humor out on you, when you've been so accommodating."

"What? Are you going to ring a peal over your brother, then, for giving you a megrim?"

Jemima sighed and splayed her fingers over her knees. "It's not Terry, either, who has made me feel this way. He's no different than he's ever been."

Bryce settled himself in the chair that faced the hearth, crossing his legs at the ankles beneath the hem of his long dressing gown. "Let's not get into another spitting match over Troy. I'd defend my brother against all comers, and I daresay, he'd have done the same for me."

She gazed up at him. "Why are you here, Bryce?"

"I told you, I couldn't sleep."

Her mouth curved into a tiny smile. "No, I mean here at Bryce Prospect. London was all atwitter at your sudden disappearance in May. You must know that the *ton* tracks you, wherever you go . . ."

"Like a watchful herd of sheep keeps tabs on a hungry wolf, eh?"

"So you think yourself a predator?"

He shrugged slightly. "It is how I am regarded. Mothers practically drag their daughters into alleyways when I pass them on the street. Which is unnecessary . . . in most cases."

There was a long moment of silence in the shadowed room, then Jemima said, "You still haven't told me why you left London."

"It's not important. Why don't you tell me something of your own life, Jemima."

She gave a small laugh. "That *would* put you to sleep. And I'm not going to let you avoid my question. Consider it a guest's prerogative."

Bryce hesitated, and then said, "My father has been ill . . . it's his lungs, you see. Ever since my brother was killed, the old man hasn't taken proper care of himself. Laboring in the fields with his workers, riding out to inspect his herds in the worst weather. He and I don't get on . . . we haven't since I left Cambridge fourteen years ago. When I came back here for my brother's memorial service—Kip's body was never recovered after he drowned—it was the first time in nearly five years.

Jemima looked puzzled. "But you seem so at home in this house, Bryce. Not like a visitor."

"I grew up here. And as the eldest son, I was expected to take over the care of the estate. More so since my brother was mad to join the navy. But I had no interest in farming when I was a sprig. No, I wanted to seek after the glories of the Anglican church."

"I still can't credit that," she said.

"Neither can I now, looking back. It was my grandfather's doing I suspect. My mother's father was a rector in Cornwall—we used to summer there. He was a great, barrel-chested fellow, with more kindness and forbearance than any man I've met before or since. My brother and I believed that Grandfather Kipling was really Father Christmas without his red coat; sometimes I still believe it."

"Is he still alive—your grandfather?"

Bryce shook his head. "No, they're all gone. Mama and Grandad. And Kip. They had such high expectations for me to follow in my grandfather's footsteps. And I had a few expectations of my own. But all I came away with, after my unfortunate experience at Cambridge, was the conviction that the Church forgives us least, when we are most human . . . Not a very Christian sentiment, I'm afraid."

"But true, I think."

His gaze slid over her. "You agree?"

"If I may quote the illustrious Lord Troy, 'Ring out the new gods who have served our souls so ill, and raise up once more the temples, on Zeus's mouldering hill' "

" 'Olympian Twilight,' wasn't it? I recall reading it last year." He sighed and then grinned. "The boy does have his moments. So tell me, does that make you a pagan, Lady J?"

"Mmm, I'm somewhere betwixt and between. Troy is all pagan, however, in spite of his gentlemanly trappings. I think he was disappointed that your Bacchus Club offered only pleasures of the flesh—he was expecting some ancient Greek or Roman rituals, at the very least."

Bryce shook his head wonderingly. "You are the only woman I know, Jemima, who is rash enough to sit in Beecham Bryce's library—in your night rail, no less—and discuss the Bacchus Club as though it were a literary society. If I didn't know better, I'd think you were the one who was casting out lures."

Her amused chuckle surprised him. "And you are the only man I know—excepting my brother—who would not think me shockingly improper for even acknowledging that such a place as Bacchus exists. It's very liberating, not having to mind everything I say when I am with you." She smiled up at him. "But we have wandered off the subject—we were talking about your father's illness."

Bryce shifted in his chair. "He's gone off to Barbados—under duress, I might add. His doctors claim that some time in the tropics will cure him. But he refused to go until I promised to come here and look after the place while he was away."

"Then you have made things up with him?"

He looked down at his clenched hands. "Not so you would notice. There is too much discord between us—one selfless act on my part hasn't made a dent in it. After I'd disgraced myself at Cambridge, he rewrote his will and left everything to Kip. And now . . . now God only knows who will inherit Bryce Prospect."

"Then it truly is a selfless thing you are doing." she said quietly. "Overseeing a property that should have come to you and with no hope of reward. I wonder that you even made the offer."

Bryce's eyes met hers, and he was unaware of the dull pain that lay close beneath the bright surface. "I couldn't let him stay here and die, Jem."

"No," she whispered hoarsely. The pain he guarded so carefully colored his tone, even if she hadn't already seen it in his eyes. Not only were the doors of society closed to him, she realized, but the doors to his family home, as well. And by a man he claimed no allegiance to, but whose death he would do his best to prevent.

Jemima stared into the candle flame as she spoke. "Bryce, remember yesterday, when you told me you found me surprising? I think I must return the compliment." She looked up at him. "You are not at all what I expected."

"I must be losing my touch," he said. "You should be cowering in a corner by now, at the very least."

She answered with more honesty than she intended. "I tend not to cower. Fleeing is more my style."

Bryce sat back in his chair. He was afraid if he leaned too close he would be tempted to touch her, and if he did that, he couldn't answer for his actions. She looked so damned tempting, but vulnerable, too vulnerable, with her wide eyes and her elegant brow marred by a tiny frown.

"I tend to dislike women who flee," he said lightly. "Pursuit is just too wearying." His voice dropped a notch. "But then there are some women who are well worth the chase."

Jemima threw her head up, fighting back the urge to let his words affect her. A foolish inner voice insisted that he was speaking of her—that it was she who was worthy of his attentions. Her eyes drifted to Rajah, snarling down at her from the wall. Another skilled, silken predator, she thought, caught for all time in that fearsome pose.

She spoke into the silence that had enveloped them. "And how do you go on here, now that you have the running of the place?"

He made a sour face. "I have discovered that I am not cut out to be a farmer. My first week here, we lost six sheep to bloat. The second week, my father's favorite hunter colicked and I was up all night walking him. He recovered, but I'm not sure that I have. And now I've been here a month, and the cows are sick, my tenants have the grippe, and there are infernal beetles in the woodwork." He looked to see her reaction and was not reassured. "Oh, go right ahead, Lady J, and laugh at my woes."

She had put one hand over her mouth to stifle her giggles. "Sorry," she said, trying to regain her composure. "It's just that you seem so utterly on top of everything. But I can see that it's quite a change from London. All you had to worry about there were jealous husbands and presumptuous young upstarts looking to dethrone you as the king of libertines."

"Quite true," he said dryly. "Living in London is a piece of cake compared to running Bryce Prospect. I'm still furious at my brother for abandoning me—he'd have made a much better job of things."

"You must miss him dreadfully," she said in a low voice.

Bryce's tone grew clipped. "We rarely saw each other in recent years . . . he spent most of his time at sea. But, yes, I do miss him. He was a . . . a bright light in a bleak world."

Jemima sat without speaking for a moment, digesting his words. She'd had a close enough call last night, when she thought Terry had been killed, to know how such a loss would feel. Bereft didn't begin to describe it.

Her hand slid onto the arm of his chair, finding his hand, warm against the leather of the armrest. She wrapped her fingers around it. "I'm so sorry, Bryce," she said.

He leaned forward, disregarding the warning voice that prompted him to keep back, and laid his free hand on her hair. The loose waves were like strands of raw silk beneath his palm.

"Jemima," he sighed as his eyes probed hers with a curious entreaty.

She rose up at his unspoken bidding, until she was kneeling against the padded arm of the chair. Seduction now seemed the farthest thing from his mind, and yet he wanted so badly to take her in his arms. He yearned to hold her, even for the space of a few heartbeats. And he had an inkling that she might even understand and not flee from him in dismay.

He let his hand drift down from her hair, settling it on the nape of her neck. And then he slowly drew her forward. Her eyes were brimming with uncertainty, but still held no hint of fear as she gazed up at him.

But then he recalled who he was, a man who did not deserve comforting, especially not at the hands of a creature who put everyone else's needs before her own. She was in far more need of comforting than a sorry sinner like himself. But the only sort of comfort he knew how to offer a woman would do little to raise Jemima's spirits. It would more likely send her into an abrupt decline.

Bryce shifted back from her as he drew his hands away and placed them again upon the arms of his chair. His eyes hooded over and he drawled, "Best not get too close to the fire, pet."

Jemima sat back on her heels, jarred by the sudden change in him, the relaxed approachability now cloaked by wry detachment. She'd barely begun to examine the rampant stirrings that his touch aroused in her when he had pulled back. "W-what?" she stammered in confusion.

In answer he reached down to where her robe was billowing perilously close to the tilted candle. He smoothed the fabric away from the fire, letting his fingers linger for an instant on her calf.

"Don't want my guests going up in flames," he said with an attempt at humor.

"Oh!" She twisted her skirt behind her as she scrambled to her feet. His whispering touch on her leg had sent a shiver of apprehension through her and she was suddenly afraid. "I'd better go up now."

"Yes," he said, still watching her with guarded eyes. "I think that would be for the best."

She took up the candle. "Aren't you coming?"

"No, not yet. Take the candle . . . I can find my way in the dark."

I just bet you can, a little voice piped inside her head.

She stopped before the door. "Tomorrow, if you like," she said in her most matter-of-fact voice, "I could ride out with you. I still remember some things about living on an estate—maybe I can help with the cows. And we can bring food to the tenants who are ill. Though for the life of me, Bryce, I haven't a clue of what to do about beetles in the woodwork."

"Go to bed, Lady J," he said without turning his head. "Tomorrow will take care of itself."

Chapter Five

B ryce sat in the dark for a long while after Jemima left. He was still not sleepy, and in addition to that, he was now also feeling strangely depressed. His intended seduction of Jemima Vale was not following any recognizable pattern and it had him baffled. She had him baffled.

Unlike many of his brethren, Bryce had little interest in virgins. He saw no point in purposely seeking out untried women—they were new wine, unappealing to a man who craved the subtle taste of more seasoned vintages. And yet he hungered for Jemima, for a woman whose body may have been unawakened, but whose mind and spirit were richly alive.

But she was a study in contrasts that left him, for the first time in many years, unsure of how to proceed. At times she bantered with him like a carefree boy, and at others she held him off with a firm, maidenly disdain. It occurred to him that her role as traveling companion to Troy, leaving her at once experienced in life but inexperienced in matters of the heart, accounted for her perplexing duality.

Whatever its cause, that intriguing combination of blasé worldliness and guarded naiveté lent spice to his encounters with her. But he was damned if he knew how to appeal to both sides of her nature. He did not count her worldly enough to play the game he had in mind, nor was she so naive that he could cozen her into his bed with pretty promises of devotion. It was a complete stalemate.

There *was* one way that he knew he could entrap her—he could make her feel sorry for him. She had all but cast herself into his lap just now when she thought he needed consoling. But that was a scoundrel's trick, playing upon a woman's sympathy. And if he couldn't have Jemima's passion, he certainly didn't want her pity.

Bryce rose and lit one of the candles that sat upon the mantel. He needed a glass of brandy. Badly. As he lifted the decanter from the side table, something shifted in his brain. He set the decanter down again with a dull clunk and then crouched beside the table and studied the amber liquid. Last night, after he'd poured a healthy tot of brandy for Jemima, he had noticed that the level was even with the top row of crystal florets that were carved into the decanter's side. Now the level was fully three fingers below that mark.

Someone had been making inroads into his father's best French cognac.

Troy had been closeted in the library all morning, but Bryce recalled that when he'd poured the poet a glass of claret just before lunch, Troy had remarked that he'd been longing for the hair of the dog. No, Troy wasn't the culprit. The butler, Griggs, was a Methodist who drank nothing stronger than tea, and Bryce could hardly envision Mrs. Patch sneaking into the library to knock back a brandy or two. Especially since she had a store of cowslip wine laid by in her day room.

He stood up and shook his head, trying to clear away the whispering disquiet that had the hair at the back of his neck standing on end. His feelings of alarm, he told himself, were as groundless as Jemima's fear of old Admiral Hastings.

Picking up the candle, he moved to the bookshelves, needing to find something that would distract him from his unease. His father possessed a starchy collection of books, to be sure, and there was little on the shelves to tempt him. He had a mind then to look through the collection of erotica he'd brought with him from London. If he couldn't sleep, he'd at least be entertained.

The family Bible sat open and ponderous on its wooden stand before the window; Bryce crossed to it and slid one hand beneath it, relishing the fact that the key to his cache of profane literature lay beneath this sacred tome. He knelt before one of the lower library cabinets, unlocked it, and drew out a tooled leather box.

As boys, he and Kip had hidden all their less-savory reading matter in that cabinet—florid adventure stories, etchings of scantily clad women they had purchased from traveling peddlers, and the odd French novel. The great thing was that their father believed the key to the cabinet had been lost and had never, to Bryce's knowledge, tried to have it forced open. Why should he, when he had a half-dozen cabinets in which to store his dry, dusty collection of sermons? The brothers had been tickled by their own temerity—hoarding such inflammatory literature virtually under their father's pious nose. "Hide in plain sight," Kip had said with a wink to his brother. Bryce shuddered to think how his father would react to this rather more adult contribution to that cabinet of secrets, as he sat cross-legged on the floor and began to sort through the contents of the box.

Within seconds the hair on his neck was standing upright again. Three books were missing from his collection—a racy two-volume account of an unnamed gentleman's journey through the world of eros, and a rare and valuable book of Japanese woodcuts. That one in particular was Bryce's favorite.

He tapped his fingers against the edge of the open box, wracking his brain to make some sense of things. The missing brandy and the stolen books . . . one of them he could blame on the servants, but not both. Someone had come into his library, after he'd left last night, and helped himself to the best that Bryce Prospect had to offer. As though he were entitled to it. And aside from the elderly gentleman now en route to Barbados, there had only been one other person with such an entitlement.

His father's parting words drifted into Bryce's disordered brain. "Don't grieve overmuch for your brother," he had said gruffly. "Men lost at sea oftentimes return home again . . . years later, by some accounts."

Bryce thought at the time that his father had become a bit addled from the medicines he was taking. Still, it had been a strange thing to say. But no stranger than the old man's warning that Bryce was to look the other way if anything involving smugglers came to light on the estate, which had immediately followed his obscure comment about Kip's death.

Bryce had wondered then what his father had embroiled himself in, and he now had an inkling that his mention of Kip and smugglers, practically in the same breath, was no coincidence. There was only one other person who knew where the key to the cabinet was hidden. There was one other person, excepting his father, who knew that the library could be reached from a secret stairway that led up from the cellar. A cellar with a broken window that he and Kip had been sneaking in and out of since they were breeched.

Bryce carried his candle to the wall opposite the fireplace and pressed down on one of the wooden spindles that topped the wainscotting. The panel slid open noiselessly. He stepped into the narrow space. The dust beneath his feet looked like it had been disturbed recently, but that could have been the work of mice. Well, large mice, perhaps. There was a scuffed place near the top of the stairs that looked suspiciously like a bootprint.

Bryce returned to the library and poured himself a very large brandy. He raised it in salute to the glass-eyed elephant that hung opposite the secret panel. "You'd tell me, wouldn't you, Tusker, if he'd been here? You wouldn't keep something like that to yourself."

But the beast said nothing, looking blindly out from the wall with its trunk raised as if in silent greeting to Kip's ghost. Bryce muttered an oath, knocked back the brandy, and went off to seek his bed.

Jemima was deep in conference with Mrs. Patch, when her host came into the housekeeper's day room the next morning.

"There, " Jemima said, pointing to a page in the *Country Lady's Book of Housekeeping Hints*, which Mrs. Patch had obligingly pulled down from a high shelf. "A recipe for curing milk fever."

"That book is fifty years old if it's a day," Bryce remarked as he crossed the room.

"Old remedies are sometimes the best," his housekeeper pointed out tartly. "You've done everything the farrier suggested and nothing has worked. It couldn't hurt to try this. Here, sir, come and see."

Bryce shot Jemima a look of unveiled skepticism as he craned over Mrs. Patch's shoulder. "What does it call for?" he muttered. "Eye of newt, toe of bat?"

"A tisane of withies and nettles," Jemima pronounced.

He rolled his eyes. "The cure is worse than the disease, eh? Very well, we will set the imperial poet to gather nettles—that should furnish him with some interesting inspiration."

"And," Jemima added, "your cook has promised to make up baskets of calves' foot jelly and chicken broth for the ailing farmers. Mrs. Patch is contributing her own special blend of camomile tea, which she guarantees will speed their recovery."

"And what of the death-watch beetles? Is there a remedy for that plaguey nuisance in your book ?"

"Turpentine," Jemima said a bit smugly. "If there's any to be found in the house."

"I believe I can lay my hands on a tin or two. Do we pour it into the walls, do you think? The smell alone should make short work of my unwelcome house guests."

Jemima gave him an owl-eyed stare. "Are you that eager to be rid of us?"

"I was referring to the beetles," he said dryly. He then cocked his head and studied her. "I wonder, Jemima," he mused, "if Alexander the Great had a woman like you in his life. You know, someone to light a fire under him when he was too weary to go out and conquer the civilized world."

She made a rude face at him. "I am only trying to help you, Mr. Bryce. If you'd rather I didn't, I will go attend to my *knitting*."

"I believe you mean tatting. Isn't that what spinsters toil over?"

"I was being sarcastic," she sniffed.

He turned to his housekeeper. "She's a prickly little thing, don't you think, Mrs. Patch?"

That good lady also sniffed—which Jemima thought quite appropriate for a woman who was well past sixty—and said, "We could *all* use someone like Lady Jemima here at the Prospect. If you take my meaning, Mr. Beecham." And with that less-than-obscure pronouncement she went bustling out of the room, the recipe book tucked under one plump arm.

"It is never a wise idea," Bryce muttered in a low voice as he watched her bristling departure, "to keep on the servants one grew up with. They can't ever seem to forget that they knew you when you were a grubby sprat with mud all down your shirt."

"I don't recall that I was ever a grubby sprat," Jemima remarked serenely.

Bryce shifted his eyes and let his gaze wander over her. She was dressed for riding, and though her deep green habit was styled along simple lines, it had been tailored by a master hand. The unadorned bodice followed every curve of her breast, and the skirt, which she had caught up over one arm, fell in great sweeping folds. She looked, at once, straitlaced and highly provocative.

"No," he said as he raised his eyes again to her face. "Goddesses are rarely ever grubby."

She sighed. "We are back to hollow flattery, I see."

He chuckled. "I never flatter anyone before noon, Lady J. I haven't got the wherewithal. Now, come out to the stable and I'll see if I can scratch up a horse sedate enough for a lady of . . . advanced years."

Jemima put her head up and preceded him through the doorway. He hung back a little to admire her as she swept down the hall. She was all affronted dignity and long-limbed allure. And he wanted her as badly as any woman he'd met in his adult life. But if he was to succeed with her he needed time, which meant fostering the notion that there was a bloodthirsty murderer still at large in the neighborhood. He wondered if he could keep up the ruse, especially since he now had a fair idea who the murderer might be. Someone about as bloodthirsty as a lark.

Once she knew there was no real threat to Lovelace, the sublime Lady Jemima would be free to remove herself from his care and return to London. He feared that once she was surrounded by her intellectual coterie, he would have no further opportunities to pursue her. She would become just another society lady who would cut him if ever they chanced to pass on the street.

He ran his hand through his hair in frustration. She was worth the chase, worth taking the time to seduce. He had only to look at her, feel his blood heating and his desire rising, to be sure of it. And he knew that when she got wind of his duplicity, as she was bound to at some hopefully distant point, she would be furious. He had to win her now or he would never again get the chance.

Jemima had left her jauntily feathered riding hat on Mrs. Patch's work table; Bryce snatched it up and went striding after her. She was at the front door, being buttonholed by her brother. Bryce stayed back in the shadows of the hall and watched the exchange with an unpleasant expression on his face.

"You're sure you packed it, Jem?" The poet laid a hand on her arm. "You know I can't write worth a damn if I haven't got my Homer beside me."

"It's with your things, Terry," his sister replied patiently. "I packed it myself at the inn."

"And I've run out of licorice, if you're going anywhere near the village today . . . And I could use some new pen points, though I daresay Bryce has a store of them somewhere."

Bryce saw that she was trying to edge away from him.

"And I need you to get a blasted ink stain off my favorite shirt. You do still carry that French soap about with you, don't you?"

"Ask Mrs. Patch to help you Troy," she responded with more than a touch of annoyance. "I've promised to ride out with Bryce this morning."

Her brother gave her a look of petulant resignation and went striding off in the direction of the breakfast parlor. Bryce moved forward then, handed her her hat, and without one word of commentary, he offered her his arm and led her through the front door.

They rode over a large portion of the estate, stopping in at the smithy and the dairy, before proceeding on to the homes of the tenant farmers. Bryce hadn't wanted Jemima to risk contracting the influenza and had tried to prevent her from actually sitting with his tenants, but she assured him she had an iron constitution and hadn't caught so much as a sniffle since she was a girl.

She chattered with the farm wives and made a fuss over their children, watching while Bryce coaxed the ailing farmers to eat

their broth. He displayed a relaxed ease with his tenants, no easy
task in the cramped cottages which smelled overpoweringly of
stewed cabbage and wet diapers. But in spite of their size the cottages were in decent repair, and the inhabitants, except for the ones
with the influenza, seemed in good health. Bryce's father was a
proper landlord, she was pleased to note.

At the third cottage they visited, Bryce sat in the back garden,
dandling a chubby infant on one knee, watching as Jemima helped
the farmer's wife hang out her laundry. He appeared to be completely in his element, and she realized with a shock that Bryce
would have made a very decent vicar—his charm was not limited
to the drawing room and his concerns did not end at the boudoir.

The image of him with a rosy-cheeked child in his lap was not
one she chose to dwell on, however. A domesticated version of the
notorious Beecham Bryce was too appealing and far too unsettling.

It was nearly noon when they came to the bailiff's house, which
lay near the estate's northeastern boundary. It was larger than the
cottages, boasting four rooms downstairs and a gabled attic. Mr.
MacCready, a tall, spindly man with a ruddy complexion, insisted
they join him for luncheon, He had heard about the murder in the
grove, and he questioned them both intently as they shared a meal
of cold ham hock and cheese. When Bryce informed him that the
Runners had been called in, the man looked unimpressed.

"Ruddy lot a Londoner knows of country matters, sir," he grumbled, scratching his narrow chin."Lucky if he could find his own
arse with a map . . . oh, beggin' your ladyship's pardon."

Jemima grinned. The bailiff was certainly a colorful fellow, and
he lived up to his reputation as a dandy, sporting a well-tailored
suit of blue broadcloth and a nattily tied cravat. His pale blue eyes
watched her while he spoke, and Jemima had the feeling the man
was assessing her in return.

He shook Bryce's hand as they were leaving. "As I've said before, sir, it's a rare treat to have you back at the Prospect. You've
been missed . . . by everyone."

"Well, he certainly has a soft spot for you," Jemima remarked to
Bryce as they walked across the bailiffs lawn toward their horses.

"I run a poor second to Kip in MacCready's book," Bryce said
without any hint of resentment. "I was surprised the old fellow didn't
take it harder when my brother was killed. He took me aside at the
memorial service and insisted that Kip was too stubborn to give up
the ghost so easily. At the time I thought he was being a bit daft."

"It's hard to let go," she said softly. "Even when you know you must."

Bryce stopped untying his horse's reins and turned to her. There was something in her voice, a hint of poignant realization, that he knew had nothing whatever to do with his brother. When he lifted her onto her horse, his hands were, for once, impersonal at her waist.

She arranged her skirts over the horse's flanks and then put her head back and said thoughtfully, "Bryce, do you ever wish you could do things over?"

"You mean relive a pleasurable experience?" His eyes teased her, hoping to remove the somber expression from her face. "I pray for it."

She shot him an impatient frown. "No, of course that's not what I meant. I'm talking about decisions you made, courses you followed, that you now regret."

"I regret nothing," he said evenly as he mounted his horse. "But you are not speaking about me, that's plain. Tell me then, what ill roads have you unwisely decided to travel, Lady J?"

She shrugged as she moved her mare up beside his gelding. "I'm not sure if I actually made the decision. That is what's troubling me. I more sort of fell into it."

"Then perhaps it's time you fell out of it," he said softly. "You don't lack for grit, Jemima. Or brains."

She sighed and toyed with her horse's mane. "It's this country life," she said. "It leaves a person too much time for reflection."

"Then I'll just have to make sure I keep you busy. And for starters, there is something I want to show you. Come along now, and see if you can keep up."

He urged his horse into a slow canter and then increased its speed until they were flying over the green turf. Jemima watched him moving effortlessly in cadence with his horse's rocking motion and felt a hollow ache begin to well up in the pit of her stomach. It was as though all her happiness were racing away from her over the lush, green grass.

For her entire adult life, Jemima had managed to avoid the entanglements of love. She had faded into gray midlife without once stirring herself to reach out for something bright. Because, she supposed, there was always the light of her brother gleaming at her shoulder. But Troy did not belong to her. Not the way a husband or a child belonged to a woman.

It had been brought home to her as she sat among the wives of the tenant farmers and watched them with their children. Those women had little in the way of worldly goods, and yet they possessed so much that Jemima longed for. A cozy home, the laughter of children, and the care of a loving husband.

Instead of that bounty, Jemima had her artists' salons, and her ladies' charitable organizations, and her brother's never-ending jaunts to God-knows-where. Years and years of offering her services to the benefit of others. How empty and wasted those years now seemed.

"Je-mi-ma!" Bryce was calling from the middle of the field, one hand waving over his head.

She waved back and kicked her mare into a trot. The horse Bryce had chosen for her was a narrow-shouldered bay with a lop ear. He claimed the mare was a nice, sensible ride, but Jemima knew, the instant she took up the reins, that Pandora was a prime goer, for all her physical flaws. The mare now covered the distance to Bryce in a breezy gallop that left her totally unwinded.

Which was more than Jemima could say for herself. The sight of Bryce, sitting relaxed on his gelding, the breeze lifting the ends of his neckcloth against the tanned skin of his throat, his dark hair gleaming in the afternoon sun, all but took her breath away.

"Woolgathering?" he asked as she pulled up beside him.

"Sorry. I had to adjust my stirrup," she lied. "My skirt got tangled in it."

"You should have told me," he said silkily. "I'd have been happy to remove your habit. From the stirrup, that is."

Jemima looked up at the sky, assessing the position of the sun. "I see that it is past noon. And that your innuendos have returned, right on schedule."

Bryce's mouth drew up into a crooked grin. "I don't flatter before lunchtime; innuendo I can furnish round the clock."

She shook her head and grinned back. "Unrepentant to the last. I see. I shall just have to make sure that I don't offer you any more grist for your mill. Now, where are we off to? I put myself in your hands—oh, no!" She laughed. "I've just done it again, haven't I?"

He nodded slowly, his eyes narrowed in amusement. "But so charmingly that I will let it pass, unremarked."

Side by side they rode past herds of doughty beef cattle and flocks of black-faced merino sheep. Pandora shied playfully at the sound of the sheep's plaintive baahs, and Jemima easily brought the frisking horse under control, noting as she did so the open admiration in Bryce's eyes.

As they rode along an elevated ridge, with a row of close-planted cedars on their left and a field of dairy cows on their right, Jemima saw a rider coming toward them. The man was traveling parallel to the ridge on a narrow cart track that lay some distance below the spine of cedars. Bryce clearly didn't see him—he was too busy looking for ailing cows.

There was something about the rider that reminded Jemima of her companion—the set of the wide shoulders and the upright, graceful posture in the saddle. As the man drew closer, she saw that his lower face was obscured by a dark beard and that he wore a blue, nautical-style jacket. Probably a sailor just off his ship, taking a shortcut across the Bryce estate to hasten his trip home. But the man's uncanny resemblance to Bryce teased her. That, and something else that she couldn't put a name to.

As he disappeared from sight around a bend in the ridge, she found herself wondering if Bryce's father had possibly gotten a child or two on the wrong side of the blanket. And that line of thought progressed quite naturally to the question of whether Bryce himself had sired any byblows. It was more than likely, she reasoned forlornly. She had a wretched inkling that the next time she was in Hyde Park of a Saturday morning, when the nursemaids were about with their charges, she'd stumble across at least a dozen children with curling sable hair and pale gray eyes.

Bryce motioned Jemima to stop as he pulled his horse up at the edge of a wide field. It was uncultivated except for the wild grasses and flowering weeds that had proliferated there. He lifted Jemima to the ground, and then tied both horses to a dead crab apple tree. She followed him across the field, lengthening her strides to keep up with him, to where the level grass dipped abruptly down into a ravine. Bryce eased her down the steep slope, and then held on to her hand as they made their way along the narrow gully. It was strewn with round rocks, as though it might have been a streambed at one time.

"Damn," he muttered as he came to a halt.

Jemima peered around his wide shoulder. They had come to what appeared to be a small landslide—a mass of tumbled rocks was piled up against one side of the ravine.

Bryce sat down on one of the larger rocks and rubbed at the back of his head. "Well," he said sheepishly, "so much for my surprise." He motioned with his thumb to the wall of the ravine behind him. "Someone's gone and covered it up."

Jemima scrambled up a little way onto the pile, careful lest she sprain her ankle and end up hobbling beside Lovelace. "What was it?" she asked, standing upright.

"A cave," he said. " A really topping cave. Kip and I discovered it when we were boys. It's all limestone beneath these downs, and the stream that once ran through this ravine carved out an amazing tunnel in there. It's probably just as well that they've closed it off—too tempting a spot for the local lads to get up to mischief." He scraped at the charred remains of a twig fire with the toe of his boot. "Though it looks like someone's been here recently."

"I think it's a shame," said Jemima with sincere disappointment. "I've never seen an English cave. Terry and I explored one outside Athens two years ago and it was breathtaking."

Bryce swung to her and said peevishy, "Do you never do anything without that confounded brother of yours?" The breeze that was buffeting along the gully caught at his hair, sending the dark curls dancing over his brow. He brushed them back impatiently. "Don't you ever think you'd like your own life, Jemima? Not always being part of your brother's train, carted from place to place like a piece of luggage."

Jemima sat down abruptly on a round rock and frowned across at the opposite wall. "I don't wonder you're a success with the ladies," she muttered. "You've got such a way with words."

"No, I'm serious. He gives you little thought, except when you are not there to look after him. And then it's, 'Where the devil has she put my Homer?' and, 'How the deuce could she let me run out of licorice?' I see it, even if you don't ."

Jemima heaved a little sigh as she set her chin on one upraised hand. "My brother is not much different from most husbands I've seen. They, too, take their partners for granted. At least with Troy, I am not always under his thumb. He sees to it that I have my own funds, and so I can come and go as I please. But I would be very lonely without Terry in my life. I know he is childish and demanding—"

"Among other qualities."

"And it's true he does not always appreciate me. But I've seen the world, Bryce, at his shoulder. Egypt and Morocco. Greece and Turkey. He deserves to be looked after—he truly is a talented poet."

"If you like sentimental claptrap. 'The Crusade of Destiny,' indeed!"

"You were admiring his words only last night, if I may remind you. And the Prince Regent esteems him enormously."

"Prinny's taste is all in his posterior end."

"Bryce!"

"So you sit at the feet of your gilded brother, and let your own talents go fallow."

"You follow your muse, *Mr.* Bryce—Venus, I believe she is called—and I follow mine."

He gave a dry laugh. "My muse is a deal more entertaining than yours, *Lady* Jemima. At least the pursuit of Venus allows for some pleasure. You are no more than a dogsbody to that self-inflated sprig."

Her eyes flashed dangerously. "You have no right to speak that way about him."

"Good Lord, Jemima, the man is twenty-six years old. Isn't it time you cut the apron strings?"

"I told you, I am not his caretaker. And he is very fond of me." *Like a faithful hound,* she couldn't prevent herself from adding silently.

Bryce cocked his head back so that he could look her in the eyes. "He brought you to the Tattie and Snip, and then went haring off to a prizefight without any thought to your safety. He learned you were staying in the home of a notorious rake and never even raised an eyebrow. And he practically offered you to me, on a platter. No, I am not making it up . . . I only wish I were. Do the pretty, he said to me. Charm her, Bryce." He drew a breath. "Is that fondness, my pet? Sounds more like pandering to me."

Jemima stood up and stumbled down from the rock pile. She spun to him, her hands curled into fists. "Why do you always do this to me? We cannot speak together for five minutes before you begin to insinuate the most wretched things."

He blinked. "Was I insinuating? I thought I was saying it right out."

"Then I will say this right out," she cried raggedly. "You are jealous of Troy—yes, jealous. Because he has a rare gift, something that one man in ten thousand possesses. He is clever and charming, he draws people to him. He visits with royalty and heads of state wherever he travels.

"While you, sir, are a wastrel and a rake, who has nothing to your credit but a string of ex-mistresses and God-knows-how-many byblows. My brother will leave the world enriched by his genius. You will leave the gutters full of your baseborn brats."

Jemima almost clapped a hand over her mouth. If he had struck her for such harsh words, it wouldn't have surprised her. But he only laughed, his head tipped back, and his eyes regarding her with amiable humor. "You," he said, once his laughter had subsided, "have been eavesdropping on my father. Only I believe his expression was 'my ill-gotten brats.' I give you points for alliteration, but then what else should I expect from the great Troy's sister?"

Jemima flashed him one last look of extreme irritation before she swept past him. She wished the blasted gully wasn't so full of rocks—it was difficult keeping her chin up when she had to watch out for her footing. And she knew he was following her stumbling retreat with his eyes—she could feel them burning a tiny hole between her shoulder blades.

How dare he criticize my choices? she raged to herself. How dare he draw her into his life and then presume to sit in judgment on her? And most of all, how dare he see inside her, and with such cuttingly accurate insight?

How could he know that the complacencies of which he had accused Troy were the very things that had lately begun to chafe at her? Her brother's lazy expectations, his need for constant coddling. Genius or not, he had no right to expect her to fetch and carry for him. She again recalled his words, "She follows me like a faithful hound," and nearly screamed in vexation.

It wasn't Bryce she should be angry with, she realized, as she clambered up the sloping entrance to the ravine. It was herself. She was the one who had given up any dreams of a husband or children to nurture her brother's talent. So that he could have it all—fame and wealth and the love of the multitude. And in due time he would doubtless marry and father a family. And where would Lady Jemima Vale be then? Trapped in the role of faded spinster aunt, who would then be required to transfer her solicitous care from her brother to his offspring.

Bryce had accused her of living in Troy's shadow and she saw now that it was true. She had lived in the darkness for too long. She knew she would never marry—there were circumstances in her life that precluded that possibility, things that even Troy knew nothing about. But if she was truly going to experience her own life, and not some vicarious version of her brother's, then she had to decide what it was she wanted. The years were racing past and she had allowed herself to experience so little.

As much as she questioned Bryce's morality, there was no doubt the man had seized life and tasted it. Tasted it and drunk from it and never regretted one moment. And he had loved. Surely not in the romantic manner that schoolgirls prattled about, but he had given his passion free rein and reveled in that heady blossoming of the senses. She, on the other hand, was as withered and parched as the dead crab apple tree that loomed before her.

With an oath, she scrambled up the canted trunk of the tree, tugged her mare closer, and levered herself onto the sidesaddle.

The need she had denied for so many years now positively raged through her. She wanted to be loved by a man. Not thought of as a faithful pet, or, worse yet, a piece of luggage—but adored, worshipped, and esteemed. But barring those urealistic expectations, she would happily settle for being desired. And unless she missed her guess, Beecham Bryce, that blunt, infuriating, and unaccountably attractive man, already desired her. So maybe it was time she stopped fleeing. For once in her life she would meet her fate head on.

She untied his horse's reins and led the gelding back to the entrance of the ravine. Bryce looked up in surprise as he came up the grassy incline. "I imagined you'd be halfway back to the house by now."

"I don't know where the house is," she said with less than total honesty.

He reached for his horse's reins, then stretched them tight between his fingers. "Jemima, I . . ."

"No, Bryce." She leaned from the saddle and laid her hand for an instant on his hair. It was warm from the sun, the loose curls soft beneath her palm.

This is what I want, she thought with a little shiver. *And what I just might be able to have.*

"Don't say anything," she said softly. "We are like oil and water sometimes. That's all it is."

Bryce was looking at her with an expression of cautious assessment. "I still believe I need to apologize. I have an unfortunate tendency to speak my mind, and devil take the consequences."

She narrowed her mouth as she shook her head. "I am the one who needs to apologize. For letting idle gossip color my judgment of you. Inexcusable, I think, now that I have met you." She offered him a tentative smile. "The man is wholly different from the myth."

Bryce disregarded her smile as he wrapped the reins over his hand until the knuckles showed white. "The gossip is true, Jemima," he said in a gruff voice. "At least part of it. I am not a victim of slander . . . I'm not a victim of anything but my own wayward nature."

She would not be swayed from her intent. "Wayward or not, Bryce," she proclaimed, "you possess a few redeeming qualities. For one thing, you have never uttered an unkind word to Lovelace, whatever you might think of her. My sainted brother sent her off to the garden in tears yesterday morning. And I've seen how your servants respect you . . . and the farm people. I wager Mr. Mac-

Cready is not easily won over, and he admires you a great deal. I refuse to believe you are so black as you have been painted."

If she thought this declaration would be met by approval on his part, she was sadly mistaken. He looked away from her, off toward the line of cedars, his face hovering close to a scowl. "You might not think me so black today, Jemima," he said in a low voice. "But there will come a time when you will."

Turning his horse away from hers, he swiftly mounted. "I have some business with one of my neighbors," he said over his shoulder. "If you ride back along the ridge a mile or so, you will see the housetop beyond the trees."

He spurred his horse forward and rode off without so much as a backward glance. She had the uncanny feeling that this time he was the one who was fleeing.

Once he was sure Jemima was headed back toward the house, Bryce returned to the ravine. It took him several minutes of rolling rocks off the landslide, before he had cleared enough space at the top of the pile to see into the cave. Mindless of his pristine buckskins and gleaming topboots, he slithered through the narrow opening and fell with a thump onto the pebbled floor.

A lantern sat conveniently at his feet. He lit it from the tinderbox he carried in his coat pocket and surveyed the small cavern. It was a tidy bivouac, all things considered. A pallet was spread out under one limestone outcropping with a small metal trunk beside it. A crate containing pots and plates and a variety of utensils had been shoved against the opposite wall. He only wondered that the bent fork he plucked up from the crate wasn't part of the Bryce family silver. Because the fine linen sheets and soft woven coverlet on the pallet had surely come from his home, as had the silver flask, which was half hidden beneath the pillow. Filled with his father's cognac, no doubt.

He knelt beside the metal trunk and traced his fingers over the two small books that lay there. A third book had been carefully wrapped in a large linen napkin. At least the thieving troglodyte had had the sense to protect Bryce's rare volume of Japanese woodcuts from the dampness of the cave.

Grinning like an idiot, he shifted onto the pallet, sitting with his hands pressed hard over his eyes as he tried to quell the fierce, hopeful beating of his heart. But it would not be stilled. No matter how much the voice of reason intruded, telling him over and over that he was a bloody fool to believe in miracles, he couldn't hold back the elation that was bubbling up inside him.

Chapter Six

Bryce arrived back at the house to find a stranger standing on the front porch, smoking a clay pipe.

"Good day to you, sir," the man called merrily, as Bryce dismounted from his horse and handed the reins to a waiting groom.

"And good day to you."

"We've been awaiting your return. I came here with Sir Walter—he's inside with your guests. Not a happy man, that one. Not to be in company with such fine ladies . . . and such talkative ladies." He grinned and held out his hand as Bryce came up the steps. "Lawrence Fletcher, at your service. Of Bow Street, as you might have guessed. Most folks just call me Mr. Fletch."

"Very pleased to make your acquaintance, Mr. Fletch. I am Beecham Bryce."

Bryce had never had occasion to meet a Runner in person, his own crimes being more amatory in nature than strictly unlawful. He studied the man briefly and was not impressed. Though of middle height, Mr. Fletch was possessed of an unfortunately disproportionate body—his melon-shaped head quite overwhelmed his thin, angular frame. A fitted moleskin jacket and pipestem breeches did little to flesh out that reedy architecture. His bony wrists protruded noticeably form the worn edges of his shirtsleeves and an oversized Adam's apple bobbed above a carelessly knotted Belcher handkerchief. Not exactly the sort of man to strike fear into the hearts of wrongdoers. Crows, perhaps, but certainly not bloodthirsty murderers. So it was a good thing, Bryce reflected wryly, that there was no one of that ilk hanging about in the district.

Mr. Fletch bore his scrutiny with relaxed tolerance. He then gave Bryce a wide smile. His eyes, neither black nor brown, glittered brightly in his swarthy face. "I note your nag sir." He nodded toward Bryce's departing horse. "Won the Derby in '08, unless I miss my guess."

Bryce gave the man a swift, approving look. Perhaps there was a brain after all in that oddly shaped head. "You've a good eye for horseflesh, Mr. Fletch. I bought Rufus from his owners—the ungrateful rascals were going to put him down when he started to lose his races."

"Gelding," the man said with a wink. "No use a'tall for breeding. But a nice country hack, I reckon."

"He's a grand horse, and since I won a great deal of money on him in that particular Derby, I thought he deserved better than a trip to the knackers."

Mr. Fletch bowed slightly. "A man after my own heart, Mr. Bryce. Now if you will join your guests in the drawing room, I believe we can get down to business." He knocked his pipe against the stone railing of the porch and followed Bryce into the hall.

Everyone looked up as the two men entered, their faces full of anticipation and a touch of unease. Lovelace was sitting primly on the sofa, her injured foot resting on a little stool, with Troy beside her, sprawled back against the cushions. Jemima was seated at the window in a delicate side chair. She looked at Bryce for an instant, and then lowered her eyes to her lap. He could have sworn she blushed.

Sir Walter was the first to greet him, rising from his chair near the fireplace and muttering worriedly, "He's French, Bryce. Confound it, the fellow is French."

Bryce looked from the magistrate to the Runner. "He sounds English enough to me, Sir Walter."

The man hissed, "Not Mr. Fletch, dash it all, the corpse."

Mr. Fletch coaxed Sir Walter back into his chair. "Mr. Bryce, if you will make yourself comfortable."

Bryce went to stand beside Jemima, murmuring, "This looks to be a farce that will outshine anything the Minstrels could produce."

"Sssh!" She shot him a warning look.

Mr. Fletch situated himself before the fireplace, his knobby hands hanging loose at his side. "Now that Mr. Bryce is returned, we can begin. I am going to tell you what I have discovered, but if any of you have something you would like to add, please feel free to interrupt me."

Lovelace gave a little shiver of anticipation.

Mr. Fletch clasped his hands before him. "I have thoroughly examined the body of the murdered man, which Sir Walter has been good enough to keep in his spring house."

Bryce gave a little snicker of amusement, which he immediately covered with a dry cough.

Jemima gave him another dark look, as Mr. Fletch continued. "He was killed by a single knife thrust through the thorax, which penetrated the heart." He glanced at the two women, as if assessing the possibility of potential swooning. Both Jemima and Lovelace were regarding him with avid, bright-eyed attention. "From the tailoring of the man's clothing, and from the coins in his pocket, I can deduce that he is, if not himself French, someone who has spent some time in that country."

Lovelace raised her hand. "Mr. Fletch," she said, once he had acknowledged her. "I heard the man speaking and he sounded just like me."

"She means, he spoke English," Troy translated with a wry glance at his sister.

Mr. Fletch was unperturbed. "It has on occasion happened that a Frenchman has learned to speak our language. Quite well, in fact, and with a barely detectable accent."

Jemima made a noise of impatience. "Mr. Fletch," she said haltingly, "I do not wish in any way to tell you your business, but I have myself owned gowns that were from Paris. And I'm sure in the bottom of my reticule you might find the odd coin from Greece. These facts make me neither French nor Greek."

Mr. Fletch nodded. "Just so, ma'am. I have not said that this man is French, only that his clothing is. Which begs the question, how is it that a man who spoke English, who was murdered in England, was wearing clothing from a country with whom we have been at war for over a decade?"

Lovelace raised her hand again, waving it back and forth. "I know!" she cried. "Oh please, call on me."

"He ain't a schoolmaster, Sheba," Troy muttered.

"Yes, Miss Wellesley?" Mr. Fletch tried not to roll his eyes.

Lovelace looked around, making sure that all eyes were on her as she proclaimed, "He was a spy!"

"Or a smuggler," Bryce said under his breath.

"Or an emigré," Jemima mused aloud.

"Ladies, gentlemen, please. We are not here to conjecture on anything. We are here to establish facts. Now with Miss Wellesley's assistance, I would like to recreate the murder. Mr. Bryce, Lord Troy, if you would join me up here. And Miss Wellesley, of course."

Troy rubbed his hands together enthusiastically. "Theatricals, how lovely."

Bryce leaned for an instant over Jemima. "If you make so much as one cutting remark . . ."

She hid her grin behind her hand, but could not prevent her eyes from dancing up at him.

After a great deal of deliberating, Lovelace arranged her two actors into the proper positions. "Now you must argue and glare fiercely at each other."

The men took antagonistic stances opposite each other and began to mutter nonsense in a low tone.

"Perfect!" Lovelace cried. "Now Lord Troy must say, 'This is all I found, I tell you!' "

They did as she asked, and then on her further instructions, Bryce caught Troy's wrists in his hands and began to force him back toward the fire breast. "Now!" Lovelace crowed. "The knife."

Bryce drove an imaginary dagger into his opponent's chest. Troy staggered melodramatically around the room for far longer than was necessary, and then collapsed in an inert heap upon the sofa. Lovelace screamed then, full out and with every bit of lung power she possessed. It lasted a full fifteen seconds, and Bryce swore later to Jemima that he heard Sir Walter's foxhounds baying in response all the way off in Withershins.

"Oh, s-sorry," Lovelace stammered when she was through, once she realized that everyone in the room, including the corpse, was looking at her with their mouths hanging wide open. "It was what came next. I—I forgot we were in a drawing room. I am stage-trained, you know."

"Ought to be house-trained," Troy murmured, but then gave her a broad wink. "We'll see you in Covent Garden yet, Sheba."

Mr. Fletch thought it was time to get his reenactment back on track. "What now, Miss Wellesley?"

"He," she said pointing to Bryce, "crept stealthily up to the tree where I was hiding. And then he grabbed me by the arm."

Bryce walked casually across the carpet.

"Stealthily, old chap," Troy coached from the sofa, his chin on his fisted hands.

"You're dead." Bryce dismissed him with an amused scowl. He grasped Lovelace lightly by her wrist and swung her toward him.

"Now," Mr. Fletch said quickly. "Tell me what you see."

"Mr. Bryce," Lovelace said with a perplexed frown.

"No," the Runner said between his teeth. "The man who caught you in the woods. Describe him."

Lovelace closed her eyes, her face working into a tight squint as she concentrated. "A tall man . . . dark hair . . . tanned face . . . pale eyes."

"You are still describing Mr. Bryce," the Runner said impatiently.

"Indeed I am not," she cried. "It's true there is a resemblance . . . when Mr. Bryce came to my aid, I thought he could have been the murderer. Well, actually, at first I thought the cow was the murderer . . ."

Bryce saw the bewildered expression on the Runner's face and shot him an apologetic grin. "You get used to it after a while, Mr. Fletch," he assured him. "It actually almost grows on you."

Lovelace continued, undeterred. "The man in the woods resembled Mr. Bryce—at least from the nose up. Because you see, I just now recalled that the murderer had a beard. A short, dark beard. I cannot think how I could have forgotten such a thing."

"That, Miss Wellesley," Mr. Fletch responded briskly, "is why we perform reenactments. They stir the memory something fierce. So tell me, what did you do next?"

"I ran away," she stated.

"Pretend, Lovelace," Jemima piped in quickly. She had a vision of them all chasing after the girl as she hightailed it at a hobbling run across the west lawn.

With a great deal of huffing and puffing, Lovelace ran slowly in place. "I fell into a rabbit hole then."

"Very large rabbits hereabouts," Troy drawled.

"But if you please, Mr. Fletch," she said, "I'd rather not reenact that. Acting it the once was hard enough on my ankle."

"Of course, miss. You may sit down now. And I must say, you did very well."

As Lovelace limped back to the sofa, her audience gave her a smattering of applause. She performed a curtsy, and then pinched Troy on his arm, so that he would sit up and make room for her on the sofa.

"But I'm the corpse," he protested as he shifted to one side.

"So," Mr. Fletch said, as he paced across the room. "We have seen the murder through this young lady's eyes. Two men, an argument, a scuffle, and then a knife thrust. Mr. Bryce finds Miss Wellesley, takes her to the inn, speaks to the landlord for . . . how long?"

"Five minutes at the most," Bryce replied.

"And when they return to the scene of the murder, and meet up with Lady Jemima, the corpse has already been disposed of. Now, even if our murderer was a behemoth, I doubt he had the strength to remove a man's body and carry it overland. Earlier today, Sir Walter took me to the clearing where the murder took place, and afterward I found hoofprints in the lane where it curves around the wheat field."

"I never took Rufus into the lane that day, except quite near the inn," Bryce said. "But there are others who sometimes use that lane, tinkers and farmworkers. The butcher's boy."

"So I've been told. But there was also an interesting bit of evidence left on the rail fence."

Jemima closed her eyes and winced. She had a fair idea of the evidence a bloodied corpse left behind.

"Ah," Mr. Fletch said. "I see Lady Jemima anticipates me."

Her eyes met the Runner's. "It was all over my folding stool and my gown. The blood, that is." Her glance shifted to Lovelace. "Miss Wellesley has a deal of fortitude to have witnessed such a grisly crime and not fainted dead away. I can't say I'd have had the strength to flee, after such a thing."

Bryce bent and whispered, "But you excel at fleeing, Lady J. I have your own word on it."

She chose to ignore this. "But tell us, Mr. Fletch, how did the murderer carry off the body?"

He nodded toward Bryce. "If the man was built along similar lines to our host, he could have moved the victim a short distance."

Troy leapt up from the couch with an eager expression on his face. "Want to try, Bryce? Carry me around the room?"

"Oh, sit down, Troy," Bryce muttered. "I already carried you half across the stable yard . . . in case you have forgotten your intemperate arrival here."

Troy sat down and winked at Lovelace. "I was completely jugbit."

"Mr. Bryce has made my point for me," the Runner said with a scowl at the unrepentant poet. "If the murderer had a horse waiting in the lane, he had only to carry the body, what? . . . twenty or thirty feet."

With a shock of recollection, Jemima had a vision of the peddler she had seen as she crossed the wheat field. Just after the murder it would have been. She toyed with the idea of mentioning this occurrence to the Runner. But then Bryce had just pointed out that local tradesmen often used the lane. Just another case of the maiden lady starting at shadows, she thought with a small scowl.

"It's a bad business," Sir Walter grumbled. "Two strangers having at each other in our quiet little burg. I'd never have brought you in, Mr. Fletch, if I hadn't thought it was Lord Troy who had been killed."

The Runner said, "But as I am here, Sir Walter, I think I can be of assistance. Now we know that our unknown corpse was carrying the items which had been stolen from Lord Troy's room at the Iron Duke. The landlord cannot say with any certainty if there were strangers lurking around the inn that morning—a great many people were coming and going, and all because of a mill that was being held in Barcroft.

"Best fight I ever saw," Troy reminisced softly.

"But someone took Lord Troy's things and we have no reason to think it was anyone other than the unidentified victim."

"But why break into Troy's room?" Jemima asked as she shifted away from Bryce, who was leaning against the window frame with his long legs canted perilously near her hip. "Why was he singled out?"

Mr. Fletch gave her a nod of approval. "That is a pertinent question, Lady Jemima. Why indeed? And I have a theory. A man called Sir Richard Hastings was staying in the room beside your brother's. I believe the thief entered the wrong room. Sir Richard is a retired naval officer, but he is still active in government circles. He is rumored to be involved in rooting out a spy network which operates on this coast. I wager a member of the Admiralty would be a more likely target for a French thief than a poet."

"See!" Lovelace crowed to Troy. "I was right about the spies. Now you shall write a poem about spies and foul murderers, and Papa can turn it into a stage play. And I can play . . . I can play myself." She twinkled at him.

"I never write about politics and such," the poet said darkly. "Not enough pith." Lovelace looked forlorn until Troy said, "But I will write something for you, Sheba. How about, 'Little Lame Lovelace, or the Fortitudinous Foundling'?"

"Oh, yes," she breathed.

Mr. Fletch coughed pointedly to regain everyone's attention. "There is one problem with my theory. If the dead man was part of a spy network, why then did his compatriot in the woods murder him?"

"Why do you assume they were compatriots?" Bryce asked in a matter-of-fact voice.

"It stands to reason. The two men clearly knew each other. 'Tis unlikely that two strangers would be arguing in such a manner.

Miss Wellesley overhead enough of their exchange for us to conjecture that they were in league."

"Do you think she is in any danger now, Mr. Fletch?" Jemima
asked intently.

The Runner nodded slowly. "I do not wish to frighten Miss
Wellesley. But this man has done murder once; I doubt he would
shrink from it a second time. Especially since the young lady was
the only witness to his crime."

Lovelace gave a small whimper. Troy took up her hand and
began to pat it reassuringly.

Jemima turned to gaze up at Bryce. "I thought you were being
overly cautious, insisting she stay here. But it appears I was
wrong."

At the moment, Bryce looked like his thoughts were a million
miles away. He moved forward into the room. "No one will come
to any harm, if they stay within the confines of the estate," he said
a bit brusquely. "Mr. Fletch, have you had a chance to speak with
Sir Richard? In light of his connection with the Admiralty, he
might be able to tell you what the thief was looking for."

"Papers!"

Bryce looked down at Lovelace, thinking she had again ventured a solution. But she was sitting subdued and pale and quite
silent.

"It was papers he was after," Jemima repeated, her eyes on
Bryce. "That was why Terry's notebook was ripped up. The man
took the poems, thinking they were some sort of naval documents."

"Don't be daft, Jemima," Troy uttered. "Who could mistake poetry for perishing naval documents?"

"No, wait—" Mr. Fletch held up one hand. "The thief might
have thought they were written in code. It's not an uncommon
practice. Messages are sent using phrases from newspapers or
books, and the recipient deciphers them using a decoding chart."

"Good luck to him deciphering 'Ode to Persephone,'" Troy
chuckled. "It's more than I was able to do with the blasted thing."

"There were no papers found on the man's body," Mr. Fletch remarked. "So the murderer must have taken them. And if that's the
case, the dead man was killed, not for a cache of naval secrets, but
for a silly bit of foolscap. Oh, sorry, Lord Troy." He gave the poet
an affable grin that did little to hide the wry twinkle in his bright
eyes.

Jemima shifted forward in her chair. "I'm still confused on one point, Mr. Fletch. When the Frenchman said, 'This is all I found,' wasn't he admitting to his confederate that the papers were not those he expected to find at the inn? Why would the bearded man commit murder over worthless papers?"

Mr. Fletch nodded. "A nice observation, ma'am. Perhaps he killed our Frenchman not to get his hands on the papers but rather in a fit of rage, because the thief had so badly bungled the job. Then the murderer took the pages with him to cover his tracks, never realizing that his victim was carrying your brother's jewelry, which would allow us to trace the Frenchman back to the inn."

There was a grim silence in the room, as everyone digested the concept of such a vengeful villain.

Mr. Fletch gazed about him with narrowed eyes, like a heron surveying a teeming pond. "Now, do you have any other questions?" he waited a moment. "No? Very well then. I must thank you all for your time. We've made a good start here today. All I request is that you not discuss this matter except amongst yourselves. Secrecy," he intoned, "is paramount at this point."

He moved forward to shake Bryce's hand. "And thank you for the use of your home, sir. I'll have a word with Sir Richard in Canterbury. Let's hope he can shed some light on the matter."

"You're not going to stay here and guard us, Mr. Fletch?" Lovelace asked with a throb in her voice.

Bryce nearly laughed. Mr. Fletch looked barely able to guard a biscuit tin, let alone a house full of people. Though the man had a keen enough grasp on things, he had to admit. Too keen, perhaps.

Mr. Fletch gave Lovelace a tight smile. "I investigate things, miss. We Runners tend not to get involved in the watchdog end of the business. But I believe Mr. Bryce and Lord Troy will see that you come to no harm. And if the murderer has any brains, he'll have left the district."

"Probably gone back to France, by now," Sir Walter muttered sourly as he rose from his chair. "Bloody frogs. Well, come along now, Mr. Fletch. You can drop me home and then have the use of my gig. I pray Hastings will be able to put an end to this sorry business."

Mr. Fletch turned in the doorway. "I've taken a room at the Iron Duke, so if you happen to think of anything else I might need to know, you can leave a message with the landlord."

As Bryce escorted Sir Walter and the Runner from the room, Jemima noted that he again wore that distracted expression on his face. As though he were fretting about something. Troy sat looking thoughtful a moment, and then he jumped up from the sofa and, after a brief aside to Jemima, went striding out the door in the wake of the three men.

Lovelace turned down Jemima's offer to sit with her in the garden, moaning that she didn't dare go out of the house, even in daylight, with a crazed French murderer on the loose. Jemima understood totally—she wasn't sure she cared to venture outside herself.

"I wish Mama and Papa were here," Lovelace said mournfully as Jemima settled beside her on the sofa. "And Charlie. And even that wretch, Percival Lancaster—he is our leading man, you know. And even though he drinks like a fish and calls me a scene-stealing little harpy, he is a strapping, robust fellow. I think he would probably defend me from peril . . . if only because he fancies himself to be something of a hero."

"I'm sure he would defend you, " Jemima said soothingly. "We all would, Lovelace. And I think you should know why Troy went after Mr. Fleltch just now—he want to send for another Runner to look into your parents' whereabouts. Surely someone from Bow Street should be able to trace a large traveling coach and a prop wagon with WELLESLEY'S WANDERING MINSTRELS painted on the side."

Lovelace looked slightly less crestfallen. "Did he really do that for me, Lady Jemima?" A fresh batch of tears welled up in her pansy brown eyes. "You and your brother are so kind."

"Now, I think you should have a look in on the library—there are some very entertaining books in there, and you need a distraction. And if all else fails, you can always talk to the animals."

Lovelace appeared bewildered.

"You'll see what I mean," Jemima said with a knowing grin, as she walked the hobbling girl to the door.

Bryce returned to the room a few minutes later and found Jemima standing at the window, gazing out over the lawn. "Looking for spies in the underbrush?" he asked as he came up beside her.

"It's all so preposterous," she said, turning to him. His expression was now relaxed and held a hint of amusement. "French spies and coded messages . . . like something from one of Lovelace's melodramas."

"Unfortunately those things do exist." he said softly. "All part of warfare between civilized nations."

Jemima bit at her lip. "In London it is easy to forget we are at war. One sees the military everywhere, of course, but the men seem like play soldiers, their uniforms merely a bit of pretty color to set off a lady's gown." She sighed. "I am ashamed to admit it, but I have given the war little thought. It . . . it has had no impact on my life until now."

"What?" he asked as he moved closer. "Haven't lost a dashing beau to artillery fire, Lady J?"

She shook her head crossly. "Don't make a joke of it, Bryce. You of all people know how it feels to lose someone you love because of the war. Even if it wasn't in a military engagement, your brother died in service to the King. But my friends in London are artists and writers and the like—they are indifferent to the war at best, and at worst, well . . . I fear some of them actually admire Bonaparte."

He gave her a tolerant smile. "It's not a crime to admire your enemy. You think Wellington doesn't look upon Napoleon as a worthy foe?"

She lowered her head and said softly, "I think it's time I came down from my ivory tower."

"Bravo, Lady Jemima." Bryce took up her hand. "Shall I fetch a ladder from the barn?"

She snatched her hand back and gave him a searing frown. "Can you never be serious?"

"I avoid it at all costs. Especially since you appear to be serious enough for the both of us, at the moment. Will it reassure you if I promise that Lovelace will come to no harm while she is here?"

"You are very cocksure of your ability to protect her."

There was a strange light in his eyes as he replied, "I am a dangerous man to cross."

She was about to point out that any reputation he might have in the *ton* as a man not to be trifled with had certainly not filtered into France. But her protest died on her lips. He did indeed look very dangerous at that moment, fierce and quietly menacing. And if half of England knew that Beecham Bryce was deadly with a pistol or a sword, then who was to say that a Kent-based clutch of spies had not also learned of it?

Bryce leaned toward her, his mouth almost brushing her ear as he added in a low tone, "Do you think I would let you remain here, if I thought there was the slightest risk?"

"No," she said, quickly moving away from him. He was too compelling up close; even from half across the room she could feel the heat of his presence. "I think you will keep us all safe, Bryce.

And perhaps we are starting at shadows. It's possible there is no risk involved."

"Not for Lovelace, not at the hands of spies," he said as he closed the gap between them in three easy strides. "For you, however, there is a deal of risk."

She looked up, startled. And then smiled wryly. "Oh, I see. More innuendo?"

Bryce wasn't grinning. "I believe I'm beginning to weary of innuendo."

"Amen," Jemima murmured under her breath.

"No," he continued, "I think it's time for a more direct approach."

"What, is the fox to be warned then, that the hounds are about to be loosed?"

"Mmm. Let us say that I am giving you a sporting chance. Though I'm damned if I know why."

"You must know by now that I am not easily cozened," she said evenly. "You've plied your rakish wiles on me these past three days, flung your hints and unsubtle flatteries, and I am still unmoved."

Bryce gave her a long look through his forelock and then shook his head. "Lady Jemima, you are much greener than you appear, if you think my behavior to date has been an attempt at seduction."

She felt herself begin to flush with embarrassment. "B-but you've been flirting with me . . ." she nearly sputtered. "At least . . . I thought you were."

"I flirt with Lovelace. Idle, meaningless words. I wouldn't waste my time flirting with you, Jem."

Jemima didn't know whether to be outraged at the insult inherent in his words, or gut-wrenchingly disappointed that he didn't desire her after all.

But then he added in a deep, provocative whisper, "There is nothing idle or meaningless about what I say to you." He compounded the effect of his words by leaning forward and slowly brushing his chin over her cheek.

She had never felt anything so remarkable—the slight rasp of his skin against the soft planes of her face left a shivery trail of fire. His husky voice had held a promise of sensual pleasures and earthly delights. Jemima had to fight off her inclination to walk up to him and lay her head against his chest. It would be so easy to raise her lips to his and so rewarding to feel that steely mouth soften into tender passion. But not here in this room where a gruesome murder had been acted out. Not now, when her fears for Lovelace were so close to the surface.

Bryce had moved to the arm of the sofa, and now sat watching her, his eyes intent and his lips curled into a cryptic expression that was neither grin nor scowl.

"I . . ." Jemima opened her mouth, but had no idea of what to say. *Take me,* occurred to her. *Have me, own me . . .* But as much as she admitted to her desire for him, she knew she needed to set her own pace. She had no intention of being an easy conquest, only an ultimately willing one.

She drew a breath, seated herself beside him on the sofa, and said in an airy voice that would have done Lovelace proud, "I fear you will never succeed in luring me into dalliance, Bryce. I am too often amused or infuriated with you to ever take anything you say seriously."

He swiveled around to face her, his mouth now relaxed into a genuine grin. "You know little of the matter, that's clear," he said. "Humor and anger are two of a libertine's greatest tools—humor makes a woman lower her guard and think herself secure."

"And anger?"

He cocked his head and said reflectively, "Anger heats the blood—which is the desired outcome when a man seeks to bed a woman." His gaze slid to her. "Lord, Jem, you must think seduction a bland thing. How do you picture it? An oily cad whispering wet kisses up your arm, while he mouths pretty platitudes? If that's been your experience of seduction, then I can only say you have put yourself in the hands of cawkers."

"I have never intentionally put myself in any man's hands," she replied briskly, neatly disguising the fact that she wanted desperately to put herself in Bryce's strong, tanned, and very experienced hands.

"Oh, women rarely acknowledge that they are accomplices to their own seduction—they pretend dismay, which allows them a clear conscience once they are enjoying the results of their acquiescence."

"Perhaps they truly do feel dismay." She added a bit sharply. "Would you even notice if they did?"

He shot her a withering look. "If you are implying that I have ever forced myself on a woman—"

"Why wouldn't you? You are a tall man, fit and strong. I doubt a woman's feeble protests could keep you from achieving your goal."

His scowl softened. "It's true there are those who enjoy forcing a woman to comply. There is an ugly word for such men. But I have never been remotely interested in coercion." He reached down and lifted her hand from her lap, turning it over and flattening out her fingers. He then laid his hand directly over hers, less than an inch above the palm. "Here, what do you feel?"

She looked questioningly into his eyes, then down at their two hands.

"Nothing," she said softly. "I feel nothing."

"Relax," he said. "And close your eyes."

She did as he asked, more out of curiosity than in any faith that something magical was going to occur. Then she felt it, the subtle electric vibration arising from her palm. It quivered in the air between their two hands, and within seconds her own hand had raised to his. His fingers closed over it.

"That," he breathed, tightening his grip, "is what *I* am interested in. The pull . . . the tug . . . the magnetic force that draws two people together. Not coercing a woman, Jemima. Never that."

He dropped her hand abruptly, stood up, and crossed over to the nearest French window. "Enough for today. I've got to see to my horses." He disappeared through the arched opening.

Jemima looked down at her hand, still raised before her. It was shaking—no longer from his touch, but from the intensity of the emotions that were flooding through her. The warm clasp of his fingers had sent a ripple of pleasure through her body, but more than that, she was reacting to the blinding surge of need that had erupted from her heart. Like Bryce, she longed to succumb to that fierce magnetic pull, but she knew there was much more that she wanted from him. Last night she had seen a glimpse of the real Bryce behind the libertine's facade—a man who worried over his father, even though there were years of enmity between them. A man who mourned the death of his brother—a brother who would have deprived him of his own patrimony. She had a vision of Bryce as a young man, his idealism soured by the harsh response of the Church he aspired to serve—to what was nothing more than a youthful dalliance. *The Church forgives us least, when we are most human.* Those words had been laced with bitterness, even more than a decade after the fact.

And so he had turned from the light, given up his vocation, and become a reprobate—a man who allowed all his appetites free rein. And yet some traces of honor lingered; she was sure of it.

She raised her hands to her face. "Don't, Jemima," she breathed into her palms. "Don't look for redeeming qualities in him. He makes no excuses for his behavior—why then should you presume to make excuses for him?"

The answer rose up from deep inside her and shocked her in its clarity.

"No!" she said aloud in a trembling voice. "I won't let it happen. I refuse to let it happen."

Her decision that morning, to participate in her own seduction, began at once to falter. She couldn't let Bryce get that close to her, not now. Not in light of the feelings that were currently making a whirlygig of her heart. How could she have been so blind to her own desires? She wanted Bryce all right. But not only as a skilled and accomplished bedmate. There was a world of things she wanted from him. He had only to touch her in the most casual way, for all her long suppressed yearnings to rise up.

She had lied to herself in the meadow that morning—merely being desired by a man was not enough. But she knew it would be a chilly day in hell before a man like Beecham Bryce would adore, worship, or esteem her. A very chilly day.

Bryce went to the stable and hid in the dark recesses of the tack room, idly buffing one of the bridles with a cloth, while he waited for his blood to cool.

Damn the woman! Sitting there demure and proper, like a sainted school mistress, gazing up at him with her bright, azure eyes. So innocent, so bloody trusting. Blithely announcing to him that she was not about to be led down the garden path. She'd almost made it sound like a challenge.

What he'd told her was true, at least in his experience—women were always accessories to their own seduction. Their protests were rarely more than lip service to convention. His theory had been validated on the rare occasions when he'd been turned down. Women who were not interested in dalliance said no. And then did not linger in range.

But Jemima Vale had confounded him. He'd made no secret of his interest in her, practically from the start, and she'd made it equally clear that she had no intention of letting him seduce her. But then she did not go away, as prudence would have dictated. It was true she was more or less trapped in his home until Lovelace was freed from threat of the unknown murderer. But the house was large—she could have easily kept away from him. Instead she made herself available to him at every turn. She had gone driving

with him, and hadn't fled from the library last night, even though
it was highly improper for them to sit and talk in such an intimate
setting. And she had willingly accompanied him on his ride over
the estate that morning.

If he didn't know better, he'd think she was throwing herself at
him.

But as much as he wished that were true, he suspected Jemima
sought him out only because, in her immeasurable nàiveté, she assumed he had accepted her rebuff and had subsequently lost all interest in pursuing her. When, in fact, just the opposite was the case.

Blind little fool! To believe she could discuss the techniques of
seduction with a hardened libertine, as though they were chatting
about archery, without making herself a target for his lust. It gave
her a vicarious thrill, he saw quite clearly, to question him on such
an indelicate topic. But she would learn, if she didn't take care,
that if you danced too close to the fire, you were bound to get
scorched.

At dinner, any discussion of the murder was avoided as if by
mutual accord. The conversation was restricted to commonplace
topics—the merits of the various dishes that were carried to the
table, the state of the nation, and that trusty standby, the weather.
Each of the diners seemed preoccupied by his or her own thoughts.
Lovelace was fretting with worry over the prolonged absence of
her family, as well as the threat of the vengeful murderer. Jemima
was trying, in vain, to tamp down her unruly and wholly irrational
feelings for Bryce. By the end of the meal she had lapsed into an
edgy silence.

Bryce was still reeling from the discovery he had made in the
cave that afternoon. He chatted amiably enough with his guests,
but his thoughts were drawn back to that limestone cavern. In spite
of his insistence to Jemima that she was not at risk—and he truly
believed that to be the case—until he knew exactly what sort of
game his nighttime visitor was playing, he had no right to offer
such a guarantee. For the first time since her advent into his home,
he was rethinking Jemima's presence there.

Bryce's attention shifted to Troy, who seemed full of high spirits as he entertained the table with the tale of his first meeting with
the Prince Regent. But then in a matter of minutes he became
oddly deflated, picking listlessly at his salmon as though the
weight of the world sat upon his immaculate shoulders.

Jemima knew the reason behind Troy's mercurial behavior, and when she took him aside in the drawing room, he merely smiled at her question. "Of course I'm working on a poem. When am I not? But this one is something different—not an epic tale, but rather a dark, shadowy piece. It's this house, Jem. It puts me in mind of specters and hobgoblins."

Troy's creativity, she knew, had always been affected by his surroundings. After visiting Holyrood House, Mary Stuart's castle in Edinburgh, he had been inspired to write one of his best short poems—"The Queen's Consort." And in Egypt and Greece, where Troy had steeped himself in the ancient, sun-burnished landscape of the Mediterranean, exquisite cantos had flowed nonstop from his pen.

"Yes," she said, casting a quick glance at their host, "I do find this house to be full of shadows. Though I can't say I find them particularly inspiring."

"Ah, but then you don't require inspiration," he said in his offhand way. He excused himself then, and went off to the small parlor Bryce had given him to use as a study. In less than a day, Troy had filled it with books and papers, pens and ink pots, as well as his collection of talismans.

Jemima went to her own room shortly after Troy's departure, eager to escape before Bryce could seek her out for conversation. She had not been alone with him since their tête-à-tête in the drawing room, an interlude that she still looked back on with great misgiving. She had left him playing at jackstraws with Lovelace. His gaze had followed her as she went from the room, showing puzzlement and a measure of unguarded hunger. As she went slowly up the stairs, Jemima was able to convince herself that the yearning she'd seen in those pale eyes was nothing more than a trick of the light.

Chapter Seven

The next morning Jemima breakfasted in her room and then decided to take advantage of the fair weather to practice her sketching in the garden. As she hurried from the house, her sketchbook tucked under one arm, it occurred to her that she was again fleeing from Bryce. The thought did not trouble her overmuch; the less she was in his company, the better for her ragged, newly breached heart.

She wandered along the curving brick pathways of the large garden, delighting in the hidden nooks and picturesque cul-de-sacs that each turning presented. The end of the garden near the dovecote was overhung by ornamental willows, but there were also stands of cedars, enclosing moss-encrusted stone benches, and groupings of lime trees, their slick green leaves shining above small urns of yew. Jemima had rarely seen such an inviting place.

At the center of the plantings lay an Elizabethan knot garden, with its characteristic boxwood hedge, neatly trimmed and pungent. Here the June sun was unrelieved by any shade, so Jemima continued along the path, passing colorful beds of primrose, dianthus, and foxglove, until she came to a small trickling fountain that lay in the shadow of a lone hemlock. It was surrounded by lilies and backed by a white trellis, which was covered with climbing vines, the tangled growth a charming combination of cultivated plants and opportunistic wildflowers. She sat down on the narrow stone bench opposite the fountain and began to draw, hoping to distract herself from her troubling thoughts of Bryce by discovering the true nature of a nasturtium vine with her pencil.

She was deeply immersed in her sketching, following her usual method of draw, smudge, erase, smudge, erase, draw, when an all-too-familiar voice said softly from behind her, "May I see?"

Jemima resisted the urge to clasp the sketchbook to her chest.

Bryce hunkered down beside her on one knee, and gently drew the book from her hands. He looked at the ungainly, smeared drawing and then at the gracefully twisting vine that she had attempted to reproduce.

"Mmm," he said after a moment, "I think I see your problem."

He opened the book to a clean page and, without so much as a by-your-leave, plucked the pencil from her fingers. Then, leaning one elbow on her lap—which nearly caused her to gasp aloud—he began to draw, holding the sketchbook upon his raised knee. Jemima watched with wide eyes as the nasturtium came to life on the page. With deft, sure strokes he captured the very essence of the vine, its twisted tendrils, its upthrust leaves and its wide-open blossoms.

"There," he said, as he held the book up, without removing the pressure of his arm upon her thigh. "What do you think?"

What she thought wasn't the half of it. What she was feeling was a deal more to the point. The man had exceptional talent—she had spent enough time with artists to recognize a real gift when she saw it.

"Where did you learn to draw like that?" she asked, trying to disregard the fluttering of her pulse, which was caused by the heady combination of raw physical desire and genuine artistic admiration.

She felt him shrug as he replied, "I've always been a dab hand at it. Now you try."

He uncovered a fresh page, but when Jemima took up the pencil his hand closed over hers. "Loosely, pet. You're hanging on to it like a miser clutches a groat. Relax."

That was fine for him to say, she thought crossly. His heart wasn't spinning about in his chest as hers was. His breath wasn't coming in painful gasps, when it was coming at all.

He turned to her, his fingers still splayed over her hand. "You've got to see the whole subject, Jem, not just one little patch. And then draw your line in a single motion." He opened the book to her original drawing of the vine. "See . . . all these scratchy little marks. Much too crabbed and awkward." He returned to the pristine page and guided her hand in a long sweeping line. "And don't be so literal—you've got to hint . . . imply . . . suggest."

"Sounds like more innuendo," she muttered under her breath.

"Exactly," he said with a grin. "You need to flatter your subject, not attack it like an enemy."

He watched, his head bent below her shoulder, as she again attempted the nasty nasturium. She could see the tiny strands of silver that laced his dark hair, and the tanned rise of one cheekbone.

There was a humming in the air between them that had nothing to do with bees. She realized she was observing Bryce far more than she was the nasturtium vine, yet somehow her drawing turned out surprisingly well.

He nodded as he traced his thumb over the edge of the page. "Much better, don't you think?"

"Mmm. And I didn't have to erase once."

"Or smudge."

He shifted away from her lap, and the loss of his warm weight on her thigh felt like a gaping hole in the universe.

"But tell me this, Jemima," he said. "You hang about with artists in London; why hasn't one of them, taken you in hand? You clearly enjoy sketching, not like some ladies who only do it because it is expected of them. Why haven't you gotten yourself a bit of professional guidance."

She gnawed her lip. "It would be ridiculous to ask a real artist to waste their time teaching someone as untalented as I am. A waste of both our time, I expect."

He gave her a bearish look. "You can be the most exasperating woman. Who better to ask than someone who is talented? You won't learn anything from a novice, sweeting. Only more ways to erase and smudge."

He stood up and stretched, his hands at the back of his waist. Then he looked down and gave her an easy smile. "Looks like I'm going to have to take you in hand, Lady J. Pass on my own smattering of technique. But not right now, unfortunately. I've got some business along the coast this afternoon. Actually I came out here to tell you the latest development in the case of the missing Minstrels. Tolliver rode over from the Tattie and Snip this morning with some news. It turns out one of his scullery maids has confessed."

Jemima's head snapped up. "To the murder?"

"No," he said, laughing. "To sending Lovelace's family off on a wild-goose chase."

Her eyes widened in dismay. "When did that happen?"

"The same afternoon as the murder. It seems the Wellesleys had a look in on Lovelace about an hour after they left the inn. Young Charles needed to stop to . . . ah, well, you get my drift. As soon as they saw she wasn't in the prop wagon, they came haring back to the inn and met Mary the maid, in the front yard. She told them she had seen Lovelace ride off with a gentleman on a horse. . . . The girl must have seen me taking Lovelace back to the grove."

Jemima put one hand over her mouth. "Her parents think she eloped with you?"

"No, someone named Randolph. Mary heard Mr. Wellesley say 'It's that blasted Randolph whelp who's carried her off.' "

"Why didn't Mary explain that Lovelace had merely gone off with you? And why didn't she say anything to Tolliver about the Wellesleys returning here? Surely Mary knew we were all fretting over their disappearance."

Bryce rubbed at his chin. "Mary is not what you would call awake on all suits. And she was afraid she would get into trouble for loitering in the front yard, when she supposed to be washing linens in the stable yard. She had a beau, you see—that goose boy who almost broke my horses' necks the other morning. He passes by the inn every afternoon. Mary was playing truant from her duties and waiting for him near the road when the Wellesleys came back."

"What made her tell Tolliver now?"

"Mr. Fletch, in all his fearsome splendor, was asking questions at the inn yesterday. Mary thought she would be sent to prison if she didn't confess."

"Poor girl," Jemima murmured.

"Oh, Mary will bounce back. Tolliver merely ripped into her a bit."

"No," Jemima said with a chuckle. "I meant Lovelace. She must be devastated by this latest news. The Minstrels could be anywhere."

"Actually Lovelace thinks they've gone to Grantley, as we suspected, which is where the Randolph whelp's family lives. Although she said they might possibly have gone to Brighton, where she was being courted by another young man who offered to carry her off to Gretna and marry her over the anvil." Bryce gave her a wry smile. "She has led a . . . rather eventful life for a girl not yet turned seventeen."

Since Jemima could recall no suitors who offered to take her driving in the park, let alone carry her off to Scotland, she made no comment, except to say, "Perhaps I should go in and sit with her."

"No," Bryce said. "Your brother has taken a break from his opus and is at present composing limericks in the front parlor to distract her." Leaning down, he tapped his forefinger on her book. "I think you should stay right here and practice. I'll want to see what you've accomplished when I get back. Remember, loose, easy strokes. And keep your wrist fluid and flexible . . ."

His words drifted off. She was looking up at him intently, her face dappled with a sprinkling of sunlight that had filtered down from between the hemlock boughs. He was torn between the desire to draw her in that pose, her face tilted up to him, the pinpoints of sunlight playing over her hiar—and the urgent need to rip the sketchbook from her hands and tumble her back onto the soft moss that grew beside the fountain. His indecision hung in the air between them, a shimmering tension that was broken when a linnet flew into the pine tree behind them and began to carol out a song.

Bryce knew his opportunity had passed. Jemima was now fussing with her book, her gaze returned to her lap. He bowed briefly, flicked the back of one finger over her cheek, and then went striding away along the bricked path.

After a brief luncheon with her brother and a fretful Lovelace, Jemima returned to her sketching in the garden. By midafternoon, she had mastered not only the nasturtium, but a stand of hollyhocks, and a grouping of lupines. She was too engrossed in capturing the dovecote and its overhanging willows to notice when an elegant traveling coach came bowling up the drive. She was too far from the front of the house to hear the hearty shouts of "Halloa!" or the sound of her brother's voice raised in welcome.

Three gentlemen climbed down from the dark blue coach and formed a semicircle around Troy, who had come out onto the porch wearing a beaming smile of surprise.

"This is all that is wonderful," he pronounced. "I had no idea you were staying in the neighborhood."

"We weren't," a whip-thin young man with a high forehead and thinning, sandy hair replied. "We heard in London that you were involved in some sort of murder—"

"And we thought to ourselves, why should Troy have all the fun?" This was from a brown-haired fellow with a pair of genial blue eyes and the extreme shirt points of a confirmed dandy.

"London is grown dashed dull," the thin man added.

"Leave it to you, Troy, to be in the thick of things, even here in this little backwater."

Troy's glance shifted to the speaker, a man somewhat older than his two companions. He was handsome in a florid way, with broad shoulders and a wide, muscular torso that was just beginning to thicken at the waist. The afternoon breeze fluttered his black curls out of their stylish arrangement.

"It wasn't my doing, Army," Troy responded. "Jemima's the one who landed us in this place. She's playing duenna to the chit who witnessed the murder."

"Ah, the fair Jemima," Harold Armbruster purred. "It's been an age since I've seen your sister, Troy."

"Well, she's about somewhere. Pity Bryce isn't here to receive you; he rode out hours ago. But I'm sure he won't mind putting you up. Er . . . you were planning on staying on, weren't you?"

The thin man stepped forward. "Don't like to descend on a fellow unannounced, Troy. We've taken rooms at the Iron Duke—left our baggage coach there. Likely looking place, that."

Troy shook his head. "No, Bryce will see to you, I'm sure of it. He's a capital fellow, Kimble, in spite of what the tabbies say about him. And you and Carruthers"—he bowed to the brown-haired dandy—"and Army, can help me to pass the time. Come inside now, and we'll have drinks in the drawing room." He put an arm companionably over Kimble's narrow shoulders. "There's a trout stream here, old chap. Now, doesn't that whet your appetite to stay on?"

When Jemima returned to the house, her brother was just coming down the main staircase. He was dressed for riding, the claret-colored coat a rich contrast to his gilt hair.

"Where are you off to, Terry?" she asked with a slight frown.

He gave her a wide smile. "It's the greatest thing, Jem. Some of my friends have come down from London. They heard about the murder . . . and well, you know my friends . . . they want to be in at the kill, so to speak. I've left a note for Bryce, asking if they can stay with us here at the Prospect. We'll have a jolly house party with those fellows about."

Jemima wanted to point out that there wasn't anything very jolly about hiding out from a murderer, but merely said, "So which of your cronies has been rash enough to abandon the excitement of London for the quietude of Kent?"

"Kimble and Carruthers . . . you know they live in each other's pockets. Oh, and Armbruster is with them, as well."

A sudden pallor had washed over Jemima's face.

"Don't know how I could have forgotten to mention Army," he continued, oblivious to his sister's distress. "I didn't think to see him with Kimble and Carruthers, though—he's not part of their usual circle. They're a bit too sporting mad for Armbuster's taste. But all three of them joined Bacchus this winter, so maybe that explains the connection. I'm to have dinner with them tonight at the Iron Duke."

Jemima drew in a sharp breath. "Troy, I want to return to London."

"London?" He stopped toying with his riding crop. "That's a daft notion, Jem. Now that I have my friends with me, we'll have a splendid time. You'll see."

"I do not wish to stay here any longer," she said forcefully. "I miss *my* friends, for one thing."

"But what of Lovelace?" he asked with a puzzled frown. "I thought you needed to stay here and play chaperon."

"She can come with us. Bryce has some nonsensical notion that the murderer might follow her to London, but I cannot credit such a thing."

Troy leaned toward her. "What's really bothering you, Jem?"

She shot him a disgusted look. "Is it so wrong that I should desire to return to my own home?"

"Ah," he said, pointing a finger at her. "Don't foist Socratic method on me, Button; answering a question with another question. You are obviously avoiding the truth."

"Don't call me Button," she huffed. "I disliked it when I was a girl and it hasn't improved one whit with time."

"Well, then, stop acting like a cranky child." Troy ruffled her hair and received another dark look. He winced. "Lord, I don't know what's gotten into you lately. Bryce has been generous in the extreme to let us stay here. He's given us the run of the house and of the grounds. I told Kimble I can't wait to have a go at his trout stream."

"*Trout*," she muttered under her breath.

"And," he continued, overlooking her grumbling, "he's got a stable full of high-bred horses who are at present languishing for lack of use. I'm taking one of them out for a gallop before I head to the inn. There's some interesting countryside hereabouts and I could use a bit of inspiration for my new poem. Why don't you change into your habit and ride out with me? There's plenty of time before dinner."

"I've already seen the countryside," Jemima hissed darkly. "I want to see London."

"Well, London ain't going away, Jem. It will still be there when we get back. Now I'm for the stables."

He was just reaching for the latch of the front door, when Jemima cried out, "Terry!"

Troy rolled his eyes as he turned to her. There was a great deal of the elder-sister-who-would-not-be-brooked in her tone. "Yes?" he said wearily.

She closed the gap between them. "I am very . . . uneasy in this house." She struggled furiously to come up with a valid excuse, one that would free her of Bryce Prospect before her brother's friends descended on them. She opted for a reason that was very close to the truth. "Bryce makes me very . . . uncomfortable."

"Bryce?" Troy looked baffled. "He's a topping fellow, Jem. Sets a better table than most, I can tell you. And his cellar is sublime, though I reckon that's because he's so near the coast—smugglers, you know."

"I am not talking about his wine cellar," she said between her teeth, barely keeping a leash on her temper. "I am talking about his reputation."

Troy raised her hackles another notch by actually having the gall to laugh. "Oh, you mean all the *on-dits* about his many amours?" He waved his fingers through the air. "You of all people needn't worry about that. By all accounts Bryce's taste runs more to well-endowed little ladybirds with ebony curls. No, you're not his style at all, Jemima. Even if your age didn't preclude the possibility."

Squeezing her shoulder solicitously, he added, "There, now. Haven't I eased your mind? Though I must say, you surprise me. You've never been a stickler before this. Lord knows, most of my friends are in the petticoat line and you haven't held it against them."

He gave her an encouraging smile and without waiting for a response he went out the door. Jemima heard his boots crunching over the graveled drive.

Damn the boy! She nearly screamed out the words. She had a mind to appropriate Troy's carriage and hie herself off to London alone.

Because there were some people she feared more than crazed French murderers and langourous libertines. And one of them was about to visit Bryce Prospect at Troy's instigation. And if her sainted brother wouldn't stir himself to protect her from Beecham Bryce, he certainly wouldn't protect her from one of his bosom boys.

Chapter Eight

Jemima had to fight off a light-headed feeling of disbelief as she made her way up to her room. She knew she should probably seek out Lovelace, now that Troy was no longer there to distract her, but she was too overset by her own worries to face the girl. And there was, in truth, a bit of simmering resentment toward Lovelace in her heart. If the girl hadn't been wandering in the woods that first afternoon, Jemima would not now be under siege in this house—beleaguered by the unwanted stirrings her host aroused in her and frightened out of her wits by the prospect of seeing her nemesis again.

She had assiduously managed to avoid being in company with the man for close to a year, since the night she and Terry had stayed in Leeds during their journey to Scotland. The night an idle, harmless flirtation had turned into something ugly and degrading. Jemima still couldn't recall the incident without a frisson of fear and a mortifying, deep-seated shame.

As she lay on her bed, trying to compose herself, she had a startling insight—she could enlist Bryce as an ally. He had vowed yesterday that he wouldn't let any harm come to her in his home, and she knew she could hold him to that promise. At least where any outside threats were concerned. She suspected he hadn't been referring to his own designs on her when he'd uttered those words of reassurance.

And there was also the possibility that Bryce would refuse his hospitality to Troy's friends. He already had enough on his plate without the addition of three town beaux cluttering up the landscape. But she of all people knew how persistent Troy could be when he wanted something.

After she laid out her gown for dinner, she rang for the housemaid that Bryce had assigned to assist her. Prudie was a local girl with a merry face and deft hands. She prattled on in a soft voice as she skillfully arranged Jemima's hair into a loose chignon.

"My sister and me," she said, as she coaxed a few tendrils to whisper down along Jemima's throat, "we can't hardly sleep at night, what with this Frenchy on the loose."

Jemima wondered how Prudie knew the man was French, in light of Mr. Fletch's insistence on secrecy. But then she recalled how frequently servants knew of things that went on behind closed doors, oftentimes more than their masters themselves did.

"And there's more, miss. My brother who works down at the mill swears he's seen a strange man ridin' about on the estate. Seen him more than once, he has."

"I saw a stranger yesterday," Jemima commented idly. "That is, I don't know if he was a stranger to the estate or not. But he didn't look like a farmworker, more like a sailor, with his blue jacket and beard—"

"That's him!" Prudie squealed. "You saw the murderer!"

Jemima started to protest. "Surely he wouldn't be riding about in broad daylight."

Prudie merely pursed up her round mouth. "Who is to say what a murderer will or won't do?" she said sagely. "Especially a French one!"

As Jemima made her way down to dinner, she wondered if the rider she'd seen was the same tall, bearded man Lovelace had described to Mr. Fletch. She shivered a bit at the thought. Though beards were uncommon in London, having been out of fashion since the Tudor era, some countrymen still sported them. And sailors, of course. But they were still enough of an oddity to occasion notice.

She'd best tell Mr. Fletch about the stranger when he returned from interviewing Sir Richard. The sooner the mystery was solved, the sooner she could drag her indolent brother away from the bucolic pleasures of Bryce Prospect and back to London.

As she entered the drawing room, Bryce curtly informed Jemima that they would be dining alone. Lovelace, he told her, was still upset by the news that the Wellesleys were mistakenly pursuing her and a phantom swain half across Kent and had asked to have her dinner sent to her room on a tray.

After that pronouncement, he went to stand at the window, gazing out at the dark sky while he toyed idly with his glass of sherry. Jemima noticed the tension in his shoulders and the taut line of his cheek. He'd been so mellow in the garden, playful and charming, and not at all high-handed when he had coached her with her drawing. But now he seemed distracted and remote. She had thought to show him the sketches she had so carefully—but loosely—toiled over, and had purposely left her sketchbook in the drawing room so she could demonstrate her progress to him. Now she moved to the sofa where the book lay and casually slipped it behind one of the cushions. He looked to be in no mood for offering criticism, or rather, he looked far too critical for her to risk another scathing string of "dreadfuls."

During the meal Bryce still seemed preoccupied. Jemima attempted to fill in the frequent conversational gaps with a stream of amusing anecdotes, which even to her ears sounded brittle and forced. She wished once again that she possessed a smattering of Lovelace's easy coquetry.

At one point, during a particularly convoluted tale involving Troy and the driver of a Greek donkey cart, Bryce stopped her and suggested brusquely that she "save her conversation for her brother's friends from town." He then motioned to the footman to refill his wineglass for the sixth time.

"Oh," she said, feeling suddenly deflated. "So you have agreed to let them stay here."

He shot her a look of exasperation. "Your brother didn't leave me much choice. I was just riding into the stable yard as Troy was setting off to meet them. He insisted it was what you would want—something to distract you until this murder business gets sorted out." He then added in a clipped voice, "I gather the present company is not stimulating enough for your tastes."

Her eyes flashed. "Troy has a great deal to answer for. It was concern for his own comfort, not mine, that motivated his request."

She expected that Bryce would snatch up this opportunity to elaborate on his favorite theme—Troy's cavalier treatment of his sister, but he merely raised his glass to his mouth and drank deeply.

"More to the point," she continued as she leaned forward, her elbows on the table, "why would you want a gaggle of idle coxcombs lounging about your home?"

Bryce shrugged and looked away from her. "Perhaps *I* do not find the present company stimulating."

Jemima was too stunned to answer. He had never been overtly rude to her before. Something had riled him, and he was taking it out on her. She wondered, as she poked at her green beans, what could have vexed him so dreadfully in the relatively short space of time since they had been together in the garden. Maybe something had happened while he was on the coast to put him in such a beastly mood.

They subsided into an awkward silence until the port was brought in. After the footman had filled his glass, Bryce sent the man out of the room. Jemima started to rise, but he motioned her to stay seated.

"I'm sorry you don't want Troy's friends here, Jemima," he said in a slightly conciliatory tone. "But it's too late now for me to rescind the invitation. Besides, your brother claims he writes better with his friends about. It doesn't make any sense to me, but who am I to stand in the way when his muse calls."

Her glance swung to the glass of port he was raising to his mouth. "As does your own," she murmured.

His eyes narrowed. "Don't snipe at me, Jem. Not because Troy's gotten one past you."

She put her fists on the table. "You pander to him as much as I do. Perhaps even more. I feel like I am caught in the coils of some male conspiracy."

He grinned then, a slow twisting of his mouth. "Most ladies would relish such a situation. And Troy's friends are not a bad lot. in fact, I know Kimble slightly—he and my brother were friends at Cambridge. I don't mind offering them my hospitality, and if you were thinking clearly—"

"Who says I am not?" she snapped.

"If you were thinking clearly, you would see that a houseful of guests will help to ensure Lovelace's safety. She'll be surrounded by men, the pink of the *ton* . . . excepting myself, of course. And if that doesn't make her feel safe, it will at least make her feel vastly admired.

"And," he continued as he refilled his glass, "they will furnish you with protection as well."

"Me?" She blinked twice.

"Safety in numbers, pet. You'll have all your familiar squires around you—and even a hardened rake has to admit defeat when faced with such daunting odds."

Jemima wanted to lay her head on the table and weep. Bryce was being so confoundedly logical. He couldn't know that she feared the attentions of one of those men far more than his own.

Instead, she put her head up and stated, "You are quite mistaken. Troy's friends are not in the least interested in squiring a maiden lady. Their taste runs, as I am sure yours does, to women of another sort."

Bryce leaned his chin on his hand and observed her through his long lashes. She thought it was a wickedly provocative thing to do to a lady—maiden or otherwise.

"You have no idea what my tastes are," he murmured.

"And I haven't any desire to be edified on that score," she said in her most quelling voice.

He chuckled softly. "It's the damnedest thing, Jemima. Most people mellow out after a good meal. You, on the other hand, turn waspish and bristly as a hedgehog. Three nights running, it's been."

"I wasn't waspish last night," she protested. He was a fine one to be casting stones, in light of his own crusty mood. "I was . . . a bit quiet, is all."

"It wouldn't surprise me," he mused, "if you came down to dinner tomorrow night with a pistol in your reticule and started taking potshots at my dinner guests."

Bryce could have no idea how much that notion appealed to her at that moment. She could at once rid the world of an impudent rake, a self-indulgent poet, *and* a loathsome, heavy-handed "pink of the *ton*."

"Maybe you need to take a stomach powder before dinner," he continued in the same teasing voice. "I have heard that spinsters of a certain age often suffer complaints of their digestion . . ."

Jemima rose to her feet and all but threw her napkin across the table. "I know I am not young, Bryce,'" she bit out, feeling the angry color wash over her face. "I certainly don't need you to point it out to me. Though I think it most unfair that you, who can give me only three or four years, are thought to be in your prime, while I . . . I am put on the shelf and considered an ape-leader."

Bryce had risen to face her, his eyes dark as granite. "Yes, I bait you, Jemima. But only so you will see how ridiculous it is to think of yourself in such a way."

"Oh, no," she cried softly. "Not ridiculous . . . realistic. I am not blind. I saw how easily Lovelace won you over. Even Troy sits at her little lame feet. Her youth and beauty easily make up for any lack of intellect. Women of my age, on the other hand, have little to offer a man, saving the workings of their minds. A poor recompense, I think. But it doesn't matter . . . I am well past the age where it is proper or fitting to have any illusions about myself, regardless of what I might feel inside."

"What *do* you feel, Jemima?" he asked as he came around the edge of the table toward her. "Tell me."

She shook her head, avoiding his eyes. And wondered what the devil had come over her, that she could be so pitifully maudlin in front of him. Whining about her illusions and revealing her creeping jealousy of Lovelace.

"I must ask you to excuse me," she whispered hoarsely as she turned and hurried across the room.

"No, I will not!"

Bryce vaulted away from the table and caught her halfway to the door, blocking her path with his body, as one hand clamped hard on her wrist—harder than he realized. The sherry he'd drunk in the drawing room, the quantity of wine he had consumed with his dinner, and the two glasses of port he had just finished, were making only slight inroads on his senses. His head for liquor was legendary, but his head for long-limbed, chestnut-haired women with hauntingly beautiful azure eyes was notoriously poor.

Jemima glared at him. "What is this?" She raised her arm where his fingers still bit into the skin of her wrist. "Making your last stab at seduction before my squires appear tomorrow? Lord, Bryce, I'd have expected a defter touch from you."

He released her wrist slowly, his eyes full of heat. "They've had their chance with you, Jem—Troy's friends. A parcel of blithering fools they must be if they never saw what was beneath their noses."

"Wh-what do you mean?" She took an involuntary step back from him. There was such intensity in his gaze, masculine power and raw hunger. The climate in the room had altered suddenly— she felt the air thinning out, so that her breath now came in tiny gasps.

"You, Jemima," he said. He drew her closer until his body was mere inches from her own. "I see you, even when you try to hide in your brother's shadow . . . your intelligence, your humor . . . and your spirit. They shine from you as much as the beauty in your face or the light in your dazzling blue eyes—"

"They're green—" She sighed raggedly.

"Green as the verdant, patchwork hills of Ireland," he replied, never taking his eyes from hers.

Something snapped inside her then. Roused her from the intoxicating haze that his voice had sent drifting over her like a seductive net. "Ireland," she repeated sharply. "Yes, you've been to Ireland, haven't you? To woo Harriet Travers, I believe."

Bryce's mouth curled into the semblance of a grin. "You sound almost jealous, pet. I had other business in Ireland. Harriet was just a . . . pleasant diversion."

"As I'm sure all your conquests are to you. Now if you will let me pass . . ."

She tried to negotiate her way around him. He stepped back and leaned against the door, splaying his fingers behind him on the carved oak. His eyes challenged her as much as his provocative posture. As his glance raked over her, his mouth widened into a knowing smile. "Gad, Jem. You are hungering for this down to the tips of your toes, but will be damned before you let me see it. Do you know how much that tempts me? To wonder what you'll be like once I've broken through that icy disdain?"

Her nails dug into her palms. "I am neither hungering nor icy, Mr. Bryce. I am extremely cross."

"Oh, no," he said with infuriating calm. "I've seen you cross, Jemima. This is a whole different animal."

He reached out one hand and laid it for an instant on the skin above the low-cut bodice of her gown. She had to prevent herself from looking down to see if it had left behind a searing handprint, so fierce was the heat she had felt at that momentary touch.

"No," he said, "I take back icy. You're warm. And so soft beneath my hand. And there is a pulse beating in your throat . . . trip-a-trip, like a tiny drum . . . do you feel it, sweetheart?"

"I . . ." Her hand crept up to her throat of its own volition. Her body seemed to be floating now, held aloft by the soothing, melodic timbre of his words and the sensual promise in his smoky eyes.

"Bryce," she said with a catch in her voice "I can't do this."

"You don't have to do anything, pet," he said with an earnestness that even Jemima, in her bemused state, had to acknowledge. "You do enough for everyone else, God knows. This time, let me do for you."

His raised hand drifted across the slight gap that separated them, his fingers spread wide as he sketched a light caress upon the peach-tinted flush that had colored her cheeks. His touch was swansdown soft and delicately arousing. Those strong, elegant fingers, that could control a team of high-bred horses or hold a pistol level in the face of outraged propriety, were now whispering over her face, coaxing, soothing, easing, and always with the gentlest hints of pressure.

She felt the room spin; time and dimension skewed breathlessly as his fingers traced over her ear. He touched the lobe fleetingly with his thumb, before his hand came to rest on the rise of her collarbone. A bolt of pure desire lanced through her, and she nearly groaned at the unfamiliar sensation.

"Let me, Jemima," he coaxed as he brought his hand up to cup the soft underside of her jaw.

It was a revelation to discover just how many places he could stir to surface heat just by the touch of his fingers. But the surface heat wasn't a patch on the growing fire that was licking through her insides. Jemima wanted to sink down into the blissful cocoon of pleasure that was curling all around her.

She heard Bryce utter a soft, ragged sigh, heard herself moan slightly in reply as his hand drew away from her. Her eyes opened—which surprised her a little, since she hadn't realized they were closed. Bryce was gazing at her intently, his expression a mixture of guarded expectation and open desire.

"Yes?" he whispered.

"Yes," she breathed, at that moment willing to do anything at his bidding.

He took her hand then and led her from the dining room. The paneled hallway was dimly lit, and she thought she saw a servant or two hovering back in the shadows. She spent an idle moment wondering if they would be shocked and decided she didn't care. Bryce wanted her, and not because she was the sainted Troy's sister, but because he thought her beautiful and clever, and even if those were the facile lies of a practiced rake, she needed for once in her life to believe they were true.

She followed him up the wide staircase, her hand still enfolded in his. He stopped before the entrance to her bedroom and opened the door, coaxing her through with a hand at her back. When he didn't follow, she turned and looked up at him in confusion.

"Come to me, Jemima," he said, bending low so that his voice purred against the side of her throat.

"I don't under—?"

He raised one hand and placed it soft against her mouth. "No coercion," he said gently. "Come to me freely. Or not at all."

He was gone then, his footfalls lost in the thick Persian carpet that ran the length of hall.

Jemima leaned back against the door and stood unmoving for several seconds. He hadn't kissed her, hadn't so much as embraced her, and yet she was trembling as though he had made passionate love to her—with his warm hands, his silky voice, and his smoldering hawk's eyes. She feared that any further demonstrations of his desire would send her over the brink of reason into a sort of honeyed madness.

She drifted into the room in a daze, wondering what the protocol of seduction demanded. Was she to array herself in her most alluring bed gown and douse herself with French perfume before she made her way to his bedroom? Should she comb out her hair into glistening waves and smooth lotion over her body before she presented herself to him?

It was too arch, she thought. Too calculated. Bryce could have taken her there on the floor of the dining room like a round-heeled housemaid, and she knew she wouldn't have protested. But this enforced separation was giving her too much time to think. And that, she realized, as she sank down onto her vanity bench, was exactly what Bryce had intended. That she be an accomplice to her own deflowering. That she make up her own mind, without his compelling presence to sway her.

Was she brave enough to do it? Brave enough to put her heart at risk so that she might ease the overwhelming physical longing he had awakened in her? Could she abandon all caution, let herself be his plaything for an hour or two, and then return to the staid strictures of her everyday life?

A thought whispered through her brain, reminding her that she would never again have a chance to fulfill her fantasies with such a man. She had been sullied once, by a ham-handed lout, and perhaps she needed Bryce's exquisite touch upon her skin to wipe away that wretched memory.

But then she knew it for the rationalization it was. She didn't need any reasons to go to him other than the sureness in her soul that he would not hurt her or be anything less than kind.

Somehow that was enough.

Nevertheless, she thought defiantly, *I will not present myself to him like a concubine preening before a Turkish pasha. If Bryce wants me, he can dashed well deal with hooks and corsets and hose.*

Bryce looked up from his chair beside the hearth as she entered his room. He was holding a glass of tawny liquor in one hand and there was another filled glass sitting on the small table at his elbow. He had removed his dinner coat and waistcoat, but aside from that, he was fully dressed. He eyed her satin gown and said with a mock leer, "You must be very eager, my lady, that you didn't take the time to change."

"And you, sir, are very smug," she said as she crossed over to the fireplace.

He rose and after taking a quick swallow, he handed her his own glass. "Not smug," he said as he watched her sip at the cordial from the spot where his lips had rested. "Just very, very relieved."

Her gaze darted to his face. In truth, he looked nearly giddy. "You didn't think I would come?"

With a graceful shrug he replied, "I never know what to expect from you, Lady J. It's one of your greatest charms."

The inevitable spill of curls lay tumbled over his forehead; Jemima reached up and smoothed them back, delighting in the sensation as the silky strands whispered through her fingers. Lord, she had been longing to do that very thing since she had first seen him in the wooded grove.

He said almost sheepishly, "We Bryces are famous for our unruly hair. It's a curse, I think, visited on the family for some ancestor's misdeed."

"I like it," she said, as she combed her fingers through the soft, springing curls that gathered along the nape of his neck. "It's one of *your* greatest charms," she added with an impish grin as she tugged playfully at the dark waves.

She felt him tremble, a noticeable shiver that swept over his entire body. He knocked the glass from her hand, sent it crashing to the hearth, before he swung her back against the firebreast. His arms tightened around her swiftly, crushing her against his chest. She was overwhelmed by his power, by the tensile flex of his arms that revealed, she suspected, only a fraction of his true strength.

No man had ever drawn her full against his body, so she wasn't prepared for the thrill of contact. His chest was an expanse of supple steel beneath the fine cambric of his shirt, and as his lean belly and muscular thighs molded to her, aroused her, she became mindless with the need to return the pressure.

He lowered his head, nudging aside the tendrils that danced along her throat, murmuring her name again and again. "Ah, Jemima," he crooned. "Jemima. What a fine and lovely name. I whisper it each night before I sleep and hear it echoing back to me in my dreams."

She tipped her face up and wriggled in protest. "You said it was a useful sort of name," she complained.

His eyes danced down at her. "Did I really? I must have been out of my mind. Can you remember everything I've ever said to you, I wonder?"

"No, only the truly wretched things. Sly comments about my advanced age and slighting references to my being a piece of luggage in my brother's train. Beyond that, I've hardly taken any note of you at all." She grinned.

"Liar," he said between his teeth. His mouth lowered at once and caught her still grinning. He curved his lips to match her smile and then when she gasped in surprise, he coaxed her mouth open slightly and drew her into a proper kiss.

Jemima hadn't been expecting it—that one moment he could be bantering with her and the next be kissing her with such open-mouthed hunger. She had envisioned a more studied approach, not this sudden overtaking of her senses. But then he had never behaved in the unctuous manner commonly attributed to rakes. He was no perfumed coxcomb, but a man simmering with unbridled appetite.

Bryce shifted her abruptly away from the marble hearth, leaned hard into her, forcing her head back as his mouth urgently explored her lips, murmuring soft sounds of pleasure all the while. She felt the room dip, as he teased his tongue against her teeth and then let it dart deeper into her mouth. It felt so strange, so powerful, so amazingly right.

Her knees were warm toffee now, pliant and yielding. His strength alone was keeping her from melting onto the floor, his strong arms and the incredible seeking heat of his mouth, which she reached for, craning her head up and up, to find. The taste of him, all sweet wine and smoky port, the mind-numbing scent of him, a heady combination of sandalwood, tobacco, and potent, animal musk. Every particle of him invaded her senses, until she was shorn of any hesitation.

She twined her fingers into his hair, cradling his head between her hands. "Ah, Beecham," she cried softly. His response was to deepen his kisses, thrusting hard against her willing mouth, marking his possession of her with his lips and tongue, and with tiny, exquisitely painful bites.

Jemima cursed her own lack of expertise—surely a man like Bryce required someone with more finesse, a woman who wasn't awkward and unsure, with gangling arms and jellied legs. She made a tentative foray with her own tongue, thinking only to reciprocate the pleasure he was giving her, and she heard a deep groan erupt from the muscular cavern of his chest.

"Oh," she cried, pulling back. "Wasn't I supposed to do that?"

Bryce drew a breath to steady himself. He looked down at the woman in his arms, her face flushed with passion, her lips rose red and swollen from his kisses, and her eyes, her remarkable azure eyes, alive with light and quickening desire, and he knew he had strayed far into uncharted territory.

If only because, he realized with a shock, he was thoroughly content to keep kissing her. For a millennium or two. Not that his body wasn't aching to take her. But his mind, and more specifically his heart, were entranced by her tentative but wholly passionate unfurling. He'd never kissed a woman like Jemima, who was so unschooled and yet so utterly responsive.

She stood now, quivering like a newborn foal in the circle of his arms, still a little afraid, but curious and full of wonder. And when he kissed her again, she would arch into him, her body liquid and supple. He didn't know if he could stand to do more than kiss her. The thought of her slim body, naked beneath him, of her legs, drawing him into a sublime carnal embrace was more than he could bear.

"Beech?" she coaxed, tugging at his shoulders. "Did I do something wrong?"

"No," he said, shaking off his distracting thoughts. "Nothing wrong, sweetheart. Only right. Only ever right."

"Oh." Her eyes brightened. "You made such an odd noise."

He shook his head, as he drew one hand from the small of her back and raised it to stroke his fingers over her velvety lower lip. Then he slid one long finger past her lips and into her mouth. She caught it between her teeth and bit down gently until he groaned again.

"You see how easy it is, sweeting, to make me sigh for you. Say my name again . . ."

"Beech," she crooned. "Beecham . . ."

He bent her back and laid his mouth on her throat, savoring the taste of her flesh, feeling less like predator than prey, as the scent of her perfume and her heated skin stole into his befuddled brain. He bit gently at the smooth white skin, wanting to mark her there, mark her as his own, so that any man, any festering pink of the *ton*, would know that she was his alone.

But prudence restrained him. Lady Jemima would face her peers on the morrow without having to blush for her indiscretion. She sighed as he lifted her into his arms and carried her to the brocaded chaise that lay at the foot of his wide tester bed.

The ideal piece of furniture for seduction, Jemima thought, still slightly irreverent even in the face of her imminent deflowering.

No arms to impede access to a woman's body and just wide enough to accommodate two, providing they were lying very close together. Or one on top of the other. Jemima nearly moaned—the thought of lying beneath that lean body was enough to send her heart reeling.

He instantly busied himself at the back of her gown, undoing the myriad hooks, until the heavy satin fell away from her shoulders. Then he knelt beside her, one knee on the carpet, and lowered the bodice, drawing it down slowly, letting the fabric whisper over her skin. She watched his eyes darken, as he slid the lace sleeves of her chemise from her shoulders.

"You've made me work for this," he remarked.

"You seem to be doing fine," she answered boldly. "I fancy not all your conquests have come to you conveniently dressed in their night rails. You appear to know your way around a lady's gown."

He sat back on his heels, a frown surfacing on his brow. "You're not one of my conquests, Jemima."

"What then?"

He leaned forward, bracing his arms on either side of her. "You are a woman . . . who is wise enough to recognize the attraction between us, and who is brave enough and honest enough to respond to it."

She touched his nose with the tip of her finger and then traced a path down to his chin, letting her finger linger a moment on the divine, sculpted arch of his upper lip. She wondered how she had ever thought him harsh featured. His face, ardent and full of earnest intensity, bore so much rugged beauty. And his eyes, deepset and glistening like a lake of silver, were dazzling in their bright regard.

"Is that what I am, Beech?" she asked softly. "I suppose I understand now what you meant about women being . . . accomplices to their own seduction. The truth is, I wanted you to . . . well, do this . . . for some time now. Not very ladylike, I'm afraid, but there you have it."

Bryce lowered his head and whispered a sustained kiss along the length of her throat. "Ah, Jem," he sighed against her skin. "This isn't a seduction . . . I . . . I'm not sure what it is." He raised his head and met her eyes. "I almost wish that perishing poet of a brother of yours would come bursting in here and knock me about. But I'd still come after you. I think I'd always come after you."

Jemima closed her eyes. They were only pretty words, she knew, and whether or not Bryce wanted to name it a seduction, that's exactly what it was. But it thrilled her beyond measure that he could say such heartstoppingly lovely things to her. As though he meant them.

With his chin, he rucked down the bodice of her chemise, and before the cool evening air could assault her skin, he had covered her breast with his mouth. Any heat she had felt before was immediately supplanted by the searing fire that lanced through her as he drew on her nipple. Her low, wavering cry echoed up to the high ceiling. Bryce's response was to increase the pressure of his mouth, until she was arching up from the chaise, fighting off the hands that pinioned her wrists to the cushions. She needed to touch him, his hair, his face, his lean, hard body. But still he held her down, heedless of her frustration, as he sated himself.

When at last he raised his head, after leaving a tiny love bite just below the carmine crest, there was still no surcease for her. He caught her mouth in a fierce, ragged kiss, bruising her already tender lips. She was gasping now, her need for him blinding her to any trivial considerations, like breathing or thinking. The ache that had spiraled up from her belly was keening for resolution. When he did release her hands, she immediately brought them up to grasp his shoulders, holding him there against her, not ever wanting to let him go. She cried his name as he ran one hand along her torso, his fingers discovering every curve and plane of her trembling body.

He gave a strange, stuttering moan against her mouth and then spun himself away from her. He sat there, crouched on the carpet, one hand still resting on the chaise. Jemima hiked herself up onto her elbows and watched him with anxious eyes, again fearful that she had done something wrong.

Bryce's heart felt like it was ramming its way out of his chest. His body was taut as a bowstring, and the heavy ache in his loins was a painful reminder that he would soon be beyond any coherent thought. But he needed to stop, needed desperately to think. Jemima was the first gently bred woman he had been with in three years, and furthermore, she was untouched. He desired her with every fiber of his being, but something was stopping him from acting on that desire.

He had marked her as he'd wanted to, in a place that only he could see. But he wanted to mark her in another manner, for all the world to see. He wanted to claim her, hold her, against any who would take her from him. And, sweet Jesus, he had never felt that way before. Not about any woman.

He turned to her, saw how still she was as she watched him.

There was confusion in her eyes, along with the fledgling fire of passion. He gave her an encouraging smile and raised his hand to touch her face.

"Sweet Jemima," he whispered. "I wanted to go slowly for you. And look at me, I'm having at you like a cow-handed stripling."

"No," she said, covering his hand with her own. "It is . . . you are . . . I don't know if there is even a word for the way you make me feel."

He rose to his feet, needing to remove himself from her potent lure while he sorted out his thoughts. He began to slowly untie his neckcloth. Very slowly. Jemima gave him an impatient frown.

"What?" he asked, his fingers still twisted in the knot at his throat. "Hate to see me destroy all my valet's hard work? I'll leave it on, if you like . . ."

She laughed outright.

"One is not supposed to laugh during a seduction," he uttered in mock affront.

"Oh, sorry," she said, biting her lip as she tried to control her wayward humor. "I am only amazed that, along with everything else I am feeling, I have an overwhelming desire to grin."

"Grinning is allowed," he said. He realized he too felt like grinning. He was very, very pleased. About something. About her. Because she was quaint and charming and surprisingly self-assured. And more lovely than a sonnet. When Jemima Vale stopped fleeing, she was something to behold.

A little snippet of feeling stirred inside him then, like a salamander shifting beneath the fallen leaves of a forest. A tiny ripple of remorse. He tried to disregard it as he slid the length of muslin from his throat. She had come here, as he'd hoped she would on this last night before they were inundated by Troy's pestilential cronies, of her own free will. Who was he to deny her any pleasure, merely because he had a passing concern for her honor? She had taken him up on his offer, and there was an end to it.

And how could he face the cold, empty night alone? She was surely the warmest creature on God's earth. He recalled how much he had wanted to hold her in his arms the night he'd found her in the library, how he'd longed to avail himself of that warmth. But it wasn't the voice of passion that had so stirred him that night, it had been something far more tender.

He let his gaze linger on her—she had tugged her chemise up over her breasts, but her lovely, magnolia-petal shoulders were still bare, still flushed from his kisses. As he watched her he knew, with a sinking feeling of inevitably, that he couldn't take her. Not like a doxy or a woman of easy virtue, in spite of her willingness to be so used. Not here in his boyhood home with all its lingering reminders of a younger and as-yet untarnished version of Beecham Bryce.

But he couldn't very well send her away, not without causing her a deal of pain. A man didn't carry a woman to the brink of passion and then dismiss her out of hand. Especially not a woman like Jemima Vale, who would see his rejection as sure proof of her lack of feminine allure. But he had to think of some way to make her leave.

Conscience was a bloody nuisance; and he knew now why he'd never cultivated one before this.

She cocked her head at him, clearly puzzled by his long, silent scrutiny, and then said, as if she had read his thoughts. "Are you sure about this, Bryce?"

So, he was back to being Bryce now. That boded well for his cause.

"I only wonder that you should want me," she continued hesitantly, "when you could have any woman in the *ton*."

He raised one brow devilishly and condemned himself to the torment of celibacy as he said archly, "I've *had* every woman in the *ton*, sweetheart."

With relief, he watched the shocked expression rise up in her eyes. Jemima Vale was about to experience the callous rake in action, and he prayed that such a display would send her fleeing back to bed. Her own bed.

"And modest to boot," she remarked. "I forget that I am merely the last in a long line of women."

"Hardly the last," he observed with brutal honesty. "Let us say you are something new and fresh." He might as well have called her useful again, so languid was his tone.

"Fresh," she echoed slowly, wincing at his words. She then said in a reedy voice, "May I ask you something, Bryce?"

"You are chock full of questions tonight. Putting off the inevitable?"

"No. Well, maybe just a bit." He saw that she had twisted the skirt of her gown into a corkscrew of satin. "I need to know if the reason you want me . . . is b-because I'm a virgin."

He stopped unbuttoning his waistcoat, letting his hands fall to his sides. It was the last thing he'd expected her to ask. "I place no premium on that, Jem," he said. "It would be the height of hypocrisy for someone like me to require that his paramours be untouched. I am hardly in a position to throw stones." He gave a dry chuckle, but she did not respond, only sat gazing down at her lap. His voice lowered. "But then again, it would be the height of discourtesy not to acknowledge the rare gift you are offering me."

She looked up swiftly. Her face had paled, the glowing peach of her cheeks now gone a stark white. There was a vivid emotion in her eyes, but it was no longer passion. Unless Bryce missed his guess, it was something very like shame.

He sat down beside her and took up her hand. "And in case you're worried about unpleasant repercussions when it comes time for you to wed, let me reassure you that I am the soul of discretion." He said the words with just a hint of practiced ease.

Jemima tugged her hand back from his. "I . . . I do not intend to wed. Never. What occurs here tonight will make no difference to me."

He raised one hand melodramatically to his breast. "Ah, you wound me to the quick."

"I didn't mean it like that," she said with a stern frown. "The fact of the matter is, I have no 'rare gift' to offer you, Bryce. Whatever happens between us will not alter my state—because I have every reason to believe I am not a virgin."

His dark brows knit as he blew out a long breath. "Well, that's possibly the oddest statement I've ever heard. And how, pray, could you be in doubt of something so . . . significant?"

She cast him a look of entreaty and then turned her head away. "Don't make light of it . . . oh, please don't. It's not something I look back on with anything but disgust."

"I take it you were not exactly a willing participant." His tone was gentle now, all his feigned arrogance driven away by his concern for her.

She shook her head slowly. "No, I was not."

"Do you want to talk about it?" He purposely kept his voice remote as he rose and moved away from the chaise.

"No. I'm sorry I even brought it up. It's just that I thought you should know . . . in case it made a difference . . ."

"Tell me," he urged her softly. "Don't hold back, sweetheart. You know I am the last man on the planet who would condemn you."

She sat in silence for a moment and then said with a sigh, "Very well. I don't suppose there's any harm in telling you. It happened last summer while Troy and I were on our way to Scotland. We overnighted at a large, rambling country house. I couldn't sleep, so I went looking for the servants' staircase, to fetch up a glass of milk from the kitchen. One of Troy's friends found me wandering lost in the hall. He . . . he was quite drunk. I thought he was only being playful at first—Troy's friends sometimes flirt with me . . . in an innocent way. But then—" She choked slightly, and Bryce was glad he was no longer beside her—he'd have surely tugged her into his arms. "He . . . he dragged me into an empty bedroom. I fought back, but he was quite strong and . . . and I think he took me." Her voice shook as she added weakly, "He didn't even bother to lay me on the bed."

Bryce barely restrained an oath. "Who was it, Jem? Roncaster? Carruthers? Who did this to you?"

She spoke from between her raised hands. "It doesn't matter. He never mentioned it to anyone, thank God. And I hadn't the heart to tell Troy. He thinks his friends are all such fine fellows." She drew a steadying breath. "Now you see how impossible it would be for me to marry. Not after that."

Bryce was gazing away from her, his face grown taut. He would discover who had used her in such a way. He still had plenty of connections in the *ton* who could ferret out where Troy had stayed on his way to Scotland and who had made up the house party at each stopover. He'd find the man and bring him to his knees. At this moment, he knew he could do murder for Jemima's lost honor. But since he was a civilized fellow, he'd settle for horsewhipping the wretch and leave it at that.

And now, more than ever, he needed to end this charade. He saw how very fragile Jemima was, for one thing. And how misguided to think herself unfit for marriage. If Troy's drunken friend hadn't succeeded in taking her maidenhead, she could go to a husband untarnished. And if it was true that the lout had had his way with her, well, what man would hold that against a woman he loved? But in either case, Bryce was not going to make things worse by taking her virtue himself or, heaven forbid, by repeating the other man's crime.

"I see now that this has changed things," she said quietly as he continued to keep his eyes trained on the wall behind his bed. "You only wanted me because you thought I was untouched—fresh and new and ripe for deflowering." She made an effort to sit up.

He returned to her side and knelt down. Placing his hand on her chest, just above the neckline of her chemise, he gently forced her back against the cushion. His hand stayed there, warm and intimate against her skin. "No," he remarked silkily, returning to his role of heartless libertine in spite of his overwhelming desire to comfort her. "You are ripe, all right. And virgins are tiresome. On the other hand, women who have been broken, but not yet schooled, are infinitely intriguing."

Her eyes narrowed as she said cuttingly, "Such as young wives whose husbands are off fighting Napoleon?"

He looked at her and blinked slowly. Jemima knew how to get in a body blow, right enough. He wondered if she suspected how much that particular episode still troubled him.

He forced an attitude of unconcern and shrugged negligently. "He also serves, who sits and waits."

Jemima gingerly removed his hand from her chest, let it drop to the cushion, and then sat up. "I've changed my mind, Bryce. I choose not to be party to my own seduction." Her eyes met his squarely. "At least not at *your* hands."

He stood up at once. "I knew you weren't hot-blooded enough for this sport," he said under his breath. And then cursed himself for letting his wounded pride get the better of him.

The sting of his reproof jolted through Jemima and she flung her head back. The candlelight played over the angular planes of his face, darkening a portion here, highlighting another there. His eyes, however, were totally obscured. Then he moved his head slightly and she saw something that twisted her heart. The jaded weariness in those hooded gray eyes had been replaced by an expression of regret. Her heated retort died on her lips.

"And you are not cold-blooded enough," she said evenly as she rose to her feet, "to take a woman for the wrong reason."

His glance shifted to her face. "There is never a wrong reason, Jemima. Only a wrong time."

She gathered her skirts in one hand, held up the bodice of her gown with the other, and gave him a brief nod. "Good night," she said as she hastened to the door.

Chapter Nine

Jemima paced her bedroom in agitation, sweeping the skirt of her robe behind her as she crossed and recrossed her chamber, all the while muttering to herself. She had been wrong, so dreadfully wrong, to think Bryce wouldn't hurt her. Had he slashed her with a knife, the pain could not be more acute than what she was feeling.

He had seemed so genuinely pleased when she'd first gone to his room. He'd held her in his arms and kissed her until she was dizzy with delight. Those caresses had made her feel so . . . so incredibly alive. But then he had turned disdainful and cruel. For no reason that she could fathom. She only knew that she had made a grave error about his nature. Bryce truly was a hardened rake, coldhearted and remote from all tender feelings. He'd stood there like . . . like an iceberg, while she told him about her ravishment. He'd made not one consoling remark, nor offered her a single gesture of comfort. He had been curious, certainly, but in such a horridly detached way.

Thank God, she'd gotten her wits back before things had progressed any further.

But after what had transpired between them, it was unthinkable to remain at Bryce Prospect. How could she make idle small talk over the dinner table, knowing that Bryce had seen her half naked, that he had kissed her in places where her own hands rarely strayed? And more to the point, knowing that she had allowed these familiarities, nay, had wholeheartedly encouraged them.

It was utterly humiliating.

She had to prevail on Troy, and insist that they return to London in the morning. She didn't care if half the *ton* was to come calling on Bryce Prospect tomorrow, Troy had to take her away from this place. His friends could go hang—especially one friend in particular.

Jemima hastened into the dimly lit hallway without her candle, intent on accosting her brother. She passed Bryce's door with a

silent tread, barely daring to breathe until she came to Troy's room.
There was no response when she scratched at the door. She
knocked a bit more forcefully and was met with continued silence.
He's drunk again, she thought with dismay as she opened the door
and went into the chamber. Even in the darkness she could see that
the bed was empty, its counterpane pulled neatly up to the pillows.
It had to be after midnight, but Troy was apparently still carousing
with his cronies. She thought to wait up for him, but her instincts
told her he might be gone for hours yet. Tolliver stocked a rare cellar, and she knew Terry's friends were quite capable of making
merry until dawn. Her demand would have to wait until morning,
but it would lose none of its urgency for having been delayed.

She was walking swiftly in the direction of her room, her slippers
making little noise on the carpeted floor, when a tall figure loomed
out of the darkness and careened into her. Crying out in pain and surprise, she threw both hands up to ward him off. Iron hands fastened
onto her wrists, and she struggled for several long seconds before
she was thrust roughly away. She fell back, jarring her hip against a
side table, and then sank down to the floor, lying there in a half
swoon, listening to her assailant's footfalls thudding rapidly away.

A door opened some distance behind her and Bryce stepped out
into the corridor. "Who's there?" he called softly.

"Bryce!" It was a shivery bleat of fear. In spite of her anger at
him, he was the only person she wanted beside her right now.

He flew down the hall. "Sweetheart," he cried, falling to his
knees and wrapping his arms tight around her. "Jesus, what's happened?"

"It was him!" she said raggedly. "He was here, in the house."

"Who, Jem. Who was here?"

"The murderer. The man that Lovelace saw in the grove is in
your house."

"Jemmie," he said earnestly, "it's nearly pitch dark out here. You
couldn't tell a pumpkin from a post chaise in this light."

"No," she insisted, trying to stifle her rising panic. "I touched
his face, I felt his beard." She pushed away from him and scrambled to her feet. "We must check on Lovelace, Bryce." She
clutched the fabric of his shirt as her voice rose. "What if he has
already murdered her?"

He held tight to her hands, to prevent her from racing down the
hall. "No," he said, and when she continued to resist, he scooped her
off her feet and carried her back to his room. He deposited her on one
of the chairs and stood looking down at her, his eyes full of caution.

"Think now, Jemima, before you rouse the whole house and have Lovelace thrown into hysterics. Perhaps you merely encountered one of the servants."

She shook her head vehemently. "No. A servant would have apologized for knocking into me so roughly. He . . . he hurt me, Bryce." She lifted her wrists and he immediately knelt down beside her and began to examine the irregular red blotches that still marked her skin.

"I'll flay him alive," he muttered under his breath as he traced his fingers over the marks.

"What?" she asked, blinking.

"Nothing," he said. "You're sure he wore a beard."

"Yes, I put my hands out to ward him off and they ended up on his face. He was monstrous . . ."

"Tall was he?"

"Yes, just as Lovelace said, nearly as tall as you."

Bryce sank back on his heel sand laughed softly.

She did not think levity was at all what was called for at the moment and she gave him a stormy frown.

"I think I know who ran into you, pet. Old Simmy Wilcox." He soothed the knot from her brow with one finger. "He's a whiskery beanpole of a fellow who used to be a smuggler. Sold the odd cask of brandy to my father. He had the run of the place when I was a boy. My father mentioned he was still about. He probably came here tonight to see the old man—not knowing he was away, you see—and didn't expect to meet you creeping about in the hall."

"I wasn't creeping!"

"Old Simmy is a bit slow-witted. Took a marlinspike on the skull in his youth. He meant you no harm, I'm sure of it, and you probably frightened him as much as he frightened you." He stroked the palm of the hand he was holding. "There, now, don't you feel better?"

"Indeed I do not." She rose from the chaise and for the second time that night brushed past him. "I will not feel better until I have assured myself that Lovelace has suffered no harm."

Bryce also rose and took hold of her shoulders. "Don't alarm her, Jem. Not over Old Simmy. If she is asleep, don't awaken her with this foolish story, for God's sake. We'll have her weeping until dawn, in that case."

Jemima sniffed back her own tears. "It wasn't Old Simmy," she said forcefully. "It wasn't 'old' anyone. The man who was here tonight is young."

"Why do you say that?" Bryce asked slowly.

"Because I have seen the bearded man myself. Twice. Only I never made the connection until now."

Bryce appeared to lose a bit of color. "Tell me . . ."

"I saw him the day of the murder—a youngish man with a dark beard. He was riding along the edge of the wheat field, in the opposite direction from the inn."

"You never mentioned this."

"It seemed insignificant at the time. Just a peddler with a pack-horse." Jemima now turned pale and her eyes widened. "Oh, sweet Lord, it wasn't a packhorse, was it?"

Bryce shook his head. "Perhaps a man's body thrown over his saddle, shrouded in his own overcoat?"

Jemima reeled back onto the chair. "This is frightful, Bryce. Oh, God, I am shivering."

Bryce tugged the comforter off his bed and wrapped it around her. "There's nothing to be afraid of, Jem. I have men posted outside and in the downstairs hall."

"Maybe they should be posted in the upstairs hall," she remarked with a bit of her usual spirit.

"Yes, well, I'll see to that tomorrow. Now tell me, when was the second time you saw this man?"

"Yesterday morning," she said. "While we were riding along that ridge of cedars. The man was coming toward us on the track below the ridge. Almost no one wears a beard these days, and so that was the first thing I noticed about him. He was dressed like a sailor, and I thought that accounted for the beard. I also noticed that he looked remarkably like you, Bryce."

"What? You could see behind the beard?"

She grinned. "No, it wasn't his face so much—I was too far away to make out his features. It was more a case of his bearing, his posture . . . Oh, I know this sounds daft, but I thought he might have been one of your father's by-blows."

Bryce put his head back and gave a low chuckle. "Let's hope the old man never gets wind of your theory. Unlike his unregenerate son, Father never so much as glanced at another woman."

"Oh." Jemima looked down at her lap. "Then I am sorry to have implied such a thing."

"Well, even if your bearded man was the murderer, riding about in daylight for all to see, I doubt he'd be fool enough to wander about a strange house in the dark, hoping to stumble across his prey. Murderers tend to be a bit more methodical."

Jemima grumbled, "I hope you are right."

"Come now, I'll take you for a quiet look in on Lovelace, so you can assure yourself that she is unharmed. Then I will return you to your own room. Want me to sleep on the threshold, like a devoted retainer?"

"No," she said, as he drew her to her feet. "I don't think that will be necessary."

"And tomorrow," he said as he led her into the hall, "I will ask MacCready to see if he can't located Old Simmy. I'll have him brought here so he can apologize for rattling you so badly."

Lovelace was sleeping soundly when Jemima peeked into her room. Her blond curls were tangled on her pillow, and Jemima thought she looked very young and vulnerable. It was strange, how fond she had become of the girl, in spite of her sometimes wearing personality.

She returned to the hall where Bryce was waiting with a candle. He raised his brows questioningly.

Jemima smiled, and then said, "Innocence slumbers, at peace in her bed, while all about her villainy fills the world with dread."

"More Lord Troy?"

She grinned. "No, I just made it up."

"Well, then, you can't be shivering in your slippers any longer, if you are composing odes to sleeping beauty. Come along, pet, things will look brighter in the morning."

Jemima was at least relieved that Bryce had shrugged off his odious rake persona and was once again his amiably sarcastic self. This, now, was the man she had come to . . . to esteem. She wondered, as she followed him along the hall, why that winning version of Beecham Bryce had evaporated from his bedroom just when she most wanted him to be there.

He preceded her into the room, holding his candle aloft. "No intruders," he said as he beckoned her inside.

She went up to him and laid a hand on his arm. "You did that on purpose, didn't you?"

He cocked his head. "Did what?"

"Behaved like the worst sort of bounder back there in your bedroom. To make me flee from you. You don't have to admit it; I don't expect you to. But I know it's true just the same."

He sucked in his cheeks thoughtfully. "You might chalk it up to conscience, Jemima. But I doubt you would credit me with possessing such a thing. Suffice to say, I will forget that little episode ever occurred."

That was as great an untruth as he had ever spoken, he mused to himself. He would be weeks forgetting the feel of her velvety skin under his hands. And who knew if he would ever stop hungering for her honeyed kisses?

She nodded slowly. "We will both put it behind us, Bryce. Remember, we were *equal* contributors."

He raised his hand, wanting to touch her one last time. But then reason prevailed. He clasped his hands together and said in a brisk voice, "Well, I think I'll have a look around the house . . . make sure everything's locked up tight."

He left before she could say another word.

Jemima climbed into bed, lay back against the lavender-scented sheets, and mulled over his ruse—the feigned arrogance that had so successfully effected her flight from his bedroom. She knew she should be furious with him for doing such a thing. It was odiously manipulative. But all she could muster up at present was a feeling of complete bewilderment.

The most notorious rake in the *ton* had been incoherent with desire for her—she knew what condition he'd been in when he pulled back from her on the chaise, since even maiden ladies could recognize a state of arousal—and yet he had somehow been tweaked enough by his conscience to halt his seduction, practically in midcaress. She'd always suspected Bryce possessed an honorable streak, and so wasn't nearly as surprised to discover he had a conscience as he appeared to be. But she was much too exhausted by all that had transpired to probe the ramifications of his selfless behavior.

In the morning, she thought with a deep yawn. *I'll think about it in the morning.*

When she did fall asleep, however, it was with a tiny, satisfied smile on her face.

Bryce went directly to his library, after nudging the sleeping footman who was guarding the lower hall into a more wakeful state of watchfulness. He poured himself a large brandy and sat sipping it as he sorted through his options. There weren't many, he reckoned. The advent of the intruder had brought home to him the fact that, though he was fairly sure whom he was dealing with, he had no guarantee that the man's intentions were harmless. Especially after the troubling information he had gleaned that afternoon on the coast. Nothing made sense any longer. Which meant that it was time for a confrontation with the intruder.

Bryce looked up at the mantel clock and groaned. He didn't fancy a midnight ride across the countryside, more so since it meant leaving Jemima and Lovelace alone in the house with only the sleepy servants to stand guard.

He took a slow swallow of brandy, trying to regulate his thoughts, which was a deal more than he could do for his pulse, which continued to trip erratically. When he'd heard Jemima's muffled cry in the hallway, his heart had instantly begun a fierce thudding in his chest, and even after he'd seen that she had come to no real harm, his pulse still had not eased.

And he was also recovering from his earlier encounter with her, which had left him trembling and aching with desire. He'd had little experience with sexual frustration in his lifetime, and in this instance it had left him with unaccustomed feelings of self-doubt. When he should be feeling noble, he reminded himself. And righteous. But all he felt was confused and agitated and hellishly irritable.

He let his hands dangle over the sides of his chair, the glass he held tipping precariously above the rug. *Jemima*. He sighed the word aloud. Even with the remnants of the brandy on his tongue, he could still taste her. Sweet and hot, like the very best cognac, and with ten times the power to intoxicate him.

As he pondered this unaccountable longing for a woman who was neither very young nor precisely willing, he recalled his baiting words to her on the day they had met. *It's so hard to know what will strike a libertine's fancy.* She'd struck his, all right. Like an arrow straight to the heart. And that image frightened him more than any outraged spouse he'd ever faced over pistols.

As he sat, trying for the hundredth time to understand his insatiable craving for Jemima Vale, he heard a noise from behind the panel on the far wall. He instantly snuffed out the solitary candle beside his chair, and then waited, barely breathing in the darkness. His hand crept to the pocket of his waistcoat—where he kept a small pistol—and he cursed silently when he remembered shedding it in his bedroom.

With a low-pitched creak the panel moved aside. Someone slid out of the opening and moved into the room. There was a sound of a match being struck, and then a candle flame glowed into life. Bryce looked upon the tall young man who was cupping the candle with one hand. A raggedy fellow he was, in a threadbare blue coat and canvas trousers, his bearded face nearly obscured by a wide-brimmed hat. Bryce watched in silence for several long seconds, and then smiled as he felt his heart leap with joy, his wariness all fled away at the sight of that mobile, good-natured face.

"Hello, Kip," he said from the shadows.

"Jesus, Beech!" his brother cried crossly as he bobbled the candle and nearly dropped it. "Do you want to give a fellow an apoplexy?"

Bryce rose from his chair. "You're not happy to see me?"

"Why should I be?" Kip asked with a barely contained grin. "You're sitting here, playing lord of the manor, while I'm reduced to living in a bloody cave. And that is my favorite chair you've appropriated."

Bryce crossed the room. "Put down the candle, Kip."

"Why, so you can plant me a facer for deceiving you?"

"No," Bryce said as he took the candle from his brother and set it on the library table. "So I can give in to this unaccountable urge to hug you, you great blithering clodpole."

He wrapped his arms around his brother and nearly lifted him off his feet.

"Hey, now," Kip warned him. "Mind the ribs. That Frenchman sliced me in the side, before I put an end to him. Thank the Lord it's healing nicely."

Bryce released him at once and stepped back. "That's a blessing, at least. But I need to speak to you about your Frenchman . . ." He made a tsking noise. "Carrying bloody corpses about in my woods. And frightening half the female population in the county, to boot. I think I'm entitled to some explanation."

"And you shall have one. But first I need a drink . . . and an answer to my own question—how the devil did you know I was about?"

"Aside from the dwindling contents of the brandy decanter, and the fact that several books have gone missing from our secret cabinet, and the curious coincidence that a man who could be my twin has recently been seen on the estate, I couldn't possibly say. Oh, and there was also the cryptic message the old man gave me, before he sailed off to Barbados. Something to do with not taking your death to heart." Bryce's voice lost its bantering tone. "When did you tell him, Kip? How long has he known you were alive?"

Kip rubbed fretfully at the side of his bristly jaw. "I've been working on a delicate problem for the Admiralty, one that requires total secrecy. But when Sir Richard Hastings told me Father's health was failing . . . well, I had to risk telling him. I had no idea he'd taken my death so hard. I'd been off fighting Napoleon for the past four years, after all. It was always a possibility that I might be killed."

Bryce wondered if Kip had any idea how hard *he* had taken the news. "Without divulging any state secrets," he drawled, "could you give me some of the pertinent details? Were you really lost at sea?"

Kip nodded as he poured himself a brandy. "It was during a squall that blew up off Romney. I lost my footing running to help one of the men with a line, and the next thing I knew, I was in the water. I managed to make it to shore, but I got cut up on the rocks off the headland. When a group of smugglers found me on the beach, I was barely conscious. Fortunately, my uniform jacket was gone . . . a good thing, or they would have coshed me and tossed me back in the water. The men took me to one of their storage caves and looked after me—I'd gotten a nasty gash on my head."

"But, thank the Lord, it is an unusually hard head," Bryce remarked with great fondness as his brother settled into the chair opposite him.

"I was ill for nearly a week, but afterward, once I'd gotten my strength back, I asked to join up with the smugglers. Said I'd been first mate on a merchant ship with a hellish captain and swore I'd never go back into service."

"Why not just come home, Kip? Why the pretense?"

His brother leaned forward and said in a low voice, "One night while I was ill I heard Tarne, the leader of the smugglers, plotting with his men. They thought I was asleep, I suppose, because what they spoke of was nothing less than treasonous. It appears Tarne's been taking orders from someone in London, orders to carry French spies back and forth across the Channel. French gold can be pretty persuasive in these lean times, and I bore the smugglers no real ill will—they had rescued me, after all. But I knew I needed to win Tarne's trust so I could discover who was at the head of the operation."

"And I gather you did . . . win his trust, that is."

Kip sat back. "Yes, and I was able to furnish the Admiralty with descriptions of every man who came over from France. They've apprehended three of them, so far."

"I understand your need for secrecy, but surely your family was entitled to know you hadn't perished."

Kip shook his head. "I couldn't risk anyone outside Whitehall discovering I was still alive. If Tarne got wind of the fact that I was Captain Kipling Bryce of His Majesty's Royal Navy, I'd end up forty feet under, with an anchor tied to my legs. Not a pretty end, Beech."

"Well, I must say this has been quite a week for dead brothers returning from the grave."

At Kip's bewildered expression, Bryce grinned and said, "No, it would take too long to explain. So what brings you inland?"

"Our most recent import, a Mr. Perret, needed an escort to London. Tarne usually accompanies the Frenchmen to the city, but he was suffering from a bad case of the influenza."

Bryce gave a low chuckle. "It's been going around."

"Since I professed some knowledge of the city, I was chosen to take him. The first night we were there I led him to Bacchus, at his request. In fact, our informants in London have trailed at least three of these French fellows to Bacchus. Perret obviously met with someone there."

"Who?"

Kip shrugged. "I'm not sure. Your doorman wouldn't allow me to follow him inside."

"You should have written me for an introduction," Bryce said smoothly. "I believe I could have gained you admission."

Kip's eyes lit. "Someday you'll have to take me through the place. I hear there are all sorts of . . . interesting goings-on."

"I rarely go there myself anymore," Bryce muttered.

"Anyway," Kip continued, "Sir Richard, who has been my contact in the Admiralty, decided we could use Perret to pass some false information back to France. I engineered a meeting between Perret and a supposed traitor in the Admiralty. He informed the Frenchman that Sir Richard would be carrying some important naval documents with him when he traveled down to Withershins for a prizefight—reports of our current squadron positions in the Channel. They were to be passed from Sir Richard to Admiral Beston in Dover the day after the fight."

Bryce frowned. "Why risk a spot so close to Bryce Prospect to do the deed? If you were so intent on keeping your identity a secret, I mean."

"It was Sir Richard's idea. He thought it best to pick a location where I knew the lay of the land. And he wanted the documents to be stolen close to the coast, so that the Frenchman wouldn't be tempted to return to London, where he might have the means to discover they were patently false. We wanted him away from England and back in France as quickly as possible."

"And you didn't fear that you would be unmasked once you were here?"

Kip shrugged. "I'd let my beard grow while I was with the smugglers; it altered my appearance enough so that I knew few would recognize me. And besides, I only planned to be here for one afternoon. I was to wait in the grove while Perret went off to search Sir Richard's room at the Tattie and Snip."

"It's the perishing Iron Duke now," Bryce muttered.

"So I've heard. Tolliver is fallen under Old Hookey's spell like the rest of us. Lord, Beech, do you remember when you and I were boys, we stole Tolliver's fattest pig and hid it in our cave?"

"Of course I remember . . . I also recall the whipping that prank earned us at Father's hands. I think I still bear the marks." The words were uttered with a rueful grin.

Kip nodded. "He was harsh sometimes, but in his own way fair."

Bryce kept his own counsel on the matter and chose to say nothing, except to inquire why the Frenchman would think Sir Richard would leave important papers lying about in his room at the inn.

"Because," Kip said, "I assured him the old man wouldn't carry them with him to a prizefight. Perret entered the inn once Sir Richard rode off, and when he returned to the grove, he was in a towering rage. He said he'd located the right room, complete with an admiral's hat in the window, but the only papers he'd found were worthless bits of scribble. He claimed I had lured him there on false pretenses. I swore that I was Tarne's man to the end, but Perret began to fear a trap. He got the wind up then, pulled out a knife, and tried to stick it between my ribs." Kip's eyes darkened. "I never intended to kill him, Beech, but he didn't leave me much choice."

"You always were too tenderhearted," his brother said.

"It wasn't that. Since he'd clearly botched the theft of the papers, I thought I could salvage something by bringing him back to the Admiralty for interrogation. I hoped we might be able to shake the name of the ringleader out of him. But he pulled his knife before I could draw my pistol . . . and now he's beyond any questioning."

"At least on this plane," Bryce commented dryly. "And so now you are back where you began."

"Not quite. I don't like to say this, Beech, but the Admiralty suspects the ringleader is a member of Bacchus. It could be anyone in that rackety group."

"Including myself?"

Kip looked noticeably uncomfortable. "There has been some discussion of that possibility. You do live rather high, and with no income to speak of."

"And treason is not beyond a man as morally decayed as I am." Bryce's voice was dangerously quiet.

"I never wanted to believe it; you must know that. But you aren't only a member of Bacchus, you own the damn place. And when you left London so abruptly last month and came down here, the Admiralty was sure you were involved in some unsavory business along the coast. It only confirmed their suspicions about you."

Bryce rose from his chair and turned toward the hearth, trying to restrain his anger. How typical, that the one good deed he'd performed in a decade would give rise to such damning speculation.

"And did you explain to them that there was another reason why I might have come here?"

"What? To look after things for Father?" Kip gave a brittle laugh. "I had a difficult time crediting that, even when the old man himself told me. I thought there had to be another reason."

"So what changed your mind about me?" His jaw tightened. "Or am I being premature?"

Kip shook his head. "I knew you were not in London the night the Frenchman visited Bacchus. I bribed the porter afterwards and got a list of the men who had been there, some twenty names or so."

"Hmm? I shall have to speak to Tompkins about that. We can't have every rascal in London getting wind of our private members."

"Oh, stow it, Beech," he snapped. "I don't care who takes their pleasure at a bawdy house. But at least I now have a list of possibilities." Kip fished a paper from his inside coat pocket and handed it to his brother. "Here. Have a look and tell me what you think."

Bryce gave his brother a long, steady stare, and then his mouth relaxed into a smile. "Thank you," he said, acknowledging Kip's act of faith in sharing the list with him.

"There are a few men here I think you can eliminate," he said when he'd read it. "Lord Troy, for one."

"How can you be so sure? I know the man is a celebrated poet, but that don't mean he's a patriot."

"No, he might not be a patriot, but he is possibly the least political man I've ever met. And the most indolent. Treason takes too much work."

"Rumor has it that Lord Troy is staying here with you."

"Rumor, for once, speaks the truth. That was his sister you trampled in the hall tonight."

"A tasty bundle," Kip observed blithely. "Hope I didn't do any permanent damage."

Bryce growled. "I'd prefer it if you didn't manhandle my guests. Especially that particular guest."

Kip gave a soft whistle. "So, the wind sits in that direction."

"Don't jump to any conclusions, boy. She is merely a diversion until I get back to London. Unfortunately your encounter with Lady Jemima convinced her that a bearded murderer was loose in the house. I had to tell her you were old Simmy Wilcox."

"The smuggler? Lord, Beech, the man's a halfwit."

"Yes," he purred as his eyes lit up. "And by the by, what were you doing in the upstairs hall? Besides waiting to frighten maiden ladies out of their skins, that is."

"I was after a blanket from the linen closet—it gets damned chilly in that cave once the sun goes down. I came through the library out to the main staircase and nearly tripped over one of the footmen. Fortunately he was asleep on the floor. I had to go up the back stairs on my belly, like a snake."

"I thought it prudent to post guards in the house. I still wasn't sure who we were dealing with."

"Jesus, what's the world coming to, when a man can't burgle his own home in peace?"

Bryce merely grinned in reply. "So why did you come back to the library? I was just girding myself to ride out to the cave and confront you—in your den, as it were."

Kip held up his glass. "I needed a drink after running into your Amazon. I swear she took ten years off my life. I shinned down the drainpipe from the old schoolroom and slipped into the cellar. Oh, and I fetched a blanket from one of the guest bedrooms . . . I hope you don't mind."

Bryce rolled his eyes. "You could always stay here at night. I'll make you up a nice little pallet in the attic, just the spot for a demented relative."

His brother made a rude face. "This all probably sounds daft to you, but I know what I'm doing. And I promise, when we find the spy master, I'll come out of hiding."

"You weren't exactly in hiding in the east meadow yesterday afternoon. Not the most prudent way to avoid detection."

"You saw me?"

"Lady Jemima did. She thought you were one of Father's byblows."

Kip gave a hoot of laughter. "That pious old parson. He was lucky to have got us, Beech."

"So why did you risk riding about in broad daylight?"

Kip stalled a bit. "MacCready's been leaving food near the cedar ridge, for me and my nag. And no, don't start ripping up at me for telling him and not telling you. I needed an ally while I was here. And you are too visible."

"Not to mention still a suspect," Bryce murmured under his breath. "So why haven't you returned to the coast, now that the Frenchman is dead?"

"Hastings thinks the ringleader will send someone to follow up on Perret's disappearance. He wants me to watch for any unusual comings and goings in the area."

"You've picked a fine week for that, my boy. The house is over-run with guests, with three more due to arrive tomorrow. You'll be interested to hear that one of those men is on your list—Harold Armbruster, a crony of Troy's. Ralph Carruthers will also be here, and your old school friend, James Kimble. At least *he's* not on your list of suspects." Bryce stopped a moment. He misliked the idea of anyone even remotely suspected of involvement with the spy ring under the same roof with Jemima.

"What do you know of Armbruster?" he asked. "Any reason I should forbid him my home?"

Kip thought a minute. "He is in tight with several highly placed ministers, but I doubt he's the man we're after. Armbruster's not the brightest bullock in the herd, and the man who is operating this ring is a pretty cagey fellow. He's led us all a merry dance for nearly six months."

"And what if this ringleader decides to come down from London himself? He's not going to feel very charitable toward the person who killed his pet spy."

Kip nodded. "Actually that's what Sir Richard hopes will occur. But the man doesn't know the true circumstances of Perret's death. I sent a message to Tarne in Romney and told him that Perret and I were attacked by footpads on the road from Withershins, and that after Perret was killed, I managed to get away with the papers. Tarne thinks I was wounded—well I was, actually"—Kip gingerly touched his side—"and he believes I am waiting in the area for instructions on where to dispose of the stolen papers."

"Well, that is what you're doing, isn't it?"

"Not precisely," Kip responded with a smug wink. "I'm setting a nice little trap. If the ringleader does show up—and he might, because he won't trust anyone else to carry the papers after Perret failed him—we will be ready for him."

"What if he merely sends Tarne to retrieve the papers?"

"He'll come. I feel it in my guts. The man has been feeding the French tidbits of information, but getting these plans to Napoleon would be a coup. No, he won't risk anyone else taking them to France. I instructed Tarne to have my contact hire a room at the

Iron Duke under the name of Marlborough. I thought that name would appeal to a man who has delusions of grandeur." Kip grinned. "MacCready's been checking to see if anyone has registered using that name. It's only a matter of time."

Bryce looked unimpressed. "Hasn't anyone ever told you that only a fool uses himself as bait?"

Kip smiled slowly. "I'm not completely alone. Hastings has a man staying at the inn and several posted in the village. But I'm already a dead man, so if our spy master turns vengeful . . . well then . . ."

"Well, nothing," Bryce snapped. "You've only just been resurrected, and I'm damned if I'm going to let you risk your neck for the Admiralty."

Kip nearly blushed at the intensity of his brother's words. "I value my neck as much as you do, old man. It's a waiting game I'm playing—just need to keep out of sight until my contact arrives."

"To retrieve the nonexistent naval documents," Bryce added.

"Oh they exist all right. They were conspicuously hidden under Sir Richard's mattress, but that Perret, damn his eyes, missed them." Kip again reached into his pocket and drew out a tattered clutch of papers. "All he came away with was this—nothing but a blasted poem—"

" 'Ode to Persephone,' " Bryce quoted, not needing to see the title scrawled on the top sheet.

Kim started back. "How the devil—?"

Bryce twitched the sheets from his brother's hands. "It's Lord Troy's latest opus. And if you don't mind, I'll keep these until I can return them to their rightful owner." He rose and carried the papers to his desk, where he locked them in the center drawer. His brother was still gaping at him.

"Your canny spy searched the wrong room," Bryce said, and then shook his head. "Lord, I wonder how the French have managed to stay out of our grasp, if that is the best they can send against us."

Kip still looked perplexed. "I told Perret that Sir Richard was in the third room on the right."

"Sir Richard's was the third room, but if you recall the layout of the inn, it's actually the fourth door along the passage. The first door is to the privy closet."

Kip put his hands over his face and shook his head. "Bloody hell! Our careful plan done in by a privy!"

Bryce chuckled. "I don't wonder Perret was a trifle out of twig. I saw Troy's room—it looked like an Algerian street bazaar. I am amazed your spy was able to find anything at all in there. Although he did help himself to Troy's gold watch and his signet ring."

Kip rolled his eyes. "Clearly not a gentleman, my Monsieur Perret. I'm almost glad I had to put an end to him." He rose and turned toward the opening in the wall. "Now I'd best be off to my cozy cave."

"I should mention that there's a Bow Street Runner poking around the place. A genial enough fellow, but hardly a bloodhound."

"MacCready told me the magistrate called him in to investigate the murder."

"Well, what else was Sir Walter to do? The poor man's never had to deal with anything more serious than a drunk on fair day or a tinker with light fingers. You'd have done better than to hide the corpse in a hay rick, Kip, and then set fire to it, if you'd wanted to keep the law out of things."

He grumbled, "I didn't set the blasted thing on fire. I just wanted to dispose of Perret as quickly as possible, until Sir Richard could send someone after the body. There were some lads coming along the lane as I rode off—maybe they set the fire. It was bad enough I had to kill the man, but then to hear he'd been roasted afterward . . ." Kip shuddered. "And there was a chit in the woods who witnessed the murder. Screamed her head off like a banshee before she ran away. That's why I couldn't leave Perret where he was."

"Small blessings," Bryce said. "I mean, that you didn't leave a dead man in my cow pasture. By the by, the banshee's name is Lovelace Wellesley and she happens to be residing under this very roof. Hiding out from you, as it were. I owe you a debt of gratitude for sending her to take refuge here."

Kip looked baffled. "I thought Troy's sister was the one who'd taken your fancy."

"She is. But she'd never have come here if it wasn't for Lovelace. Now if the Minstrels would only turn up and cart the girl off to London, I could get on with my life."

"The Minstrels?" Kip appeared even more baffled.

"Nothing. Just another muddle I've been hoping to clear up, along with the milk fever, the grippe, and the death-watch beetles."

"I gather it hasn't been a bed of roses for you this past month."

"It's been . . . challenging. I only hope the old man appreciates my sacrifice."

Kip's voice lowered. "How is he, Beech? I don't suppose you've heard from him yet."

"It's too soon. I only hope that the climate can work a cure."

"The doctors told him that—"

"Hang the doctors," Bryce muttered. "He needs one of us with him. To see that he doesn't overtax himself. If you would end this game of cat and mouse you are playing, I could leave the Prospect in your hands and sail off to Barbados."

He squirmed a bit. "I'm sorry all this has fallen on your shoulders."

"I can barely wait for you to return to the land of the living, so you can take over the damned place."

"Oh, no." Kip put his hand up. "I'm not cut out for this farming business. The sea is my life."

"I think intrigue is your life. But I am at least reassured that you are fighting for the right side. I rode to Romney this afternoon and spoke with a few of my old smuggler friends. Real smugglers, not spy smugglers. They'd seen someone who fit your description near the Marsh . . . but they were hesitant to tell me who you were keeping company with. That Tarne is an ugly customer, from all accounts."

"You thought *I* was working for the French?"

Bryce ran his tongue over his teeth and shrugged. "You thought the same of me."

"Christ, Beecham, I never did. It's just that I've always wondered where you got your blunt from, after Father cut you off."

"That's my affair."

"Well, if you can't tell your own brother . . ."

"Look who's talking," Bryce said with a grin. "And Kip"—his brother turned in the opening to the passage—"I'm very glad you're still alive. Now, if you could just endeavor to stay that way . . ."

The panel slid closed, but Bryce heard the muted laughter through the wall.

God bless Kip, he thought.

Chapter Ten

It was shortly before noon the next day when Jemima left her room. She managed to reach the stable without meeting up with her brother or her host, which marched nicely with her plan to avoid *all* men—she was that out of charity with their species. She needed all her courage to face her nemesis later in the day and couldn't afford being rattled by a chance encounter with Bryce. Last night he had invaded her dreams, which shouldn't have surprised her, as he had also invaded her waking thoughts with increasing and disturbing frequency. And she had no armor against such an onslaught—when love struck, she now knew, it was with an errant arrow, at best.

She'd spent the morning mooning over her hot chocolate, again trying to fathom his behavior toward her last night. What had brought on the unlikely chivalry he'd displayed by refusing to take her into his bed? Especially since he'd spent the past days in dogged pursuit of that goal. Her only answer was so preposterous that it didn't even warrant consideration.

But whatever his motivation, his selfless concern for her honor had battered down the last of her defenses. By turning her away, he had won her heart—that formerly steadfast organ—and she was as ill at ease at the loss of it as she imagined Bryce would be at the gaining of it.

Jemima asked one of the stable lads to ride out with her. She intended to visit the ailing tenant farmers, a plausible reason to delay her encounter with her nemesis, who was due to arrive at midday. It was unlikely, she now believed, that she would come to any harm from him while under Bryce's watchful eye, but that didn't mean she wanted to rush into company with the man.

When she spotted Mr. MacCready riding along the lane that led from the Iron Duke, she hailed him with pleasure. They spent a pleasant hour together, and when they parted at last, she carried away the bailiff's firm opinion that Mr. Bryce was the only man fit to inherit the Prospect. He had further conveyed to her the general consensus that old Mr. Bryce was dicked in the nob to have written his eldest son out of his will.

Jemima entered the drawing room before dinner with a stout-hearted determination not to show fear. Kimble and Carruthers were seated beside Lovelace on the sofa, expressions of rapt admiration on their well-bred faces. *That didn't take long*, she thought, chuckling silently. Bryce was near the windows, in conversation with Troy and Armbruster. He looked up as she came into the room, a smile playing around the edges of his mouth. But before he could move in her direction, Armbruster had crossed over to her.

"Dearest Lady Jemima," he said as he took up her hand. "Such a delight to see you again."

"Mr. Armbruster," Jemima said evenly as he lifted her hand to his mouth.

Carruthers and Kimble had both risen from the sofa, and each in turn made his bow to her. "London has been but a pale shadow of itself, without you there to brighten its avenues," Carruthers pronounced.

"Watch that," Troy called out. "You're treading on my turf with all that folderol."

"I have been gone from London less than a week," Jemima pointed out to the brown-haired dandy.

"Ah, but each day is an eternity without your presence," he murmured smoothly.

Offering him a fleeting smile, she sat beside Lovelace. "We'd do well to ignore them," she whispered.

"Yes," Lovelace agreed with a grin. "I doubt I have heard so much fustian in so short a time."

"Ladies, you wound me," Carruthers protested, his hand over his heart.

"We had no idea when Troy asked us to stay here," Kimble said, shooting a smug grin at Carruthers as he sat down beside Lovelace, coopting the only available space on the sofa, "that we'd have not one, but two fair ladies gracing us with their presence."

Carruthers added, "Miss Wellesley has just been telling us about her misadventure in the woods."

"Oh?" said Jemima in some confusion as she turned to Lovelace. "I thought we weren't . . . that is . . ." She looked up at the two men. "You see, we were instructed to secrecy by the Runner from Bow Street."

Lovelace was instantly dismayed. "Oh, Lady J, I never meant—"

"Don't concern yourself." Kimble smiled at the girl with genial reassurance. "We are all friends here, are we not, Lady Jemima? And if Miss Wellesley restricts her audience to the gentlemen present, why then you may be assured the tale will not pass from this room."

Jemima soon forgot the matter when Carruthers inquired after her Aunt Sophie, who was one of his grandmother's bosom bows. As she dutifully detailed her aunt's sojourn in the Lake Country, she watched Kimble doing his manful best to disguise his admiration for Lovelace, who was furnishing him with a meticulously detailed account of her brush with murder.

"Do you ride, Miss Wellesley?" Kimble asked when she at last paused for a breath.

Lovelace nodded. "A little. I portrayed Lady Godiva last year in Devon; outdoors it was and in a high wind"—both gentlemen began attending her with increased interest—"but my horse grew agitated and refused to take the stage. It was very mortifying to play Lady Godiva while being pushed about in a wheelbarrow, I can tell you that."

The two men looked properly abject, though not quite for the reason Lovelace had intended. Jemima grinned and then looked across at Bryce; he was attending their conversation with narrowed eyes.

"Perhaps you and Lady Jemima might ride out with us, Miss Wellesley," Kimble continued. "I fancy a look at Bryce's property— my father is forever after me to spend time on our estate in Cheshire."

Carruthers snorted. "Not that there's much left of it, after your pater paid off your brother's gaming debts."

Kimble shot him a look of irritation, but then said pleasantly, "I don't suppose there are any particular sights to be seen here. You know—Norman ruins, standing stones, quarries . . ."

"There is a trout stream," Jemima said, rolling her eyes. She then added, "And there is a limestone cave . . . in a ravine near the east boundary. Bryce took me there earlier this week. But unfortunately the entrance had been sealed off with rocks, and we couldn't get inside."

"I cannot ride in any case," Lovelace said fretfully. "Not until my ankle mends."

"Then we will stay close by and seek to distract you," Kimble said.

By the time dinner was announced, Jemima was breathing more easily. She had fallen back on drawing room banter to see her through, and so had managed to keep Troy's friends, if not at bay, at least from seeing how edgy she was. Bryce was watching her, she knew, even though he kept his distance. His eyes probed hers whenever their glances chanced to meet, and so she spent dinner gazing down into her plate and speaking only when she was spoken to. If her nemesis was paying her any special attention she was not aware of the fact. She was thankful that Lovelace possessed such a nonstop stream of amusing tales, and for once did not begrudge the girl all the attention she received.

"Your brother's friends are so charming," Lovelace said as she and Jemima made their way toward the drawing room after dinner, leaving the gentlemen to their customary excesses in port, cigars, and braggadocio. "Especially Mr. Kimble. He is not precisely handsome, but he has such a pleasing manner."

"Bryce thought their company would help to distract you," Jemima said.

"They treated me like a lady." Lovelace sighed as she seated herself on the sofa. "Even Troy does, when he is not teasing me. It makes me feel . . . well, quite special."

Jemima sank down beside her and said in a voice she hoped was not too prim, "Try not to let them turn your head, Lovelace. When you are the toast of London, you will undoubtedly have any number of young bucks tossing rose petals at your feet. So you must learn to tread carefully if you are not to step on the thorns."

Lovelace giggled. "There aren't any thorns on rose petals, Lady J. But I take your meaning. Young men do offer all sorts of flummery, but I'm not so green as to think they are in earnest."

Then you are a wiser creature than I am, Jemima responded silently.

By the time the gentlemen joined the ladies in the drawing room, Jemima was beginning to think her fears were groundless. Perhaps her assailant had forgotten the incident in the country house, perhaps he had been too drunk to even recall it. There was also the possibility that he regretted his actions and had no intention of causing her any further distress. She relaxed then and offered to accompany Lovelace on the piano. While the girl sang a series of country ballads, Jemima lost herself in the music, letting the room and all its inhabitants drift far into the background. Well almost all its inhabitants.

When a man's hand touched upon her shoulder, she grinned to herself. Was Bryce possibly making a public claim to her with that gesture? She turned to smile up at him and her fingers slipped to the wrong chord. The man leering down at her was not her host.

Her hands started to tremble and lost their place on the keyboard, as the pressure of the man's fingers increased slightly. Lovelace's song drifted to a halt.

"Please, sir!" Jemima hissed up at him. "You are distracting me."

He leaned to her ear. "I *live* to distract you, Jemima."

After he returned to his seat on the sofa, Jemima mumbled an apology and began to play again, forcing herself to concentrate on the music. When the song ended, she looked up at last. Bryce was standing at the very back of the room, his glass of brandy held near his chin. His face was in shadow, but she could have sworn his eyes were ablaze with light. He moved forward and said in a languid, relaxed voice, "Gentlemen, I believe we have taxed these ladies enough tonight."

Troy rose. "I'm for my bed, Bryce. These scoundrels kept me up till cock's crow last night and I'm completely done in."

To Jemima's relief the party broke up then. She attached herself to Lovelace, saw her to her room and stayed there, chatting idly, until she was sure all the gentlemen were abed.

Bryce watched Jemima's bedroom door from the darkest portion of the hall. He had settled himself in a window seat that was partially obscured by a large potted palm. Nearly half an hour had passed before he saw a solitary figure making its way toward him from the wing where Troy's friends were quartered. He tucked his feet back into the shadows as the man knocked softly on Jemima's door. When there was no response he knocked again.

"Who is it?" Her voice was muffled.

"Troy," the man replied. "I need to talk to you."

The door opened a crack. The man thrust his body through the opening, forcing his way into the room. As the door began to close, Bryce moved like a shot across the carpet. He shouldered his way through the entrance before the lock could be turned.

Jemima stood in the middle of the floor, her face ghost white in the candlelight, except for two splashes of crimson high up on her cheeks. Her hands were clenched against the skirts of her dressing gown as she stared openmouthed at the wide-set man before her.

Harold Armbruster spun to face Bryce with an expression of surprise, which then twisted into a sneering smile. "Treading on your turf am I, Bryce?" he inquired sanguinely. "But I believe I can claim a prior . . . um, connection."

Bryce saw Jemima's complexion turn a sickly gray. He stepped past Armbruster and clasped his hand over her arm. "Don't you dare swoon," he ordered gruffly.

She threw her head back and drew a deep, steady breath. "I'm fine."

He turned back to Armbruster, who had not moved from the spot where he stood. The man outweighed Bryce by a stone or more, and in spite of his thickening waistline, he was known to be handy with his fists in the boxing ring.

"Please excuse us, Ma'am," Bryce said smoothly. He grasped Armbruster's shoulder and tried to shift him toward the door. "Mr. Armbruster has apparently wandered into the wrong bedchamber by mistake."

Armbruster shook off his hand and laughed softly. "Give over, Bryce, there's a good fellow. I know you rakes hate to surrender the field to any man, but this lady and I have an understanding."

"Understand this," Bryce snarled, trying to keep the red hot rage that was coursing through him at bay, at least until they were away from Jemima. "You will leave her room this instant. And you will leave this house before daybreak. I do not welcome men of your ilk under my roof."

"Only room for one cock in the henhouse, eh?" Armbruster chuckled. His gaze slid to Jemima, who nearly wilted back before that oily perusal. "For myself, I'm not adverse to sharing." He tapped one finger on Bryce's chest and said silkily, "And from what I know of your reputation, old chap, neither are you."

Bryce felt it then, the fierce jolt of his past crimes slamming into him, brought home by Armbruster's gleeful assumption that any woman beneath the same roof as Beecham Bryce was fair game for dalliance. Bryce knew then that he had sullied Jemima merely by offering her his hospitality. He might just as well have taken her last night, rather than giving in to his conscience and standing away. He could have had her, and made truth of the lie that would surely spread through London, once Armbruster returned there with his poisonous tongue.

With inarticulate fury he thrust the man away from Jemima, catching his arm by the wrist and twisting it up behind his broad back. Armbruster bellowed in rage. Bryce tightened his hold and growled, "If you make another sound, I will break your arm like a twig. I swear it." He dragged him to the door and motioned Jemima to open it. She flew across the room and swung it wide.

"Lock it," he ordered brusquely as he tugged Armbruster out into the hall.

"We are going to have a nice little chat," he muttered as he strong-armed the man toward his room. Armbruster twisted and writhed, but Bryce's anger had lent him a nearly superhuman strength. When they got to Armbruster's chamber, Bryce kicked open the door and swung the man inside. A single candle burned on the nightstand. Bryce released him and quickly stepped back out of range of his fists.

"Have you gone mad!" Armbruster cried, as he tried to rub the feeling back into his arm. "Christ, man, you fly to defend the chit as though she were untouched. I know better, even if you don't."

"I am not here to discuss Lady Jemima's virtue," Bryce responded, trying to regain his composure. "But I will tell you this— if I hear anything to her detriment in London, anything the least slanderous, I will know whose foul tongue was at work, and I will see that you suffer for it."

Armbruster made a noise of disparagement. "And who has appointed you guardian over her? Troy lets her go her own way, he always has. If her own brother sees fit to let her become a byword—"

Bryce lost his battle with restraint. He landed a blow somewhere below Armbruster's heavy lips and sent the man sprawling back onto the carpet. Armbruster was on his feet in an instant, his agility surprising Bryce. But there was no stopping the righteous rage that had overcome him—he knocked Armbruster down two times more before the man subsided into dazed surrender on the carpet.

"Damn, you've got a punishing right," Armbruster said raggedly, running one hand along his jaw. "Never seen you at Jackson's . . . thought you were more of a pistols-at-dawn sort of fellow."

Bryce stood white-faced and unmoving. "I would be happy to accommodate you, if that's your desire."

A look of alarm twisted Armbruster's face. "No, no. I believe we've settle things here between us."

"Have we?" Bryce asked dangerously.

Armbruster climbed shakily to his feet. "I'll leave after breakfast, as you asked."

"Before dawn," Bryce intoned. "I'd make you leave this minute, but I never like to trouble my grooms over trifling matters."

Armbruster took the insult—that Bryce placed his servants' comfort before that of a gentleman—without a word of protest. But when Bryce turned for the door, Armbruster forestalled him.

"You're nothing like I expected, old chap," he mused. "From the tales I've heard about you, and from the goings-on at Bacchus, I expected to find this place a haven of vice. And when I saw that delectable bit of muslin in the drawing room, the alluring Miss Wellesley, I knew I was correct in my assumption. Yet now you tell me I need to mind my manners around the ladies." He shook his head in disbelief. "You must be losing your touch, Bryce. Or else the fair Jemima has beguiled you."

"There is nothing between Lady Jemima and myself," Bryce said, "excepting that I am her host. Even *I* have some notion of propriety when I am in my father's home. Now I bid you good night."

"Trotting off back to her room, eh?" Armbruster said under his breath.

Bryce spun back to him and grasped a handful of his neckcloth. "Don't make me sorry I didn't horsewhip you, Army. And remember what I said—" His fingers tightened on the man's throat. "One word, one whisper that sullies her reputation, and you'll learn precisely how good I am with a pistol."

Bryce thrust him away and went striding from the room. His blood was still simmering, but his head had cleared enough for him to realize that the man had been correct on one count—he did intend to seek out Jemima, if only to assure her that Armbruster would be no more than an unpleasant memory by morning. It would be prudent to wait until then to tell her, prudent to wait until his anger had cooled completely. Because he knew—just as he'd told Jemima—that while anger heated a man's blood, it also heated his loins. And he had no business going near her in that condition.

She answered his knock with a shivery whisper. "Bryce?"

"Yes, it's me." Good. He could deliver his message from his side of the door. "I just wanted to tell—"

The door swung wide. She stood before him clutching a fireplace poker to her chest.

"I think you can dispense with the weapon," he said as he was lured into the room by her wide, frightened eyes. He gently took the poker from her and returned it to the hearth.

"I was determined not to be a simpering damsel this time," she said with a sigh. "I can't believe I let him in here. What an utterly stupid thing to do."

"You didn't open the door for Armbruster, Jem. You thought it was Troy."

"Armbruster," she proclaimed, "sounds nothing at all like Troy. At least when I am wide awake. But I was half asleep when he knocked."

"You don't have to make excuses, pet. The man is a bounder."

"I only thank God that you happened to be nearby." She sank down onto her vanity bench.

"I didn't *happen* to be anywhere." Her gaze darted up to him as he continued. "I was waiting outside your room for him to come along."

"You were?" Her face took on a wondering expression.

Bryce nodded as he crouched down before her. "I watched him all through supper. He looked at you with more appetite than he displayed for his *boeuf en croute*."

Jemima gave a tiny chuckle.

"I saw the way you shrank back when he touched you while you were at the piano." His voice lowered. "Armbruster was the man, wasn't he, Jem? The one you spoke of last night."

She nodded slowly and said in a wavering voice, "I've managed to avoid him since last summer. A happy circumstance, you may be sure. I was so afraid when I learned he was to come here with Troy's friends. But I hoped that he would not attempt to renew his . . . attentions to me. He was drunk that night, after all, and I thought he must surely have forgotten the whole incident."

Bryce nearly growled. *Christ, what man could forget holding Jemima in his arms?*

"But it was a foolish hope. Even though he's not sought me out in London, I must have done something to encourage him tonight."

He growled in earnest this time and rose abruptly to his feet. "I am to blame for that, Jemima. As you pointed out that first day in the woods, Bryce Prospect is now a libertine's home. And men of indifferent morals assume they may come here and sin with impunity."

"I never said that," she cried, rising to face him. "You have done nothing wrong. It was my brother who invited that creature here. It was Troy who welcomed Armbruster into his circle of friends last summer."

"You should have told him, Jem," he said softly. "Troy would have kicked the fellow down two flights of stairs once he knew how he had trifled with you."

"And you did?"

"What?" He cocked his head.

"Kick him down the stairs?" she said.

"I am more civilized than your pagan brother. I merely ordered him to leave at daybreak."

"Yes," she said, taking his right hand in hers and placing a gentle kiss upon his raw, swollen knuckles. "I see how very civilized you are." Her eyes beamed up at him.

He sighed hoarsely as her lips trailed over the tender, broken skin. He was rapidly losing his determination to leave her to her slumbers.

"How many times did you hit him?" she murmured against his hand.

"Only three." He choked out the words as her soft mouth moved to the base of his wrist.

"That's a nice, righteous number," she said as she pressed his palm to her cheek.

He somehow managed to disengage his hand and tuck it behind him. It was trembling like a leaf on an aspen. Which was not surprising, considering the tremors of heat that were coursing along his lower spine and swirling down to his belly.

"You should have told me about Armbruster last night," he said, trying to sound dispassionate. "You needed only to say that Troy's friends made you uncomfortable and I would have forbid them the house."

She made a noise of exasperation. "I did tell you last night. I repeatedly questioned you on your decision to let them come here."

"It's not the same thing, pet. You never came right out and said that one of my house guests was the man who attacked you. Good God, Jemima! Do you think I'd have let Armbruster within a mile of you, if I'd known who he was? The damned cad! I've a mind to tell Mrs. Patch to burn his bed linens."

With him in them, he added wickedly to himself.

Jemima smiled. "I can't account for this sudden change in you, Bryce. All righteous and indignant. What's happened to the notorious libertine?"

He shifted away from her, went to perch on the arm of a chair, and sat silent for a moment. Jemima followed him and laid a hand on his hair, tracing her fingers over the waves that lay upon his collar.

"You don't want the libertine, Jem," he said with great weariness. "When I heard the way Armbruster spoke of you just now—as though you were a commodity to be haggled over—I heard echoes of my own vice. Traces of my own damned arrogance . . . Oh, I like women. God, too well. But respect them or honor them. . . ?"

"Or esteem them," she added in a tiny voice.

"No," he answered, lowering his eyes before she could see the anguish that had dulled them. "I can't say that I've ever felt any of those things for a woman. They are playthings . . . pretty trifles . . . pleasing diversions to be used and discarded at whim." He slowly let his head fall back. "I have rarely taken anything from a woman but idle amusement. And so suspect I have missed out on the best they have to offer—compassion and comfort . . . and love." His words were laced with bitterness.

"Have you never loved, Bryce?" she asked softly. "Not ever?"

He opened his eyes and looked at her without one shred of armor. The fierce light she saw there frightened her, even as it answered her question. It was no languid fawning look of adoration he bestowed on her—it was, at once, a white hot blaze of hunger, longing, and bleak resignation.

Then the look was gone, and his mouth formed into a tight smile.

"I came close once," he said musingly. "Though I never speak of it. Oddly enough, it relates to what you said before you fled from me last night." He added in an undertone, "Lord, Jem, you've been fleeing from men since you got here, it seems. And only one of them was me." He gave a dry laugh. "But I at least can make amends to you, even if Armbruster and last night's intruder can't."

He rose, and then coaxed her down into the chair.

"It's a point of pride with me, not explaining my actions to anyone," he said as he settled himself at her feet. "But for you, Jemima, I am making an exception."

She laid a hand on his shoulder. "You don't owe me any explanations."

"I do. I owe you this." He paused to draw a breath. "Last night, before you left my room, you made a stinging reference to young wives of men serving in Spain. I am aware of the unsavory scandal that arose from my association with that particular young wife."

"You must know I didn't mean to—"

He reached up and laid a finger firmly against her mouth. "Hush, now. Let me say it out. Lady Anne Webster was deeply in love with her husband, but she was also an extremely jealous young woman. She'd heard through malicious friends that her husband, Major Webster, was keeping a Portuguese woman in Lisbon . . . If you take my meaning."

"The woman was his lover," Jemima ventured.

"Exactly. Whether it was true or not, Lady Anne took it to heart. She decided to draw her errant husband back to London by being blatantly unfaithful to him and I, I am ashamed to admit, was not dismayed at the prospect of being the object of her dalliance."

"Why would you agree to such a detestable scheme?" she asked with a frown.

"Because, my little moralist, I was unaware of her motives at first. Do you think I stop and assess what is on a married woman's mind, when she casts out her lures to me?"

She muttered, "I am being hopelessly naive, I see."

"Mmm. At any rate, she convinced me to travel with her to the Lake Country, where she had rented a small manor house. I fell completely under her spell—she was vivacious, breathtakingly alive, and I began to wish Webster at the very devil. Lady Anne had convinced me that her feelings were engaged, and in spite of all my years as a profligate, I believe I felt the . . . sting of Cupid's arrow for the first time."

"You say it with such scorn," Jemima said. "Didn't she return your love?"

He shook his head slowly. "I was merely a pawn, so besotted that I played straight into her hands. She'd done what she intended—set the *ton* on its ear by openly consorting with a libertine, and so made sure her husband would hear of it in Spain. She had only to wait for him to come for her."

He turned his face toward her; it bore a grim expression. "I never realized it until later, but the coldhearted Lady Anne had every expectation that her husband would kill me when he arrived from Spain. But he did not come for her, alas. He merely sent a letter, informing her that he was beginning divorce proceedings." His voice grew strained. "She tried to kill herself with my pistol the day his letter arrived."

Jemima gasped. "Sh-she tried to shoot herself while you were there?"

"She came into our bedroom carrying the pistol . . . and a note she'd written, swearing that I had forced myself on her, badgered her, until she had no will to resist. I crossed the room barely in time to stop her from putting a bullet in her brain. She flew at me like a harpy then, spewing her rage. I realized at that moment that any tender feelings she'd shown me were only a pretense."

She took his face between her hands. "Oh, my poor Beech."

He shook off her touch. "Don't pity me! Pity the wretched creature who loved so desperately that she wanted to die rather than lose her husband's affection. Christ, you should have seen her . . . After she read Webster's letter something snapped inside her and I . . . I think it drove her mad. I brought her myself to her parents' home—she was nearly incoherent by then—and saw to it that they were given the note she'd written. It seemed the least I could do . . . taking the blame for her distress."

"Another man would have destroyed that note," she said quietly.

He gave a mirthless laugh. "Why should I bother? Even without her damning words, it was what the world believed of me. The merciless predator, remember?"

Jemima protested, "But she made herself available to you . . . she leased the house." Her voice trembled. "She made you fall in love with her."

Bryce tore his gaze from her. "If *that* was love, then I am forever done with it. But I suspect it was nothing more than a fleeting chemistry, which I foolishly mistook for a more enduring emotion."

Jemima chose not to comment on his sudden glibness. "Did the major ever come back to her?"

He nodded. "But by that time her family had placed her in a private asylum and fostered the rumor that she had died mysteriously. When Webster met me over pistols, I never even raised my gun. I think I wanted him to kill me, Jem. Pity his aim was off." He rubbed absently at his shoulder, where the major's pistol ball had buried itself. "I . . . I stayed away from women for a long time after that."

"I wonder you didn't become a monk," she said sharply.

His smile was tolerant. "I'd done with religion, as you recall. Besides, the leopard doesn't change his spots so easily. And I discovered later that a streak of madness ran through Lady Anne's family—she had an older brother who'd lost his wits before he turned twenty. It eased some of my guilt."

"So there were no more married ladies after that?"

"No, only whores and trollops and bits of muslin."

"And aging spinsters," she added with a sigh.

He rose to his knees, slid his hands up to her shoulders, and shook her slightly. "Don't say it in that way, Jemima. There is such life in you, such beauty. And humor and intelligence and warmth." His voice grew wistful. "I thought I could make you see those things in yourself. I wanted to so very much."

Jemima felt her throat close, as tears gathered on her lashes. "I thought you wanted only to seduce me . . . I thought it was a game you were playing to pass the time."

His voice rasped close against her ear. "It's not a game any longer."

His kiss was not schooled by expertise this time. It did not speak of skilled, single-minded conquest, but of deep-seated need. His lips sighed against hers, touched her with gentle caresses and warm, buttery strokes. Jemima melted against him, finding a sure haven in his embrace.

"Ah, Beech," she whispered. "You don't have to lie . . . but thank you for making the attempt."

"Not lying," he said raggedly and followed the pronouncement with a brusque kiss. "I have never lied to you, Jemima. I swear I never will." He carried her back against the cushions, her body bracketed by his arms, as his lips bore tender testimony to his words. They danced gently over her opened mouth, as he murmured wordless endearments. She gave a small gasping sigh, as his tongue glided over her lips and sought the warm recess of her mouth. She was drowning in heated nectar, so sweet was the taste of him on her lips and the feel of him against her skin, where his fingers curled over her bared shoulder.

There was more seduction in these gentle, earnest kisses, did he but know it, than in any heated onslaught. He was winning her with his restraint. Last night he had been lusty, bantering, an experienced man of the world. Tonight he was cautious, uncertain, and so very, very giving. Last night he'd wanted to take his pleasure with her. Now he was bringing her joy. Such immeasurable joy.

"Beech," she sighed against his mouth. "I am so happy."

"Are you, Jemima?" He stroked one finger over her lips in an achingly slow caress.

"Not just from this." She captured his hand and pressed it to her mouth. "You gave me something tonight—your trust. And whatever happens between us, I will always treasure that."

He sat back on his heels. "Is it such a valuable commodity then?"

"I think it is," she said. She leaned forward and tucked her head into the well of his throat. His hands rose up to hold her there. "And it is more than I ever thought to gain from any man."

Bryce's heart wrenched, twisted in dismay that this lovely creature had such niggardly expectations from the world and from men. She should have everything a man could bestow on a woman: adoration, admiration . . . and love. No one deserved love more than Jemima Vale.

He cursed the life he had led, the life that had hardened him and sullied him. He raged at the foolish choices he had made that placed him outside the realm of decent people. Rakehell, they called him and profligate. And he was all those things and more. He had reveled in his chosen vices, and believed himself well lost to propriety. It was not until his home had been invaded by Jemima Vale that he realized how much he'd carelessly tossed away. It was not until his heart had been wrested out of its icy armor by this warmest of women, that he understood what it truly meant to love, and how it felt to know that his love would never be allowed to blossom.

He put her from him, gently setting her back on the chair. "It's late," he said gruffly.

"Yes," she echoed, "it's very late."

Too late, she wanted to cry, seeing the remote expression again obscure all the ardent emotion in his face. If he could kiss her like that, feeling her respond to him with every fiber of her being, and then take his leave of her with such calmness and composure, then she reckoned he would always be beyond her.

"Good night," he said from the doorway. "And make sure you lock up."

"Yes," she said dryly, looking away from him, "I haven't the strength to fend off any more intruders."

He grinned wistfully and thought, *Gallant Jemima*. For two nights running he had refused her offered favors, and she was still trying to make jokes. He went into the hall, softly closing the door behind him. He glanced down the hallway toward Armbruster's room. The blasted cad had assumed Bryce would avail himself of Jemima's bed, having vanquished the foe and won the lady for himself.

But Bryce had got the last laugh, after. A lot of bloody good it did him.

Chapter Eleven

The next morning, as Jemima toyed with the toast on her bed tray, she realized she had been at the Prospect for five days and had not once breakfasted with Bryce. Was he grumpy in the mornings? she wondered, lounging back against her pillow. Or was he brisk and bright and tiresomely cheerful? Some part of her regretted that she'd not made the attempt to find out, and another part wished she had a lifetime to spend with him to discover all his moods—in the morning, at noon, and especially at night.

She loved him so fiercely, that at times it was an acute pain, slicing relentlessly at her insides like the sawblade in a timber mill. Other times a soft flush of tenderness washed over her, filling her with warmth and delight. When she recalled his amused teasing and his halting confidences, her heart sang. When she thought of his sordid past and his uncertain future, her stomach plummeted in dismay. And so the cycle repeated over and over, until she didn't know whether there was great wisdom in loving him or pure folly.

She only knew that the heat of his kisses and the simmering ardor in his eyes fired her with such unmaidenly longings that she forgot any notions of chastity. All she desired was the thrill of his embrace and the bliss of his hard body, arching unrestrained against her own.

But Bryce would have no further opportunities to tempt her. She would not place herself in his path. Her pride would not allow it. He had rebuffed her twice in the past two days, and the lesson was well, if painfully, learned. Whether from a lack of desire, or a more noble disinclination to put her honor at risk, Bryce had thrust her away. Nothing would ever induce her to offer herself to him again. Nothing.

If that was love, then I'm forever done with it. Those bitter words he'd spoken last night were a clear warning, one she had to heed. Even the delicious thought of being once more dazzled by his kisses could not override her certainty that skilled passion was a pale substitute for true caring. And she would settle for nothing less from him.

There is no solace in these reflections, she told herself mournfully as she pushed aside her uneaten breakfast and climbed from her bed. *Only frustration and unspeakable pain.*

In the distance the church bell in Withershins was pealing softly. With the vague notion that a morning spent in devout worship would wipe all traces of Bryce from her soul, Jemima sought out Lovelace once she left her room and insisted they attend the service at the local church.

But even after she and the girl had been seated in the Bryce family pew in the ivy-draped Norman church, Jemima found herself unable to concentrate on the service. In the hushed and sacred confines of the sanctuary, her mind wandered again and again to the pagan stirrings Bryce aroused in her. When the rector, a stately gentlemen with a crown of white hair and a faint lisp, began his sermon, she realized he had uncannily chosen the parable of the wise and foolish virgins. Jemima thought that this was no more than the penance she deserved for encouraging a rake's attentions, but she was squirming in her seat by the time the service ended.

As she and Lovelace came through the arched doorway of the church, Sir Walter accosted them. He hemmed and hawed a bit at first, and Jemima realized he did not wish to speak in front of Lovelace. She suggested the girl go on ahead with Sir Walter's son, a well-favored young man with a cleft chin who, Jemima knew, would be a prime target for Lovelace's particular charms. Once she was gone, Sir Walter took Jemima's arm and led her toward the stone wall that abutted the graveyard.

"I don't like to trouble you, Lady Jemima," he said, wiping at his brow with a handkerchief. "But the fact of the matter is, Mr. Fletch sent a message to my home late last night. He had spoken with Sir Richard Hastings and was able to ascertain nothing."

Jemima frowned. "Surely Sir Richard would have told him if there was any sort of plot afoot."

"That's what I thought. But Sir Richard all but ordered Mr. Fletch to halt his investigation. He insisted the dead man was not a French spy, and that he himself had been staying at the Iron Duke only to see the prizefight. Claims he had no papers of any sort on him that would interest a spy. Sent Mr. Fletch away with a flea in his ear, by all appearances."

"Oh, dear," she said softly. "That puts us back where we began. I mean with an unidentified corpse."

Sir Walter scuffed his boot on the shaley ground. "He'll never be identified now," he said. "Had to bury him yesterday, in potter's field. Poor blighter, set down in an unmarked grave. I didn't mind so much, when I thought he was a Frenchy, but I wouldn't wish that sort of burial on any God-fearing Englishman."

Jemima forbore to point out that a great many French people were God-fearing, or that the dead man, of whatever nationality, had undoubtedly been a thief and therefore less God-fearing than most.

"So will you let the investigation drop?" she asked.

"Haven't got much choice, have I? Mr. Fletch is not happy to have been called down from London on such a wild-goose chase."

"Perhaps he can focus his attentions on finding Miss Wellesley's missing family."

"I sympathize with Miss Wellesley's distress, ma'am, but chasing after a theatrical troupe is small fish for a man of Mr. Fletch's talents. I expect he'll be returning to London now."

"Do you think it's safe for her to remove to the Iron Duke?" she ventured.

"What? Why would she want to leave Bryce Prospect? I know Bryce has the devil of a reputation where ladies are concerned, but demme, the chit's barely out of leading strings. No, no, I think she should stay on there until her family can be located. Well, I'd best be off now. Tomorrow I'll be back to my usual duties—fining the local drunks and checking the cellars of the Bo'sun's Mate for smuggled goods." He chuckled. "Now let me get my son home before he makes a fool of himself over a pretty face."

She glanced at the young man, who was standing tongue-tied as he gazed at Lovelace.

"Sir Walter—" she called out as he started toward the couple. His mention of smuggled goods had jogged her memory. "One more thing . . . Have you ever heard of a smuggler called Simmy Wilcox?"

Sir Walter turned and scratched the back of his ruddy neck. "Now there's a name I've not heard in donkey's years. Old Simmy Wilcox. He drowned as I recall, ten years ago it must have been."

"Drowned?" she echoed blankly. "At sea?"

"No, in a vat of ale. Poor fellow was never right in his head. Why do you ask?"

"No reason," she replied, schooling her face into polite disinterest. "I heard someone at the Prospect mention him and I thought it an odd name."

"Odd name for an odd fellow. Give my regards to Bryce,

ma'am. And tell him I'll ride by to see him tomorrow to discuss this turn of events regarding Sir Richard."

Jemima was quiet on the drive back to the Prospect, listening with only half an ear as Lovelace nattered on about Sir Walter's son. Why had Bryce lied to her about Simmy Wilcox? What reason could he have for resurrecting a dead half-wit? It led to only one conclusion, one she had a hard time giving voice to, even inside her own head—he'd done it to put her off the scent. Because he knew the identity of the intruder in the hallway and was trying to protect him. And if the intruder was the murderer, then Bryce was sailing very close to being an accomplice to that deed. And if the man he was shielding was a French spy, which, in spite of Sir Richard's disclaimer, she still had a strong suspicion was the case, then Bryce was involved in treason, as well.

She sat swaying in the carriage, trying to stifle her creeping uncertainty. It was lowering enough to have fallen in love with a libertine, but it now looked as though he might be something far worse.

The *ton* had speculated for years over where Beecham Bryce found the money to support his extravagant mode of living after his father had cut him off. Gambling, procuring, and smuggling were some of the opinions ventured. Jemima now feared she had another occupation to add to that list of unsavory possibilities— spying for French gold. It was rumored that Bacchus included in its membership many high-ranking military men and several cabinet ministers. And even a maiden lady could deduce that when gentlemen were in their cups and in the presence of a toothsome ladybird, all sorts of state secrets might come spilling out.

By the time they reached the house, she was no longer sure of anything. But she would not damn Bryce until she had something more conclusive to go on than her own fretful imaginings. Still, she had a hard time greeting him cordially when he came up to the carriage with a shotgun slung over his arm.

"Troy's friends are mad to go shooting," he said with an easy smile. "They've gone out back to the kennels . . . probably stirring my dogs to·a frenzy."

"I thought you didn't hunt," she said, eyeing the shotgun with distaste.

"Not big game, Jemima. But taking down a few pheasants is hardly in the same league, especially when they're destined for the pot."

"I doubt you need to hunt to put food on your table," she uttered as she sailed past him into the hall.

He turned to Lovelace, who was watching Jemima's departure with a perplexed expression. "She's in such a queer mood, Mr. Bryce," she said as he handed her onto the porch. "She barely said one word on the drive back from church. I'm parched from having to furnish all the conversation."

Bryce grinned. That was one skill Lovelace had in spades.

"Perhaps it was something Sir Walter said that upset her," she added. "He particularly wanted to speak to her alone." She shrugged and then limped into the hall.

Bryce tapped one hand against the butt of his rifle. He toyed with the idea of letting the shooting party go on without him, so that he could discover what had turned Jemima so waspish. But he knew Troy's friends were still curious about Armbruster's sudden and sketchily explained departure, and he reckoned he needed to distract them. Jemima's problem would have to wait until he returned from the field.

Not that he had any great fondness for hunting, he thought as he made his way around the house and toward the kennels. Blasting defenseless birds out of the sky with buckshot. Hang the woman for making him feel like a barbarian. It was damned inconvenient, having a conscience all of a sudden.

After luncheon, Jemima settled Lovelace in the sitting room with a novel and a box of chocolate bonbons. She then lingered in the lower hallway, hovering on the edge of indecision. Any search for evidence of Bryce's involvement with the spies was tantamount to admitting her lack of faith in him. How could she claim to love him, if she had so little belief in his character? But then she thought of the women in her circle of friends, those who had had the misfortune to love hopeless gamesters, heavy drinkers, and chronic adulterers. The husband of one of her own dear sisters fell into that last category. Love, it appeared, was not predicated on sterling credentials or upright behavior.

Anyway, she reasoned as she shook off her hesitation and made her way up the stairs, she'd just have a quick peek into some of the places where Bryce might have hidden incriminating evidence—if only to reassure herself that it was all a hum. She'd begin in his bedroom.

Fortunately, most of the servants were taking advantage of their Sunday afternoon off, but she left the door open a crack, just in case someone came along the hall. In spite of the sunlight streaming in through the opened draperies, Bryce's bedchamber still held a seductive aura. His scent seemed to permeate the room—brandy, tobacco, sandalwood, and something she couldn't quite name. It was a masculine blend that was heady, rich, and very potent.

She stood in the center of the floor, her eyes drawn to the wide tester bed, where, but for a man's misplaced gallantry, she might have found heaven. Dragging her gaze away from the brocaded coverlet, she caught sight of a painting that was propped up on a table near the window. She had not noticed it the night she had been there, indeed she could have sworn it had not been in the room on that occasion.

She was drawn to it now, drawn by the luminous play of light on water, which the artist had captured with only the faintest of brush strokes. She stopped in her tracks when she got close to the painting. It was surely one of Canaletto's Venetian landscapes, and unless she was very mistaken, she had seen that exact painting last autumn in London, at an ambassador's home.

Her heart began to drum unevenly. How had the painting come to be sitting in a Kentish manor house? Was it possible that, in addition to being a murderer's accomplice and a spy, Bryce was also an art thief? Then the odors of fresh paint and linseed oil assailed her nose. It was a scent she often encountered while visiting the studios of her artist friends in London. It was also the scent she had identified when she first entered the Prospect. Oil paint, linseed oil, and the sharp tang of turpentine.

The landscape was newly painted; she suspected if she touched a fingertip to the surface of the water, it would come away smudged with a trace of cerulean blue.

I've always been a dab hand at it, Bryce had said about his ability to draw. This was something more than a dab hand, she thought, peering more closely at the canvas. This was downright forgery.

One of her impoverished artist friends had traveled to Amsterdam last year and had returned with several splendid Rembrandts—which he had himself painted. Jemima had jokingly suggested that, since they appeared so authentic, he should try to peddle them as the genuine article. But her jest had fallen flat. The artist had puffed himself up and pronounced dolorously that no one who called himself a true artist would ever condone the selling of forgeries.

Jemima spun away from the painting and fled from the room, overset by the notion that a man with the talent to recreate the haunting beauty of a Canaletto might so misuse that ability by hawking fakes to unsuspecting buyers. Could he have sunk so low?

In truth she knew little of Bryce's ethics, and his morality, unfortunately, spoke for itself. But it wasn't a crime, she countered, as she made her way down the staircase, merely to copy a classic painting. It was only reprehensible if the work was passed off as genuine. And she had no proof that Bryce intended anything underhanded with his Canaletto. For all she knew he, like her friend in London, merely copied masterpieces to hone his own skill.

She put it from her mind as she made her way to the library. It was best to focus on the more immediate task, which was discovering why Bryce had lied to her about the addled smuggler.

Bryce watched as Kimble took down a brace of quail with two quick shots. Troy and Carruthers clapped the marksman on the back, while Jenkins, the gamekeeper, looked on in disgruntled silence. It was technically not birding season, and Bryce knew the man resented this intrusion on his coverts by a group of boisterous dandies. Bryce himself was not pleased to be tramping about in the underbrush when he most heartily wished to be back at the Prospect with Jemima.

He suspected that the house party would soon be dispersing. Even though Troy's friends had arrived only the day before, they'd been noticably unsettled by Armbruster's abrupt departure. Furthermore, Bryce knew they would quickly grow bored with the limited entertainments the countryside had to offer. Jemima's tenure in his home would soon be ending, and Bryce hadn't a clue as to how to keep her there.

Not your home any longer, he reminded himself glumly. Especially not now, now that Kip was again in line to inherit. He didn't even have a proper home to offer her. Nothing but a small rowhouse in Knightsbridge. Maybe he could install her in Bacchus, he thought with a wry grin.

Then he frowned when he realized where his unrestrained musings had taken him.

Christ! What was he thinking? What did it matter whether or not he had anything to offer her? She was a passing fancy, an amusing diversion.

The lie assaulted him, even as he gave voice to it in his head. Jemima had never been a diversion, not from the first moment she had flashed her incredible eyes at him and given him a proper setdown. He'd been as done in as one of the hapless quail Kimble had so neatly blasted from the air.

He threw off his disturbing thoughts with a muttered curse and went trailing after his guests.

"Your shot, Bryce," Troy called, as the two liver-and-white spaniels went casting back and forth over the field, their stub tails wagging as they got down to the important business of flushing gamebirds.

"No." Bryce held up one hand. "I'll let you gentlemen take all the honors."

"Demme, Bryce, don't disappoint us," Kimble called out. "One hears that you're the finest marksman in London. They say you can shoot out the eye on the jack of hearts without disturbing his smile."

"I'm not in the mood for shooting today," Bryce replied evenly. To make his point, he broke open his shotgun and laid it over his arm. "And I have some business awaiting me back at the house. If you gentlemen will excuse me, Jenkins will look after you."

He turned without waiting for their response and headed back toward the Prospect, his long strides carrying him away at a brisk pace. As he cleared the wood and topped the rise that overlooked the house, sitting snug and serene in its bright green skirt, his heart slammed in his breast.

This was his home, the only true home he'd ever known. Even during the many years he'd spent away from it, Bryce Prospect had remained a haven in his dreams. In spite of the bleak months after his mother's death, in spite of the difficult years with his father, it was here he'd experienced the greatest joy.

And that joy had returned to him during this visit. The feeling of expectation and excitement. The sense that the world was a bright and happy place. Two things had brought that joy back to him— the knowledge that his brother still lived, and his growing feelings for Jemima Vale.

And therein lay the rub. Had Kip remained no more than a beloved ghost, Bryce might have been reinstated as the heir. He suspected the old man would have come about eventually. And then he would have had a prosperous estate to place at Jemima's feet. He could take up the reins of his ancestral home and mellow into old age with his wife and children around him. He'd gladly have given up his life of dissipation in London; how could the lures of vice compare to the wonder of a life shared with Jemima?

But in gaining Kip, he had surely lost Jemima. She had been an earl's daughter, was now an earl's sister, and traveled in the world of literary and artistic royalty. He knew enough of her nature to believe that his past would weigh little with her, but there were other issues. There were things a man needed to offer the woman he wed. Stature and position. And wealth. And while he was by no means a pauper, Bryce knew that without his inheritance, his various business dealings would not be able to keep Jemima in pearl necklets or allow her the scope of travel she had grown accustomed to under her brother's care.

"Bryce's prospects don't look good," he muttered to himself, and then he laughed aloud. Lord, he was totally besotted if he was reduced to making bad puns.

At least he knew Kip was being looked after. There was some consolation in that. After he'd seen Armbruster off at dawn, Bryce had ridden to the Iron Duke and had a most satisfying early breakfast with a gentleman who was biding there. He'd made his choice—keeping Kip alive was paramount, regardless of how it affected his chances with Jemima.

He angled down the slope of the hill, the tails of his greatcoat lashing behind him as he headed for the kitchen entrance. As he walked, he pondered whether the things he did possess were enough to tempt Jemima away from her life with Troy. It was a questionable inventory—a sordid past, a tarnished soul, a hopeful heart, and a most enduring love.

Why not ask her if it's enough? the voice of reason argued. *At least allow her the courtesy of making up her own mind.*

The notion intimidated him as much as it appealed to him. Because as skilled as he was at seduction, he was a rank novice when it came to courtship. But then he realized that he'd been wooing Jemima all along—his uncharacteristically noble behavior toward her was proof of that.

"I'll do it," he muttered as he went through the door. "And devil take the consequences."

The library was cool and full of shadows. Jemima stepped cautiously into the room, her determination to unmask Bryce's involvement with the murderer waxing and waning in turn. She recalled the old adage about curiosity and the cat, but she also remembered Plato's essays on the virtues of knowledge. She weighted the proverb with the words of Plato, and Plato won.

Bryce's slant-top desk was the natural place to begin her search. It was locked, but Jemima quickly overcame that obstacle by the judicious use of a hairpin. She rapidly sorted through the pile of estate papers and bills which had been shoved haphazardly into the cubbyholes, feeling the whole time like the worst sort of sneak.

But nothing looked at all suspicious. The shallow carved drawer in the center of the desk was also locked but, again, it proved no match for her hairpin.

A sheaf of crumpled, folded papers lay there, atop a jumble of pen points and wafer seals. She lifted the papers out, shut the drawer, and closed up the desk. Moving to the nearest window, she stood beside the oak Bible stand and unfolded them. The words, "Ode to Persephone," danced before her eyes. It was Troy's poem, the one that had been ripped from his notebook by the dead thief. The poem that everyone, including the Bow Street Runner, assumed was in the possession of the thief's murderer.

She stood arrested in a posture of disbelieving shock. Until that moment she hadn't truly believed Bryce could be involved in the murder, but now she held irrefutable proof. He had to be in league with the bearded man, and maybe even—dear Lord—with the French spies, as well.

No wonder he'd insisted that Lovelace stay at the Prospect, she reflected wretchedly. Where better to keep an eye on the only person who could identify his accomplice?

As the reality sank in, Jemima felt herself growing light-headed. She reeled sideways against the Bible stand. The heavy, Moroccan-bound Bible began a gradual slide off the angled top. Jemima watched its slow descent with horrified eyes—a book that size would sound like a thunderclap when it hit the parqueted floor. With a muffled *oomph*, she caught it in her arms just before it cleared the ledge.

She hefted the book against her chest and was about to set it back on the stand when she saw the brass key lying upon the aged oak. She removed it before she replaced the Bible and then stood for a moment tapping it against her palm. It was too large to fit in the desk's keyhole, and she gazed narrow-eyed about the room, wondering what other secrets the library might offer.

The mahogany cabinets beneath the bookshelves had distinct possibilities. The first four she searched were unlocked and held a collection of musty papers dating back to the previous century. The fifth cabinet was locked, however, and she was not surprised when her key opened the door. Kneeling on the carpet, she drew out the tooled leather box, holding her breath as she lifted the embossed lid.

"Books," she muttered. No letters from France, no naval plans, nothing whatsoever incriminating. Not that she needed anything more than the poem, now tucked in her bodice, to damn Bryce. She picked up the top book on the pile. *The Secrets of the Hindi*, it proclaimed in a gilt script. Some sort of travel book, she thought, as she opened the cover.

"Good Lord!" was all she could utter when she saw the first illustration.

The hand-colored picture showed an exotically garbed couple, with their bodies entwined in a manner that Jemima knew had to be anatomically impossible. The subsequent drawings were similarly lurid—portraying a variety of contorted couplings in shocking detail. She held her hands up to her burning cheeks. This was far beyond her ability to assimilate—her scant knowledge of what men and women did together in the dark did not allow for these erotic, sensual poses. Surely proper English gentlemen did not expect their partners to disport themselves in such a manner. It was unthinkable.

But as she continued to look through the books, powerless against her own curiosity, her blood began to heat. As horrified as she was by Bryce's link with the murderer, her body was still in his thrall. She wondered with a sigh what it would be like to reenact these provocative poses with him, a man skilled and practiced and so sublimely—

She heard footsteps in the hall—she'd again left the door ajar—and quickly dropped the books into the box, shoved it into the cabinet, and shut the door. As she scrambled to her feet, she saw that one slim volume still lay on the rug. She swept the hem of her skirt over it just as Bryce came into the room.

"I thought you were off shooting," she said in a strained voice, unable to meet his eyes.

He shrugged. "I left Troy and his friends happily tramping after my father's dogs. I came back because I wanted to talk to you." He started toward her across the carpet.

"I'm afraid I don't feel much like talking," she said coolly. "I have a bit of a headache, in fact."

Another gentleman would have begged her pardon and gone off about his business. But Bryce just came closer and cocked his head. "You are looking pale, Jem. Has Lovelace chattered you into a megrim? Perhaps you should sit on the couch and put your feet up." He offered his arm to her.

Jemima grit her teeth. If she moved even one inch, he would see the book peeking from under her hem. "I was looking for something to read," she said. "Something restful." With a languid motion she waved to the stack of books behind her. And prayed he would take the hint and leave.

"Or perhaps you have already chosen something." As he spoke he leaned down and retrieved the book from beneath her hem. "This might be a bit . . . um, warm for your taste." He looked at the book's title and his eyebrows rose. "*Definitely* too warm." He knelt down and returned the book to the cabinet, and then held out his hand without looking up at her. "The key," he said.

She dropped it into his palm as though it were a red hot ingot.

"Thank you," he murmured as he relocked the door. When he rose, his eyes held more than a hint of rebuke. "I believe an explanation is in order, Jemima."

She put up her chin. "I choose to say nothing at present."

He gave a harsh laugh. "You sound as though you were in a court of law. I merely want to know why you have been poking around in my private things. Feeling bored?" His voice took on a honeyed tone. "Maybe I can relieve your boredom." He raised a hand to her face, stroking one finger along her cheek.

She drew back with a hiss.

His eyes widened and his voice lost all its seductiveness. "What is it, Jem? Lord, you look ready to swoon." He moved even closer and she had to prevent herself from shrinking back.

"It's nothing," she said, trying to sound matter-of-fact. "I'm just a bit upset. You see, I met the magistrate at church—he told me that Sir Richard has ordered Mr. Fletch to abandon his investigation."

Bryce looked thoughtful. "It appears Sir Richard's playing a deep game."

He's not the only one, she wanted to cry out. "I haven't told Lovelace yet," she said. "But I think, since Sir Richard doesn't believe the murderer is a threat any longer, that she and I should remove to the inn."

Bryce took hold of her wrist. "Don't be daft. Sir Richard's edict only proves that he doesn't want a Runner nosing about in Admiralty business. Not that Mr. Fletch appears to be much of an investigator."

Her mouth tightened. "In that case, I imagine you would be grateful for his ineptitude."

"What is that supposed to mean?" he asked in a low voice.

Jemima realized she was about to let her fear and her anger at him overcome her prudence. "Nothing," she said more calmly. "I can't think why I said such a thing. And yes, you are right . . . I believe I will go upstairs and rest awhile." She looked meaningfully at his hand, which still encircled her wrist.

"Not until you tell me what you meant about Mr. Fletch." He tightened his hold.

"*Bryce*—" she said warningly.

"Tell me. Tell me why you are behaving like a skittish foal and why you won't look me in the eyes." His hand drifted from her wrist to her cheek. "Tell me what is troubling you, Jemima."

Her head twitched back, away from his fingers. Even now, even in the midst of her shock over his apparent treason, she knew she could not prevent herself from responding to his touch.

He observed her for a moment and then said, "Are you cross because I went out shooting? You'll be happy to know I never even raised my gun." He offered her a lazy grin, which was met with stony displeasure.

Jemima knew she couldn't keep the truth from him for long. It was one of the remarkable things about Bryce—she felt she could tell him anything. *Anything.* And perhaps there was a logical explanation for why he had Troy's poem in his desk. Though for the life of her, she couldn't think of a single one.

"I believe you know who the murderer is," she whispered hoarsely.

Bryce didn't school his features quickly enough. Jemima caught the swift expression of startled surprise that tightened his jaw. "What nonsense is this?" he asked in a voice of controlled caution.

"Can you deny that you know who killed the Frenchman?"

As he started to reply, Jemima raised one hand in warning. "Tread carefully, Bryce. You vowed last night that you would never lie to me."

His mouth closed and compressed into a thin line, and she swore she could hear his teeth grind.

"Then I will toss your own words back at you—" he said bluntly. "I choose to say nothing at present."

"Because you can't deny that you are in league with the man," she observed grimly.

"I won't dignify such a ridiculous accusation with a denial," he said. "What reason can you have to accuse me? Haven't I aided the investigation? Haven't I kept Lovelace safe?" His voice grew insistent as he grasped her by the arms. "How can you condemn me so easily . . . after last night?"

She shook off his hands and stepped back. "Do you think this is easy for me, Bryce? To discover the man I . . . I trusted is an accomplice to murder. And maybe even to treason."

"Damn it, Jemima!" he said with a fierce scowl. "I am not an accomplice to anything."

"Liar!" she spat.

"It is not a lie," he said, running a hand through his already windblown hair. His temper was starting to rouse as it had when Kip had accused him of trafficking with the spies. How had his reputation as a rake given people—especially those he was close to—such a mistrust of his character? Just because a man hankered after women, it didn't follow that he would sell out his country for a handful of *louis d'or*.

He bit back his anger and said slowly, "There are things afoot here, things I am not at liberty to reveal to anyone." Her expression still challenged him. "Ah, Jem, let this alone for now . . . until I am free to tell you the truth. I am on the side of right in this, you must believe me."

Her eyes narrowed. "You are a cozening libertine, who lies to women as soon as look at them."

"Yes," he said. "I have been a libertine and even a knave at times. But before God, I have never raised a hand against my country. And I have never lied, Jem. Not to you."

She drew a breath, and then said in a flat, empty voice, "Simmy Wilcox is dead these ten years. Drowned in a vat of ale."

Her words hung in the air between them for several seconds. Bryce saw the resolve in her face and in the remote emptiness of her eyes he read the demise of his own bright future.

"Yes," he said, nodding. "He is dead. And so I thought him a safe scapegoat. I lied only to keep you from fretting. I . . . I can't believe that one lie has made you think me such a villain."

"It's been my experience that one lie begets a thousand. But no, it wasn't only that Banbury tale you spun for me, Bryce, that makes me think ill of you."

"So what other misdeeds have you laid at my door?" he asked sourly.

She drew the notebook pages from her bodice and held them up. He didn't attempt to take them from her; he knew well enough what was contained on those pages. Troy's cursed "Ode to Persephone." He vowed he'd never read another line of poetry as long as he lived.

He turned from her and crossed to his desk, levering the slant top open a few inches just to satisfy himself that she had purloined the papers from the drawer. "You've been busy, Jemima," he said in a voice of ice. "I wonder you didn't ransack my bedroom. Ah, I can see your blush from across the room. So even my most private chamber did not escape your prying eyes."

"Your private chamber, indeed," she parroted with disdain. "I fancy a rake's bedroom is the most public room in his house."

He bowed with great irony, acknowledging her riposte. "I stand corrected. You of all people should know about the goings-on in my bedchamber."

She gasped in shock. "I assure you, I will make every effort to forget *anything* about that place."

Except the forged painting, she added silently. She'd keep that little tidbit to herself for now.

"I'm leaving now for the Iron Duke," she said. "And I'm taking Lovelace with me."

"That's a foolish notion," he said irritably. "You'd do better to remain here until tomorrow. You can leave for London in the morning."

She snorted. "Yes, I expected you'd say that. But you have no right to question my wisdom."

"Oh, don't I?" he muttered as he recrossed the room. "You've just proven how unwise you can be."

"In what way?"

He snatched the notebook pages from her hands and rattled them under her nose. "Only the greatest nitwit in the world would have shown these to a man she thought was in league with spies and murderers. What if I *were* those things, Jemima? Do you think I would blithely let you leave here, carrying away the evidence that would damn me?"

"I . . . I didn't think—" She took a tiny step back. "I only wanted to—"

"Here, take the blasted things!" He thrust the pages into her hand, forcing her fingers to close around them. "Now does that prove to you that I'm not in league with the confounded spies? No? . . . I see that nothing short of a good shaking will remove this idiotic notion from your brain."

"Don't!" she cried, pushing his hands away. "What else can I believe, Bryce? Everything points to you—the stolen papers, your lies to protect the bearded man. Tell me, please . . . what am I to believe?"

His voice lowered. "You could start by believing in me. But no, Lady Jemima Vale doesn't stray from the path of her narrow convictions." His bitterness was like a blade. "God forbid she should take a chance on something, or take a man's word on faith alone."

She stood unmoving, her eyes huge in her pale face. "I . . . I'm trying . . ."

"It doesn't matter. Nothing matters any longer." He motioned abruptly to the door. "Go," he said wearily, drawing in a long breath. "Take yourself off to the Tattie and Snip. Lord knows you've been hankering to do just that thing since you first set foot in my house. And take the Tragic Muse with you. I promise you there is no danger to her. There never has been any threat from the murderer."

"Never?" she echoed softly in disbelief.

"It was all a ruse. I used it to keep you here."

An expression of pure pique welled up in her eyes. "You mean you let us stay here, shivering in our beds with fear, knowing the whole time that there was no danger?"

Bryce shrugged. "I told you repeatedly that no harm would come to you or Lovelace. It was you who refused to believe me."

Jemima's bosom swelled. "What possible reason could you have to do such an infamous thing?"

He narrowed the gap between them. "It was a foolish notion I had. I wanted to keep you here . . . I thought you had possibilities, Jemima."

"The less that is said about that, the better," she uttered in her most caustic voice.

"You intrigued me, if you want the truth. And I needed something to distract me . . . from the milk fever and the beetles in the wainscotting." He paused, hoping to at least see a glimmer of humor in her fine eyes. But they only flashed at him dangerously.

"So it was another lie—"

"Not a lie," he protested. "An opportunity, more like. To spend time with you, to learn who Jemima Vale was when she wasn't hovering behind her brother. I knew you would be angry when you found out about my little game. But I thought you would forgive me when I told you why I'd done it."

"Spare me your idle flattery. You saw me as just another woman to be seduced."

"Yes," he said, determined to offer her honesty, at least in this matter. "At first. But it wasn't long before I realized I wanted more from you. A great deal more."

"You've gained nothing but my scorn, Bryce. There is nothing you can say that will convince me of any nobility of purpose in your behavior."

He growled softly. "Nobility of purpose, is it? I tell you the unsullied truth, and still you rail at me about honesty? I'll give you honesty in spades, then, and say right out why I came back to find you."

"It is of no interest to me," she said, half turning from him.

He caught her by the shoulder, forcing her to look at him. "I came back here . . . to ask you if you would consider having me."

"Having you?" she repeated blankly.

"Having me for your husband. Because I thought, fool that I am, that you cared for me. And this is what I am met with . . . ridiculous accusations and foul inferences. But that's all I deserve, isn't it? Because I'm a rake and a scoundrel. A man beneath contempt." There was now a white-hot anger in his voice. "Not a fit mate for the great Troy's sister, eh?"

He watched with satisfaction as she blanched noticeably. He wanted to wound her, as she had wounded him. But then, when he saw how she trembled under his hand, his anger shifted to irritation.

Christ! Did she honestly think she had anything to fear from him besides harsh words?

"Oh, for God's sake, Jemima," he cried. "Stop wilting against the bookshelf. I'm not Armbruster—I'm not going to force myself on you."

He turned and took two steps away from her. But the magnetic pull was too strong—he had gotten too close. And the anger in his blood had done its work.

In an instant he spun back. "The hell I'm not—"

He thrust her hard against the bookcase, twisting her arms behind her in a crushing embrace. The thin veneer of civilization shattered as he kissed her. His mouth was wild, scorching, as it battered against her lips. His head swam with the sensation, while the rest of him drowned in her scent and her taste and the stirring shape of her beneath his hands.

The last time . . . his brain keened. *The last time you'll ever touch her . . .*

That inevitability lent added heat to his assault; he needed to imprint every part of her on his soul. The thrust of her breasts, the arch of her hips, and the thready sound of her breathing, as she gasped against his hungry mouth.

She wasn't wilting now, she was fighting him, trying to free her hands from his implacable hold. She cried out as he braced his body against her and caught her chin with one hand to hold it steady. Over and over he let her taste his pain and his frustration, until her thrashing ceased. He felt her go limp beneath his hands as she groaned softly.

He released her abruptly and stepped back. Her mouth trembled like a child on the edge of tears.

"Take that with you to your spinster's bed," he whispered raggedly just before he stalked away.

Jemima leaned back against the mahogany shelves, unable to move, barely able to breathe. She was still stunned by Bryce's declaration that he wanted to marry her and equally shaken by the fact that he had rescinded his proposal in practically the same breath.

Oh, but how he had kissed her! As though every fiber in his body were crying out for her touch, as though he were consumed by his need to brand her with the fire that raged inside him.

She had never felt so confused. Or so full of self-loathing. Because she knew that the things she had accused him of, in her monumental arrogance, had placed them beyond any possibility of reconciliation.

He was facing away from her now, standing directly before the window with his arms crossed over his chest, the bright light creating a nimbus around his dark curls.

"I c-can't bear—" she stuttered, trying not to sob out the words.

"The sight of me," he said from over his shoulder. "Yes, I've gotten your drift. Well, I won't stop you, if you want to go running off to the inn. You can go to perdition for all I care."

She blinked several times, then lifted her skirts and walked with slow, studied steps to the door.

He watched her with a curiously detached expression on his face; he wasn't attending her rather shaky retreat from his library. In his mind he was seeing a frightened, white-clad version of Jemima Vale as she was forced up against a wall and overpowered by a tall, strapping man. He felt her panic and distress as she was rudely groped and cruelly kissed, all the while held captive, like a rabbit in a snare.

His stomach lurched.

Don't flatter yourself that you're any better than Armbruster, his inner voice rasped. *In truth, you're a damned sight worse.*

Jemima was too far away to hear it when he slammed his fist into the front panel of the desk—leaving a noticeable dent that would be remarked upon by subsequent generations of Bryces.

Chapter Twelve

Jemima decided to leave most of her clothing behind. She threw a few gowns and some underthings into a valise and then changed into her riding habit. She was doing up the buttons when she heard a commotion in the hallway outside her room. Men's voices, low-pitched and muffled.

"Jemima!" Troy called through the door.

"Go away!" she called back. He was the last person she wanted to see.

He opened the door and came cautiously into the room, his windblown hair and muddied boots proclaiming he was not long away from the fields. Jemima saw Kimble and Carruthers hovering in the hall, trying not to gawk. Count on Troy to make her humiliation a public spectacle.

"What the devil is going on, Jemima?" he asked, shutting the door behind him. It caught on the edge of the carpet and didn't quite close. "I come in from shooting and discover from the butler that you have ordered the pony cart and are leaving for the inn."

"That is correct," she said. As he started to protest, she leaned forward and said intently, "I want to leave this place, and so I shall."

"Without a word to me?" He plucked her parasol from the bed and leveled it at her accusingly. "You've clearly lost your wits. Bryce is barricaded in his library and refuses to see anyone, but I know this has something to do with him."

She crossed her arms and stuck out her chin. "I don't owe you any explanations."

"This is intolerable, Jem. How can I work when you are forever distracting me with these bizarre fits of yours? It's hard enough keeping my mind on poetry, without worrying about you half the livelong day."

Jemima tugged the parasol from his hands and jabbed him in the chest with it. "Worrying about me?" Her voice rose a notch. "*Worrying about me?* That is the most preposterous thing I have ever heard. When have you ever spared a thought for me, Troy? No, it's Jemima fetch this, Jemima fetch that. It's pack for me, unpack for me, order up a dinner for me. It's soothe the butler, calm down the cook, fire the footman, hire the housemaids. *All* the livelong day!"

Troy stood with his mouth gaping open and his eyes round as bright blue marbles. "Jem . . ." he at last managed to utter. "Is . . . is that what you think?"

"That is my life with you, Terence Vale. But not any longer. I will not take another farthing from you. Not another penny. I will live on my own resources . . . I have a small inheritance from Great Aunt Clarice. It will be enough. It must be enough."

"No," he said, crossing his own arms. "I won't allow it. You'll be next to a pauper."

"Better a pauper than a piece of luggage in your train. Better my own woman than a supplicant in your house." She saw him wince, but did not apologize for her words.

Troy took a step closer. "A supplicant? You are talking twaddle, Jemima. I've looked after you, as a brother should, and hope I've never made you feel you owed me for anything. I can't comprehend this change in you. We've rubbed along very well until now, haven't we?"

"Until now," she said. "But things change, people change. I . . . I can't live that way any longer. I need my own life." Her voice sank to a whisper. "What there is left of it."

He ran his hands over his face and said irritably, "I think I'd best fetch Bryce up here. He'll make you see reason. Knows his way around women, that one."

"No!" she cried. "If Bryce sets one foot inside this room, I will climb out that window, walk to the inn, and get on the next coach to London, or to Canterbury." Or to perdition, she thought, recalling Bryce's harsh words. "You have no idea what that man has done, Troy."

"Bryce?" Troy appeared unruffled. "If he flirted with you, I suppose I'm to blame. I told him you needed a bit of cheering up. Where's the harm in that?"

Her eyes narrowed. So it was true, what Bryce had told her.

She gave her brother another sharp jab with the umbrella. "You set a notorious libertine on my trail," she inquired in disbelief, "and then ask where's the harm? Are you completely witless?"

Troy held out his hands and stepped back from her anger. And her parasol.

"It might interest you to learn," she said acidly, "that the man kept us in this house under completely false pretenses. There was never any risk to Lovelace. Bryce swears the murderer has no interest in her."

"H-how can he possibly make such a claim?" Troy sputtered.

"He knows who the murderer is," she said darkly. "He's known all along."

Troy's brows furrowed. "You believe Bryce is in league with the French? I take leave to doubt it. Why, the man is no more a spy than I am . . . or Kimble or Armbruster, for that matter."

Jemima drew a breath. "He says he is not. And I want to believe him. But I found the poem that was taken off the dead man locked in Bryce's desk. And he would not tell me how it came to be there."

Troy sighed. "I am convinced you are starting at phantoms, Button. And if you have a nice lie-down, and a bit of cordial, I am sure you will come to your senses. What's more, I've promised Carruthers a game of whist tonight, and you know I can't play worth anything, if you aren't there to partner me."

"Whist!" she cried, flinging the parasol across the room, where it bounced against the door, effectively shutting it. "Is that all you can think of? Your own petty pursuits? When I tell you that we have been living with a man who lied to us, who cozened us . . ."

"He hasn't cozened *me*," Troy uttered blithely. "Been the soul of generosity. Gave me my own place to write, after all. And let my friends run tame in his house. I heard he even saw Army off this morning."

At the mention of Armbruster, Jemima felt her temper begin to rise beyond her ability to control it.

"You'd better go now," she said between her teeth. "There's no point in arguing with you."

"Jemima!" Troy implored her. "I refuse to let you leave!"

"And I refuse to discuss it. Now, if you will excuse me, I need to fetch Lovelace."

She tugged her valise off the bed, swept past her brother, and headed for the door.

But Troy knew the value of making a good exit. He rushed to the door and flung it open.

"I will leave you then, Madam Ingrate!" he proclaimed in affronted tones. "I am off to Withershins with *my friends*. The mayor's spaniel bitch has just whelped six prime youngsters, so I won't waste my breath brangling with you, Jemima, when I can be having a jolly time looking at puppies."

He spun out the door and went striding off. Jemima stood fuming for all of ten seconds before she stormed into the hall in his wake and wailed out, "Puppies!" in pure frustration.

Lovelace was drowsing on the drawing room sofa, a novel clasped to her dimity-clad bosom, when Jemima found her. To her credit, the girl at once fell in with the plan. Jemima had no way of knowing that it was the expression of lost hope in her eyes that made Lovelace so amenable, rather than Jemima's insistence that there was no longer any danger and, therefore, no reason to stay on at Bryce Prospect.

"Might I not say good-bye to Mr. Bryce?" Lovelace asked, popping one last bonbon into her mouth.

"He is closeted in his library," Jemima explained. "You can write him a note from the inn, if you like."

Lovelace nodded. She followed Jemima out of the house and down the path to the stables behind the house. She was still using the cane and had to hobble along livelylike to keep up with her companion.

"Isn't your brother coming with us?" Lovelace inquired breathlessly.

"Troy has chosen to stay here, but it's of no matter. I have enough money to hire a carriage at the inn. We'll be back in London by tomorrow night."

"London?" Lovelace said. "But what of my family? How will they find me?"

Jemima laid a hand on her arm. "Tolliver will have my direction. They'll find you, never fear."

Jemima helped Lovelace into the pony cart, politely refusing the head groom's offer to drive them. She didn't take an easy breath until they were on the main road heading for the inn. It was all behind her now. Tomorrow she would be back in London, and then she could have a good, long cry. But not now, she thought, as she wiped a stray tear from her eye. This was neither the time nor the place for regrets.

An hour later, the ladies were sharing tea in a private parlor at the Iron Duke. A very quiet tea. Since Jemima had refused all of Lovelace's conversational gambits, the girl had subsided into a pouting silence.

"Mr. Bryce is in love with you," she remarked when the boredom had quite overcome her.

Jemima looked up from her teacup, which she had been gazing into as if it held the secrets of the universe. "What?"

"I am something of an expert on love," Lovelace continued. "Oh, I don't mean because of all the young gentlemen who have pursued me," she added with uncharacteristic humility. "It's the plays I perform, you see. By Mr. Shakespeare and Mr. Sheridan and even those my own papa has written. I understand what real love is. Do you recall in *Romeo and Juliet*, when Romeo says, 'Ah, that I were a glove upon that hand, that I might touch that cheek.' Mr. Bryce is forever looking at you like he wished he were a glove."

Jemima nearly chuckled. But then she grew annoyed. Who was Lovelace to preach to her about true love? A feather-headed, simpering coquette who hadn't the wit to hold on to her own family.

"I don't wish to discuss Mr. Bryce," she said stiffly.

"Did you two have a row, Lady J? Lover's quarrels are at the heart of most romantical plays. You've only to recall Beatrice and Benedick in *Much Ado About Nothing*—"

"This *isn't* a play, Lovelace," Jemima said crossly as she rose to her feet, setting her cup down with a distinct clink. "And I wish you would not rattle on in such a way—it is giving me the devil of a headache. Can't you find something else to occupy you besides this mindless chatter?"

Lovelace's face fell. She rose, hobbled to the doorway, and then said in a hollow, wavery voice, "Perhaps I should take myself off to the stable. Mrs. Tolliver told me there is an orphan lamb in there."

Jemima nodded without meeting the girl's eyes. She felt as though she were the one who had orphaned the lamb. And skinned it to boot. This was all it required, Jemima thought wretchedly. She'd quarreled with Bryce, alienated her brother, and had now sent Lovelace off nearly in tears. Maybe she should go outside next and kick the stable dog.

Maybe you should kick yourself, Jemima, her conscience taunted. *For leaping to conclusions, for presuming to sit in judgment, and for having so little faith in the man you love.*

She refilled her teacup and sank back on the sofa, again trying to make sense of Bryce's behavior. But as much as she twisted the facts in her head, trying to find some way to exonerate him, she always arrived at the same conclusion—even if he wasn't involved with the spying, Bryce was guilty of protecting the man who had killed the Frenchman. A man who, if her recent nighttime encounter with him was any indication, was hiding somewhere in the nearby vicinity.

But where? Certainly not at the Prospect—even Bryce would have balked at allowing that. It was a pity she knew so little of the surrounding area. There might be abandoned cottages or shepherd's huts where a hunted man could take refuge. There could be remote farm sheds or caverns . . .

She sat up so abruptly that her tea sloshed onto the carpet.

Of course! It all makes sense now—Bryce's cave in the ravine.

She recalled that the remains of the twig fire near the cave's entrance had still smelled pungently of smoke. Bryce had brushed at the charred wood with his boot and blamed it on local farm children. It was clear he hadn't known anyone was using the cave when he'd brought her there. But she also recalled how briskly he'd dismissed her that afternoon with some nonsense about visiting a neighbor. Without a doubt he had gone back to the cave to discover who was sheltering there.

Oh, Lord! She'd have to alert Sir Walter. One of Tolliver's grooms would have to ride to Withershins.

She was hurrying out the parlor door when she ran smack into Mr. Kimble.

He gave a low chuckle and swung her from his path. "Steady on, Lady Jemima."

She nearly hugged him with relief as she blurted out, "Oh, Mr. Kimble, thank goodness you are here. I must get a message to Sir Walter."

He offered her a low bow. "I am completely at your service. But come now, there's no need to alarm the entire inn." He drew her back into the parlor. "Things are already at sixes and sevens at the Prospect. Bryce is acting like a bear—won't let a soul near him. Troy and Carruthers have gone off to Withershins—I know you and Troy have had words, Jemima. And I thought . . . um, that you might need a bit of support. So tell me, what has distressed you so? It's not that murder business again, is it?"

"That's exactly what it is," Jemima stated. "I have some information for Sir Walter."

"Yes?" Kimble stopped fussing with his neckcloth and raised his brows.

"I need to tell him that—" She stopped in midsentence as the gravity of what she was about to do struck her. She might not only be setting the law on the murderer's trail, she could also be imperiling Bryce. Treason in wartime was a serious offense. She had no care for the bearded man, but she couldn't face being the instrument of Bryce's disgrace.

"What is it, Lady Jemima?" Kimble took up one of her hands and drew it comfortingly to his chest.

Lovelace was right, she thought, Kimble was truly a kind soul. "I don't know what to do," she said forthrightly. "I believe I can help to catch this man, but there are others I don't wish to imperil."

Kimble shrugged. "When a man runs with the foxes," he pronounced softly, "he risks being taken by the hounds. Dear lady, surely anyone who is in league with a murderer isn't worth your concern."

"It's not exactly as black or white as that."

"Few things are," he agreed with a gentle smile. "Why not tell me what you suspect, and let me advise you. Oh, I know you think me just another foolish town beau, but I've a sound head in a crisis. I might surprise you."

"Thank you for the offer, Mr. Kimble." She closed her eyes for a moment. "But I would prefer to speak to someone in a . . . legal capacity, in confidence. In case I am mistaken in my suspicions, you see."

Kimble looked a tiny bit miffed. "Surely you trust me, Jemima. We've known each other forever."

"I . . . I . . . Oh, please. Just say you will carry a note to Sir Walter for me."

Kimble shot her a mutinous look, but then he nodded. "As you will."

She went to the writing desk in the corner of the parlor and quickly penned a message to Sir Walter. She wrote of her suspicions about the cave and asked him to meet her at the inn. She sealed it with a wafer and handed it to Kimble. He gave her an encouraging smile, and then went from the room.

After he left, Jemima tried to involve herself in the novel Lovelace had left on her chair. When she found herself rereading the same paragraph for the eighth time, she set the book down. She tried gazing out the window to compose herself, but she was just too agitated to sit and do nothing. Maybe she should fetch Lovelace back from the stable and entice her with a game of cards, by way of apology.

Jemima went in search of her. But she was neither in the stable nor anywhere in the yard. The serving girl, Mary, stood beside the kitchen door, beating carpets with a broom handle.

"Have you seen Miss Wellesley?" Jemima asked.

Mary goggled as she thumped up a cloud of dust. "You mean the purty 'un wif all the gold hair? She's gone orf wif a gentleman on horseback."

Jemima, who'd never been rude to a servant in her life, had an urge to box the girl's ears. "No, Mary," she said with forced patience. "It was days ago when she went off with Mr. Bryce. I meant today, now."

Mary rolled her eyes and stopped thumping. "I tol' yer. She just now rode orf with a gentleman."

"Did he force her to go?" Jemima asked, fearing, in spite of Bryce's assurances to the contrary, that the murderer had come for his reckoning.

Mary considered a moment. "Din't appear so to me."

Jemima relaxed slightly. "Who was he, Mary? Someone from Bryce Prospect?"

The girl scrunched up her face. "Din't see 'im from the front. He had on a blue coat, though."

Well, that limits the candidates to half the male population of Kent, Jemima muttered to herself. Not to mention the bearded man also wore a blue coat. Though even Mary would have been hard put to describe *him* as a gentleman.

She hurried into the inn, calling for Tolliver, who promised to have a horse saddled for her at once. She paced restlessly in the front hall while she waited. There was nothing for it now—she'd have to ride back to the Prospect and enlist Bryce in the search for Lovelace. Because Troy had gone off with Carruthers to see spaniel puppies, and Kimble was doubtless in Withershins by now. Which left Bryce as her only ally. And in her heart she wanted to turn to him. He had never failed her before, and she had no reason to think he would send her away this time. They had quarreled, it was true, but what was a quarrel when Lovelace might be in danger?

There was a second reason she wanted to see him—so she could tell him that she had alerted Sir Walter. It was the only fair thing to do. Bryce had rescued her from Armbruster, and she couldn't just cold-bloodedly betray him to the magistrate without some forewarning. She'd do everything in her power to prevent him from being implicated. Though, knowing how riled Bryce was at present, he'd probably admit his guilt boldly and damn anyone's eyes for judging him.

She recalled the look on his face after he had kissed her so fiercely up against the bookcase. Anger had warred with hunger in those blazing platinum eyes. He had every reason to expect betrayal from her. He had already received the full measure of her scorn and mistrust.

Lord, there was no point in replaying that scene. They had both been guilty of intolerable behavior—she'd been precipitous for assuming he was in league with the spies, and he had been unforgivably highhanded for misleading her about the threat to Lovelace.

Tolliver came into the hall then, to announce that her horse was ready. He grinned and pointed to the register book, which lay open on the reception table beside Jemima. The name "Marlborough" had been scrawled at the top of the right-hand page in a bold, rounded hand.

"Just a prank," he said. "One of my guests must have gotten a bit bosky yesterday and written it. Not a bad notion. It appears we've both a Wellesley *and* a Marlborough staying at our humble inn. Next thing you knew, a Hanover will come bowling up in a gilded coach and request a room." He chuckled dryly.

"If Sir Walter comes here," she said as Tolliver handed her onto the mounting block, "tell him to wait for me."

She quickly guided the horse out of the stableyard, along the lane, and through the gate that led to Bryce's cow pasture. As she crested the hill that edged the pasture, she saw a figure on horseback off to her right. It was Bryce. She couldn't mistake his easy grace or wide shoulders even from that distance.

Her first instinct was to call out to him. Lovelace needed rescuing after all. But when she saw he was riding in a northeast direction, she had a sudden inkling of his destination. She turned her mount and sent if after the lone rider, staying some distance behind him—not difficult with the less-than-spirited horse Tolliver had given her. After following him for several minutes, she watched him ride across a wide field and then disappear in its center. She was smiling smugly as she drew her horse up beside the dead crab apple tree.

It was exactly as she had anticipated. She was finally going to see the bearded man up close.

She quickly tied her horse to the tree and went forward until she came to the edge of the ravine. Bryce's chestnut gelding was grazing in the distance, halfway down the grassy slope of the incline.

Jemima crawled along the rim until she was opposite the cave. Then she crouched down in the tall grass that overhung the lip. Bryce was fifteen feet below her, speaking with the bearded man. It was a wonder they couldn't hear her heart beating, it drummed so loudly in her chest.

"It's impossible," the bearded man was saying. "I'm not the only one at risk. There are fellows in London who are involved in this; they'll be targets too, if this gets out. And I found out only this morning that someone registered at the inn yesterday as Marlborough."

Jemima frowned. That was the name Tolliver had pointed out to her. A prank, he'd said.

"Christ," she heard Bryce mutter. "That's all the more reason for me to tell Jemima the truth, so I can get her to return to the Prospect. Who knows what sort of trouble she'll get into at the inn."

"The fellow ain't at the inn," the man said. "Just signed in and left. He wants me to know he's here, Bryce, but he obviously suspects a trap. So you see, it's still too dangerous to reveal anything. It's even dangerous for you to have come here."

"What? Afraid that I'll scare off Marlborough?" Bryce said.

His companion grunted. "He'll make himself known to me in his own good time, I suspect."

"As for Jemima," Bryce went on, "I believe we can trust her. I feel I've got to trust her."

"What if you're wrong? I've yet to meet a woman who could keep a secret for five minutes."

"She's not like other women," Bryce said. He added softly, "Not at all like other women."

The bearded man cuffed him on the arm. "So you've fallen at last, eh, Beech. I'm surprised the earth didn't tremble when you hit the ground."

"Oh, it trembled, right enough," Bryce responded.

Jemima felt herself blushing. She grit her teeth; she had other fish to fry right now—chiefly, discovering the identity of this unkempt man with whom Bryce clearly shared the secrets of his heart.

"She found the poem I'd locked away," Bryce said. "And is furious with me for keeping the truth from her. Not that I blame her. I fear she won't stop prying until she discovers your identity. She's relentless."

The bearded man chuckled. "Well, then, there's nothing for it, old chap. If she does discover who I am, we'll just have to put her out of the way."

Jemima nearly gasped at his words, and then waited for Bryce to rush to her defense. To her dismay, all he did was shrug. "I wish you luck," he drawled. "She'll not go peacefully, I can promise you that."

Jemima pushed herself away from the edge of the ravine, still simmering at Bryce's callous response. As she drew back, a few pebbles dislodged themselves and went clattering down into the gully.

"Who's there?" a voice hissed up.

Oh, Jehosephat! She winced and closed her eyes as she froze in place, her breath trapped in her lungs.

She heard a slight movement from below her and then all was

quiet again. She waited, unmoving, for the men to resume their conversation. She waited and waited . . . all the while feeling enormous empathy with Lovelace who had endured a similar torture in the wooded grove.

"Good afternoon, Jemima."

She opened one eye. And saw Bryce's top boots. She opened the other eye and twisted her head up to gaze at him. He was observing her with a taut expression of extreme displeasure on his face.

Wonderful, Jemima thought. *The ultimate humiliation—Bryce discovers me belly down in a field.*

"Who is it?" the bearded man shouted up.

"Who do you think?" Bryce called back as he reached down for her. "My own personal bloodhound."

She rolled away from his hand and scrambled up. Then she was off and running, as fast as her long legs would carry her. Bryce cried out for her to stop, but she only increased her speed.

Suddenly, a tall, brawny man sprang up from the grass, directly in her path. She tried to avoid his outstretched hands, but his long arms snagged her. He caught her up and held her against his chest. When she started kicking against his shins, he drew a wide-bladed knife and set it at her throat.

"Belay that!" he growled as he began to drag her back in the direction of the ravine.

She refused to look at Bryce, couldn't bear to see his smug expression. Like an idiot she'd run straight into the arms of his accomplice. But when they finally came up with Bryce, his face was pale and taut.

"Be a good lad and throw down your pistol," the burly man purred, "if you want the lady left alive."

"I am unarmed." Bryce held his arms away from his body as the man quickly patted down his waistcoat and coat pockets with his free hand.

"So you are. Now move." He nodded toward the incline. "I've a hankering to visit yon hermit."

Bryce walked in front of the man, along the edge of the ravine. "Let her go, Tarne," he said softly through his teeth. "She's no part of this. Cosh her if you must, but don't make her a witness to anything—"

"Stow it!" the man snarled. "And keep movin'."

Jemima met Bryce's eyes. "I'm sorry," she rasped.

He gave her a thin-lipped smile before he started down the slope. The man called Tarne tugged her down in Bryce's wake and half carried her along the streambed. There was no one else in the bottom of the ravine.

"Where the hell is Ripley?" Tarne roared directly into her ear. "I know he's been hiding down here."

"He's gone, Tarne," Bryce said calmly. "I rode out here to see him and found the place deserted." His eyes beseeched Jemima not to contradict him.

"How is it that you know my name?" Tarne swung to Bryce. "You in league with Ripley?"

"Yes," he said. "Most assuredly I am in league with him. My name is Bryce."

Tarne looked dubious. "My man in London never mentioned you."

Bryce shrugged. "Perhaps he does not tell you all his secrets." He added matter-of-factly, "I happen to be the owner of Bacchus."

Tarne grinned. "Well, then, you must be a mate of my friend in London. He particlly likes that place."

"And that woman you are about to eviscerate happens to be my current ladybird. I would appreciate it if you'd let her go."

Tarne looked down at Jemima. He shook his head. "She looks a bit long in the tooth for that rig." He tightened his hold and winked at Bryce. "Not that I'd hold that against her, if I was of a mind to sample her wares." He nuzzled her neck and Jemima felt her insides go liquid.

"Ripley's bolted," Bryce said with white-lipped restraint. "But he might have left the papers behind."

"There are no papers." Tarne sneered. "Leastwise not the naval papers my master was after. Bleedin' frog pinched the wrong lot. My master was fairly vexed over that."

"Indeed there are papers," Bryce assured him. "I've seen them myself. Your man, er, Ripley, went back to Hastings's room and took them. It's possible they're still inside the cave."

Tarne nibbled his lip and looked uncertain. Clearly decision-making was not his forte.

"Go on, then." Tarne motioned with his head. "Climb in there and have a look."

"And leave you alone with her? Not bloody likely." Bryce narrowed his eyes. "Get them yourself."

Tarne's response was to pull a wicked-looking horse pistol from his waistband. Jemima was immensely relieved to discover it was merely the butt of that pistol that had been boring into her spine.

Tarne aimed at Bryce and cocked the hammer back meaningfully. "If you don't, you're a dead man."

"If I find the papers, will you leave us, leave her, unharmed?"

"I ain't making no promises."

"So be it." Bryce shrugged. He moved to the rock pile and proceeded to climb toward the opening.

Jemima began to squirm. She'd had enough of Tarne's foul breath and overly familiar hands.

"Jemima, no!" Bryce called across to her. "Jesus, don't fight him!"

"It's more than you're doing!" she shouted back.

Tarne shifted the knife slightly and pushed her chin up. He cocked an eye at Bryce, and then lowered his mouth to Jemima's. She writhed in his hold, wriggled until she got one arm free. Heedless of the weapons he held, she cocked her elbow and jabbed him sharply in the belly. Low in the belly.

With a bellow of pain he thrust her away. She scrambled back and to one side, crouching to grope for a rock to use as a weapon. When she stood up, clutching a large stone, Tarne's pistol was leveled at her head and he was grinning evilly. She flashed a panicked glance to the rock pile and whimpered, "Bryce."

Bryce lurched upright, braced his legs apart, and swiftly raised his arm. A shot rang out, echoing against the ravine's walls. A spray of shale exploded to her right.

Jemima waited . . . for the pain and the rush of blood. And for the blackness to engulf her.

Tarne was weaving, rocking unsteadily from front to back. She watched in amazement as he swayed toward her and then toppled over at her feet. A small crimson stain had blossomed on his temple.

She felt the blackness closing in; Bryce scrambled down from the rock pile in time to break her fall.

"You're not hurt," he crooned as his hands swept over her, reassuring himself that his words were true. "He missed you, sweetheart."

He carried her away from Tarne, to the foot of the rock pile, where he laid her down gently.

"Bring the brandy," he called out as he stroked the hair back from her face. The bearded man climbed out of his hiding place and then knelt beside her, holding a silver flask to her lips.

He grinned at Bryce. "I see what you mean about her being a handful."

"A blasted idiot, more like. I nearly didn't get to the pistol in time. Did you have to bury it so deep?"

"Well, I couldn't very well leave it up there on the rocks, gleaming in the sun."

They were bickering, Jemima realized in a daze. Like siblings did. Like she and Troy did. Bickering fondly, tolerantly. She twisted up and squinted at the bearded man. He had Bryce's nose and Bryce's hair.

"Kip?" she said weakly.

"Aye," he said as he raised one of her hands. "Captain Kipling Bryce, of his Majesty's Royal Navy."

Her gaze shifted to Bryce. "That's why you couldn't tell me. Your brother is the spy."

Bryce looked at his brother, one dark brow raised.

"Oh, tell her," Kip said brusquely. "By the look of things, she's to be part of the family in short order."

Bryce drew a long breath. "Kip's been working for the Admiralty, helping a ring of smugglers bring spies over from France. None of the smugglers know his real identity, and he can't end the charade until he discovers who the ringleader in London is. Someone who is a member of Bacchus, by all indications."

Kip whistled softly. "You're a quick study, Beech. Couldn't have said it better myself."

"And who was that dreadful man?" She motioned weakly in Tarne's direction.

"The leader of the smugglers," Bryce said. "Kip's been waiting here to give him the naval papers."

"But I thought you weren't a real spy?" She craned around to look at Kip.

"I'm not. The papers are fakes. But the French won't know that. Pity Bryce had to kill Tarne, because he was our only link to the ringleader. It's going to play havoc with my report to the Admiralty."

"I'm sorry you had to shoot him, Bryce," she whispered. "I didn't know how else to get away from him. I was going to be sick, you see."

Bryce laid his hand on her brow and drew her head back against his shoulder. "Unlike my brother, I am not at all sorry that Tarne is dead."

"He always was the bloodthirsty Bryce," Kip remarked.

Bryce was helping Jemima to her feet when they heard a faint noise from the end of the ravine. A slim, sandy-haired man was walking along the streambed, picking his way delicately among the stones, his eyes on the ground. Kip quickly scrambled up the rock pile and again slid into the cave.

"It's Kimble," Bryce growled softly over his shoulder. "Don't tell me *he* knows about this. It's bad enough Father and Mac-Cready knew. Was I the only one left in the dark, Kip?"

"Of course he doesn't know," his brother hissed back.

"Then what the devil is he doing here?"

Jemima swallowed. "I told him about the cave," she said bleakly. "Yesterday before dinner."

Bryce looked away from her in mute frustration.

"Mr. Kimble," Jemima called out. He looked up but made no sign of acknowledgement. "I am so relieved that you have not yet gone to Sir Walter's. Because I was wrong about the murderer—"

Bryce squeezed her arm in warning. "Keep quiet, Jem. Till I know what he wants, we need to go cautiously. I tossed my only pistol down to Kip when Tarne appeared, so I am unarmed."

When Kimble reached the spot where Tarne's body lay, he nudged it with his toe. "Dead?" he asked with an expression of distaste. "Pity."

"We have reason to believe he was the spy," Jemima proclaimed, in spite of Bryce's edict.

Kimble raised his eyes to her, and she swore the hair at her nape stood straight up on end. His gaze was as icy and remote as an arctic glacier. The pleasant young man with the genial air had vanished.

As she watched in disbelief, he pulled a dueling pistol from his waistcoat. He came right up to them, smiling serenely.

"Lady Jemima, I didn't think to find you here." He gave Bryce an exaggerated wink. "Pleasant spot for an assignation, eh, Bryce? Private and remote. Well, except for the occasional smuggler." He nodded over his shoulder to where Tarne lay facedown. "Too bad you had to shoot him."

"He displeased me," Bryce said softly as he shifted Jemima behind him, keeping one hand on her arm.

A fierce, focused energy seemed to emanate from him; it disturbed her by its intensity and reassured her with its intent. Bryce had called himself a dangerous man, and she now believed it. Not just because he was a crack shot or a devil in a duel, but because his nerves were of honed steel. There was not the slightest particle of deference or uncertainty in his manner as he regarded Kimble.

Kimble frowned slightly. "Yes, well, he pleased me. And since I've got the pistol, my opinion is the one that counts." He smiled then. "Actually, I've come here to find your bearded friend, Bryce . . . the one I saw scrambling into the cave." His voice rose. "You can come out now, Ripley. Unarmed, if you please."

Kip's head appeared at the dark opening to the cavern. "I could shoot you where you stand."

Kimble shrugged and called out, "Army!" He pointed with is free hand to the top of the ravine. Harold Armbruster knelt there, holding a shotgun trained on Bryce.

Jemima's hands clutched at Bryce's coat. His hand slid to her wrist and tightened. "Steady, Jem."

She leaned her face against his back, whispering, "Bryce, I'm so sorry. I've muddled things so badly."

"No secrets," Kimble interrupted with a tiny moue. "Not that any of you were exactly clever at keeping secrets. I learned from Miss Wellesley that a tall bearded chap—obviously Tarne's man, Ripley—killed my Frenchman, and that the blasted Frenchman had not stolen the naval papers, but rather one of Troy's tedious poems. And, Lady Jemima, you had such an informative talk with your brother—with the bedroom door ajar. About Bryce having the stolen poem. And then you were so eager to give me the note for Sir Walter, which described the exact location of this cave—"

"You read my note!" she fumed. Her outrage overrode the fear she ought to be feeling.

He nodded. "I'd gone to see you at the Iron Duke, because I was afraid you'd go haring off to Sir Walter with the information that Bryce had mysteriously acquired the poem. Couldn't have a magistrate nosing about in my business, now, could I? Happily you let me be your emissary. After that everything fell into place. I rode to the Bosun's Mate to fetch Tarne and Armbruster, then we came here to dispatch Ripley. I sent Tarne in alone—we didn't want Ripley to get the wind up until Tarne had him at gunpoint—but none of us was counting on Bryce being here. That turned out to be something of a nuisance."

Bryce bowed his head toward Kimble and drawled, "It was my pleasure. I gather you signed in as 'Marlborough' at the inn before you came to the Prospect yesterday."

"Mmm. I'd never have revealed myself, but I didn't suspect it was a trap until later." He turned his head and his voice rose impatiently. "Ripley . . . Now! I have a small score to settle with you."

Kip heaved himself onto the rocks and skittered down to the streambed. He made his way slowly toward Kimble, holding his hands away from his sides, palms up. He stopped several feet in front of Bryce and Jemima. Kimble glowered at him.

And then he saw the man behind the beard and the tattered clothing and he blanched.

"Going to shoot me, James?" Kip challenged him. "Your best friend . . . the friend who bailed you out of a hundred scrapes at Cambridge?"

"Ch-christ, you're supposed to be dead," Kimble stuttered. He shook himself. "How the devil did you get mixed up in this?"

"That's what I should be asking you," Kip snarled. "Why did you turn your back on your country, Jamie? Was it for the gold? Or the sense of power? You always were under your father's thumb."

"It doesn't matter," Kimble said, visibly pulling himself together. "What matters now is that I can repay you for the trouble you have caused me." He called up to Armbruster without taking his eyes off Kip. "Come down now. We need to end this farce."

"Armbruster was at Bacchus the night Perret went there," Kip said musingly. "He was acting as your go-between. That was cleverly done, Jamie. Put me right off the scent."

"They'll eventually connect Armbruster to you, Kimble," Bryce added. "Hastings knows he was at Bacchus that night. It's only a matter of time before he makes the connection."

"I'll be living in France by then. Living very nicely. And I'm afraid Army isn't going to survive to tell any tales. Tarne would have ended up the same way—if you, Bryce, hadn't done my work for me."

Jemima ventured, "You could go to France now, Mr. Kimble. No one would stop you."

He offered her his most genial, reassuring smile. "Sweet Lady Jemima. Do you know the only reason I tolerated Troy was because of you. Though his visit to Bryce Prospect did furnish me with an excellent excuse for coming down here and discovering what had happened to my Frenchman. Still, Troy is so tiresome . . . but you were always such a bright light."

She was beginning to beam at him in spite of herself, when he added, "It's a pity I've got to kill you."

Her hands clenched tight on Bryce's arm.

"Not today, laddie!" a merry voice rang down from the edge of the ravine.

Kimble's head jerked up. Mr. Fletch stood above him holding a small pistol, which seemed a negligible threat. The blunderbuss MacCready was holding, however, was a deal more intimidating.

"Now if you will just drop your pistol, I'll keep this fellow from blowing a nice, wide hole in you."

"Army!" Kimble cried out in a strident voice. "Army!"

Mr. Fletch chuckled. "Aye, you can call for the army, the navy, and the blasted bluestocking league. It won't do you any good."

The Runner prodded Armbruster to the edge of the gulley; he had been trussed up like a prize capon.

Kimble put up his chin and flung his gun far behind him. "You've no proof of anything," he said calmly to Kip. "I'll say I found you here and, believing you to be the spy, thought it best to hold you at gunpoint."

"Is everything in order, Mr. Bryce?" the Runner called out. "We're coming down now to take that scoundrel off your hands."

Bryce nodded up to Mr. Fletch. The two men disappeared from his sight. When Bryce looked back at Kimble, he was holding a small pistol aimed at Kip's chest.

Kip took a cautious step backward, so that he stood directly in front of his brother.

"No," Bryce muttered.

"Only just got him back, eh, Bryce?" Kimble purred. "Would be a shame to lose him again so soon."

Bryce took a deep breath and held Kimble's gaze. He forced himself not to let his eyes wander to Kip's back, to where his second best dueling pistol was tucked beneath the hem of the short blue jacket.

"If I'm to lose everything," Kimble added with a slow grin, "I'll make damned certain I exact a price."

Bryce saw the murderous intent glittering in his eyes. It chilled him to the bone. Kimble was done for and he knew it. He was bound for the gallows and had nothing to lose by killing Kip.

Kimble raised his arm and the sun glinted off the pistol barrel.

"Take me!" Jemima cried sharply, darting out from behind Bryce.

Kimble's gaze swung to her; his concentration wavered for an instant. In one fluid motion, Bryce plucked the pistol from under Kip's jacket and fired over his brother's shoulder.

Kimble's mouth slewed open in surprise. His hand moved jerkily to his right arm, to where the bright blood was already staining his coat. He stared at it in bewilderment, and then sank to his knees.

"Demme," he murmured faintly as his pistol clattered to the ground.

Bryce spun to Jemima and tugged her toward the end of the ravine, where Mr. Fletch and MacCready, alarmed by the sound of gunfire, were approaching them at a run.

"I'm not going to faint again," she told him shakily, clutching at his lapels as the men pelted past them to where Kimble lay.

"That was the most damnably foolish thing you've done to date," he growled as he shook her.

"I couldn't think of what else to do," she said. Her teeth were chattering so uncontrollably she could barely speak. "I saw Kip's gun . . . I knew you'd use it . . . I . . . I couldn't bear it if he shot your brother."

"Jemima!" he cried, shaking her even harder. Then his voice broke. *"Oh, Jemima."*

The next instant he dragged her against his chest, holding her tight in his arms. She started to cry then, clinging to him as she sobbed out endless apologies.

"I sh-should never have d-doubted," she stuttered into his neck-cloth. "How could I think such things of you? . . . That you were a traitor . . . a murderer's accomplice . . . I'm sorry I sent for Sir Walter . . . I was coming to warn you . . . Can you forgive me for not believing in you?"

He coaxed her head up. "You believed in me when it counted, sweetheart."

"And I saw the painting . . . the Canaletto . . . in your room . . ." Jemima was unaware that his hands had tightened on her upper arms; she merely gave him a weak grin. "I thought you were forging paintings, and somehow that seemed the worst crime of all. Oh, I don't know how I could have been so foolish."

Bryce shifted her to MacCready and went to his brother. Kip was kneeling beside Kimble, trying to staunch the flow of blood with the man's neckcloth.

"I left this one alive for you," Bryce said sourly. "I hope you're properly grateful."

Kip nodded. "The Admiralty will be grateful, at any rate. You might even end up with a knighthood."

"Spare me," Bryce muttered. He looked across to Mr. Fletch. "Sir, I believe I am in your debt."

The Runner smiled. "All in a day's work, Mr. Bryce."

"Well, I'd like to know how he got here," Kip complained. "He's not one of Hastings's men."

"This is Lawrence Fletcher, from Bow Street," Bryce said. "Since I was unable to keep an eye on you myself, I enlisted him this morning to do the job. And not a moment too soon."

"Mr. MacCready and I have been watching your cave from the ridge of cedars. Lord love us," Mr. Fletch observed, "we could have held a cotillion in this field, for all the people who were milling around in it this afternoon. We spotted Tarne easy enough, but by the time we got down off the ridge, he was already dead. We managed to surprise Armbruster after Kimble had gone into the ravine. And thanks to Mr. Bryce's skill with a pistol, Kimble won't be troubling us any longer either."

"I thought you said you didn't have much faith in him," Kip whispered audibly to Bryce.

Mr. Fletch's bright eyes gleamed. "Mr. Bryce realized it never pays to underestimate the Runners. Indeed, it never does."

After Mr. Fletch and MacCready had ridden off with their prisoners, Kip fetched his horse from the thicket where it had been tethered. The three rode back to the Prospect in subdued silence, Bryce and Kip on either side of Jemima. They dismounted in the stable yard, and Kip went in through the kitchen door. Mrs. Patch gave a strangled shriek when she saw him and collapsed in a boneless mass before the hearth.

Jemima's wisdom prevailed then. She insisted Bryce call the staff together in the library, to explain to them that his brother was alive. She knew the elderly Griggs would not have survived the shock of seeing Master Kip returned from the grave. After the servants had been apprised of Kip's return and shared a celebratory toast, they dispersed back to their tasks, leaving her alone with the two brothers.

Bryce moved to stand before Kip and gave him a long look from beneath hooded eyes.

"Well, you're back home now, boy. And London is calling me. I'm sure you can handle things from here on. I've got some business to attend to before I leave, so I'll make my farewells." He turned and offered Jemima a brief, tight smile. "It's been a pleasure knowing you, Lady Jemima. Give my regards to your brother." He bowed and went striding out of the room.

Jemima's mouth was still opened in shock when she turned to Kip.

He appeared less perplexed. "He'll come around, Lady Jemima. Beech is always edgy after a fight. You'd never know it to look at him, but he hates this killing business. Wanted to be a parson, you know."

Kip poured them each a drink and then raised his glass to Tusker. "It's so good to be home," he said with a smile that was an eerie replica of Bryce's.

"Yes," she said numbly. "Home."

I can't wait to be back in my own home, she thought wistfully.

Though it would not be her home for long. She had every intention of doing what she'd told Troy; of finding a way to lead her own life. And when Bryce came to her—she amended quickly—*if* Bryce came to her, she would examine her feelings for him at that time. For now, she was too bone-weary and too emotionally exhausted to prod at the wound he had inflicted when he'd offered her such a terse farewell.

She was about to take her leave of Kip, when Troy and Carruthers came bursting into the room.

"Jemima, thank God! I've ridden to Jericho and back looking for you, and you've been sitting here the whole time, having a nice pleasant cose with Bryce." He stopped and peered at Kip. "Oh . . . er, you're not Bryce. Oh, I say, you're not the murderer by any chance?"

Kip rose and bowed. "Kipling Bryce, at your service. And you must be the celebrated Lord Troy. And Carruthers, I believe." He bowed again. "Yes, I'm afraid I am the murderer."

"Well, that's a relief," Troy pronounced inexplicably. "Lovelace can go back to London now without fearing for her life."

"Lovelace!" Jemima cried. "Oh, Lord! I'd completely forgotten about her. She went riding off with a strange gentleman, Terry. And I have no idea—"

"That's what I've come to tell you," Troy said. "Sir Walter's son rode here earlier today to find her and the butler told him she was at the Iron Duke."

"And he ran off with her?" she moaned.

"No," Troy crowed, "he brought her to his father's house. Her family turned up there, you see. They thought the magistrate might be able to help them locate her. They're on their way here now."

There was a commotion in the front hall. The library's occupants spilled out into the foyer in time to see Lovelace come tripping over the threshold, holding the hand of a younger male version of herself.

"See, Charlie," she was saying. "Isn't it the most wonderful house." She caught sight of Jemima. "Lady J!" she trilled. "They found me! Oh, you must come out and meet my dear mama and my dearest papa."

Lovelace drew her out the door—quite oblivious of the tall, bearded man behind Jemima—and with one sweeping motion of her hand indicated the traveling coach and the garishly painted prop wagon that were drawn up in the drive. "Lady Jemima, may I present Wellesley's Wandering Minstrels."

The four adults beside the coach all bowed theatrically.

Troy put an arm around Jemima's waist. "Well, Jem, everything's fallen neatly into place. Lovelace can go off and conquer London, Kip has returned to Bryce Prospect, and we can get back to our own home."

She nodded wearily. It was going to be some time before Troy understood her need to get away from him. She wasn't going to tax him with it now. He'd have enough on his plate with the loss of his two friends.

"There's only one thing I don't understand," he added. "Where the devil has Bryce gotten to?"

Where indeed? Jemima echoed silently.

Bryce sat unmoving on Rufus in the woods that edged the lawn and watched the cavalcade roll up to his front door. A group of people emerged from the coach and another group came out of the house. They mingled on the porch steps. Lovelace was there and a youngster who had to be her brother. The two more imposing adults he assumed were her parents. Troy and Carruthers were there. And Kip. And of course, Jemima. It was the last time he'd see her. The last time he'd allow himself to even go near her.

He suspected how much he'd hurt her just now. But he also knew that a clean wound healed more quickly than a jagged one. And so he'd taken his leave of her abruptly, and with every expectation that her recovery would be swift. It was true she had most eagerly come to his arms, but he accounted that behavior to be an aberration—the result of her naturally passionate nature fanned into desire by his skillful manipulations. Once she was no longer in his company, Jemima's good sense would prevail and she would doubtless look back on their encounters with a shudder of dismay.

She wouldn't lament the loss of a dear confidante, a clever and delightful companion, as he would. She wouldn't burn for a thousand nights to come, as he surely would, with the mindless need to lose himself inside her.

Any notions he'd harbored that she possessed tender feelings for him had been laid brutally to rest in the library. The expression of near revulsion on her face when he'd declared himself to her had been all the proof he needed of his wretched folly. It had been madness to believe he could have any future with her. She'd never trust him again, for one thing. Not after all his convenient lies. It was true she had turned to him in the ravine, seeking the comfort of his arms. But she had been overwrought. Once she was rational again, she would recall how he had forced himself on her in the library, and her heart would be closed to him forever.

And even if she retained some small charity toward him, there was another impediment—she'd seen the painting in his bedroom. Pray God she never discovered how low he had sunk—bartering his art for a foolish, gullible man's gold—or she would feel nothing for him but disgust.

No, they would both be best served by ending things now. He had been reminded again that afternoon of how dangerous it was to care deeply for a person. He felt anew the pain that shredded your soul when love turned to loss. He'd lost enough people in his life—his mother, and beloved grandfather. Kip, for a time. and he'd lost his father, though not to death. He'd lost his respect and his regard. It still hurt, but it was an old pain. His love for Jemima and his ruthless determination to give her up had replaced that ache in his heart.

He'd sworn three years earlier, at Lady Anne's bedside, that no one would ever render him defenseless again. But Jemima had done just that. Nothing had ever frightened him like the sight of her in the hands of that cutthroat, Tarne. Or the vision of Kimble's pistol barrel swinging toward her. Both times he had been momentarily powerless to think or act. And that was an intolerable state. When he'd told Jemima he wanted to marry her, he still had no idea how much she meant to him. It was only when he'd seen death hovering close around her, that he realized the full measure of his love. It was crippling to be that connected to another person. Christ, it was nearly paralyzing.

It wasn't wrong to retreat, he assured himself as he watched her from his hiding place, when your emotions were so very tangled.

When Jemima at last disappeared through the front door with her brother's arm about her waist, Bryce whispered a hoarse "Good-bye" and turned Rufus in the direction of MacCready's cottage.

Chapter Thirteen

The London debut of *The Rake's Reform* was a resounding success. Troy had written an endpiece for Lovelace, and when she tripped up to the footlights and recited it, in a breathless voice that carried up to the highest tiers, there was not a dry eye in the house.

"Love tarnishes without the cloth of care, and bright regard is vapor in the air,

"Without the breath of constancy in reach, it withers like the last forgotten peach.

"Faith grows not in an altitude of scorn, and passion dies before it can be born,

"If doubting clouds the soul and fogs the brain, then love forever hidden will remain."

Jemima added her applause to the crescendo that rose from the pit and from the boxes. Troy merely sat back and said smugly, "See, I knew she could to it. My little Lovelace."

She shifted in her seat. "You're not forming a *tendre*, are you, Terry? The two of you have been living in each other's pockets these past weeks."

He shook his head. "I just needed a distraction. I've lost two of my friends, after all. And you know how I feel about Lovelace . . . she's . . . like a sister to me. Like you used to be, before you stopped hanging on my every word. Not that I mind the change."

And there had been a change, Jemima reflected. A remarkable change.

It had begun on the carriage ride back from Kent. Troy had drawn up his horses at one point and turned to her with a troubled expression on his face. "There's something I need to ask you, Jem. Bryce left a note in my room before he disappeared yesterday. He said I should ask you about our journey to Scotland. It made no sense to me, but I don't think he would have bothered to write it, if it wasn't important."

Jemima clasped her hands in her lap and wondered why Bryce

had done such a thing. But then the answer became clear. She couldn't have an equitable relationship with Troy until there was truth between them. Bryce knew that—his own brother had kept him in the dark, and she could imagine how that must have pained him. She had spent her life concealing her own spirit from Troy. Hiding her light, Bryce had called it. She would never break free of Troy's shadow as long as she avoided telling him what was in her heart. Her passions, her aspirations, *and* her fears.

So she told him of Armbruster's assault in the dark country house. When she was done, he laid one hand on her sleeve. "Ah, no, Button. No."

"Yes," she said simply. "I'm sorry I never told you."

He lowered his head. "I've failed you, haven't I? I see it now. Too busy playing the poet to notice what was going on around me."

Jemima had to resist the urge to comfort him; it was a lifelong habit. But she knew she was the one who needed consoling. She only wondered if her brother would ever be selfless enough to notice.

"And Bryce?" he said after a long silence. "Did he also try to force himself on you? Is that why he needed to leave me the note—was he prompted by a guilty conscience?"

She gave a tiny shrug. "He was very attentive at times. But I doubt I was ever at risk." That much was true. It was she who had encouraged him, out of curiosity, and need, and budding desire.

"I may not be getting points for observation right now, Jem, but I could have sworn you liked Bryce."

"Oh, I liked him very much," she said in a trembling voice. And then the tears came, streaming down her cheeks, unchecked and barely noticed. The pain in her heart was all she was aware of, the wrenching, twisting, knife-sharp pain.

Troy dropped his reins and enfolded her in his arms. "I'll tear out his black heart," he whispered fiercely, "if he's made you fall in love with him and then spurned you."

"He said he wanted to marry me," she wailed into his collar.

Troy held her away from him. "But then what's amiss? I certainly won't throw a rub in your way. The man's got an unsavory past, but then they do say rakes make the best husbands."

"He went away, Terry. Left me without a word of hope. I doubt we will ever meet again."

Troy kept his own counsel on the matter and promised Jemima

that he would be the best, most caring brother in the whole blasted universe.

So she and Troy made their peace, and so far it seemed to be an enduring one. He had hired a young man as his secretary, to look after his creative requirements—and to keep him in licorice and pen points. He had given Jemima one of the spare bedrooms in their house to use as an art studio. And he was careful not to intrude there unless expressly invited.

She was glad he had thrown himself into helping the Minstrels with their play. After the truth about Kimble and Armbruster came to light, Troy hadn't wanted to go to any of his clubs or visit his usual haunts. She suspected he felt some complicity in their nefarious deeds, if only for being so obtuse. Lovelace was a harmless diversion, as long as he wasn't about to throw his heart over the windmill. She knew the girl thought of her brother only as an amusing companion, and the last thing the Vale household needed was two brokenhearted lovers creeping through its halls.

Not that she was prone to creeping, she amended, but she was certainly brokenhearted. It was three weeks since she had left the Prospect and there had been no word from Bryce in all that time. Kip had written to tell her the aftermath of the spy business. He'd also informed her that he'd sold out his commission and was taking over the estate, at least until he could convince his father that he didn't want the place. He never once mentioned Bryce in his letter. It was a notable omission.

Jemima had kept her feelings for him at bay—until the week before, when she had read the final draft of Troy's endpiece. She had burst into tears and stood weeping uncontrollably until Troy had taken her into his arms and soothed her. He really was a very understanding brother these days.

Once the players had taken their curtain calls, she and Troy drifted down the crowded staircase. There was to be a celebration in the theater's reception room, and Lovelace had insisted they join the Minstrels in raising a glass. As they neared the foyer, which was lit on both ends by branches of candles held aloft by towering statues of scantily clad muses, the crowd parted slightly.

Beecham Bryce was standing in the gap. There was a woman on his arm, exactly the sort of woman Jemima expected to see there— petite and rounded, with a mass of ebony curls and a clinging gown that gave the torch-bearing muses a run for their money. She tried to look away, thought of slipping back up the stairs until he was gone, but the crowd behind her was unrelenting. They formed a wall of humanity, all of them with the single-minded intention of moving down to the foyer.

Troy hadn't seen Bryce, and he continued speaking to her as though the world hadn't turned upside down.

And then Bryce turned his head and saw her. She nearly stumbled. And she surely blushed. Her only consolation was that she was wearing a dazzling new gown, a pale green sweep of silk that shimmered with spangles. But he wasn't looking at her gown, he was looking directly into her eyes.

Like an arrow, that gaze pierced her.

Troy tugged on her hand when he realized she had stopped moving. He saw where she was looking and muttered, "Damn!" under his breath. Then the crowd shifted and Bryce was lost from her sight.

"Button?" Troy touched her cheek.

"I'm fine," she said, drawing in a deep breath. "I just hadn't expected to see him here."

"I feared he might come," he said. "Lovelace invited him, you see. But I didn't expect to see the Stanhope woman. She and Bryce are ancient history according to the betting book at White's. The odds favor Lord Henley to be her next—" Troy's voice drifted off. "Sorry, Jem. I'm so used to talking to you about everything . . . I forgot you probably don't want to hear about Tatiana Stanhope."

She made a valiant attempt at a smile. "It doesn't matter. He doesn't matter."

They went backstage, and Jemima did her best to enjoy Lovelace's success. but she kept a wary eye on the door to the reception room, fearing that Bryce's invitation to the play might have also included a summons to the celebration. But he never appeared, and when Troy's carriage was at last brought around, she felt greatly relieved. She dozed restlessly on the short drive back to their townhouse, until Troy roused her gently and coaxed her up the front steps.

Troy didn't notice the caped figure standing across the street, hidden in the shadows of a wide oak. He was intent on getting Jemima to bed and fetching her a glass of hot milk, as she used to do for him when he was ill. His nurturing skills needed a deal of honing, but he reckoned he wasn't doing badly for a novice. And after all, Jemima had furnished him with an excellent example.

Bryce watched Troy assist his sister into the house with a curious pain in his chest. *I should be the one she leans upon*, he muttered to himself. As glad as he was to see that Troy had finally developed some proper fraternal feelings, Bryce would have usurped his role in an instant.

Why had he risked going to the play, knowing the pain he would feel seeing her face-to-face? God, she had looked so bewitching, there on the theater steps. The green gown had trembled with light, and her eyes, the eyes that haunted him in his sleep, had slashed through his cloak of pretense—his air of studied unconcern had dissolved beneath that bright, unwavering gaze. He would have gone to her, like a man under a spell, if Tatiana hadn't pinched him on the arm and asked peevishly where he was taking her for supper. He'd taken her all right, straight back to her rooms on Half Moon Street. And left her there.

Had he really been thinking of rekindling that affair? Did he imagine the cold, practiced skills of a courtesan could remove Jemima's heated imprint from his soul?

You have to stop doing this, he growled to himself.

He had to stop seeking Jemima out in secret. He had thought he could give her up, but it was hell living in the same city with her, breathing the same air, traveling the same streets. Every night he found himself on the pavement across from Troy's house, waiting for Jemima to return from her evening's entertainments. And every night he told himself it would be the last time.

But in a week it wouldn't matter. He'd be away from England, and the temptation to seek her out would be gone. Though his feelings for her wouldn't be; he doubted they would ever diminish. He was a proper fool, all right, caught for all eternity in the unrelenting grip of the one emotion he'd spent his lifetime avoiding.

As he turned away from Jemima's house, he recalled the last line of Lovelace's speech. *When doubting clouds the soul and fogs the brain, then love forever hidden will remain.* Showed how little Troy knew about the matter. As clouded by doubt as he was, Bryce knew the love he felt was hidden only from Jemima. He couldn't hide it from himself . . . not when it coursed through him with every breath.

But then as he walked on through the quiet streets toward his own house, he rethought the lines. If love was hidden from the person who had your heart, then it might as well not exist. Maybe that's what Troy meant. And in that case he was more astute than Bryce ever realized.

"Damned, perishing poet," he muttered into the night.

Chapter Fourteen

Bryce stepped back from the painting. It needed a bit more carmine in the woman's face. Devil take it if those Dutch didn't love their apple-cheeked women. For himself, he preferred them with magnolia skin . . . and azure eyes . . . and a mouth of lush, blushing rose.

"Ahem."

Bryce turned. Liston, his butler, was standing in the doorway of the studio bearing a silver tray. "A young lady wishes to see you, sir. She sent up her card."

Bryce plucked up the card in his paint-smudged fingers. And then placed it gently down on the salver. "No."

When the butler did not move, he leveled a basilisk glare at him and repeated the word. *"No."*

"But, sir . . ." the man protested. "If I may say . . . you've not been yourself since you returned from Kent. I think . . . that is, we downstairs all think . . . er, knowing from your valet what occurred there, that perhaps you should—"

Bryce's jaw tensed and his fingers clenched on the paintbrush. "I don't care what you think. I need to finish this painting today. Or His Highness will have a royal conniption and refuse to pay me. Now, if I don't get paid, Liston, you don't get paid. So tender my regrets . . . oh, and best lock the door behind her."

The butler nodded in a crestfallen manner and went out of the room. Bryce had to restrain himself from going to the window to watch as his visitor exited the town house.

He was screwing the lid back on the small jar of carmine paint, when he heard the breathless gasp behind him. He shut his eyes and prayed there was something wrong with his hearing.

"Oh, Bryce . . ." she crooned. "I never thought . . . I couldn't even imagine . . ."

He turned, saw her standing in the doorway, awestruck as she gazed around his studio. In her walking dress of palest orange striped with vertical bands of sea green, he thought she looked as completely edible as a marzipan peach. And just as bad for his digestion.

"No, Jemima!" he cried, trying to block her entry into this most sanctified room in his home. But she managed to elude his outstretched hands and went directly to the Frans Hals on the easel.

"It's remarkable," she said. "Look how you've captured the gleam in her eye. Oh, and look at this—" She had flitted over to a Titian Madonna which sat on a tarpaulin and crouched down before it.

"How in blazes did you get in here?" he said, his hands fisted at his side.

That she had come here to accost him and had been instantly distracted by his paintings was gratifying to his artistic pride, but it somehow tweaked his male vanity. He wanted to pick her up bodily and toss her into the hall. Better yet, throw her out the window. It was three flights to the street—that should slow her down a bit. But he dared not touch her. That would spell the beginning of his downfall.

"I bribed your butler," she said simply, looking up over her shoulder. Her gaze shifted back to the Titian. "How did you get her gown to be so very blue and so very green at the same time?"

I made it the color of your eyes, he wanted to answer. Instead he turned away from her and drew a drape over the portrait of the merry Dutch lady.

"I'm not going to even acknowledge that you're here," he said, refusing to look at her. "Though I doubt the *ton* will be so obliging. But if you choose to become a byword, who am I to . . ."

She was moving again. Before he could stop her, she went to the wooden rack at the rear of the studio and began to slide a painting from its storage slot. He strode over to the rack and grappled with her, trying to pry the unframed canvas from her hands. His fingers touched her skin and he drew back as if he'd been burned.

She traced her hands above the painting, which showed two children huddled in the shadows of a dark alley. In spite of the decay and detritus around them, their expressions were as hopeful and as poignantly wise as that of the Titian Madonna on the tarp.

"How?" she cried softly, grasping the painting between her hands. "How could you paint this?"

Bryce shrugged. "I am drawn to low things. I thought you knew that."

"No," she said. "I meant how did you capture them, their spirit and their pain?"

She drew several more paintings from the rack—a lone harlot in a blue-lit avenue, her scarlet lips a stark contrast to the pale, consumptive cast of her skeletal face . . . a group of men idling in a grog shop doorway, their clothing tattered and their eyes glazed with gin, each of them regarding the other with companionable affection. More children, some with their careworn mothers . . . more whores with the weight of shame and the cocky pride of endurance in their faces.

When Jemima rose to her feet, her eyes were bright with unshed tears, and when she turned that gaze on him, Bryce thought that perhaps he should throw *himself* from the window.

"Studio tour's over, Jemima," he said brusquely, still trying to rally from the blow of seeing her again. "I won't ask for the ten bob I usually charge nosy females."

"I knew about those paintings," she said, sketching a motion toward the covered easel. "Prinny was in his cups last night and started bragging to Troy. He told him he'd found the best artist in Christendom to copy paintings for him. He said he sends you off to the homes of those in the *ton* who won't part with their masterpieces, and that you make studies in watercolor and complete them back here in London."

"Like any good forger," he said, still not letting himself look at her. Her scent, however, a delicate blend of tuberose and gardenia, had managed to reach him in spite of the more pungent studio odors.

"No," she countered. "This isn't forgery . . . not when you're selling your work to the Prince Regent. I would call you a copyist," she added primly, "for lack of a more illustrious name."

He scowled broadly. "And so now that you know I'm not engaged in any criminal activity, but rather in mere commerce, I gather you've come to tender your apologies for again misjudging me."

"Devil take you, Bryce!" she cried. "You sound like . . . like what I imagine your father sounded like when he was reading you and Kip a lecture. Oh, don't you see . . . I wouldn't care if you were forging masterpieces. I'd have honed my painting skills, just so that I could work with you . . . be with you."

Her voice drifted to a reverent whisper as she knelt beside the painting of the street Arabs. "But even if I studied for a thousand years, I would never be able to paint like this. It's such a gift,

Bryce. And it's a crime to keep them hidden away here." She tipped her head up. "I know people who could sponsor you, the directors of the Royal Academy . . ."

That's it, he thought, *the very last straw*. She thought he'd allow her to pander for him.

He walked to the door, pointed to the hall with an imperious finger, and uttered, "I don't need a patroness, Lady Jemima. And as you've so often pointed out to me, I already have a muse. Now, if you would kindly take yourself away from here, I need to get back to work."

She sighed as she rose to her feet and walked up to him. "You're going away," she said. "Prinny was complaining to Troy about it. And I saw your trunks in the downstairs hall."

"Yes," he said, keeping his eyes trained on the doorpost opposite him.

"To Barbados? To your father?"

"I can't imagine that my destination is of any concern to you." He stopped himself in midsneer. "But, yes, that is where I'm going."

She clutched her reticule so tightly that the tendons in both hands stood out in relief beneath her lace mitts. "Let me come with you," she said in a barely audible whisper.

Bryce's eyes showed a brief flicker of brightness but then clouded over instantly. He hitched his shoulders. "I can't stop you if you want to go haring across the ocean. What, does Troy fancy a sojourn in the tropics?"

"I don't want to go with Troy," she said crossly. "He's turned into a monster, for one thing."

"A monster?" he echoed. "How is this? I've seen how he looks after you now, how he caters to you."

"Have you?" she mused. "I wonder how you've seen those things. But I blame you that he's become like this. You left him that note, you see. And now he is riddled with guilt and barely leaves me alone for an instant. I can't so much as return a book to the subscription library without him dancing attendance on me. He coddles me unmercifully—a pillow for my head, a footstool for my feet. It's toddies and warm milk and nourishing broths. I feel like an invalid, Bryce. This is not the way I want to live my life . . . I am not a hothouse blossom. But he is determined to make things up to me, and it's all your fault."

Bryce nearly grinned. *Poor Jem.* Troy had switched his single-minded obsession from pursuing idle entertainment to ruthlessly ensuring the well-being of his sister.

"Hmm? First he was too neglectful and now he is too attentive. I perceive that you are a difficult woman to please, Jemima."

"I'm not difficult," she cried in frustration. "You of all people know how easy I am to please."

He steeled himself and looked down at her. Once his heart had stopped flailing in his chest, he said, "I can't say that I ever really gave it much thought."

She hung her head in defeat; the bright spirit had been siphoned right out of her in the space of an instant.

I can't do this much longer, he reflected grimly. *Every time I strike at her, another gaping wound tears open inside me.*

He stepped back into the room, to allow her to pass into the hall. But she just stood there. He watched her shoulders quiver and damned himself thrice over for his own bloody pigheadedness.

"I realize now," she said in a ragged voice, "that I never once told you how I felt about you. I made you believe I was girded against your flattery and immune to your charm. Even when I lay in your arms, I never let down my guard. And so I can't blame you if you are callous to me, or even cruel. You think your words cannot pierce my maidenly armor." She paused. "But they can . . . they do."

"You'd better go, Jemima," he said quietly. "There is no profit in baring your soul to me."

She turned her head even farther away from him and rubbed surreptitiously at her nose. "Yes," she said, putting her chin up as she faced him. "I expect you've saved us both from an awkward scene."

She went from the room in a rush; he heard her slippers tap-tapping on the wooden stairs. This time he couldn't prevent himself from hastening to the window. He'd allow himself at least this token. It was some relief to lean his face against the cool glass, while he waited for his heart to walk out of his home.

Jemima barely saw the stairs beneath her feet; her vision was still clouded with unshed tears. She stumbled onto the landing of the first floor and nearly collided with two porters who were carrying a painting through the open door of what appeared to be a bedroom.

She apologized quickly and was about to make her way down the next flight of stairs, when the porters swung toward her and she was able to see the front of the canvas. It was a portrait of a woman reclining in a field of wildflowers. The breeze whispered tendrils of chestnut hair away from her brow as the sunlight played over her upraised face. The woman was beautiful, full of life and vitality, in spite of her relaxed pose.

Jemima caught sight of her own face in the rectangular mirror that hung beside the bedroom door and wondered how the plain, unremarkable person who gazed back at her could have inspired this glorious painting. And when the answer came to her, her face broke into a tremulous smile of joy. And though she did not note it, the woman whose face was now reflected back to her was anything but plain.

"Excuse us, ma'am," one of the porters grumbled.

"Put it down," she said to the man, imploring him with her eyes. "Please. Just for a moment."

They set the painting against the doorpost and retired into the shadows at the end of the hall. Jemima crouched down before it and touched the gilt frame in wonder. She didn't hear the rapid footsteps coming down the stairs, but she knew it the instant he came to stand behind her.

"I'm not surprised you'd rather take her with you," she said. "She is much more beautiful than I am."

He leaned forward and rested his hands on her shoulders. "I painted what I saw, Jemima. Only what I saw."

She turned to look up at him, placing her hand over his. And then she frowned. "You painted this," she whispered in bewilderment. "And yet you could send me away?"

He shook his head as he knelt down behind her and pulled her back against his chest. His arms crossed over her waist, holding her tight and strong. "I . . . I was coming down to stop you. To chase you through the streets, if necessary. Because I don't want the blasted painting, Jemima. I want you."

"You've an odd way of showing it, then." She was trying to hold on to her caution. Though it was difficult with the feel of him so warm against her back.

"I am an idiot," he said against her hair. "A blind fool."

"Who would have sailed away from England without a word to me."

He sighed so deeply she felt it rumble in her own chest. "Perhaps. I thought you would get over this . . . over me, if I left you alone. I never expected you to come here, to seek me out." His voice teased her. "It's not the sort of thing Lady Jemima Vale would do."

"It is now," she stated intently. "I seem to have strayed off the . . . what was it? . . . the narrow path of my convictions."

"Ah, Jem." He leaned forward and stroked his mouth over the delicate rise of her collarbone. Jemima's spine melted like hot wax and she sank back into him. When he canted her head back with his chin and set his mouth on hers, she moaned and sighed. And then she chuckled deep in her throat.

Bryce chided her gently. "I thought I'd warned you that laughing was not allowed during a seduction. You've got to pay more attention, my heart, if you expect to make any progress."

"I forgot," she said with false contriteness. "Besides that wasn't a proper laugh. But your porters are goggling at us from the end of the hall. I thought you might like to know."

"Hmm? Not very good for my reputation. I do have standards to keep up."

With that he plucked her off her feet and carried her into his bedroom. "Get on with it," he called to the porters just before he kicked the door shut. He tumbled Jemima onto the bed, then stood looking at her with fond irritation. She was laughing outright now, trying to stifle her giggles with one hand.

"I think you've caught a bad case of melodrama from Lovelace," she said. "A pity you don't have a nice theatrical mustache, like Percival Lancaster in *The Rake's Reform*."

He lay down beside her and raised her hand to his lips. "I could grow one if you like. I'd look a proper villain then."

She leaned up on one elbow and traced her fingers over the elegantly molded line of his mouth. "No," she crooned in the same reverent tone she had used to praise his paintings. "You're perfect the way you are."

With an impatient sigh he tugged off her lace mits and drew her hands again to his face. He wanted to feel her touch on his skin with no barriers between them.

"This might be a good time to tell me—" he began. And then he groaned as she danced her fingers over his earlobe. "Tell me . . . what you feel for me. Not that I am without some vague notion . . ."

She leaned over him until they were nearly mouth to mouth. "You make me feel young, Beech," she whispered. "And alive, and . . . so . . . complete. No one's ever seen me the way you do. I'm not speaking of looks or beauty. You see inside me. It frightened

me at first, that you could do that. And then I felt as though I could
not live without it. Without you knowing me . . . That was the
dream I spoke of in Sir Walter's meadow—that some man would
see me, in spite of Troy's long shadow."

He lay there with a thoughtful expression on his face, his eyes
drifting over the painted clouds that adorned the sky blue ceiling.
"Not exactly what I expected, Jem. But nice . . . very, very nice."

"Well," she said. "What about you? Can't drum up a few platitudes?"

When he did not answer at once, she shifted away from him.
"Here's a fine how'd you do. I come to your house like any brazen
hussy, to throw myself at you quite shamelessly. And you can't
even—"

"Hush, pet," he said, laying a finger on her mouth. "It's not easy
to find the right words."

Her frown deepened. "This is your last chance—I've offered
myself to you three times now . . ."

"Three is a nice, righteous number, Jem," he said softly. "I
learned that in divinity school."

"You also learned how to kiss like a fallen angel while you were
there," she said crossly.

He rolled over and caught her beneath him, trapping her with his
long legs and lean body. "Are you complaining?" His mouth hov-
ered dangerously over hers, his eyes turned to molten pewter. "I
thought you liked my kisses. Except for that wretched day in the
library, when I forced myself on you."

She touched his cheek. "I prayed you'd never stopped kissing
me that day. I still dream of those kisses."

"You do?" His brows knit. "Well, I was a benighted fool to stop
then, wasn't I?" Lowering his mouth, he drifted it over her lips. "I
won't make that mistake again," he murmured.

Jemima was quite satisfied with the quality and duration of his
kiss this time, even if her toes were curled into hard little knots and
her belly felt as if a sawmill blade were whirring out of control.

When he was done ravishing her mouth, Bryce leaned over and
drew a book from his night table. "Here," he said, still a bit shaky.
"Perhaps this will explain it better than my feeble attempt at
words. This lies beside me while I sleep."

She took it from him. It was her sketchbook, which she'd inad-
vertently left behind at the Prospect.

"You'd gotten rather good," he said as he opened it to the drawings she'd made in the garden. "But I also treasured the not-so-

good ones. Every smudge and erasure. Because . . . you made them."

"Oh, Bryce." She sighed. "I think you must love me . . . to be so daft over my horrid drawings."

He removed the book from her hands and clasped them between his own.

"I don't know if what I feel for you is love," he said haltingly. "I've shied away from that emotion since Lady Anne. I can tell you this—there is not one minute of each day that I don't think of you, or miss your voice or your smile. Or your touch. I reach for you in my darkest dreams, Jemima, like a man who has lost the light."

She bowed her head over their entwined hands. "I can't ask for more than that."

"You should," he said, tipping her face up. "You deserve to be loved." He gazed at her, his eyes unguarded. "And whatever name you want to give to this feeling, it's all I have to offer you. I have no wealth, no stature, no expectations, only a heart that longs to be taken into your keeping." He drew her to his chest and cradled her there, a balm to his troubled spirit. "If you will have such a tarnished creature. I dare not turn you away again, Jemima. It would surely kill me this time."

She tucked her head under his chin and smiled deliriously.

"So you'll marry me?" he asked in a matter-of-fact voice, unaware that Jemima could hear the anxious tumult of his heart beneath his shirt. "And sail with me to Barbados in three days' time? I expect your illustrious brother can procure a special license—my days of trafficking with the clergy are behind me, I'm afraid. That way we can be wed before we go. I . . . I don't fancy a sea voyage in separate cabins."

He's babbling, she thought with a shivery thrill. The cool, collected, utterly composed Beecham Bryce, he of the honeyed tongue and unshakable poise, was babbling.

She drew back from his chest and nodded. "But only on two conditions."

He eyed her with skeptical humor and muttered, "Here is where I pay the piper."

"I can live with the fact that you are an exceptional artist—I see now it's my fate to be always in the company of genius. But you must promise me that you will never, ever, take up writing poetry."

"What? No sonnets to your beautiful green eyes?"

"They're blue," she retorted, and then grinned when she realized that he'd caught her out.

He grinned back. "Whatever color they are, they're the eyes I want to see when I awake each morning." He frowned thoughtfully. "Still, it's a shame about the poetry business . . . I was feeling inspired only moments ago to take up my pen. It went something like, 'Nothing could be finer, than to marry my Jemima—' "

"Bryce!" she moaned. "That poem is far worse than anything I ever *drew*."

He chuckled as he lay back on the pillow, his hands behind his head. "Done, then. I promise to stay far away from poesy. And the other condition?"

"Your books," she said, mustering a stern, maidenly expression. Which was difficult, as she wasn't feeling the least bit maidenly with Bryce stretched out, languorous and seductive, beside her. "The ones from the cabinet in the library."

"Oh, Lord," he said wincing. "I suppose you want me to burn them."

"No," she said with a wicked smirk as she rolled right on top of him. "I want you to *bring* them. On the ship. To Barbados."

He looked startled for an instant, and then he laughed out loud.

"God, I do love you, Jemima," he breathed as he took her face between his hands and kissed her in proof of it, like the not-quite-so-fallen angel he was.

Lovelace and her brother, Charlie, came strolling down the street, arm in arm. They stopped across from Bryce's row house, where Troy was leaning up against a streetlamp. Lovelace sent her brother off to buy them lemonade from a vendor at the corner, and then turned to Troy.

"Well? Did she do it? Did she really walk in there and throw herself at his feet?"

He nodded. "Hard to tell the outcome, though. She's only been inside for twenty minutes or so."

Lovelace considered this a moment, and then she smiled. "If I know Mr. Bryce, he'd have tossed her out after five minutes if he wasn't going to come around. Oh, Troy, this is so romantical. You will have to write a poem in their honor."

"Already did," he said smugly. "Though I didn't know it at the time." He pulled some tattered sheets from his waistcoat pocket. "Been carrying the deuced thing around with me. A talisman of sorts, I guess."

She took up the first page and read aloud, " 'Ode to Persephone.' "
Recognition dawned. "Oh, Troy . . . this is the poem that—"

"Yes, yes. That started the whole blasted business. Read on,
Sheba, just the first stanza should do it."

Lovelace continued in her most eloquent stage voice:

"Virtue is a smug estate, without the lure of vice,
A feast upon an empty plate, a cider without spice.
Who writes upon this barren slate, who carves a sure device?
The rake, the rogue, the reprobate, who lives to thus entice,
Sweet virtue from her pristine state, with potent, pretty lies,
And flatteries intemperate, till blushing she complies,
Unable further to debate, this willing sacrifice,
Relinquishes a heavenly fate, for earthly paradise."

She drew a breath as she lowered the sheet. "It's perfect, Troy.
And Papa shall write a play for me based on it—*Persephone, Goddess of the Underworld*, and I shall play—"

"Persephone," he interjected with a wink. "Yes, I know. Come
along now, Sheba. I think we'd better help your brother. It appears
he has his hands full."

He chuckled as he took her arm and led her toward the corner.
"Which is exactly the state Bryce will find himself in, if my
sainted sister gets her way. I hear he's already put Bacchus up for
sale . . . which is a sad state of affairs." He added under his breath,
"Can't think of anything I'd like better than a brother-in-law with
a bawdy house."

SIGNET REGENCY ROMANCE (0451)

TALES OF LOVE AND ADVENTURE

☐**SHADES OF THE PAST by Sandra Heath.** A plunge through a trapdoor in time catapulted Laura Reynolds from the modern London stage into the scandalous world of Regency England, where a woman of the theater was little better than a girl of the streets. And it was here that Laura was cast in a drama of revenge against wealthy, handsome Lord Blair Deveril. (187520—$4.99)

☐**THE CAPTAIN'S DILEMMA by Gail Eastwood.** Perhaps if bold and beautiful Merissa Pritchard had not grown so tired of country life and her blue-blooded suitor, it would not have happened. Whatever the reason, Merissa had given the fleeing French prisoner of war, Captain Alexandre Valmont, a hiding place on her family estate. Even more shocking, she had given him entry into her heart.

(181921—$4.50)

☐**THE IRISH RAKE by Emma Lange.** Miss Gillian Edwards was barely more than a schoolgirl—and certainly as innocent as one—but she knew how shockingly evil the Marquess of Clare was. He did not even try to hide a history of illicit loves that ran the gamut from London lightskirts to highborn ladies. Nor did he conceal his scorn for marriage and morality and his devotion to the pleasures of the flesh.

(187687—$4.99)

Prices slightly higher in Canada

Payable in U.S. funds only. No cash/COD accepted. Postage & handling: U.S./CAN. $2.75 for one book, $1.00 for each additional, not to exceed $6.75; Int'l $5.00 for one book, $1.00 each additional. We accept Visa, Amex, MC ($10.00 min.), checks ($15.00 fee for returned checks) and money orders. Call 800-788-6262 or 201-933-9292, fax 201-896-8569; refer to ad #SRR1

Penguin Putnam Inc.　　　　Bill my: ☐Visa ☐MasterCard ☐Amex _____(expires)
P.O. Box 12289, Dept. B　　Card#_____
Newark, NJ 07101-5289　　Signature_____
Please allow 4-6 weeks for delivery.
Foreign and Canadian delivery 6-8 weeks.

Bill to:
Name_____
Address_____City_____
State/ZIP_____
Daytime Phone #_____

Ship to:
Name_____ Book Total $_____
Address_____ Applicable Sales Tax $_____
City_____ Postage & Handling $_____
State/ZIP_____ Total Amount Due $_____

This offer subject to change without notice.